THE
AUTOBIOGRAPHY OF A FLEA
and Other Tart Tales

THE
AUTOBIOGRAPHY OF A FLEA
and Other Tart Tales

Anonymous

Carroll & Graf Publishers, Inc.
New York

Copyright © 1995 by Carroll & Graf Publishers, Inc.

All rights reserved.

First Carroll & Graf edition 1995.

Carroll & Graf Publishers, Inc.
260 Fifth Avenue
New York, NY 10001

ISBN 0-7867-0292-3

Manufactured in the United States of America.

10 9 8 7 6 5 4 3 2 1

THE
AUTOBIOGRAPHY OF A FLEA

CHAPTER I

Born I was—but how, when, or where I cannot say; so I must leave the reader to accept the assertion ''per se,'' and believe it if he will. One thing is equally certain, the fact of my birth is not one atom less veracious than the reality of these memoirs, and if the intelligent student of these pages wonders how it came to pass that one in my walk—or perhaps, I should have said jump—in life, became possessed of the learning, observation and power of committing to memory the whole of the wonderful facts and disclosures I am about to relate. I can only remind him that there are intelligences, little suspected by the vulgar, and laws in nature, the very existence of which have not yet been detected by the advanced among the scientific world.

I have heard it somewhere remarked that my province was to get my living by blood sucking. I am not the lowest by any means of that universal fraternity, and if I sustain a precarious existence upon the bodies of those with whom I come in contact, my own experience proves that I do so in a marked and peculiar manner, with a warning of my employment which is seldom given by those in other grades of my profession. But I submit that I have other and nobler aims than the mere sustaining of my being by the contributions of the unwary. I have been conscious of this original defect, and, with a soul far above the vulgar instincts of my race. I jumped by degrees to heights of mental perception and erudition which placed me for ever upon a pinnacle of insect-grandeur.

It is this attainment to learning which I shall evoke in describing the scenes of which I have been a witness—nay, even a partaker. I shall not stop to explain by what means I am pessessed of human powers of thinking and observing, but, in my lucubrations, leave you simply to perceive that I possess them and wonder accordingly.

You will thus perceive that I am not common flea; indeed, when it is born in mind the company in which I have been accustomed to mingle, the familiarity with which I have been suffered to treat persons the most exalted, and the opportunities I have possessed to make the most of my acquaintances, the reader will no doubt agree with me that I am in very truth a most wonderful and exalted insect.

My earliest recollections lead me back to a period when I found myself within a church. There was a rolling of rich music and a slow monotonous chanting which then filled me with surprise and admiration, but I have long since learnt the true important of such influences, and the attitudes of the worshippers are now taken by me for the outward semblance of inward emotions which are very generaly non-existent. Be this as it may, I was engaged upon professional business connected with the plump white leg of a young lady of some fourteen years of age, the taste of whose delicious blood I well remember, and the flavour of whose—

But I am digressing.

Soon after commencing in a quiet and friendly way my little attentions, the young girl in common with the rest of the congregation rose to depart, and I, as a matter of course, determined to accompany her.

I am very sharp of sight as well as of hearing, and that is, how I saw a young gentleman slip a small folded piece of white paper into the young lady's pretty gloved hand, as she passed through the crowded porch. I had noticed the name Bella neatly worked upon the soft silk stocking which had at first attracted me, and I now saw that the same word appeared alone upon the outside of the billet-doux. She was with her Aunt, a tall, stately dame, with whom I did not care to get upon terms of intimacy.

Bella was a beauty—just fourteen—a perfect figure, and although so young, her soft bosom was already budding into those proportions which delight the other sex. Her face was charming in its frankness; her breath sweet as the perfumes of Arabia, and, as I have always said, her skin as soft as velvet. Bella was evidently well aware of her good looks, and carried her head as proudly and as coquettishly as a queen. That she inspired admiration was not difficult to see by the wistful and longing glances which the young men, and sometimes also those of the more nature years, cast upon her. There was a general hush of conversation outside the building, and a turning of glances generally towards the pretty Bella, which told more plainly than words that she was the admired one of all eyes and the desired one of all hearts—at any rate among the male sex.

Paying, however very little attention to what was evidently a matter of every-day occurence, the young lady walked sharply homewards with her Aunt, and after arrival at the neat and genteel residence, weat quickly to her room. I will not say I followed, but I "went with her," and beheld the gentle girl raise one dainty leg across the other and remove the tiniest of tight and elegant kid-boots.

I jumped upon the carpet and proceeded with my examinations. The left boot followed, and without removing her plump calf from off the other, Bella sat looking at the folded piece of paper which I had seen the young fellow deposit secretly in her hand.

Closely watching everything. I noted the swelling thighs, which spread upwards above her tightly fitting garters, until they were lost in the darkness, as they closed together at a point where her beautiful belly met them in her stooping position; and almost obliterated a thin and peach-like slit, which just shewed its rounded lips between them in the shade.

Presently Bella dropped her note, and being open, I took the liberty to read it.

"I will be in the old spot at eight o'clock to night," were the only words which the paper contained, but they appeared to have a special interest for Bella, who remained cogitating for some time in the same thoughtful mood.

My curiosity had been aroused, and my desire to know more of the interesting young being with whom chance had so promiscuously brought me in pleasing contact, prompted me to remain quietly ensconced in a snug though somewhat moist hiding place, and it was not until near upon the hour named that I once more emerged in order to watch the progress of events.

Bella had dressed herself with scrupuleus care, and now prepared to betake herself to the garden which surrounded the country-house in which she dwelt.

I went with her.

Arriving at the end of a long and shady avenue the young girl seated herself upon a rustic bench, and there awaited the coming of the person she was to meet.

It was not many minutes before the young man presented himself whom I had seen in communication with my fair little friend in the morning.

A conversation ensued which, if I might judge by the abstraction of the pair from aught besides themselves, had unusual interest for both.

It was evening, and the twilight had already commenced: the air was warm and genial, and the young pair sat closely entwined upon the bench, lost to all but their own united happiness.

"You don't know how I love you Bella," whispered the youth., tenderly sealing his protestation with a kiss upon the pouting lips of his companion.

"Yes I do," replied the girl, naively, "are you not always telling me? I shall get tired of hearing it soon."

Bella fidgetted her pretty little foot and looked thoughtful.

"When are you going to explain and show me all those funny things you told me about?" asked she, giving a

11

guick glance up, and then as rapidly bending her eyes upon the gravel walk.

"Now," answered the youth. "Now, dear Bella, while we have the chance to be alone and free from interruption. You know, Bella, we are no longer children?"

Bella nodded her head.

"Well, there are things which are not known to children, and which are necessary for lovers not only to know, but also to practice."

"Dear me," said the girl, seriously.

"Yes," continued her companion, "there are secrets which render lovers happy, and which make the enjoy of loving and of being loved."

"Lord!" exclaimed Bella, "how, sentimental you have grown, Charlie; I remember the time when you declared sentiment was "all humbug.""

"So I thought it was, till I loved you," replied the youth.

"Nonsense," continued Bella, "but go on, Charlie, and tell me what you promised."

"I can't tell you without shoving you as well," replied Charlie; "the knowledge can only be learnt by experience."

"Oh, go on then and show me," caried the girl, in whose bright eyes and glowing cheeks I thought I could detect a very conscious knowledge of the kind of instruction about to be imparted.

There was something catching in her impatience. The youth yielded to it, and covering her beautiful young form with his own, glued his mouth to hers and kissed it rapturously.

Bella made no resistance; she even aided and returned her lover's caresses.

Meanwhile the evening advanced: the trees lay in the

gathering darkness, spreading their lofty tops to screen the waning light from the young lovers.

Presently Charlie slid on one side; he made a slight movement, and then without any epposition he passed his hand under and up the petticoats of the pretty Bella. Not satisfied with the charms which he found within the compass of the glistening silk stockings, he essayed to press on still further, and his wandering fingers now touched the soft and quivering flesh of her young thighs.

Bella's breath came hard and fast, as she felt the indelicate attack which was being made upon her charms. So far, however, from resisting, she evidently enjoyed the exciting dalliance.

"Touch it," whispered Bella, "you may."

Charlie needed no further invitation: indeed he was already preparing to advance without one and instantly comprehending the permission, drove his fingers forward.

The fair girl opened her thighs as he did so, and the next instant his hand covered the delicate pink lips of her pretty slit.

For the next ten minutes the pair remained almost motionless, their lips joined and their breathing alone marking the sensations which were overpowering them with the intoxication of wantoness. Charlie felt a delicate object, which stiffened beneath his nimble fingers, and assumed a prominence of which he had no experience.

Presently Bella closed her eyes, and throwing back her head, shuddered slightly, while her frame became supple and languid, and she suffered her head to rest upon the arm of her lover.

"Oh, Charlie," she murmured, "what is it you do? What delightful sensations you give me."

Meanwhile the youth was not idle, but having fairly

explored all he could in the constrained position in which he found himself, he rose, and sensible of the need of assuaging the raging passion which his actions had fanned, he besought his fair companion to let him guide her hand to a dear object, which he assured her was capable of giving her far greater pleasure that his fingers had done.

Nothing loth, Bella's grasp was the next moment upon a new and delicious substance, and either giving way to the curiosity she simulated, or really carried away by her newly-roused desires, nothing would do, but she must bring out and into the light the standing affair of her friend.

Those of my readers who have been placed in a similar position will readily understand the warmth of the grasp and the surprise of the look which greeted the first appearance in public of the new acquisition.

Bella beheld a man's member for the first time in her life, in the full plenitude of its power, and although it was not, I could plainly see, by any means a formidable one, yet its white shaft and redcapped head, from which the soft skin retreated as she pressed it, gained her quick inclination to learn more.

Charlie was equally moved; his eyes shone and his hand continued to rove all over the sweet young treasure of which he had taken possession.

Meanwhile the toyings of the little white hand upon the youthful member with which it was in contact had produced effects common under such circumstances to all of so healthy and vigourous a constitution as that of the owner of this particular affair.

Enraptured with the soft pressures, the geatle and delicious squeezings, and artless way in which the young lady pulled back the folds from the rampant nut, and disclosed the ruby crest, purple with desire, and the tip, ended by the tiny orifice, now awaiting its opportunity to send forth its slippery offering, the youth grew wild with lust, and Bella, participating in sensations new and strange, but which carried her away in a whirlwind of passionate excitement, panted for she knew not what of rapturous relief.

With her beautiful eyes half closed, her dewy lips parted, and her skin warm and glowing with the unwonted impulse stealing over her, she lay the delicious victim of whomsoever had the instant chance to reap her favours and pluck her delicate young rose.

Charlie, youth though he was, was not so blind as to lose so fair an opportunity; besides, his now rampant passions carried him forward despite the dictates of prudence which he otherwise might have heard.

He felt the throbbing and well-moistened centre quivering beneath his fingers, he beheld the beautiful girl lying invitingly to the amorous sport, he watched the tender breathings which caused the young breast to rise and fall, and the strong sensual emotions which animated the glowing form of his youthful companion.

The full, soft and swelling legs of the girl were now exposed to his sensuous gaze.

Gently raising the intervening drapery, Charlie still further disclosed the secret charms of his lovely companion until, with eyes of flame, he saw the plump limbs terminate in the full hips and white palpitating belly.

Then also his ardent gaze fell upon the centre spot of attraction—on the small pink slit which lay half hidden at the foot of the swelling mount of Venus, hardly yet shaded by the softest down.

The titillation which he had administered, and the caresses

which he had hestowed upon the coveted object had induced a flow of the native moisture which such excitement tends to provoke, and Bella lay with her peach-like slit well bedewed with nature's best and sweetest lubricant.

Charlie saw his chance. Gently disengaging her hand from its grasp upon his member, he threw himself frantically upon the recumbent figure of the girl.

His left arm wound itself round her slender waist, his not breath was on her cheek, his lips pressed hers in one long, passionate and hurried kiss. His left hand, now free, sought to bring together those parts of both which are the active instruments of sensual pleasure, and with eager efforts he sought to complete conjunction.

Bella now felt for the first time in her life the magic touch of a man's machine between the tips of her rosy orifice.

No sooner had she perceived the warm contact which was occasioned by the stiffened head of Charlie's member, than she shuddered perceptibly, and already anticipating the delights of venery, gave down an abundance of proof of her susceptible nature.

Charlie was enraptured at his happiness, and eagerly strove to perfect his enjoyment.

But Nature, which had operated so powerfully in the development of Bella's sensual passions, left yet something to be accomplished, are the opening of so early a rosebud could be easily effected.

She was very young, immature, certainly so in the sense of those monthly visitions which are supposed to mark the commencement of puberty; and Bella's parts, replete as they were with perfection and freshness, were as yet hardly prepared for the accomodation of even so moderate a champion as that which, with round intruded head, now sought to enter in and effect a lodgment.

In vain Charlie pushed and exerted himself to press into the delicate parts of the lovely girl his excited member.

The pink folds and the tiny orifice withstood all his attempts to penetrate the mystic grotto. In vain the pretty Bella, now roused into a fury of excitement and half mad with the titillation she had already undergone, seconded by all the means in her power the audacious attempts of her young lover.

The membrane was strong and resisted bravely until, with a desperate purpose to win the goal or burst everything, the youth drew back for a moment, and then desperately plunging forward, succeeded in piercing the obstruction and thrusting the head and shoulders of his stiffened affair into the belly of the yelding girl.

Bella gave a little scream, as she felt the forcible inroad upon her secret charms, but the delicious contact gave her courage to bear the smart in hopes of the relief which appeared to be coming.

Meanwhile Charlie pushed again and again, and proud of the victory which he had already won, not only stood his ground, but at each thrust advanced some small way further upon his road.

It has been said, "ce n'est que le premier coup qui coute, "but it may be fairly argued that it is at the same time perfectly possible that "quelquefois il coute trop," as the reader may be inclined to infer with me in the present case.

Neither of our lovers, however, had strange to say, a thought on the subject, but fully occupied with the delicious sensations which had overpowered them, united to give effect to those ardent movements which both could feel would end in ecstasy.

As for Bella, with her whole body quivering with delicious impatience, and her full red lips giving vent to the short excursive exclamations which announced the extreme gratification, she gave herself up body and soul to the dehghts of the coition. Her muscular compressions upon the weapon which had now effectually gained her, the firm embrace in which she held the writhing lad, the delicate tighs of the moistened, glove-like sheath, all tended to excite Charlie to madness. He felt himself in her body to the roots of his machine, until the two globes which tightened beneath the foaming champion of his manhood, pressed upon the firm cheeks of her white bottom. He could go no further and his sole employment was to enjoy—to reap to the full the delicious harvest of his exertions.

But Bella, insatiable in her passion, no sooner found the wished for junction completed, than relishing the keen pleasure which the stuff and warm member was giving her, became too excited to know or care further aught that was happenning, and her frenzied excitement, quickly overtaken again by the maddening spasms of completed lust, pressed downwards upon the object of her pleasure, threw up her arms in passionate rapture, and then sinking back in the arms of her lover, with low groans of ecstasic agony and little cries of surprise and delight, gave down a copious emission, which finding a reluctant escape below, inundated Charlie's balls.

No sooner did the youth witness the delivering enjoyment he was the means of bestowing upon the beautiful Bella, and became sensible of the flood which she had poured down in such profusion upon his person, then he was also seized with lustful fury. A raging forrent of desire seemed to rush through his veins; his instrument was now plunged to the hilt in her delicious belly, then, drawing back, he extracted the smoking member almost to the head. He pressed and bore all before him. He felt a tickling, maddening feeling creeping upon him; he tightened his grasp upon his young mistress, and at the same instant that another cry of rapturous enjoyment issued from her heaving breast, he found himself gasping upon her bosom, and pouring into her grateful womb a rich tickling jet of youthful vigour.

A low moan of salacious gratification escaped the parted lips of Bella, as she felt the jerking gushes of seminal fluid which came from the excited member within her; at the same moment the lustful frenzy of emission forced from Charlie a sharp and thrilling cry as he lay with upturned eyes in the last act of the sensuous drama.

That cry was the signal for an interruption which was as sudden as it was unexpected. From out the bordering shrubs there stole the sombre figure of a man and stood before the youthful lovers.

Horror froze the blood of both.

Slipping from his late warm and luscious retreat, and essaying as best he could to stand upright. Charlie recolled from the apparition as from some dreadful serpent.

As for the gentle Bella, no sooner did she catch sight of the intruder than, covering her face with her hands, she shrank back upon the seat which had been the silent witness of her pleasures, and too frightened to utter a sound, waited with what presence of mind she could assume to face the brewing storm.

Nor was she kept long in suspense.

Quickly advancing towards the guilty couple the newcomer seized the lad by the arm, while with a stern gesture of authority, he ordered him to repair the disorder of dress.

"Impudent boy," he hissed between his teeth, "what is is that you have done? To what lengths have your mad and savage passions hurried you? How will you face the rage of your justly offended father? How appease his angry resentment when in the exercise of my bounden duty. I apprise him of the mischief wrought by the hand of his only son."

As the speaker ceased, still holding Charlie by the wrist, he came forth into the moonlight and disclosed the figure of a man of some forty-five of age, short, stout, and somewhat corpulent. His face, decidedly handsome, was rendered still more attractive by a pair of brilliant eyes, which, black as jet, threw around fierce glances of passionate resentment. He was habited in a clerical dress, the sombre shades and quiet unobstructive neatness of which drew out only more prominently his remarkably muscular proportions and striking physiogomy.

Charlie appeared, as well, indeed, he might, covered with confusion, when to his infinite and selfish relief, the stern intruder turned to the young partner of his libidinous enjoyment.

"For you, miserable girl, I can only express my utmost horror and my most righteous indignation. Forgetful alike of the precepts of the holy mother church, careless of your honour, you have allowed this wicked and presumptuous boy to pluck the forbidden fruit? What now remains for you? Scorned by your friends, and driven from your uncle's house, you will herd with the beasts of the field, and Nebuchadnezar of old, shunned as centamination by your species, gladly gather a miserable sustenance in the highways. Oh, daughter of sin, child given up to lust and unto Satan. I say unto thee——"

The stranger had proceeded thus far in his abjuration of the unfortunate girl, when Bella, rising from her crouching attitude, threw herself at his feet, and joined her tears and prayers for forgiveness to those of her young lover.

"Say no more," at length continued the stern priest; "say no more. Confessions are of no avail, and humiliations do but add to your offence. My mind misgives me as to my duty in this sad affair, but if I obeyed the dietates of my present inclinations I should go straight to your natural guardians and acquaint them immediately with the infamous nature of my chance discovery."

"Oh, in pity, have mercy upon me," pleaded Bella, whose tears now coursed down her pretty cheeks, so lately aglow with wanton pleasure.

"Spare us, Father, spare us both. We will do anything in our power to make atonement. Six masses and several paters shall be performed on our account and our cost. The pilgrimage to the shrine of St. Engulphus, of which you spoke to me the other day, shall now surely be undertaken. I am willing to do anything, sacrifice anything, if you will spare this dear Bella."

The priest waived his hand for silence. Then he spoke, while accents of pity mingled with his naturally stern and resolute manner.

"Enough," said he, "I must have time. I must invoke assistance from the Blessed Virgin, who knew no sin, but who, without the carnal delights of mortal copulation, brought forth the babe of babes in the manger of Bethlehem. Come to me to-morrow in the sacristy, Bella. These in the precincts, I will unfold to you the Divine will concerning your transgression. At two o'clock I will expect you. As for you, rash youth, I shall reserve my judgment, and all action, until the following day, when at the same hour I shall likewise expect you.''

A thousand thanks were being poured out by the united throats of the penitents, when the Father warned them both to part.

The evening had long ago closed in, and the dews of night were stealing upwards.

"Meanwhile, good night and peace; your secret is safe with me, until we meet again," he spoke and disappeared,

CHAPTER II

Curiosity to learn the sequel of an adventure in which I already felt so much interest, as well as a tender solicitude for the gentle and amaible Bella, constrained me to keep in her vicinity, and I, therefore, took care not to annoy her with any very decided attentions on my part, or to raise resistance by an illtimed attack at a moment when it was necessary to the success of my design to remain within range of that young lady's operations.

I shall not attempt to tell of the miserable period passed by my young protegee in the interval which elapsed between the shocking discovery made by the holy Father Confessor, and the hour assigned by him for the interview in the sacristy, which was to decide the fate of the unfortunate Bella.

With trembling steps and downcast eyes the frightened girl presented herself at the porch and knocked.

The door was opened and the Father appeared upon the threshold.

At a sign Bella entered and stood before the stately presence of the holy man.

An embarrassing silence of some seconds followed. Father Ambrose was the first to break the spell.

"You have done right, my daughter, to come to me so punctually; the ready obedience of the penitent is the first sign of the spirit within which obtains the Divine forgiveness."

At these gracious words Bella took courage, and already a load seemed to fall from her heart.

Father Ambrose continued, seating himself at the same time upon the long-cushioned seat which covered a huge oak chest:

"I have thought much, and prayed much on your account, my daughter. For some time there appeared no way in which I could absolve my conscience otherwise than to go to your natural protector and lay before him the dreadful secret of which I have become the unhappy possessor."

Here he paused, and Bella, who knew well the severe character of her uncle, on whom she was entirely dependent, trembled at his words.

Taking her hand in his, and gently drawing the girl to the same seat, so that she found herself kneeling before him, while his right hand pressed her rounded shoulder, he went on:

"But I am wounded to think of the dreadful results which would follow such a disclosure, and I have asked for assistance from the Blessed Virgin in my trouble. She has pointed out a way which, while it also serves the ends of our holy church, likely prevents the consequences of your offence from being known to your uncle. The first necessity which this course imposes is, however, implicit obedience."

Bella, only too rejoiced to hear of a way out of her trouble, readily promised the most blind obedience to the command of her spiritual Father.

The young girl was kneeling at his feet. Father Ambrose bent his large head over her recumbent figure. A warm tint lit his cheeks, a strange fire danced in his fierce eyes: his hands trembled slightly, as they rested upon the shoulders of his penitent, but his composure was otherwise unruffled. Doubtless his spirit was troubled at the conflict going on within him between the duty he had to fulfil and the tortuous path by which he hoped to avoid the awful exposure.

The holy Father then began a long lecture upon the virtue of obedience, and the absolute submissions to the guidance of the minister of holy church.

Bella reiterated her assurances of entire patience and obedience in all things.

Meanwhile it was evident to me that the priest was a victim to some confined, but rebellious spirit which rose within him, and at times almost broke out into complete possession in the flashing eyes and hot passionate lips.

Father Ambrose gently drew the beautiful penitent nearer and nearer, until her fair arms rested upon his knees, and her face bent downwards in holy resignation, sunk almost unpon her hands.

"And now, my child," continued the holy man, "it is time that I should tell you the means vouschsafed to me by the Blessed Virgin by which alone I am absolved from exposing your offence. There are ministering spirits who have confided to them the relief of those passions and those exigencies which the servants of the church are forbidden openly to avow, but which, who can doubt, they have need to satisfy. These chosen few are mainly selected from among those who have already trodden the path of fleshly indulgence; to them is confined the solemn and holy duty of assuaging the earthly desires of our religious community in the strictest secrecy. To you," whispered the Father, his voice trembling with emotion, and his large hands passing by an easy transition from the shoulders of his penitent to her slender waist.

"To you, who have once already tasted the supreme pleasure of copulation, it is competent to assume this holy office. Not only will your sin be thus effaced and pardoned, but it will be permitted you to taste legitimately those ecstatic delights, those overpowering sensations of rapturous enjoyment, which in the arms of her faithful servants you are at all times sure to find. You will swim in a sea of sensual pleasure, without incurring the penalties of illicit love. Your absolution will follow each occasion of your yielding your sweet body to the gratification on the church, through her ministers, and you will be rewarded and sustained in the pious work by witnessing—nay, Bellà, by sharing fully those intense and fervent emotions, the delicious enjoyment of your beautiful person must provoke."

Bella listened to this insidious proposal with mingled feelings of surprise and pleasure.

The wild and lewd impulses of her warm nature were at once awakened by the picture now presented to her fervid imagination—how could she hesitate?

The pious priest drew her yielding from towards him, and printed a long hot kiss upon her rosy lips.

"Holy Mother," murmured Bella, whose sexual instincts where each moment becoming more fully roused. "This is too much for me to bear—I long—I wonder—I know not what!"

"Sweet innocent, it will be for me to instruct you. In my person you will find your best and fittest preceptor in those exercices you will henceforth have to fulfil."

Father Ambrose slightly shifted his position. It was then that Bella noticed for the first time the heated look of sensuality which now almost frightened her.

It was now also that she became aware of the enormous protuberance of the front of the holy Father's silk cassock.

The excited priest hardly cared any longer to conceal either his condition or his designs.

Catching the beautiful child to his arms he kissed her long and passionately. He pressed her sweet body to his burly person, and rudely threw himself forward into closer contact with her graceful form.

At length the consuming lust with which he was burning carried him beyond all bounds, and partly releasing Bella from the constraint of his ardent embrace, he opened the front of his cassock, and exposed, without a blush, to the astonished eyes of his young penitent, a member the gigantic proportions of which, no less than its stiffness and rigidity completely confounded her.

It is impossible to describe the sensations produced upon

the gentle Bella by the sudden display of this formidable instrument.

Her eyes was instantly rivetted upon it, while the Father, noticing her astonishment, but detecting rightly that there was nothing mingled with it of alarm or apprehension, coolly placed it into her hands, It was then that Bella became wildly excited with the muscular contact of this tremendous thing.

Only having seen the very moderate proportions displayed by Charlie, she found her lewdest sensations quickly awakened by so remarkable a phenomenon, and glasping the huge object as well as she could in her soft little hands, she sank down beside it in an ectasy of sensual delight.

"Holy Mother, this is already heaven!" murmured Bella. "Oh! Father, who would have believed I could have been selected for such pleasure!"

This was too much for Father Ambrose. He was delighted at the lubricity of his fair penitent, and the success of his infamous trick (for he had planned the whole, and had been instrumental in bringing the two young lovers together and affording them an opportunity of indulging their warm temperaments, unknown to all save himself, as, hidden close by, with flaming eyes, he watched the amatory combat).

Hastily rising, he caught up the light figure of the young Bella, and placing her upon the cushioned seat on which he had lately been sitting, he threw up her plump legs and separating to the utmost her willing thighs, he beheld for an instant the delicious pinky slit which appeared at the bottom of her white belly. Then, without a word, he plunged his face towards it, and thrusting his lecherous tongue up the moist sheath as far as he could, he sucked it so deliciously that Bella, in a shuddering ecstasy of passion, her young body writhing in spasmodic contortions of pleasure, have down a plentiful emission, which the holy man swallowed like a custard.

For a few moments there was calm.

Bella lay on her back, her arms extended on either side, and her head thrown back in an attitude of delicious exhaustion, succeeding the wild emotions so lately occasioned by the lewd proceedings of the reverend Father.

Her bosom yet palpitated with the violence of her transports and her beautiful eyes remained half closed in languid repose.

Father Ambrose was one of the few who, under circumstances such as the present, was able to keep the instincts of passion under command. Long habits of patience in the attainment of his object, a general doggedness of manner and the conventional caution of his order, had not been lost upon his fiery nature, and although by nature unfitted for his holy calling, and a prey to desires as violent as they were irregular, he had taught himself to school his passions even to mortification.

It is time to lift the veil from the real character of this man. I do so with respect, but the truth must be told.

Father Ambrose was the living personification of lust. His mind was in reality devoted to its pursuit, and his grossly animal instincts, his ardent and vigorous constitution, no less than his hard unbending nature made him resemble in body, as in mind, the Satyr of old.

But Bella only knew him as the holy Father who had not only pardoned her offence, but who had opened to her the path by which she might, as she supposed, legitimately enjoy those pleasures which had already wrought so strongly on her young imagination.

The bold priest, singularly charmed, not only at the

success of his stratagem which had given into his hands so luscious a victim, but also at the extraordinary sensuality of her constitution, and the evident delight with which she lent herself to his desires, now set himself leisurely to reap the fruits of his trickery, and revel to the utmost in the enjoyment which the possession of all the delicate charms of Bella could procure to appease his frightful lust.

She was his at last, and as he rose from her quivering body, his lips yet reeking with the plentiful evidence of her participation in his pleasures, his member became yet more fearfully hard and swollen, and the dull red head shone with the bursting strain of blood and muscle beneath.

No sooner did the young Bella find herself released from the attack of her confessor upon the sensitive part of her person already described, and raised her head from the recumbent position into which it had fallen, than her eyes fell for the second time upon the big truncheon which the Father kept impudently exposed.

Bella noted the long and thick white shaft, and the curling mass of black hair out of which it rose, stiffly inclined upwards, and protruding from its end was the egg-shaped head, skinned and ruddy, and seeming to invite the contact of her hand.

Bella beheld this thickened muscular mass of stiffened flesh, and unable to resist the inclination, flew once more to seize it in her grasp.

She squeezed it,—she pressed it—she drew back the folding skin, and watched the broad nut, as it inclined towards her. She saw with wonder the small slit-like hole at its extremity and taking both her hands, she held it throbbing close to her face.

"Oh! Father, what a beautiful thing," exclaimed Bella, "what an immense one, too. Oh! Please, dear Father

Ambrose, do tell me what I must do to relieve you of those feelings which you say give our holy ministers of religion so much pain and uneasiness.

Father Ambrose was almost too excited to reply, but taking her hand in his, he showed the innocent girl how to move her white fingers up and down upon the shoulders of his huge affair.

His pleasure was intense, and that of Bella was hardly less.

She continued to rub his limb with her soft palms and, looking up innocently to his face, asked softly—

"If that gave him pleasure, and was nice, and whether she might go on, as she was doing."

Meanwhile the reverend Father felt his big penis grow harder and even stiffer under the exciting titillations of the young girl.

"Stay a moment; if you continue to rub it so I shall spend," softly said he. "It will be better to defer it a little."

"Spend, my Father," asked Bella, eagerly, "what is that?"

"Oh, sweet girl, charming alike in your beauty and your innocence; how divinely you fulfil your divine mission," exclaimed Ambrose delighted to outrage and debase the evident inexperience of his young penitent.

"To spend is to complete the act whereby the full pleasure of venery is enjoyed, and then a rich quantity of thick white fluid escapes from the thing you now hold in your hand, and rushing forth, gives equal pleasure to him who ejects it and to the person who, in some manner or other, receives it."

Bella remembered Charlie and his ecstasy, and knew immediately what was meant.

"Would this outpouring give you relief, my Father?"

"Undoubtedly, my daughter; it is that fervent relief I have in view, offering you the opportunity of taking from me the blissful sacrifice of one of the humblest servants of the church."

"How delicious," murmured Bella; "by my means this rich stream is to flow, and all for me the holy man proposes this end of his pleasure—how happy I am to be able to give him so much pleasure."

As she half pondered, half uttered these thoughts she bent head down; a faint, but exquisitely sensual perfume rose from the object of her adoration. She pressed her moist lips upon its top, she covered the little slitlike hole with her lovely mouth, and imprinted upon the glowing member a fervent kiss.

"What is this fluid called?" asked Bella, once more raising her pretty face.

"It has various names," replied the holy man, "according to the status of the person employing them; but between you and me, my daughter, we shall call it spunk."

"Spunk!" repeated Bella, innocently, making the erotic word fall from her sweet lips with an unction which was natural under the circumstances.

"Yes, my, daughter, spunk is the word I wish you to understand it by, and you shall presently have a plentiful bedewal of the precious essence."

"How must I receive it?" enquired Bella, thinking of Charlie, and the tremendous difference relatively between his instrument and the gigantic and swollen penis in her presence now.

"There are, various ways, all of which you will have to learn, but at present we have only slight accomodation for the principal act of reverential venery, of that permitted copulation of which I have already spoken. We must, therefore, supply another and easier method, and instead of my discharging the essence called spunk into your body, where the extreme tightness of that little slit of yours would doubtless cause it to flow very abundantly, we will commence by the friction of your obedient fingers, until the time when I feel the approach of those spasms which accompany the emission. You shall then, at a signal from me, place as much as you can of the head of this affair between your lips, and there suffer me to disgorge the trickling spunk, until the last drop being expended I shall retire satisfied, at least for the time.''

Bella, whose jealous instincts led her to enjoy the description which her confessor offered, and who was quite as eager as himself for the completion of this outrageous programme, readily expressed her willingness to comply.

Ambrose once more placed his large penis in Bella's fair hands.

Excited alike by the sight and touch of so remarkable an object, which both her hands now grasped with delight, the girl set herself to work to tickle, rub and press the huge and stiff affair in a way which gave the licentious priest the keenest enjoyment.

Not content with the friction or her delicate fingers, Bella, uttering words of devotion and satisfaction, now placed the foaming head upon her rosy lips and allowing it to slip in as far as it could, hoping by her touches, no less than by the gliding movements of her tongue, to provoke the delicious ejaculation of which she was in want.

This was almost beyond the auticipation of the holy priest, who had hardly supposed he should find so ready a disciple in the irregular attack he proposed; and his feelings being roused to the utmost by the delicious titillation he was now experiencing, prepared himself to flood the young girl's mouth and throat with the full stream of his powerful discharge.

Ambrose began to feel he could no last long without letting fly his roe, and thereby ending his pleasure.

He was one of those extraordinary men, the abundance of whose seminal ejaculation is far beyond that of ordinary beings. Not only had he the singular gift of repeatedly performing the veneral act with but very short respite, but the quantity with which he ended his pleasure was as tremendous as it was unusual. The superfluity seemed to come from him in proportion as his animal passions were aroused, and as his libidinous desires were intense and large, so also were the outpourings which relieved them.

It was under these circumstances that the gentle Bella undertook to release the pent-up torrents of this man's lust. It was her sweet mouth which was to be the recipient of those thick and slippery volumes of which she had had as yet not experience, and, all ignorant as she was of the effect of the relief she was so anxious to administer, the beautiful maid desired the consummation of her labour and the overflow of that spunk of which the good Father had told her.

Harder and hotter grew the rampant member as Bella's exciting lips pressed its large head and her tongue played around the little opening. Her two white hands bore back the soft skin from its shoulders and alternately tickled the lower extremity.

Twice Ambrose, unable to bear without spending the delicious contact, drew back the tip from her rosy lips.

At length Bella, impatient of delay, and apparently bent on perfecting her task, pressed forward with more energy than ever upon the stiff shaft.

Instantly there was a stiffening of the limbs of the good priest. His legs spread wide on either side of his penitent. His hand grasped convulsively at the cushions, his body was thrust forward and straightened out.

"Oh, holy Christ! I am going to spend!" he exclaimed, as with parted lips and glazing eyes he looked his last upon his innocent victim. Then he shivered perceptibly, and with low moans and short, hysteric cries, his penis, in obedience to the provocation of the young lady, began to jet forth its volumes of thick and glutinous fluid.

Bella, sensible of the gushes, which now came slopping jet, after jet, into her mouth, and ran in streams down her throat, hearing the cries of her companion, and perceiving with ready intuition that he was enjoying to the utmost the effect she had brought about, continued her rubbings and compression until gorged with the slimy discharge, and half choked by its abundance, she was compelled to let go of this human syringe, which continued to spout out its gushes in her face.

"Holy mother!" exclaimed Bella, whose lips and face were reeking with the Father's spunk. "Holy Mother? What pleasure I have had—and you, my Father, have I not given the precious relief you coveted?"

Father Ambrose, too agitated to reply, raised the gentle girl in his arms, and pressing her streaming mouth to his, sacked humid, kisses of gratitude and pleasure.

A quarter of an hour passed in tranquil repose uninterrupted by any signs of disturbance from without.

The door was fast, and the holy Father had well chosen his time.

Meanwhile Bella, whose desires had been fearfully excited by the scene we have attempted to describe, had conceived an extravagant longing to have the same operation performed upon her with the rigid member of Ambrose that she had suffered from the moderately proportioned weapon of Charlie.

Throwing her arms round the burly neck of her confessor, she whispered low words of invitation, watching, as she did so the effect in the already stiffening instrument between his legs.

"You told me that the tightness of this little slit," and here Bella placed his large hand upon it with a gentle pressure, "would make you discharge abundantly of the spunk you possess. What would I not give, my Father, to feel it poured into my body from the top of this red thing?"

It was evident how much the beauty of the young Bella, no less than the innocence and "naivete" of her character, inflamed the sensual nature of the priest. The knowledge of his triumph—of her utter helplessness in his hands—of her delicacy and refinement, all conspired to work to the extreme of lecherous desires of his fierce and wanton instincts. She was his. His to enjoy as he wished—his to break to every caprice of his horrid lust, and to bend to the indulgence of the most outrageous and unbridled sensuality.

"Ah, by heaven! it is too much," exclaimed Ambrose, whose lust, already rekindling, now rose violently into activity at this sollicitation. "Sweet girl, you don't know what you ask; the disproportion is terrible, and you would suffer much in the attempt."

"I would suffer all," replied Bella, "so that I could feel that fierce thing in my belly, and taste the gushes of its spunk up in me to the quick."

"Holy Mother of God! It is too much—you shall have it, Bella, you shall know the full measure of this stiffened machine, and, sweet girl, you shall wallow in an ocean of warm spunk.''

"Oh, my Father, what heavenly bliss!''

"Strip, Bella, remove everything that can interfere with our movements, which I promise you will be violent enough.''

Thus ordered, Bella was soon divested of her clothing, and finding her Confessor appeared charmed at the display of her beauty, and that his member swelled and lengthened in proportion as she exhibited her nudity, she parted with the last vestige of drapery, and stood as naked as she was born.

Father Ambrose was astonished at the charms which now faced him. The full hips, the budding breasts, the skin as white as snow and soft as satin, the rounded buttocks and swelling thighs, the flat white belly and lovely mont covered only with the thinnest down; and above all the charming pinky slit which now showed itself at the bottom of the mount, now hid timorously away between the plump thighs and with a snort of rampant lust he fell upon his victim.

Ambrose glasped her in his arms. He pressed her soft and glowing form to his burly front. He covered her with his salacious kisses, and giving his lewd tongue full licence, promised the young girl all the joys of Paradise by the introduction of his big machine within her slit and belly.

Bella met him with a little cry of ecstasy, and as the excited ravisher bore her backwards to the couch, already felt the broad and glowing head of gigantic penis pressing against the warm moist lips of her almost virgin orifice.

And now, the holy man finding delight in the contact of his penis with the warm lips of Bella's slit, began pushing it in between with all his energy until the big nut was covered with the moisture which the sensitive little sheath exuded.

Bella's passions were at fever height. The efforts of Father Ambrose to lodge the head of his member within the moist lips of her little slit, so far from deterring her, spurred her to madness until, with another faint cry, she fell prone and gushed down the slippery tribute of her lascivious temperament.

This was exactly what the bold priest wanted, and as the sweet warm emission bedewed his fiercely distended penis, he drove resolutely in, and at one bound sheathed half its ponderous length in the beautiful child.

No sooner did Bella feel the stiff entry of the terrible member within her tender body, than she lost all the little control of herself she had, and setting aside all thought of the pain she was enduring, she wound her legs about his loins, and entreated her huge assaillant not to spare her.

"My sweet and delicious child," whispered the salaclous priest, "my arms are round you, my weapon is already half way up your tight little belly. The joys of Paradise will be yours presently."

"Oh, I know it; I feel it, do not draw back, give me the delicious thing as far as you can."

"There, then, I push, I press, but I am far too largely made to enter you easily. I shall burst you, possibly; but it is now too late. I must have you—or die."

Bella's parts relaxed a little, and Ambrose pushed in another inch. His throbbing member lay skinned and soaking, pushed half way into the little girl's belly. His pleasure was most intense, and the head of his instrument was compressed deliciously by Bella's slit.

"Go on, dear Father, I am waiting for the spunk you promised me."

It little needed this stimulant to induce the confessor to an exercice of his tremendous powers of copulation. He pushed frantically forward; he plunged his hot penis still further and further at each effort, and then with one huge stroke buried himself to the balls in Bella's light little person.

It was then that the furious plunge of the brutal priest became more than his sweet victim, sustained as she had been by her own advanced desires, could endure.

With a faint shrick of physical anguish, Bella felt that her ravisher had burst through all the resistance which her youth had opposed to the entry of his member, and the torture of the forcible insertion of such a mass bore down the prurient sensations with which she had commenced to suport the attack.

Ambrose cried aloud in rapture, he looked down upon the fair thing his serpent had stung. He gloated over the victim now impaled with the full rigour of his huge rammer. He felt the maddening contact with inexpressible delight. He saw her quivering with the anguish of his forcible entry. His brutal nature was fully aroused. Come what might he would enjoy to his utmost, so he wound his arms about the beautiful girl and treated her to the full measure of his burly member.

"My beauty! you are indeed exciting, you must also enjoy. I will give you the spunk I spoke of, but I must first work up my nature by this luscious titillation. Kiss me, Bella, then you shall have it, and while the hot spunk leaves me and enters your young parts, you shall be sensible of the throbbing joys I also am experiencing. Press, Bella, let me push, so, my child, now it enters again. Oh! oh!"

Ambrose raised himself a moment, and noted the immense shaft round which the pretty slit of Bella was now intensely stretched.

Firmly embedded in his luscious sheath, and keenly relishing the exceeding tightness of the warm folds of youthful flesh which now encased him, he pushed on, unmindful of the pain his tormenting member was producing, and only anxious to secure as much enjoyment to himself as he could. He was not a man to be deterred by any false notions of pity in such a case, and now pressed himself inwards to his utmost, while his hot lips sucked delicious kisses from the open and quivering lips of the poor Bella.

For some minutes nothing now was heard but the jerking blows with which the lascivious priest continued his enjoyment, and the cluck, cluck of his huge penis, as it alternately entered and retreated in the belly of the beautiful penitent.

It was not to be supposed that such a man as Ambrose was ignorant of the tremendous powers of enjoyment his member could rouse within one of the opposite sex, and that with its size and disgorging capabilities of such a nature as to enlist the most powerful emotions in the young girl in whom he was operating.

But Nature was asserting herself in the person of the young Bella. The agony of the stretching was fast being swallowed up in the intense sensations of pleasure produced by the vigorous weapon of the holy man, and it was not long before the low moans and sobs of the pretty child became mingled with expressions, half choked in the depth of her feelings, expressive of delight.

"Oh, my Father! Oh, my dear, generous Father! Now, now push. Oh! push. I can bear—I wish for it. I am in heaven! The blessed instrument is so hot in its head. Oh! my heart. Oh! my—oh! Holy Mother, what is this I feel?"

Ambrose saw the effect he was producing. His own pleasure advanced apace. He drove steadily in and out, treating Bella to the long hard shaft of his member up to the crisp hair which covered his big balls, at each forward thrust.

At length Bella broke down, and treated the electrified and ravished man with a warm emission which ran all over his stiff affair.

It is impossible to describe the lustful frenzy which now took possession of the young and charming Bella. She clung with desperate tenacity to the burly figure of the priest, who bestowed upon the heaving and voluptuous body the full force and vigour of his manly thrust. She held him in her tight and slippery sheath to his balls.

But in her ecstasy Bella never lost sight of the promised perfection of the enjoyment. The holy man was to spend his spunk in her as Charlie had done, and the thought added fuel to her lustful fire.

When, therefore, Father Ambrose, throwing his arms close round her taper waist, drove up his stallion penis to the very hairs in Bella's slit, and sobbing, whispered that the "spunk" was coming at last, the excited girl straightway opening her legs to the utmost, with positive shrieks of pleasure let him send his pent-up fluid in showers into her very vitals.

Thus he lay for full two minutes, while at each hot and forcible injection of the slippery semen, Bella gave plentiful evidence by her writhings and cries of ecstasy the powerful discharge was producing.

CHAPTER III

I do not think I ever felt my unfortunate infirmity in the matter of a natural inability to blush more acutely than on the present occasion. But even a flea might have blushed at the wanton sight which thrust itself upon his vision on the occasion I have herein recorded. So young, so apparently innocent a girl, and yet so lewd, so lascivious in her inclinations and desires. A person of infinite freshness and beauty—a mind of flaming sensuality fanned by the accidental course of events into an active volcano of lust.

Well might I have exclaimed with the poet of old:

"O Moses!" or with the more practical descendant of the Patriarch: "Holy Moses!"

It is needless to speak of the change which Bella's whole being underwent after such experiences as these I have related. They were manifest and apparent in her carriage and demeanour.

What became of her youthful lover I never knew nor cared to inquire, but I am led to believe that holy Father Ambrose was not insensible to those irregular tastes which are so largely ascribed to his order, and that the youth was led by easy stages to lend "himself," no less than his young mistress to the gratification of the insensate desires of the priest.

But to return to my own observations so far as they extended to the fair Bella.

Although a Flea cannot blush, we can "observe" and I have taken upon me to commit to pen and ink all those amatory passages in my experiences which I think may interest the seeker after truth. We can write, at least this Flea can, or else these pages would not now be before the reader, and that is enough.

It was several days before Bella found an opportunity of again visiting her clerical admirer, but at length the chance come, and, as might be expected, she quickly availed herself of it.

She had found means to apprise Ambrose of her intention of visiting him, and that astute individual was accordingly ready to receive his pretty guest as before.

Bella no sooner found herself alone with her seducer than she threw herself into his arms, and pressing his huge carcass to her little form, lavished upon him the most tender caresses.

Ambrose was not slow in returning to the full the warmth of her embrace, and thus it happened that the pair found themselves hotly engaged in the exchange of burning kisses, and reclining face to face upon the well-cushioned seat before alluded to.

But Bella was not likely now to be contented with kisses only, she desired more solid fare, which she knew from experience the Father could give her.

Ambrose, on his part, was no less excited. His blood flowed quickly, his dark eye flamed with unconcealed lust, and his protuberant dress displayed only too plainly the disorder of his senses.

Bella perceived his condition; neither his inflamed looks, nor the evident erection, which he took no trouble to conceal, escaped her—she sought to add to his desires, if possible, not to diminish them.

Soon, however, Ambrose showed her that he required no further incentive, for he deliberately produced his fiercely distended weapon in a state the bare sight of which drove Bella frantic with desire. At any other time Ambrose would have been more prudent of his pleasures than thus early to have proceeded to work with his celicious little conquest. On this occasion, however, his senses ran riot with him; and he was unable to check the overwhelming desire to revel at once and as soon as possible in the juvenile charms thus offered him.

He was already upon her body. His great bulk covered her figure most powerfully and completely. His distended member bore hardly against Bella's stomach, and her clothes were already raised to her waist.

With a trembling hand Ambrose seized the centre chink

of his wishes—eagerly he brought the hot and crimson tip towards its moist and opening lips. He pushed, he strove to penetrate—he succeeds; the immense machine slowly but surely enters—already the head and shoulders have disappeared.

A few steady, deliberate thrusts complete the conjunction, and Bella has received the whole length of Ambrose's huge excited member in her body.

The ravisher lay panting upon her bosom in complete possession of her inmost charms.

Bella, into whose little belly the vigorous mass was thus crammed, felt most powerfully the effects of the throbbing and hot intruder.

Meanwhile Ambrose began to thrust up and down. Bella threw her white arms around his neck, and twined her pretty silk clad legs all wantonly above his loins.

"How delicious," murmured Bella, kissing rapturously his thick lips, "Push me—push up me harder. Oh, how it forces me open—how large it is! How hot—how—oh my—oh!"

And down came a shower from Bella's storehouse, in response to the strong thrusts received, while her head fell back and her mouth opened in the spasms of coition.

The priest restrained himself, he paused an instant, the throbbing of his long member sufficiently announced his condition; he wished to prolong his pleasure to the utmost.

Bella squeezed the terrible shaft in her inermost person, and felt it grow harder and even stiffer while its purple head pressed up to her young womb.

Almost immediately afterwards her unwieldy lover, unable to prolong his pleasure, succumbed to the intensest of keen and all pervading sensation of glutinous fluid.

"Oh, it is coming from you," cried the excited girl. "I

feel it in gushes. Oh! give it me—more—more—pour it into me—push harder; do not spare me! Oh, another gush! Push—tear me if you like—but let me have all your spunk.''

I have before spoken of the quantity Father Ambrose possessed the power of discharging, and he now surpassed himself. He had been bottled up for nearly a week, and Bella now received such a tremendous stream of his nature that his discharge more resembled the action of a syringe than the outpouring from the genitals of man.

At last Ambrose dismounted, and Bella on standing once more upon her feet, felt a clinging slippery stream trickling slowly down her plump thighs.

Hardly had the Father withdrawn than the door leading into the church opened, and, behold, two other priests presented themselves within its portal. Concealment was of course impossible.

"Ambrose," exclaimed the elder of the two, a man apparently between thirty and forty years old, "this is against our rules and privileges, which enact that all such game shall be in common."

"Take it then," growled the person addressed. "It is not too late—I was going to tell you of what I had got, only—"

"Only the delicious temptation of this young mossrose was too much for you, my friend!" exclaimed the other, seizing, as he spoke, upon the astonished Bella, and forcing his large hand up her clothes to her soft thighs.

"I saw it all through the keyhole," whispered the brute in her ear. "You need not be frightened, we shall only treat you the same, my dear."

Bella remembered the conditions of her admittance to the solace of the church, and supposed this was only a part of her new duties. She therefore rested unresistingly in the arms of the two new comers.

Meanwhile his companion had passed his strong arm around Bella's waist, and covered her delicate cheek with kisses.

Ambrose looked stupid and confounded.

The young lady thus found herself between two fires, to say nothing of the smouldering passion of her original possessor. In vain she looked from one to the other for some respite, some means of extrication from her predic-ament.

For, be it known, that although she fully resigned herself to the position into which the cunning of Father Ambrose had consigned her, a bodily feeling of weakness and fear of the new assailants nearly overcame her.

Bella read nothing but lust and raging desire in the looks of the new-comers, while the non-resistance of Ambrose disarmed all thought of defence on her own part.

The two men had now got her between them, and while the first speaker had pushed his hand as far as her rosy slit, the other lost no time in possessing himself of the well-rounded cheeks of her plump buttocks.

Between them Bella was powerless to resist.

"Stay a moment," at length suggested Ambrose, "if you are in earnest to enjoy her, at least undress without tearing her clothes to pieces, as you both seemed inclined to do."

"Strip, Bella," continued he, "we must all share you, it seems; so prepare to become the willing instrument of our united pleasures."

"Our convent contains others no less exigent than myself, and your office will be no sinecure, so you had better remember always the privileges you are called upon to fulfil, and be ready to relieve these holy men of the fiery desires which you yet know how to assuage.''

Thus directed there was no alternative.

Bella stood naked before the three vigorous priests.

Murmurs of delight burst from all when Bella stood timidly forth in her beauty.

No sooner did the spokesman of the newcomers, who was evidently the superior of thet three, perceive the beautiful nudity now presented to his passionate glances, without any hesitation, he opened his dress, and giving liberty to a large and long member, caugnt the beautiful girl in his arms, bore her back to the couch, and then, spreading open her pretty thighs, he planted himself between, and hastily bringing the head of his raging champion to the soft orifice, thrust forward, and at one bound buried himself to his balls.

Bella gave a little cry of ecstasy, as she felt the stiff insertion of this new and powerful weapon.

To the man in full possession of the beautiful child the contact was ecstasy, and the feeling with which he found himself completely buried in her body to the hilt of his rampant penis was one of undefiniable emotion. He had no idea he should so readily penetrate her young parts, but he had omitted to take into account the flood of semen which she had already received.

The Superior, however, gave her no time for reflection, but commenced to run his course so energetically that his long and powerful strokes produced their fullest effects upon her warm temperament, and almost immediatly coused her to give down her sweet emission,

This was too much for the wanton ecclesiastic. Already firmly imbedded in the tight and glove-like sheath, he no sooner felt the hot effusion than he uttered a long growl, and discharged furiouṣly.

Bella relished the spouting torrent of the strong man's lust, and throwing out her legs, received him to his utmost length in her belly, allowing him there to satiate lust in the jetting streams of his fiery nature.

Bella's lewdest feelings were roused by this second and determined attack upon her person, and her excitable nature received with exquisite delight the rich libations the two stalwart champions had pourced out. But prurient as she was, the young lady found herself much exhausted by this continued strain upon her bodily powers, and it was therefore with dismay that she perceived the second of the intruders preparing to take advantages of the retirement of the Superior.

But what was Bella's astonishment to discover the gigantic proportions of the Priest who now presented himself. Already his dress was in disorder and before him stood stiffly erected a member before which even the vigorous Ambrose was forced to cede.

Out of a curling fringe of red hair sprang the white column of flesh, capped by the shining dull red head, the tight and closely, shut orifice of which looked, as if it was obliged to be careful and to prevent a premature over flow of its juices.

Two huge and hairy balls hung closely below, and completed the picture, at sight of which Bella's blood began once more to boil, and her youthful spirits to expand with longing for the disproportionate combat.

"Oh! my Father, how shall I ever get that great thing into my poor little person?" asked Bella, in dismay, "How shall I be able to endure it, when it does go in! I fear it will hurt me dreadfully!"

"I will be very careful, my daughter. I will go slowly. You are well prepared now by the juices of the holy men who have had the good fortune to precede me."

Bella fingered the gigantic penis.

The Priest was ugly in the extreme. He was short and stout, but built with shoulders broad enough for a Hercules.

The child had caught a sort of lewd madness; his ugliness only served further to rouse her sensual desires; her hands could not meet round his member. She continued, however, to hold it, to press it and unconsciously to bestow upon it caresses which increased its rigidity and advanced the pleasure. It stood like a bar of iron in her soft hands.

Another moment and the third assailant was upon her, and Bella, almost equally excited, strove to impale herself upon the terrible weapon.

For some minutes the feat seemed impossible, well lubricated as she was by the previous overflowings she had received.

At length a furious lunge drove in the enormous head.

Bella uttered a cry of real anguish; another, and another lunge, the brutal wretch, blind to all but his own gratification, continued to penetrate.

Bella cried out in her agony, and wildly strove to detach herself from her fierce assailant.

Another thrust, another cry from his victim, and the priest had penetrated her to the quick.

Bella had fainted.

The two observers of this monstrous act of debauchery seemed at first inclined to interfere, but it seemed as if they experienced a cruel pleasure in witnessing the conflict, and certainly their lewd movements, and the interest they evidently took in observing the minutest details argued their satisfaction.

I draw a veil over the scene of lust which followed, over the writhings of the savage, as he—securely in possession of the person of the young and beautiful child—slowly spun out his enjoyment, until his gross and fervid discharge put an end to his ecstasies, and allowed an interval in which to restore the poor girl to life.

The stalwart Father had discharged twice before he drew out his long and reeking member, and the volume of spunk which followed was such as to fall pattering in a pool upon the wooden floor.

At length sufficiently recovered to move, the young Bella was permitted to perform those ablutions which the streaming condition of her delicate parts rendered necessary.

CHAPTER IV

Several bottles of wine, of old and rare vintage, were now produced, and under their potent influence, Bella slowly recovered her strength.

Within an hour the three priests, finding that she was now sufficiently restored to entertain their lascivious advances, once more began to show signs of a desire for a further enjoyment of her person.

Excited no less by the generous wine than by the sight and touch of her lewd companions, the girl now commenced to pull from their cassocks, and to uncover the members of the three priests, whose enjoyment of the scene was evidently manifested by their absence of restraint.

In less than a minute Bella had all three of their long and stiff affairs in full view. She kissed and toyed with them, sniffing the faint fragrance which arose from them, and fingering the blushing shafts with all the eagerness of an accomplished Cyprian.

"Let us fuck," piously ejaculated the Superior, whose prick was at that moment at Bella's lips.

"Amen," chanted Ambrose.

The third ecclesiastic was silent, but his huge penis menaced the skies.

Bella was directed to choose her first assailant in this new round. She selected Ambrose, but the Superior supervened.

Meanwhile, the doors being secured, the three priests deliberately stripped themselves, and thus presented to the brilliant gaze of the youthful Bella three vigorous champions in the prime of life, each armed with a stalwart weapon, which stood once more firmly in their fronts and wagged about threateningly as they moved.

"Oh, fie! What monsters!" exclaimed the young lady, whose shame, however, did not prevent her handling alternately these redoubtable engines.

They have sat her upon the edge of the table, and one by one they sucked her young parts, rolling their hot tongues round and round in the moist red slit in which all had so recently appeased their lust. Bella lent herself to this with joy, and opened to the utmost her plump legs to gratify them.

"I propose she shall suck us one after the other," exclaimed the Superior.

"Certainly," assented Father Clement, the man of the red hair and huge erection. "But not to finish so. I want her once more in the belly."

"No; certainly not, Clement," said the Superior. "You have well nigh split her in two as it is; you must finish down her throat or not all."

Bella had no intention of again submitting to an attack from Clement, so she cut short the discussion by seizing on the fat member and putting as much of it as she could into her pretty mouth.

Up and down the blue nut the girl worked her soft moist lips, every now and then pausing to receive as much of it as possible within her mouth. Her fair hands passed around the long, large shaft, and clutched it in a tremulous embrace, as she watched the monstrous penis swell harder with the intensity of the sensations imparted by her delicious touches.

In less than five minutes Clement began to utter howlings more like those of a wild beast than the exclamations of the human lungs, and spent in volumes down her gullet.

Bella drew down the skin along the long shaft, and encouraged the flood to end.

Clement's spendings were as thick and hot as they were plentiful, and squirt after squirt of spunk flew into the girl's mouth.

Bella swallowed it all.

"There is a new experience I must now instruct you, in my daughter," said the Superior, as Bella next applied her soft lips to his burning member.

"You will find it productive of more pain than pleasure at first, but the ways of Venus are difficult, and only to be learnt and enjoyed by degrees."

"I shall submit myself to all, my Father," replied the girl; I know my duty now better, and that I am one of those favoured ones selected to relieve the desires of the good Fathers."

"Certainly, my daughter, and you feel the bliss of heaven in advance while obeying our slightest wishes, and indulging all our inclinations, however strange and irregular they may be."

With that he took the girl in his strong arms, and bore her once more to the couch, where he placed her on her face, thus exposing her naked and beautiful posteriors to the whole three.

Next, placing himself between the thighs of his victim, he pointed the tip of his stiff member at the small orifice between Bella's plump buttocks, and pushing forward his well-lubricated weapon by slow degrees, at the same time began to penetrate her in this novel and unnatural manner.

"Oh,—my!—" cried Bella, "you are in the wrong place—it hurts.—Pray—oh! Pray—ah! Have mercy. Oh! pray spare me! Holy Mother! I die!"

This last exclamation was caused by a final and vigorous thrust on the part of the Superior, which sent his stallion member up to the hairs that covered the lower portion of his belly—Then Bella felt that he was up her body to his balls.

Passing his strong arm around her hips, he pressed close to her back; his stout belly rubbed against her buttocks, and his stiff member was kept thrust into her rectum as far as it would go. The pulsations of pleasure were evident throughout its swollen length, and Bella, biting her lips, awaited the movements of the man which she well knew he was about to commence in order to finish his enjoyment.

The other two priests looked on with envious lust, slowly frigging their big members the while.

As for the Superior, maddened by the tightness of this new and delicious sheath, he laboured at her round buttocks until, with a final lunge, he filled her bowels with his hot discharge. Then drawing his instrument, still erect and smoking, from her body, he declared that he had opened up a new route to pleasure, and recommended Ambrose to avail himself of it.

Ambrose, whose feelings during this time may be better imagined than described, was now rampant with desire.

The sight of his confreres enjoying themselves gradually produced a state of erotic excitement within him that it became necessary to quench as soon as possible.

"Agreed," he cried, "I will enter by the Temple of Sodom, and you, meanwhile, shall fill with your sturdy sentinel the Halls of Venus."

"Say rather of legitimate enjoyment," rejoined the Superior with a grin. "Be it as you say; I should well like another taste of so tight a belly."

Bella still lay upon her belly upon the couch: Her rounded posterior fully exposed, more dead than alive from the brutal attack which she had just suffered. Not a drop of the semen which had been injected into her so plentifully escaped from the dark recess, but below her slit still ran with the combined emission of the priests. Ambrose seized her.

Placed accross the thighs of the Superor, Bella now found his still vigorous member knocking against the lips of her pink slit; slowly she guided it in, as she lowered herself upon it. Presently it all entered—she had it to the roots.

But now the vigorous Superior, passing his arms around

her waist, drew her down upon him, and sinking backwards, brought her large and exquisite buttocks before the angry weapon of Ambrose, who straightway bore directly at the already well moistened aperture between their hillocks.

A thousand difficulties presented themselves to be overcome, but at length the lecherous Ambrose felt himself buried in the entrails of his tender victim.

Slowly he drew his member up and down the slippery channel. He spun out his pleasure and enjoyed the vigorous bounds with which his Superior was treating the fair Bella in front.

Presently, with a deep sigh, the Superior reached his climax, and Bella felt him rapidly filling her slit with spunk.

She could not resist the impetus, and her own overflowing mingled with those of her assailant.

Ambrose, however, had husbanded his resources, and now held the pretty girl in front of him, firmly impaled upon his huge affair.

In this position Clement could not resist the opportunity, but watching his chance while the Superior was wiping his person, he drove himself in front of Bella, and almost immediately succeeded in penetrating her belly, now liberally bedewed with their slippery leavings.

Enormous though it was, Bella found means to receive the red-haired monster which now stretched her delicate body with its entire length, and for the next few minutes nothing was heard but the sighs and lustful moans of the combattants.

Presently their motions grew harder; Bella expected every moment would be her last. The huge member of Ambrose was up her posterior passage to his balls, while the gigantic truncheon of Clement made all froth again within her belly.

The child was supported between the two, her feet fairly off the ground, and, subject, to the blows, first in front and then behind, with which the priests worked their excited engines in their respective channels.

Just as Bella commenced to lose her consciousness, she became aware by the heavy breathing and the tremendous stiffness of the brute in front that his discharge was coming and the next moment she felt the hot injection flow from the gigantic prick in strong and viscid jets.

"Ah! I spend" cried Clement, and with that he squirted a copious flood up little Bella, to her infinite delight.

"Mine's coming too," shrieked Ambrose, driving home his vigorous member, and pouring a hot jet of his spunk into Bella's bowels at the same time.

Thus the two continued disgorging the prolific contents of their bodies into that of the gentle girl, while she experienced the double flood, and swam in a deluge of delights.

Anyone would have supposed that a flea of average intelligence only would have had enough of such disgusting exhibitions as I have thought it my duty to disclose; but a certain feeling of friendship as well as sympathy for the young Bella impelled me still to remain in her company.

The event justified my anticipations, and as will hereafter appear, determined my future movements.

Three days only elapsed ere the young lady met the three priests by appointment in the same place.

On this occasion, Bella had taken extra care in regard to her toilet, and the result was that she now appeared more enchanting than ever, in the prettiest of silk dresses, the tightest of kid-boots, and the tiniest of lovely and well-fitting gloves.

The three men were in raptures, and Bella was received in so warm a manner that already her young blood mounted hot to her face with desire.

The door was promptly secured, and then down went the nether garments of the reverend fathers, and Bella, amid the mingled caresses and lascivious touches of the trio, beheld their members baldy exposed and already menacing her.

The Superior was the first who advanced with the intention of enjoying her.

Boldly placing himself in front of her little form, he bore roughly against her, and taking her in his arms, covered her mouth and face with hot kisses.

Bella's excitement equalled his.

By their desire, Bella denuded herself of her drawers and petticoats, and retaining only her exquisite dress, silk stockings, and pretty kid-boots, offered herself to their admiration and lascivious touches.

A moment later and the Father, sinking deliciously upon her reclining figure, had pushed himself to the hairs in her young charms, and remained soaking in the tight conjunction with evident gratification.

Pushing, squeezing, and rubbing against her, the Superior commenced delicious movements, which had the effect of raising both his partner's susceptibilities and his own. His prick, in its increased size and hardness, bore evidence of this.

"Push, oh! Push me harder," murmured Bella.

Meanwhile Ambrose and Clement whose desires could ill brook the delay, sought to engage some portion of the girl's attention.

Clement put his huge member into her soft white hand and Ambrose, nothing daunted, mounting on the couch, brought the tip of his bulky affair to her delicate lips.

After a few moments, the Superior withdrew from his luscious position.

Bella rose upon the edge of the couch. Before her were the three men, each had his member exposed and erect before him, and the enormous head of Clement's engine turned back almost against his fat belly.

Bella's dress was raised to her waist, her legs and thighs were in full view, and between them the luscious, pinky slit, now reddened and excited by the too abrupt insertion and withdrawal of the Superior's prick.

"Stay a moment," he observed; "let us proceed with order in our pleasures. This beautiful child is to satisfy all three, therefore it will be necessary to regulate both our enjoyments, and also to enable her to support the attacks to which she will be liable. For myself I do not care whether I come first or second; but as Ambrose spends like an ass, will probably make all smoke again in the regions he penetrates, I propose to pass first. Certainly Clement must be content with the second or third place, or his enormous member would not only split the girl, but what is of far more consequence, spoil our pleasure."

"I was third last time." exclaimed Clement. "I see no reason why I should always be last. I claim the second place."

"Good, so let it be then," cried the Superior. "You, Ambrose, will have a slippery nest for your share."

"Not I," rejoined that determined ecclesiastic; "if you go first, and that monster Clement has her second, and before me, I shall attack "by the breech" and pour offering in another direction."

"Do with me as you will," cried Bella, "I will try and bear all. But, oh, my Fathers, make haste and began."

Once more the Superior drove in his stalwart weapon. Bella met the siff insertion with delight. She hugged him, she bore down against him, and received his jets of emission with ecstatic outbursts of her own.

Clement now presented himself. His monstrous affair was already between the plump legs of the young Bella. The disproportion was terrible, but the priest was as strong and lewd as largely made, and after sundry violent and ineffectual efforts, he got in and commenced to ram the whole of his asinine member into her belly.

It is impossible to relate how the terrible proportions of this man roused the lescivious imaginations of Bella, or with what a frenzy of passion she found herself deliciously crammed and stretched by the huge genitals of Father Clement.

After a struggle of full ten minutes, Bella received the throbbing mass up to the big balls, which pressed her bottom below.

Bella threw out both her pretty legs, and allowed the brute to revel at his leisure in her charms.

Clement showed no anxiety to cut short his luscious enjoyment, and it was a quarter of an hour before two violent discharges put an end to his pleasure.

Bella received them with deep sighs of delight, and gave down a copious emission of her own upon the thick inpourings of the lustful Father.

Clement had hardly withdrew his monstrous affair from the belly of the young Bella, then, reeking from the arms of her huge lover, she fell into those of Ambrose.

True to his expressed intention, it is now her beautiful buttocks he attacks, and seeks with fierce energy to insert the throbbing head of his instrument within the tender folds of her posterior's aperture.

In vain he seeks to gain a lodgment. The broad head of his weapon is repulsed at each assault, as with brutal lust he tries hard to force himself inwards.

But Ambrose is not to be so easily defeated, he essays again, and at length a determined effort lodges the head within the delicate opening.

Now is his time—a vigorous lunge drives in a couple of inches more and with a single bound the lascivious priest then buries himself to the balls.

Bella's beautiful buttocks had a decided attraction for the lustful priet. He was agitated to an extraordinary degree, as he bore forward in his fierce efforts. He pressed his long and thick member inwards with ecstasy, regardless of the pain the stretching was causing her, as long as he could feel the delicious constrictions of her delicate young parts.

Bella utters a dreadful cry. She is impaled upon the stiff member of the brutal ravisher. She feels his throbbing flesh in her vitals, and endeavours, with frantic efforts, to escape.

But Ambrose, passing his strong arms round her slender waist, restrains her, while he follows each movement made by her, and retains himself in her quivering body by a continued inward strain.

Thus struggling, step by step, the girl crossed the appartment, having the fierce Ambrose firmly imbedded in her posterior passage.

Meanwhile this lewd spectacle was not without its effect upon the beholders.

A shout of laughter issued from their throats, and both applauded the vigour of their companion, whose visage, inflamed and working, bore ample testimony to his pleasurable emotions.

But the sight also quickly roused their desires, and both showed by the state of their members that they were as yet by no means satisfied.

Bella having by this time arrived close to the Superior, the latter caught her in his arms, and Ambrose, taking advantage of this timely check, commenced to push his member about in her bowels, while the intense heat of her body afforded him the liveliest pleasure.

By the position in which the three were now placed, the Superior found his mouth on a level with Bella's natural charms, and instantly glueing his lips thereto, he sucked her moistened slit.

But the excitement thus occasioned required more solid enjoyment, and drawing the pretty girl across his knees as he sat upon his seat, he let loose his bursting member and quickly drove it into her soft belly.

Thus Bella was between two fires, and the fierce thrusts of Father Ambrose upon her plump buttocks were now supplemented by the fervid efforts of the Superior in the other direction.

Both revelled in a sea of sensual delights, both bathed themselves to the full in the delicious sensations they experienced, while their victim, perforated before and behind by their swelling members, had to sustain as she could their excited movements.

But a further trial awaited the young Bella, for no sooner did the vigorous Clement witness the close conjunction of his companions, than, inflamed with envy, and stung by the violence of his passions, he mounted the seat behind the superior, and taking possesssion of poor Bella's head, presented his flaming weapon against her rosy lips, then forcing the tip, with the narrow aperture already exuding anticipatory drops, into her pretty mouth, he made her rub the long, hard shaft in her hand.

Meanwhile Ambrose found the insertion of the Superior's member in front quickly bring on his proceedings, while the latter, equally excited by the back action of his comrade, speedily began to feel the approaches of the spasms preceding and accompanying the final act of emission.

Clement was the first to let fly, and he sent his glutinous discharge in showers down the throat of the little Bella.

Ambrose followed, and falling on her back shot a torrent of spunk up her bowels, while the Superior at the same moment loaded her womb with his contributions.

Thus surrounded, Bella received the united discharge of the three vigorous priests.

CHAPTER V

Three days after the events detailed in the preceeding pages, Bella made her appearance in her uncle's drawing-room, as rosy and as charming as ever.

My movements in the meantime had been erratic, for my appetite was by no means small, and new features always possessed a certain piquancy for me which prevented too protracted a residence in one locality.

It was thus I found means to overhear a conversation which not a little astonished me; but which, as it bears directly upon the events I am describing, I do not hesitate to disclose.

It was thus I became acquainted with the real depth and subtlety of the character of Father Ambrose.

I am not going to reproduce this discourse here as I heard it from my vantage-ground; it will be sufficient, if I explain the principal ideas if conveyed and relate the application.

It was clear that Ambrose was annoyed and discomfitted at the abrupt participation of his "confreres" in the enjoyment of his latest acquisition, and he concocted a daring and devilish scheme to frustrate their interference, while at the same time appearing himself to be entirely innocent of the business.

In short, with this view, Ambrose went direct to Bella's uncle, and related how he had discovered his niece and her young lover in Cupid's alliance, and how there was no doubt she had received and reciprocated the last tokens of his passion.

In so doing the wily priest had an ulterior object in view. He well knew the character of the man with whom he had to deal. He knew also that sufficient of his own real life was not entirely hidden from the uncle.

In fact, the pair pretty well understood one another. Ambrose had strong passions, and was amatory to an extraordinary extent. So was Bella's uncle.

The latter had confessed as much to Ambrose, and in the course of this confession, had given evidence of such irregular desires as to raise no difficulties in making him a ready participator in the plans which the other had originated.

Mr. Verbouc's eyes had long been cast in secret upon

his niece. He had confessed it. Ambrose brought him suddenly a piece of news which opened his eyes to the fact that she had begun to entertain sentiments of the same sort for others of his sex.

The character of Ambrose occured immediately to him. He was his spiritual confessor; he asked his advice.

The holy man gave him to understand that his chance had come, and that it would be to their mutual advantage to share the prize between them.

This proposition touched a chord in the character of Verbouc of which Ambrose was already not entirely ignorant. If any fact lent greater enjoyment to his sensuality, or gave more poignancy to his indulgences, it was to witness another in the act of complete carnal copulation, and then afterwards to complete his own gratification by a second penetration and emission upon the body of the same patient.

Thus the compact was soon made; an opportunity was found; the necessary privacy secured, for Bella's aunt was an invalid and confined to her room; and then Ambrose prepared Bella for the event about to take place.

After a short preliminary discourse, in which he cautioned her not to say a word of their previous intimacy, and informed her that her relative had somehow discovered her intrigue, he led her round gradually to the fact which he had all along had in view. He even told her of the passion her uncle had conceived for her, and declared, in plain terms, that the surest way to avoid his heavy resentment was to prove obedient to all he might require of her.

Mr. Verbouc was a man of hale and vigorous build, and of about fifty years of age. As her uncle he had always inspired Bella with the greatest respect, in which was mingled not a little awe of his presence and authority. He had treated her since the death of his brother, if not with affection, at least not unkindly, though with a reserve which was natural to his character.

Bella had evidently no reason to hope for any clemency on this occasion, or to expect any escape from her indignant relative.

I pass over the first quarter of an hour, the tears of Bella, and the embarrassment with which she found herself at once the recipient of her uncle's too tender embraces and of his well-deserved carless.

The interesting comedy proceeded little by little, until Mr. Verbouc, taking his pretty niece between his knees, audaciously unfolded the design he had formed of enjoying her himself.

"There must be no silly resistance, Bella," continued her uncle; "I will have no hesitation, no affectation of modesty. It is sufficient that this good Father has sanctified the operation, and I must therefore possess and enjoy your body as your imprudent young companion has already done with your consent."

Bella was utterly confounded. Although sensual, as we have already seen, to an extent not often found in girls of such tender age, she had been brought up in those strict and conventional views which assorted with the severe and repelling character of her relative. All her horror of such a crime at once rose before her. Not even the presence and alleged sanction of Father Ambrose could lessen the distrust with which she viewed the horrible proposal now deliberately made to her.

Bella trembled with surprise and terror at the nature of the crime contemplated. This new position shocked her. The change from the reserved and severe uncle, whose wrath she had always deprecated and feared, and whose precepts she had long accustomed herself to receive with reverence, to the ardent admirer, thirsting for possession of those favours which she had so recently bestowed upon another, struck her dumb with amazement and disgust.

Meanwhile Mr. Verbouc, who was evidently not disposed to allow time for reflection, and whose disorder was plainly visible in more ways than one, took his young niece in his arms, and despite her reluctance, covered her face and neck with forbidden and passionate kisses.

Ambrose, to whom the girl turned in this exigency afforded her no solace, but on the contrary smiling grimly at the other's emotion, encouraged him by secret glances to carry to the last extremity his pleasures and his lubricity.

Resistance, under such trying circumstances, was difficult.

Bella was young and comparatively powerless in the strong grip of her relative. Lashed to frenzy by the contact and obscene touches in which he now indulged himself, Mr. Verbouc sought with redoubled energy to possess himself of the person of his niece. Already his nervous fingers pressed the beautiful satin of her thighs. Another determined push, and in spite of the close pressure which Bella continued to exert in her defence, the lewd hand covered the rosy lips, and the trembling fingers divided the close and moistened chink of modesty's stronghold.

Up to this point Ambrose had remained a quiet observer of this exciting conflict; now, however, he also advanced, and passing his powerful left arm round the young girl's slender waist, seized both her small hands in his right, and having thus pinned her, left her an easy prey to the lascivious approaches of her relative.

"For mercy's sake," moaned Bella, panting with her exertions, "Let me go; it is too horrible—it is monstrous— cruel that you are! I am lost!"

"Nay, my pretty niece, not lost," replied her uncle, "only awakened to those pleasures which Venus has in store for her votaries, and which love reserves for those who are bold enough to seize upon them and enjoy them, while they may."

"I have been horribly deceived." cried Bella, little softened by this ingenious explanation. "I see it all. Oh! shame. I cannot let you, I cannot let you, I cannot. Oh, no! I cannot. Holy Mother! Let me go, Uncle. Oh! oh!"

"Be quiet, Bella; you must indeed submit; I will enjoy you by force, if you do not allow me to do so otherwise. There, open these pretty legs, let me feel these exquisite calves these soft luscious thighs: let me put my hand upon this heaving little belly—nay, hold still, little fool. You are mine at last. Oh, how I have longed for this, Bella!"

Bella, however, still kept up a certain resistance, which only served to whet the unnatural appetite of her assailant, while Ambrose held her firmly in his clutches.

"Oh, the beautiful bottom!" exclaimed Verbouc, as he slipped his intruding hand beneath the velvet thighs of poor Bella, and felt the rounded globes of her charming "derriere". "Ah! the glorious bottom. All is mine now. All shall be feted in good time."

"Let me go," cried Bella. "Oh! oh!"

These last exclamations were wrung from the pretty girl, as between the two man they forced her backwards upon the couth which stood conveniently within reach.

As she fell, she reclined upon the stout body of Ambrose, while Mr. Verbouc, who had now raised her clothes, and lewdly exposed the silk-clad legs and exquisite proportions of his niece, drew back for a moment to enjoy at his ease the indecent exhibition which he had forcibly provided for his own amusement.

"Uncle, are you mad?" cried Bella, once more, as with wriggling limbs, she vainly strove to conceal the luscious nudity now fully exposed. "Pray, let me go."

"Yes, Bella, I am mad—mad with passion for you—mad with lust to possess you, to enjoy you, to satiate myself upon your body. Resistance is useless; I will have my will and revel in those pretty charms, in that tight and exquisite little sheath."

Thus saying, Mr. Verbouc prepared himself for the final act of the incestuous drama. He unfastened his nether garments, and discarding all considerations of modesty, wantonly allowed his niece to behold in full view the plump and rubicund proportions of his excited member, which, erect into glowing, now menaced her directly in front.

A moment later and Verbouc threw himself upon his prey, firmly held down by the recumbent priest; then applying his rampant weapon point blank to the tender orifice he essayed to complete the conjunction by inserting its large and long proportions in the body of his niece.

But the continued writhing of Bella's young form, the disgust and horror which had seized upon her, and the almost immature dimensions of her parts, effectually prevented him from gaining so easy a victory as he desired.

Never had I longed so ardently to contribute to the discomforture of a champion as on the present occasion, and moved by the complaints of the gentle Bella, with the body of a flea and the soul of a wasp, I hopped at one bound to the rescue.

To dig my probocis into the sensitive covering of the scrotum of Mr. Verbouc was the work of a second. It had the desired effect. A sharp and tingling sensation of pain made him pause. The interval was fatal, and the next moment the thighs and stomach of the young Bella were covered with the wasted superfluity of her incestuous relative's vigour.

Curses—not loud, but deep—followed this unexpected contre-temps. The would be ravisher withdrew from his vantage-ground, and unable to continue the conflict, reluctantly put up the discomfited weapon.

No sooner had Mr. Verbouc released his niece from this trying position than Father Ambrose commenced to manifest the violence of his own excitement, produced from his passive observance of the foregoing erotic scene. While still retaining his powerful grasp on Bella, and thus gratifying his sense of touch, the appearance of his dress in front plainly denoted the state of affairs as regarded his readiness to take advantage of the occasion. His redoutable weapon, seemingly disdaining the confinement of his garments, protruded itself into view, the big round head already skinned and throbbing with eagerness for enjoyment.

"Ah!" exclaimed the other, as his lewd glance fell upon the distended weapon of his confessor, "here is a champion, who will brook no defeat, I warrant," and deliberately taking it in his hand, he manipulated the huge shaft with evident satisfaction.

"What a monster! How strong it is—how stiff it stands!"

Father Ambrose rose, his crimson face betrayed the intensity of his desire; placing the frightened Bella in a more propitious attitude, he brought the broad red knob to the moistened aperture, and proceeded to force it inwards with a desperate effort.

Pain, agitation, and longing coursed each other through the nervous system of the young victim of lust,

Although the present was not the first occasion on which the reverend Father had stormed the mosscovered outworks, yet the fact of her uncle's presence, the indelicacy of the whole scene, and the innate conviction, now first dawning upon her, of the trickery and selfishness of the holy man, combined to repel within her those extreme sensations of pleasure which had before so powerfully manifested themselves.

But the proceedings of Ambrose left Bella no time for reflection, for feeling the delicate sheath press glove-like around his large weapon, he hasteded to complete the conjunction, and with a few vigorous and skilful bounds, plunged himself to the balls in her body.

Then followed a rapide interval of fierce enjoyment—of rapid thrusts and pressures, firm and close, until a low, gurgling cry from Bella announced that Nature had asserted herself, and that she had arrived at that exquisite crisis in love's combat, when spasms of unspeakable pleasure pass rapidly, voluptuously through the nerves, and with head thrown back, lips parted, and fingers convulsively working, the whole body rigid with the absorbing effort, the nymph gives down her youthful essence to meet the coming gushes from her lover.

Bella's writhing from, upturned eyes, and clutching hands sufficiently bespoke her condition without the estatic moan which broke laboriously from her quivering lips.

The whole bulk of the potent shaft, now well lubricated, worked deliciously within her young parts. The excitement of Ambrose increased each instant, and his instrument, hard as iron, threatened with each plunge to discharge its reeking essence.

"Oh, I can do no more; I feel my spunk is nearly coming. Verbouc, you must fuck her. She is delicious. Her belly clips me like a glove. Oh! Oh! Ah!"

Stronger, closer thrusts—a vigorous bound—a sinking

of the strong man upon the slight figure of the girl—a hard, low grasp, she Bella, with ineffable delight, felt the hot injection spouting from her ravisher, and pouring in volumes, thick and slippery far within her tender parts.

Ambrose reluctantly withdrew his smoking prick, and left displayed the glistening parts of the young girl, from which trickled a thick mass of his spending.

"Good," exclaimed Verbouc, on whom the scene had had a powerfully exciting effect, "It is now my turn, good Father Ambrose! You have enjoyed my niece under my eyes; that is as I wished, and she has been well ravished. She has also partaken of the pleasure with you; my anticipations are realised; she can receive, she can enjoy; one can satiate oneself with her, and in her body: good—I am going to began. My opportunity has come at last, she cannot escape me now. I am going to satisfy my long cherished desire. I am going to appease this insatiable lust for my brother's child. See this member, how he raises his red head, it is my desire for you, Bella feel, my sweet niece, how hard your dear uncle's balls are—they are filled for you. It is you who have made this thing so stiff, and long, and swollen—it is you who are destined to bring it relief. Skin it back, Bella! So, my child—let me guide your pretty hand. Oh! no nonsense—no blushes—no modesty—no reluctance—do you see its length? You must take it all into that hot little slit that dear Father Ambrose has just so well filled. Do you observe my big globes beneath, Bella daring? They are loaded with the spunk I am going to discharge for your pleasure and my own. Yes, Bella, into the belly of my brother's child."

The idea of the horrid incest he contemplated evidently added fuel to his excitement, and produced within him a surabundant sensation of lustful impatience, which exhibited itself no less in his inflamed countenance than in the stiffened and erected shaft which now menaced Bella's moistened parts.

Mr. Verbouc took his measures securely. There was indeed, as he said, no escape for poor Bella. He mounted upon her body, he opened her legs. Ambrose held her firmly against his belly as he reclined. The ravisher saw his chance, the way was clear, the white thighs already parted, the red and glistening lips of the pretty young cunt confronted him. He could wait longer; parting the lips and pointing aright the dull red head of his weapon to the pouting slit, he now drove forward, and at one bound, with a yell of sensual pleasure, buried himself to his utmost length in his niece's belly.

"Oh, Lord: I'm in her at last," screamed Verbouc. "Oh! ah! What pleasure—how nice she is—how tight. Oh!"

Good Father Ambrose held her fast.

Bella gave a violent start, and a little scream of pain and terror, as she felt the entry of her uncle's swollen member; while, firmly embedded in the warm person of his victim, he commenced a quick and furious career of selfish pleasure. It was the lamb in the clutches of the wolf, the dove in the talons of the eagle—merciless, regardless of her own feelings, the brute bore all before him, until, too soon for his own hot lust, with a scream of agonised enjoyment, he discharged, and shot into his niece a plentiful torrent of his incestuous fluid.

Again and again the two wretches enjoyed their young victim. Their hot lust, stimulated by the prospect of each other's pleasures, drove them to madness.

Ambrose essayed to attack her in the buttocks, but Verbouc, who doubtless had his own reasons for the prohibition, forbade the violation, and the priest, no ways abashed, lowered the knob of his big tool, and drove it up furiously into her little slit from behind. Verbouc knelt below, and watched the act, and at its conclusion sucked, with evident delight, the streaming lips of his young niece's well filled cunt.

That night I accompanied Bella to her couch, for though my nerves had received a dreadful shock, my appetite had suffered no diminution, and it was lucky; perhaps, that my young "protegee" was not possessed of so irritable a skin as to resent to any great extent my endeavous to satisfy my natural cravings.

Sleep had succeeded the repast with which I had regaled myself, and I had found deliciously warm and secure retreat amid the soft and tender moss which covered the mount of the fair Bella when, at about midnight, a violent disturbances roughly roused me from my dignified repose.

A rude and powerful grasp was upon the young girl, and a heavy form pressed vigorously upon her little figure. A stifled cry came from her frightened lips, and amid vain struggles on her part to escape and more successful efforts to prevent that desirable consummation on the part of her assailant, I recognised the voice and person of Mr. Verbouc.

The surprise had been complete; vain was all the feeble resistance that his niece could offen, as with feverish haste, and dreadfully excited by the soft contact of her velvet limbs, the incestuous uncle fiercely possessed himself of her most secret charms, and strong in his hideous lust, drove his rampant weapon into her young body.

Then followed a struggle in which both played a distinct part.

The revisher, fired equally by the difficulties of his conquest, as well as by the exquisite sensations he was enjoying, buried his stiff member in the luscious sheath, and sought by his fervid thrusts to ease his lust in a copious discharge, while Bella, whose prudent temperament was not proof against so strong and lascivious an attack, strove in vain to resist the violent efforts of nature, which, roused by the exciting friction, threatened to turn traitor, until at length with quiverings limbs and gasping breath, she surrendered and gave down the sweet outpourings of her inmost soul upon the swollen shaft which so deliciously throbbed within her.

Mr. Verbouc was fully aware of his advantage and changing his tactics, like a prudent general, he took care not to expend all his own climax and provoked a fresh advance on the part of his gentle combatant.

Mr. Verbouc had not great difficulty in the matter, and the conflict appeared to excite him to fury. The bed trembled and shook, the whole room vibrated with the tremulous energy of his lascivious attack, the two bodies heaved rolled, plunged in an undistinguishable mass.

Lust, hot and impatient, reigned paramount on both sides. He lunged—he strove—he pushed—he thrust—he drew back until the broad red head of his swollen penis lay between the rosy lips of Bella's hot parts. He drove forward until the crisp black hairs of his belly mingled with the soft mossy down which covered the plump mount of his niece, until, with a quivering sob, she expressed at once her pain and her pleasure.

Once more the victory was his, and as his vigorous member sheathed itself to the hilt in her soft person, a low, tender, wailing cry bespoke her ecstasy as once more the keen spasm of pleasure broke over her nervous system; and then, with a groam of brutal triumph, he shot a hot stream of trickling fluid into the furthest recesses of her womb.

Endowed with the frenzy of newly-awakened desire, and still unsatisfied with the possession of so fair a flower, the brutal Verbouc next turned his half fainting niece upon her face, and contemplated at his ease her lovely buttocks. His object became evident, as procuring some of the spendings with which her little slit was now loaded, he annointed her anus, pushing his forefinger therein as far as it would go.

His passions were again at fever point. His prick menaced her plump bottom, and turning upon her recumbent body, he placed the shining knob to the tight little aperture, and endeavoured to ram it in. In this, after a time, he succeeded, and Bella received in her rectum the entire length of her uncle's yard. The tightness of her anus afforded him the most poignant pleasure, and he continued to work slowly up and down for at least a quarter of an hour, at the end of which time his prick became hard as iron, and the child felt him squirting hot floods of spunk into bowels.

It was daylight before Mr. Verbouc released his niece from the lustful embraces in which he had satiated his passion, and then slunk weakly away to his own cold couch; while, worn and jaded. Bella sank into a deep slumber of exhaustion, from which she did not awake until a late hour.

When next Bella emerged from·her chamber, it was with a sense of change in herself which she neither cared nor sought to analyse. Passion had asserted itself in her character; strong sexual emotions had been awakened, and had also been gratified. Refinement of indulgence had generated lust, and lust had rendered easy the road to unrestrained and even unnatural gratification.

Bella, young, child-like, and so lately innocent, had suddenly become a woman of violent passions and unrestrained lust.

CHAPTER VI

I shall not trouble the reader with the conditions under which one day I found myself snugly concealed upon the person of good Father Clement, or pause here to explain how it was I was present when that worthy ecclesiastic received and confessed a very charming and stylish young lady of some twenty years of ago.

I soon discovered from their subsequent conversation

that the lady was not of titled rank, though closely connected, but married to one of the wealthiest landed proprietors in the neighbourhood.

Names are of no importance here. I, therefore, suppress that of this fair penitent.

After the confessor had ended his benediction, and had concluded the ceremony by which he became the depository of the lady's choicest secrets, he led her, nothing loath, from the body of the church into the same small sacristy where Bella had received her lesson in sanctified copulation.

The door was bolted, no time was lost, the lady dropped her robe, the stalwart confessor opened his cassock, disclosing his enormous weapon, the ruby head of which now stood distended and threatening in the air. The lady no sooner perceived this apparition, than she seized upon it with the air of one to whom it was by no means a new object of delight.

Her dainty hand stroked gently the upright pillar of hard muscle and her eyes devoured its long and swollen proportions.

"You shall do it to me from behind," remarked the lady—"en levrette, but you must be very careful; you are so fearfally large."

Father Clement's eyes glistened under his large head of red hair, and his big weapon gave a spasmodic throb that would have lifted a chair.

In another second the young lady had placed herself on her knees upon the seat, and Clement coming close behind her, lifted up her fine white linen, and exposed a plump and well-rounded bottom beneath which, half hidden by the swelling thighs, were just visible the red lips of a delicious slit, luxuriantly shaded with the ample growth of rich brown hair which curled about it.

Clement wanted no further incitement; spitting on the knob of his great member, he pushed its warm head in between the moist lips, and then with many heaves, and much exertion, he strove to make it enter to the balls.

He went in—and in—and in, until it seemed as though the fair recipient could not possibly stow away any more without danger to her vitals. Meanwhile her face betrayed the extraordinary emotion the gigantic ram was occasioning her.

Presently Father Clement stopped. He was in up to his balls. His red crispy hair pressed the plump cheeks of the lady's bottom. She had received the entire length of his yard in her body. Then began an encounter which fairly shook the bench and all the furniture in the room.

Passing his arms around the fair form in his clutches, the sensual priest pressed himself inwards at every thrust, only withdrawing one half his length the better to force it home, until the lady quivered again with the exquisite sensations so vigorous a stretching was affording her. Then her eyes closed, her head fell forward, and she poured down upon the invader a warm gush of nature's essence.

Meanwhile Father Clement worked away in the hot sheath, each moment only serving to render his thick weapon harder and stronger until it resembled nothing so much as a bar of solid iron.

But all things have an end, and so had the enjoyment of the good priest, for having pushed and strove, and pressed and battered with his furious yard until he too could hold back no longer, he felt himself upon the point of discharging his metal, and thus bringing matters to a climax.

It came at last, as with a sharp cry of ecstasy he sank forward upon the body of the lady, his member buried to the roots in her belly, and pouring a prolific flood of spunk into her very womb. Presently all was over, the last spasm had passed, the last reeking drop had issued, and Clement lay still as death.

The reader must not imagine that good Father Clement was satisfied with the single "coup" which he had just delivered with such excellent effect; or that the lady, whose wanton sympathies had been so powerfully assuaged, desired to abstain from all further dalliance. On the contrary, this act of copulation had only roused the dormant faculties of sensuality in both, and again they now sought to allay the burning flame of lust.

The lady fell on her back; her burly ravisher threw himself upon her, and driving in his battering ram until their hairs met, he spent again and filled her womb with a viscid torrent.

Still unsatisfied, the wanton pair continued their exciting pastime.

This time Clement lay upon his back, and the lady lasciviously toying with his huge genitals, took the thick red head of his penis between her rosy lips, and after stimulating him to the utmost tension by her maddening touches greedily induced a discharge of his prolific fluid, which, thick and warm, now spouted into her pretty mouth and down her throat.

Then the lady, whose wantonness at least equalled that of her coufessor, stood across his muscular from, and after having secured another determined and enormous erection, lowered herself upon the throbbing shaft, impaled her beautiful figure upon the mass of flesh and muscle until nought was left to view save the big balls which hung close below the stiffened weapon. Thus she pumped from Clement a fourth discharge, and reeking in the excessive outpouring of the seminal fluid, as well as fatigued with the unusual duration of the pastime she disappeared to contemplate at leisure the monstrous proportions and unusual capabilities of her gigantic confessor.

CHAPTER VII

Bella had a female friend, a young lady, a few months older than herself, and the daughter of a wealthy gentleman who lived very near Mr. Verbouc. Julia was, however, of a less voluptuous and ardent disposition, and, Bella soon found, was not ripe enough to comprehend the sentiments of passion nor understand the strong instincts which provoke to enjoyment.

Julia was slightly taller than her young friend, slightly less plump, but formed to delight the eye and ravish the heart of an artist by her faultless shape and exquisite features.

A flea cannot well be supposed to describe personal beauty, even in those on whom they feed. All I know is that Julia was a luscious treat to me, and would one day also be to some one of the opposite sex, for she was made to raise the desires of the most callous, and to charm by her graceful manners and ever pleasing shape the most fastidious votaries of Venus.

Julia's father possessed, as we have said, ample means; her mother was a weak simpleton, who busied herself very little about her daughter, or, indeed, anything beyond the religious duties in the exercise of which she spent a great part of her time, or the visitations of the old "devotes" of the neighbourhood, who encouraged her predilections.

Monsieur Delmont was comparatively young. He was robust, he was fond of life, and as his pious better half was far too much occupied to afford him those matrimonial solaces which the poor man had a right to expect he went elsewhere.

M. Delmont had a mistress—a young and pretty woman, who I concluded was, in her turn, indisposed after the fashion of such people, to be content only with her wealthy protector.

M. Delmont by no means confined his attentions even to his mistress; his habits were erratic, and his tastes decidedly amatory.

Under these circumstances it was not wonderful that his eye should have fallen upon the budding and beautiful figure of his daughter's young friend, Bella. Already he had found opportunities to press the pretty gloved hand, to kiss—of course in a properly paternal manner—the white brow and even to place his trembling hand—quite by accident—upon the plump thighs.

In fact, Bella, wiser far and more experienced than most girls of her tender age, saw that he was only awaiting an opportunity to push matters to extremities.

This was just what Bella would have liked, but she was too closely watched, and the new and disgraceful connection in which she was only just entering occupied all her thoughts.

Father Ambrose, however, was fully alive to the necessity of caution, and the good man let no opportunity pass by, while the young lady was in his confessional, of making direct and pertinent enquiries as to her conduct with others and theirs to his penitent. It was thus Bella came to confess to her spiritual guide the feelings engendered within herself by the amatory proceedings of M. Delmont.

Father Ambrose gave her some good advice, and immediately set Bella to work to suck his penis.

This delicious episode over, and the traces of his enjoyment removed, the worthy man set about with his usual astuteness, to turn the fact he had just acquired to his advantage.

Nor was it long before his sensual and vicious brain conceived a plot which for criminality and audacity I, as a humble insect, have never known equalled.

Of course he had at once determined that the young Julia should eventually be his—that was only natural—but to accomplish this end and amuse himself at the same time with the passion which M. Delmont evidently entertained for Bella, was a double consummation which he saw his way to by a most unscrupulous and hideous plan, which the reader will understand as we proceed.

The first thing to be done was to warm the imagination of the fair Julia, and develop in her the latent fires of lust.

This noble task the good priest left to Bella who, duly instructed, easily promised compliance.

Since the ice had been broken in her own case, Bella to say the truth, desired nothing better than to make Julia equally culpable as herself. So Bella set to work to corrupt her young friend. How she succeeded, we shall duly see.

It was only a few days after the initiation of the young Bella into the delights of crime in the shape of incest, which we have already related, and the little girl had no further experience, Mr. Verbouc having been called away from home. At length, however, an opportunity occurred, and for the second time Bella found herself alone and serene with her uncle and Father Ambrose.

The evening was cold, but a pleasant warmth was imparted to the luxurious apartment by a stove, while the soft and elastic sofa and ottomans with which the room was furnished gave an air of listless repose. In the brilliant light of a deliciously perfumed lamp, the two men appeared like the luxurious votaries of Bacchus and Venus, as they reclined only lightly clad, and fresh from a somptuous repast.

As for Bella, she surpassed herself in beauty. Habited in a charming "neglige," she half disclosed and half concealed those budding sweets of which she might well be proud.

The lovely rounded arms, the soft, silk-clad legs, the heaving bosom, whence peeped two white, exquisitely formed and strawberry-tipped "pommettes," the well-turned ankle, and the tiny foot, cased in its close-fitting little shoe: These and other beauties lent their several attractions to make up a delicate and delicious whole, with which the pampered Detities might have intoxicated themselves, and in which two lustful mortals now prepared to revel.

It needed little, however, to excite further the infamous and irregular desires of the two men, who now, with eyes red with lust, regarded at their ease the luxurious treat in store for them.

Secure from all interruption, both sought in lascivious "attouchments" to gratify the craving of their imaginations to handle what they saw.

Unable to restain his eagerness, the sensual uncle stretched out his hand, and drawing his beautiful niece close to him, allowed his fingers to wander between her legs. As for the priest he seized on her soft bosom, and buried his face in its young freshness.

Neither allowed any considerations of modesty to interfere in their enjoyments, and the members of the two strong men were fully exposed and standing excitingly erect, the red heads shining with the tension of blood and muscle below.

"Oh, how you touch me," murmured Bella, opening involuntarily her white thighs to the trembling hand of her uncle, while Ambrose almost stifled her with his gross lips, as he sucked delicious kisses from her ruby mouth.

Presently her delighted hand pressed within its warm palm the stiffened member of the vigorous Priest.

"There, my sweet girl, is it not large? And does it not burn to spout its juices into you? Oh, my child, how you excite me. Your hand, your little hand! Ugh! I am dying to thrust this into your soft belly! Kiss me, Bella! Verbouc, see how your niece excites me."

"Holy Mother, what a prick! See, what a nut it has,

Bella. How it shines, what a long white shaft, and how it curves upwards, like a serpent bent on stinging its victim. Already a drop gathers on its tip, look, Bella.''

"Oh, how hard it is! How it throbs! How it thrusts forward! I can scarce hold it, you kill me with such kisses, you suck my life away.''

Mr. Verbouc made a forward movement, and at the same moment again disclosed his weapon, erect and ruby red, the head uncapped and moist.

Bella's eyes glistened at the prospect.

"We must regulate our pleasures, Bella,'' said her Uncle. "We must endeavour, as much as possible, to prolong our ecstasies.''

"Ambrose is rampant with lust, what a splendid animal he is, what a member; he is furnished like a jackass. Ah, my niece, my child, that will stretch your little slit, it will thrust itself right up to your vitals, and after a long course it will discharge a forrent of spunk for your pleasure.''

"What joy,'' murmured Bella; "I long to have it up me to the waist.''

"Yes, oh yes; do not hasten too soon the delicious end; let us all work for that.''

She would have added more, but the red bulb of Mr. Verbouc's stiffened affair at that moment entered her mouth.

With the utmost avidity Bella received the stiff and throbbing thing between her coral lips, and allowed as much of the head and shoulders as could accommodate themselves to enter. She licked at round with her tongue; she even tried to force the tip into the red opening at the apex. She was excited beyond herself. Her cheeks flushed, her breath came and went with spasmodic eagerness. Her hand still grasped the member of the salacious Priest. Her tight young cunt throbbed with the pleasures of anticipation.

She would have continued to tickle, rub, and excite the swollen tool of the lecherous Ambrose, but that worthy man signed to her to stop.

"Stay a moment, Bella," sighed he, "you will make the spunk come so."

Bella released her hold of the big white shaft and lay back, so that her Uncle could work leisurely in and out of her mouth Her eyes greedily rested upon the huge proportions of Ambrose all the while.

Never had Bella tasted a prick with so much delight, as she now did the very respectable weapon of her Uncle. She, therefore, worked her lips upon it with the utmost relish, sucking greedily the moisture which from time to time exuded from the tip. Mr. Verbouc was in raptures with her willing services.

The Priest now knelt down, and pushing his shaven head between the knees of Mr. Verbouc, as he stood before his niece, he opened the girl's plump thighs, and parting the pink lips of her delicate slit with his fingers, he thrust in his tongue, and covered her young and excited parts with his thick lips.

Bella shivered with pleasure: her Uncle grew stiffer, and pushed hard and viciously at her beautiful mouth. The girl placed a hand on his balls, and gently squeezed them. She skinned back the hot shaft and sucked it with evident delight.

"Let it come," said Bella, rejecting for a moment the glistening nut in order to express herself and take breath. "Let it come, Uncle, I should like to taste it so much."

"So you shall, my darling, but not yet, we must not be too quick,"

"Oh! How he sucks me, how his tongue licks me! I am on fire; he is killing me."

"Aha, Bella, you feel nothing but pleasures now, you are reconciled to the joys of our incestuous connection."

"Indeed I am, my dear Uncle, give me your prick again in my mouth."

"Not yet, Bella, my love."

"Do not keep me too long. You are maddening me. Father! Father! Oh, he is coming to me, he is preparing to fuck me. Holy mother! What a prick! Oh, mercy! He will split me."

Meanwhile Ambrose, driven to fury by the delicious employment he had been engaged in, became too excited to remain longer as he was, and taking the opportunity of Mr. Verbouc's temporary withdrawal, he rose and pushed the beautiful girl back upon the soft lounge.

Verbouc seized upon the formidable penis of the holy Father, and gave it one or two preliminary shakes, pushed back the soft skin which circled the egg-shaped head, and directing the broad flaming head to the pink slit, drove it up vigorously into her belly, as she lay before him.

The moistened condition of he child's parts assisted the insertion of the head and shoulders, and the Priest's weapon was quickly engulphed. Vigorous thrusts succeeded, and with fierce lust in his face, and little mercy for the youth of his victim, Ambrose fucked on. Her excitement obliterated all sense of pain and stretching wide her pretty legs she allowed him to wallow as completely as he desired in the possession of her beauty.

A loud moan of rapture escaped from Bella's parted lips, as she felt the huge weapon, hard as iron, pressing up her womb, and stretching her with its great bulk.

Mr. Verbouc lost nothing of the salacious sight, but standing close to the excited couple, he placed his own hardly less vigorous member in his niece's convulsive grasp.

Ambrose no sooner felt himself securely lodged in the beautiful body beneath him than he curbed his eagerness, and calling to his aid the wonderful power of self-control which he possessed in so extraordinary a degree, he passed his trembling hands behind the hips of the girl, and pulling apart his dress exposed his hairy belly, with which at each deep thrust he rubbed her soft "motte".

But now the Priest commenced his course in earnest. With strong and regular thrusts he buried himself in the tender form beneath him. He pressed hotly forward; Bella threw her white arms round his brawny neck. His balls beat upon her plump bottom, his tool was up her to the hairs, which, black and crisp, plentifully covered his big belly.

"She has it now; look, Verbouc, at your niece. See, how she relishes the administrations of the church. Ah, what pressures! How she nips me in her tight, naked little cunt."

"Oh, my dear, dear. Oh! good Father, fuck on, I am spending; push, push it in. Kill me with it, if you like, but keep moving. So! Oh! Heavens. Ah! Ah! How big it is; how you enter me!"

The lounge fairly worked again, and cracked beneath his rapid strokes.

"Oh, God!" cried Bella "he's killing me—it's really to muuh—I die—I am speddding," and with a half shriek, the girl went off and flooded the thick member which was so deliciously forging her—a second time.

The long prick grew hotter and harder. The knob swelled also, and the whole tremendous affair seemed ready to burst with luxury. The young Bella moaned incoherent words, in which the word fuck was alone audible.

Ambrose, also fully prime, and felling his great affair nipped in the young parts of the girl, could hold out no longer, and catching hold of Bella's bottom with both hands, he pressed inwards the whole tremendous length and discharged, shooting the thick jets of his fluid, one after another, deep into his play-fellow.

A roar like that of a wild beast escaped him, as he felt the hot spunk spout from him.

"Oh! it comes; you are flooding me. I feel it. Oh! delicious!"

Meanwhile the Priest's prick bore hard up into Bella's body, and its swollen head continued to inject its pearly seed right into her young womb.

"Oh, what a quantity you have given me," remarked Bella, as she staggered to her feet and beheld the thick, hot fluid running in all directions down her legs. "How white and slippery it is."

This was exactly the condition of affairs which Uncle most coveted, and he, therefore proceeded leisurely to avail himself of it. He regarded her beautiful silk stockings all drabbled; he pushed his fingers between the red lips of her young cunt and rubbed the exuding semen all over her hairless young belly and thighs.

Placing his niece conveniently before him, Mr. Verbouc exposed once more his stiff and hairy champion, and roused by the exceptional circumstances he so much delighted in, he contemplated with eager zeal the tender parts of the young Bella, all covered as they were with the discharge of the Priest, and still exuding thick and copious gouttes of his prolific fluid.

Bella, at his desire, opened her legs to her utmost. Her

uncle eagerly pushed his naked person between her plump young thighs.

"Hold still, my dear niece. My prick is not so thick, nor so long as Father Ambrose's, but I know well how to fuck, and you shall try whether your Uncle's spunk is not as thick and pungent as any ecclesiastic's. See, how stiff I am."

"Ah! how you make me long," said Bella, "I can see your dear thing waiting for its turn; how red it looks. Push me, Uncle, dear, I am ready again, and good Father Ambrose has plentifully oiled the way for you.

The hard and red-headed member touched the parted lips, all slippery as they were already, the spex readily enters—the big shaft quickly follows, and with a few steady thrusts, behold this exemplary relative buried to the balls in his niece's belly, and lolling luxuriantly in the reeking evidence of her previous unholy enjoyment of Father Ambrose.

"My darling Uncle," exclaimed the girl, "remember whom you fuck. It is no stranger, it is your brother's child—your own niece. Fuck me then. Uncle, give me all your strong prick—fuck! Ah, fuck, fuck, till your incestuous stuff pours into me. Ah, ah! Oh!!" and overpowered with the salacious ideas she conjured up, Bella gave way to the most unbridled sensuality, to the great delight of her Uncle.

The strong man, content in the gratification of his favourite lechery, deals his rapid and powerful strokes. Swimming as was the condition of his fair oppenent's slit, it was so naturally small and tight and he found himself clipped in the most delicious way by the narrow opening, and his pleasure rapidly advanced.

Verbouc rose and fell upon the delicious body of his

young niece; he drove fiercely inwards at every bound, and Bella clung to him with the tenacity of yet unsated lust. His prick grew hard and hot.

The titillation soon became almost insupportable. Bella herself enjoyed the incestuous encounter to the utmost, until with a sob Mr. Verbouc fell forward spending upon his niece, while the hot fluid spouted from him, and again inundated her womb. Bella also reached the climax and while she felt and welcomed the powerful injection, gave down as equally ardent proof her enjoyment.

The act being thus completed, Bella was permitted to make the necessary ablutions, and then after a revivying glass of wine round, the three sat down, and concerted a devilish plot for the defilment and enjoyment of the beautiful Julia Delmont.

Bella avowed that Mr. Delmont was certainly amorous of her, and evidently only wanted an opportunity to push matters on towards his object.

Father Ambrose confessed that his member stood straight out at the bare mention of the fair girl's name. He confessed her, and he now laughindly acknowledged that he could not keep his hands off himself during the ceremony; her breath caused him agonies of sensual longing, it was perfume itself.

Mr. Verbouc declared himself equally anxious to revel in such tender sweets of which the description made him wild with lust, but how to carry the plot into execution was the question.

"If I ravished her without preparation, I should burst her parts," exclaimed Father Ambrose, displaying once more his rubiconed machine, smoking yet with the unremoved evidence of his last enjoyment.

"I could not have her first. I need the excitement of a previous copulation," objected Mr. Verbouc.

"I should like to see the girl well ravished," said Bella. "I should watch the operation with delight and when Father Ambrose has rammed his big thing into her, you, Uncle, could be giving me yours to compensate me for the gift we were making in favour of the pretty Julia."

"Yes, that would be doubly delicious."

"What is to be done," exclaimed Bella. "Holy Mother! how stiff your thing is again, dear Father Ambrose."

"An idea occurs to me which gives me a violent erection only to think of; put in practice it would be the acme of lust, and consequently of pleasure."

"Let us hear," exclaimed both at once.

"Wait a moment," said the holy man, suffering Bella lightly to skin down the purple head of his tool and tickle the moist orifice with the tip of her tongue.

"Listen to me," said Ambrose. "Mr. Delmont is amorous of Bella there. We are amorous of his daughter, and our child here, who is now sucking my weapon, would like the tender Julia to have it thrust up to her vitals, just by way of giving her wicked salacious little self an extra dose of pleasure. So far we are all agreed. Now give me your attention, and for the moment, Bella, let go my tool. This is my plan. I know the little Julia is not insensible to her animal instincts—in fact, the little devil already feels the pricking of the flesh. A little persuasion and little mystification would do the rest. Julia will consent to have relief from those gentle pangs of canal appetite. Bella must bring her on and encourage the idea. Meanwhile Bella can lead the dear Mr. Delmont further on. She may allow him to declare himself, if he will; in fact this is necessary to the success of the plot; I must than be called in; I will suggest that Mr. Verbouc is a man above all vulgar prejudices, and that for a certain sum to be agreed upon he will surrender his beautiful and virgin niece to his impassionned embraces."

"I hardly know about that," commenced Bella.

"I don't see the object," interposed Mr. Verbouc. "We shall be no nearer the attainment of our aim."

"Wait a moment," continued the holy man. "We are all agreed so far—now, Bella shall be sold to Mr. Delmont; he shall be allowed to take his full of her beautiful charms in secrecy, she shall not see him, nor he her—at least, not her countenance, which shall remain concealed. He will be introduced to his agreable chamber, he will behold the body, utterly nude, of a lovely young girl, he will know it is his victim, and he will enjoy her."

"Me!" interrupted Bella," why all this mystery?"

Father Ambrose smiled a sickly smile.

"You will see, Bella—be patient. We want to enjoy Julia Delmont. Mr. Delmont wants to enjoy you. We can only accomplish our purpose by preventing any scandal at the same time. Mr. Delmont must be silenced, or we may suffer for our violation of his child. Now my design is that the lascivious Mr. Delmont shall violate "his own daughter" in lieu of Bella, and that having thus opened the way for us, we shall avail ourselves of the fact to satisfy our lust also. If Mr. Delmont falls into the trap, we can either allow him the knowledge of his incest and reward him with the real enjoyment of our sweet Bella, in return for the person of his daughter, or otherwise act as circumstances may dictate."

"Oh! I am nearly spending," cried Mr. Verbouc; "my weapon is bursting! What a trick! What a delicious sight,"

Both men rose—Bella was enveloped in their embraces—

two hard and large weapons pressed against her soft figure. They led her to the couch.

Ambrose fell upon his back; Bella mounted upon his body, took his stallion penis in her fair hand, and pushed it into her slit.

Mr. Verbouc looked on.

Bella lowered herself down, until the huge weapon was wholly lodged. Then she lay down on the burly Father and commenced an undulating, delicious series of movements.

Mr. Verbouc saw her beautiful bottom rising and falling—parfing and closing with each successive thrust.

Ambrose was in to the hilt, that was evident, his big balls hung closely underneath, and the fat lips of her budding parts came down to them each time she let herself fall above him.

The sight proved too much for him. The virtuous uncle mounted the couch, directed his long and swollen penis to the posteriors of the fair Bella, and with little difficulty succeeded in housing its extreme length in her bowels.

His niece's bottom was broad and soft as velvet, and the skin white as alabaster. Verbouc, however, did not care to stop for contemplation. His member was in, and he felt the tight compression of the muscle at the little entrance acting upon it like nothing else in the world. The two pricks rubbed together with only a thin membrane between.

Bella felt the maddening effect of this double "jouissance". Terrific grew the excitement, until at length the very rapture of the struggle brought its own relief and floods of spunk inundated the fair Bella.

After this, Ambrose discharged twice in Bella's mouth, where uncle also emitted his incestuous fluid, and this final closed the entertainment.

The way in which Bella performed this operation was

such as to call forth the warmest encomiums from her companions.

Seating herself upon the edge of a chair, she received them standing in front of her, so that their stiff weapons were nearly on a level with her coral lips. Then taking the velvet gland entirely into her mouth, she employed her fair hands to rub, tickle, and excite the shaft and its appendages. Thus the full nervous power of her playfellow was employed and with his bursting penis at full stretch, he enjoyed the luscious titillation, until Bella's indelicate touches proved too much, and amid sighs of ecstatic emotion, her mouth and gullet were suddenly flooded with a spouting stream of spunk.

The little glutton swallowed all; she would have done the same for a dozen, had she had the chance.

CHAPTER VIII

Bella continued to afford me the most delicious of pastures. Her young limbs never missed the crimson draughts which I imbibed, or felt, to any grave inconvenience, the tiny punctures which I was forced most reluctantly to make to obtain my living. I determined, therefore, to remain with her although of late her conduct had become, to say the very least, somewhat questionable, and slightly irregular.

One thing I remarked for certain, and that was that she had lost all feelings of delicacy and maidenly reserve, and lived only now for the delights of sensual gratification.

I was soon satisfied that my young lady had lost nothing of the lesson she had received of her share in the conspiracy in course of proparation. How she played her part I now propose to relate.

It was not long before Bella found herself within the mansion of Mr. Delmont, and, as luck would have it, or shall we say rather as that worthy man himself had expressly designed it, alone with the amatory proprietor.

Mr. Delmont saw his chance, and like a clever general instantly pressed on to the assault. He found his fair companion either wholly innocent of his intention, or else wonderfully willing to encourage his advances.

Already Mr. Delmont had his arm around Bella's waist, while apparently, quite by accident, her soft right hand pressed beneath his nervous palm, lay upon his manly thigh.

What Bella felt beneath showed plainly enough the violence of his emotion. A throb passed quickly through the hard object which lay concealed, and Bella was not without the sympathetic spasm that told of sensuous pleasure.

Gently the amorous Mr. D. drew the girl towards him, and hugged her yielding form. He printed sudden a hot kiss on her cheek, and whispered flattering words to adsorb her attention from his proceedings. He essayed more, he gently moved Bella's hand about the hard object, until the young lady perceived that his excitement was likely to become too rapid.

Throughout Bella had firmly adhered to her "role"; she was coy innocence itself.

Mr. D., encouraged by the non-resistance of his young

friend, proceeded to other and still more decided steps. His wanton hand roved along the edge of Bella's light dress, and pressed her yielding calf. Then, suddenly with a warm and simultaneous kiss on her red lips. he quickly passed his trembling fingers underneath and touched her plump thigh.

Bella recoiled. At any other time she would have glady flung herself upon her back, and bade him do his worst; but she remembered her lesson, and went on with part to perfection.

"Oh! how rude you are," cried the young lady, "what a naughty thing—I cannot let you do that. Uncle says nobody must be allowed to touch that—at any rate not without first——" Bella hesitated, stopped, and looked silly.

Mr. Delmont was curious as well as amatory.

"Without first what, Bella?"

"Oh, I must not tell you. I ought to have said nothing about it; only you, by doing such a rude thing, made me forget."

"Forget what?"

"Something that my Uncle has often told me," answered Bella simply.

"What is it? Tell me."

"I dare not—besides, I do not understand what he means."

"I will explain it, if you tell me what it was he said."

"You promise not to tell?"

"Certainly."

"Well, then, he says I must never let anyone put the hands there, and that whoever wants to do so, must pay well for it."

"Does he really say that?"

"Yes, indeed he does; he says that I am able to bring him a good round sum in that way, and that there are plenty of rich gentlemen who would pay for that you want to do to me, and he says he is not stupid as to lose such a chance."

"Really, Bella, your Uncle is a strict man of business. I did not think he was that kind of man."

"Oh, yes, but he is," cried Bella. "He is very found of money, you know, in secret; and I know scarcely what he means, but he sometimes says he shall sell my maidenhead."

"It is possible," thought Mr. Delmont.

"What a man he must be, what a wonderful eye to business he must have."

In fact, the more Mr. D. thought about it, the more convinced he became of the truth of Bella's ingenious explanation. She was to be bought. He would buy her; better far that way than to run the risk of discovery and punishment by resorting to a secret liaison.

Before, however, he could do more than revolve these sage reflections in his own mind, an interruption occured in the arrival of his own daughter Julia, and very reluctantly he had to release his companion and arrange himself with an eye to propriety.

Bella made a rapid excuse and went home, leaving the event to take its chance.

The route taken by my fair young lady lay through several meadows, and along a cartline which emerged into the great high way very near her Uncle's residence.

The time was afternoon, and the day was unusually fine. The lane had several sudden turnings, and as Bella pursued her way, she amused herself watching the cattle in the neighbouring pastures.

Presently the lane became bordered with trees, the long

straight line of trunks divided the roadway from the footpath. Across the nearest meadow she saw several men at work tilling the ground, and at a little distance, a group of women had ceased for a moment from their labour of weeding to interchange some interesting ideas.

On the opposite side of the lane was a hedge, and looking through this Bella saw a sight which fairly startled her. Within the meadow were two animals, a horse and a mare. The former had evidently been occupied in chasing the latter about the ground, and had at last pinned his compaion in a corner not far from where she stood.

But what startled and surprised Bella most was the wonderful erectioned excitement of a long and grizzly member which hung below the belly of the stallion, and ever and anon sprung up with an impatient jerk against his body.

The mare had evidently remarked it too, for she now stood perfectly quiet with her back towards the horse.

The latter was too pressed by his amorous instincts to dally long beside her, and to the young lady's wonder she beheld the great creature mount up behind the mare and attemp to push his tool into her.

Bella watched with breathless interest, and saw the long swollen member of the horse at length hit the mark and disappear entirely in the hinder parts of the mare.

To say that her sensual feelings were roused would be but to express the natural result of so salacious an exhibition. She was more than roused; her libidinous instincts were "fired". She clutched her hands and gazed with interest on the lewd encounter; and when after a rapid and furious course, the animal withdrew his dripping penis, Bella glared upon it with an insane longing to seize it for herself, and handle the great pendant thing for her own gratification.

In this excited frame of mind, she found that some sort of action was necessary to relieve her from the powerful influence which oppressed her. Making a strong effort, Bella turned her head, and at the same moment, taking half a dozen steps forward, came straight upon a sight which certainly had no tendency to allay her excitement.

Right in her path stood a rustic youth of some eighteen years; his handsome but somewhat stupid features were turned towards the meadow where the amorous steeds were disporting themselves. A gap in the back which bordered the roadway afforded him an excellent view, in the contemplation of which he was evidently as much interested as Bella had been.

But what chained the attention of the girl was the state of the lad's clothing, and the appearance of a tremendous member, rudy and well developed, which, barefaced, and fully exposed, unblushingly raised its fiery crest full in his front.

There was no mistaking the effect the sight in the meadow had produced, for the lad had already unbuttoned his nether garments of coarse material, and had his nervous grasp upon a weapon of which a Carmelite might have been proud. With eager eyes he devoured the scene enacted before him in the meadow, while his right hand skinned the standing column and worked it vigorously up and down, utterly unconscious that so congenial a spirit was witnessing his proceedings.

A start and an exclamation which involuntarily broke from Bella caused him at once to look round, and there, in full view before him stood the beautiful girl, while his nudity and his lewd erection were at the same moment completely exposed.

"Oh, my goodness!" exclaimed Bella, as soon as she could find words, "what a dreadful sight! What a wicked boy; Why, what are you doing with that long red thing?"

The boy, abashed, attempted awkwardly to replace in his breeches the object which had provoked the observations, but his evident confusion and the stiffness of the thing itself rendered the operation very difficult, not to say tedious.

Bella came kindly to the rescue.

"What is that? Let me help you—how came it out? How large and stiff it is, what a length it is! My word! what a tremendously big one you've got; you naughty boy—!"

Suiting the action to the word, the young lady laid her delicate little white hand upon the standing penis of the boy, and squeezing it in her soft warm grasp only, of course, made it the more unlikely to re-enter its retreat.

Meanwhile the lad, gradually recovering his stolid presence of mind, and beholding how fair and apparently innocent was his new acquaintance, ceased to betray any desire to assist her in the laudable endeavoors to conceal the stiff and offending member. Indeed, it became impossible, even if he had desired it; for no sooner had her grasp closed upon it, than it acquired even larger proportions, while the distended and purple head shone like a ripe plum.

"What a naughty boy!" observed Bella; "whatever shall I do," she continued, looking archly in the handsome face of the rustic.

"Ah, how nice that is," sighed the lad—"who could

have thought that you were so near me, when I felt so bad, and it first began to throb and swell so just now.''

"This is very, very wicked,'' remarked the young lady, tightening her grasp, and feeling the rankling flames of lust rising higher and higher within her; "this is dreadfully wrong and naughty, you know it is, you bad boy.''

"Did you see what those horses were doing in the meadow?'' asked the boy, looking wonderingly at Bella, whose beauty seemed to dawn upon his dull mind, as the sun steals over a showery landscape.

"Yes, I did,'' replied the girl, innocently, "what were they doing it for—what did it mean?''

"It means fucking,'' responded the youth, with a lewd grin. "He wanted the mare, and mare wanted the stallion, and so they came together and fucked.''

"Lord, how curious!'' exclaimed Bella, looking with the most childish simplicity from the great thing in her hands to the boy's countenance.

"Yes, it was droll, wasn't it? And, my goodness, what a tool he'd got, Miss, hadn't he?''

"Immense,'' murmured Bella, thinking partly all the time of the thing she was skinning slowly backwards and forwards in her own hand.

"Oh, how you tickle me,'' sighed her companion, "what a beauty you are, how deliciously you rub it. Please, go on, Miss, I want to spend.''

"Do you, indeed,'' whispered Bella, "shall I make you spend?''

Bella saw the stiffened object reddening with the gentle titillation she was giving it, until the plump top looked almost ready to burst. The prurient idea to watch the effect of continued friction took violent possession of her.

She applied herself with redoubled energy to the lewd task.

"Oh, please, yes—go on; it is near coming. Oh! oh! How nice you do it; hold tight—go faster—skin it well down. Now, again. Oh! my goodness. Oh!

The long hard tool grew hotter and stiffer, as the little hands flew upon it.

"Ah! ugh!—It's coming!—Ugh! Hoo!" exclaimed the rustic lad, in broken accents, while his knees quivered, his body straightened his head rolled back, and amid contortions and stiffled cries his large and powerful penis squirted forth a rapid stream of thick fluid over the dear little hands which, eager to bathe themselves in the warm and slippery flood, now lovingly embraces the big shaft, and coaxed from it the fast out-pouring seminal shower.

Bella, suprised and delighted, pumped out every drop—she would have sucked it, had she dared—and then, drawing out her cambric handkerchief, she wiped the thick and pearly mess from her hands.

Then the youth, abashed and stupid, put up the expiring member, and regarded his companion with a mingled air of curiosity and wonder.

"Where do you live?" at last he found words to enquire.

"Not very far from here," replied Bella; "but you must not try to follow me, or to find out, you know; if you do," continued the young lady, "it will be the worse for you, for I shall never do that again, and you would be punished."

"Why don't we fuck like the stallion," suggested the youth whose ardour, only half appeased, began again to warm up.

"Some day, perhaps, not now, for I am in a hurry. I am late; I must go at once."

"Let me put my hand up your clothes? Say, when you will come again?"

"Not now," said Bella, withdrawing herself gradually, "but we will meet again."

She cherished a lively recollection of the stalwart affair in his breeches.

"Tell me," continued she, "have you ever—ever fucked."

"No, but I should like to. Don't you believe me? Well, then—yes, I have."

"How shocking," exclaimed the young lady.

"Father would like to fuck you," said he, without hesitation, taking no notice of her movement to depart.

"Your Father! Dreadful. How do you know that?"

"Because Father and I fuck the girls together. His tool is not bigger than mine."

"You say so, But do you really mean that your parent and you do such dreadful things in company?"

"Yes, when we get the chance. You should see him fuck. Oh! gum!" and he grinned idiotically.

"You don't seem a clever boy," said Bella.

"Father's not so clever as me," replied the lad, widening his grin, and showing his prick, again half stiff. "I know how to fuck now, though I only had it once. You should see me fuck."

And Bella saw the big stool pointing and throbbing.

"Whom did you do it with then? You naughty boy."

"A little girl of fourteen? Father and I both fucked her, and split her up."

"Which of you did it first?" demanded Bella.

"I did, and Father caught me. So then he wanted his

go, and made me hold her. You should see him fuck, my gum!''

A few minutes more Bella was again on her way, and seached her house without further adventures.

CHAPTER IX

When Bella related the result of her interview with Mr. Delmont that evening a low chuckle of delight escaped the lips of her two conspirators. She said nothing, however, of the young rustic she had encountered by the way. With that part of the day's performances she considered it quite unnecessary to trouble either the astute Father Ambrose, or her no less sagacious relative.

The plot was evidently about to thicken. The seed so discreetly sown would certainly fructify, and as Ambrose thought of the delicious treat which would certainly some day be his in the person of the beautiful young Julia Delmont, his spirits rose, and his animal passions fed by anticipation on the tender dainties hereafter to be his, until the result became visible in the huge distension of his member and the excitement which his whole manner betrayed.

Nor was Mr. Verbouc less touched. Sensual to the last degree, he promised himself a luscious repast on the newly opened charms of his neighbour's daughter, and the thought of the treat to come acted equally on his nervous temperament.

There were yet some details to arrange. It was clear that the simple Mr. Delmont would come to feel his way as to the truth of Bella's assertions respecting her Uncle's willingness to sell her maidenhead.

Father Ambrose, whose knowledge of the man had led him to suggest the idea to Bella, knew well with whom he was dealing—indeed, who did not exhibit his inmost nature to his holy man in the sacred right of confession that had the privilege to count him their confessor.

Father Ambrose was discreet, he faithfully observed the silence enjoined by his religion, but he made no scruple to use the facts he thus acquired for his own ends—and what those were the reader by this time knows as well as I did.

Thus the plot was arranged. Upon a certain day to be agreed upon, Bella was to invite her friend Julia to pass the day with her at her Uncle's house, and Mr. Delmont, it was intended, should be instructed to come and fetch her home. After a certain interval of flirtation between him and the innocent Bella, all being explained to him and previously arranged she was to withdraw, and under the pretext that it was absolutely necessary that some such precaution should be taken in order to avoid the possibility of scandal, she was to be presented to him in a convenient chamber recumbent upon a lounge, where her beautiful body and charms were to be at his disposal, while her head remained concealed behind a carefully closed curtain. Thus, Mr. Delmont, eager for the tender encounter, could snatch the jewel he coveted from the lovely victim, while she— ignorant of who her assailant might be—could never there- after accuse him of the outrage or feel shame in his presence.

Mr. Delmont was to have all this explained to him, and his acquiescence was considered certain, only one reserva- tion was intended: No one was to tell him that his own daughter was to be substituted in Bella's place. He would only know that when too late.

Meanwhile Julia was to be gradually prepared in secret for what was to take place, no mention, of course, being made of the final catastrophy, or the real participator in it. But here Father Ambrose felt himself at home, and by means of well directed enquiries, and at great deal of unnecessary explanation in the confessionnal, he soon brought the young girl to the knowledge of things of which she had never previously dreamed; all which Bella took care to explain and confirm.

All these matters had been finally disposed of in conference, and the consideration of the subject had pro- duced by anticipation so violent an effect upon the two men, that they were now in train to enjoy their present good fortune in the possession of the fair young Bella with an amount of ardour they had never surpassed.

My young lady, on her side, was nothing loth to lend herself to their fantasies, and as she now sat or lay back on the soft lounge with a stiff standing member in either hand, her own emotions rose proportionately, until she longed for the vigorous embraces she knew were about to follow.

Father Ambrose, as usual, was the first. He turned her round, placed her on her belly, and directing her to extend her plump white buttocks as far back as possible, he stood for a moment contemplating the delicious prospect and the small and delicate slit which was just visible below. His weapon, redoutable as well provided with nature's essence, rose fiercely and menaced either entry into love's delightful shades.

Mr. Verbouc, as before, disposed himself to witness the disproportionate assault, with the evident intention of enjoying his favourite role afterwards.

Father Ambrose regarded, with a lecherous expression, the white and rounded promontories straight in front of him. The clerical tendencies of his education were exciting him to commit an infidelity to the Goddess, but the knowledge of what was expected of him by his friend and patron restrained him for the time.

"Delays are dangerous," said he, "my balls are very full, the dear child must have their contents, and you, my friend, must delight yourself with the abundant lubrication with which I shall provide you."

Ambrose, on this occasion at least, spoke nothing but the truth. His huge weapon, surmounted by the dull purple head, the broad proportions of which resembled the glowing ripeness of some fruit, stood stiffly up towards his navel, and his immense testicles, hard and round, appeared surcharged with the venomous liquor they were aching to discharge. A thick, opaque drop—an "avant-courrier" of that gush which was to follow—stood on the blunt apex of his penis, as, bursting with luxury, the satyr approached his prey.

Hastily bending down the stiff shaft, Ambrose put the big nut between the lips of Bella's tender slit and all anointed as it was, commenced to push it up her.

"Oh, how hard! How large you are!" cried Bella; "you hurt me; it is going in too far. Oh! stop!"

As well might have Bella appealed to the wind. A rapid succession of thrusts, a few pauses at intervals, more efforts, and Bella was impaled.

"Ah," exclaimed the ravisher, turning in triumph to his coadjutor, while his eyes sparkled and his lewd mouth watered with the pleasure he was having. "Ah, this is luscious, indeed; how tight she is, and yet she has it all. I am up her to my balls."

Mr. Verbouc took a careful survey. Ambrose was right. Nothing but his two huge balls remained visible of his genitals, and they were pressing close up between Bella's legs.

Meanwhile Bella felt the heat of the invader in her belly. She was sensible of the skinning and uncovering of the huge head within her, and instantly her lewdest emotions overtaking her, with a faint cry, she spent profusely.

Mr. Verbouc was delighted.

"Push! push!" said he, "she likes it now, give it her all—push!"

Ambrose needed no such incentive; seizing Bella round the hips, he buried himself in her at each bound. The pleasure rose upon him fast; he drew back, until he withdrew his smoking penis, all except the nut, and then lunging forward, he emitted a low groan, and squirted a perfect deluge of hot fluid into Bella's delicate body.

The girl felt the warm and trickling stuff shooting violently up her, and once more gave down her tribute. The great pushes which now came slopping into her vitals from the powerful stores of Father Ambrose, whose singular gift in this particular I have before explained, caused Bella the liveliest sensations, and she experienced the keenest pleasure during his discharge.

Scarcely had Ambrose withdrawn, than Mr. Verbouc took possession of his niece, and commenced a slow and delicious enjoyment of her most secret charms. After an interval of fully twenty minutes, during which time the salacious Uncle revelled in pleasure to his heart's content, he completed his gratification in a copious discharge, which Bella received with throbs of delight, such as no other than a thoroughly prurient mind could relish.

"I wonder," said Mr. Verbouc, after he had regained breath and refreshed himself with a large draught of rich wine. "I wonder how it is this dear child inspires me with such overwhelming rapture. In her arms I forget myself and all the world. The present intoxication of the moment carries me with it, and I enjoy I know not what of ecstasy."

The observation, or reflection, call it what you will, of the Uncle, was partly addressed to the good Father, and, no doubt, was partially the result of interior workings of the spirits which involuntarily rose to the surface and formed themselves into words.

"I could tell you. I think," said Ambrose sententiously, "only perhaps, you would not follow my reasoning."

"Explain, by all means," replied Mr. Verbouc. "I am all attention, and I should of all things like to hear your reason."

"My reason, or rather, I should say, my reasons," observed Father Ambrose, "are manifest when you are in possession of my hypothesis."

Then, taking a pinch of snuff, a habit which the good man usually indulged before delivering himself of any weighty reflections, he continued:

"Sensual pleasure must always be proportional to the adaptability of the circumstances which are intended to produce it. And this is paradoxical, because the more we advance in sensuality, and the more voluptuous our tastes grow, the greater becomes necessity that these circumstances should be themselves at variance. Do not misunderstand me; I will try to render myself more clear. Why does a man commit a rape when he is surrounded by woman willing to afford him the use of their bodies? Simply because he is not content to be in accord with the opposite party to his enjoyment, and it is her very unwillingness which constitutes his pleasure. No doubt there are instances in which a man of brutal mind, and seeking only his own sensual relief, where it is not possible to find a willing object to his gratification, forces a woman, or a child, to his will, with no other object than his immediate relief of those instincts which madden him, but search the record of such crimes, and you will find that by far the greater are the result of deliberate design, planned and executed in the face of obvious and even lawful means of gratification. The opposition to his proposed enjoyment serves to whet his lewd appetite, and the introduction of the featue of crime and violence add a zest to the matter which obtains a firm hold upon his mind. It is wrong, it is disallowed, therefore it is worth seeking, it becomes delicious. Again, what is the reason that a man of vigorous build, and capable of gratifying a fully developed woman, prefers a mere child of fourteen? I answer, because that very disparity affords him delight, gratifies the imagination, and constitutes that exact adaptability of circumstances of which I speak. In effect it is, of course, the imagination which is at work, The law of contrast is constant in this as in all else. The distinction merely of the sexes is not of itself sufficient to the educated voluptuary—there are needed further and special contrasts to perfect the idea he has conceived. The variations are infinite, but still the same law is traceable in all. Tall men prefer short women, fair men dark women, strong men select weak and tender women, and these women are fondest of vigorous and robust partners. Cupid's darts are tipped with incompatibilities and feathered with the wildest incongruities; none but the inferior animals, the brutes themselves, will copulate indiscriminately with the opposite sex, and even these have their preferences and desires as irregular as those of mankind. Who has not seen the unnatural conduct of a couple of street dogs, or laughed at the awkward efforts of some old cow, who driven to market with the common herd, vents her sensual instincts by mounting upon the back of her nearest neighbour? Thus I respond to your invitation, and thus I give you my reasons for your preference for your niece, for the sweet but forbidden playmate, whose delicious limbs I am now moulding.''

As Father Ambrose concluded, he looked for an instant upon the fair girl, and his great weapon rose to its utmost dimensions.

"Come, my forbidden fruit,'' said he, "let me pluck you, let me revel in you to my heart's content. This is my pleasure—my ecstasy—my delirious enjoyment. I will swamp you in spunk, I will possess you in spite of the dictates of society—you are mine, come!''

Bella looked upon the ruddy and stiffened member of her confessor, she noted his excited gaze fixed upon her young body. She knew his intention, and prepared herself to gratify him.

Already had he frequently entered her tender belly and thrust the full length of that majestic penis into her small and sensible parts. Pain at the distention had now given way to pleasure, and young and elastic flesh opened to receive the column of gristle, with only just enough of uneasiness to make her careful in its reception.

The good man looked for a moment upon the tempting prospect before him, then advancing, he divided the rosy lips of Bella's slit, and pushed in the smooth gland of his great weapon: Bella received it with a shudder of mingled emotion.

Ambrose continued to penetrate until, after a few fierce thrusts, he buried his length in her tight young body, and she had him to the balls.

Then followed a series of pushes, of vigorous writhings on one part, and of spasmodic sobs and stiffled cries upon the other. If the pleasures of the holy man were intense, those of his youthful playmate were equally ecstatic, and his stiff affair was already well lubricated with her discharge, were, with a groan of intense feeling he once more reached his consummation, and Bella felt a flood of spendings burn violently into her vitals.

"Ah, how you have inundated me, both of you," said Bella, noticing as she spoke a large pool which covered her legs, and lay upon the sofa-cover between her things.

Before either could reply to the observation, a succession of cries made themselves heard in the quiet chamber, and becoming weaker and weaker as they continued, at once arrested the attention of all present.

And here I should acquaint my reader with one or two particulars which hitherto, in my crawling capacity. I have not thought it necessary to mention. The fact is that fleas, although no doubt agile members of society, cannot be everywhere at once, though no doubt they can, and do make up for this drawback by the exercise of an agility rarely equalled by others of the insect tribe.

I ought to have explained, like any human story writer, though, perhaps, with a circumlocution and more veracity, that Bella's aunt, Madame Verbouc, to whom my readers were very cursorily presented in the opening chapter of my history, occupied a chamber to herself in a wing of the mansion, where she spent much of her time, like Madame Delmont, in devotional exercises, and, with a happy disregard of mundane affairs, usually left all the domestic management of the house to her niece.

Mr. Verbouc had already reached the stage of indifference to the blandishments of his better half, and but seldom now visited her chamber or disturbed her repose for purposes of exercising his marital rights.

Madame Verbouc, however, was still young—only thirty-two summers had as yet passed over that pious and devout head—Madame Verbouc was handsome, and the lady had also brought her husband the additional advantage of a considerable fortune.

Madame Verbouc, in spite of her piety, sometimes languished for the more solid comforts of her husband's embraces. and relished with a keen delight the exercise of his rights and his occasional visits to her couch.

On this occasion Madame Verbouc had retired at her usual early hour, and the present digression is necessary to explain what follows. While this amiable lady, therefore, is engaged in those duties of the toilet which even fleas dare not profane, let us talk of another and no less important personage, whose conduct it will be necessary also to investigate.

Now it happened that Father Clement, whose exploits in the lists of the amorous Goddess we have already had occasion to chronicle, rankled under the fact of the young Bella's withdrawal from the Society of the Sacristy, and knowing well who she was, and where she was to be found, had for some days prowled about the residence of Mr. Verbouc to try and regain possession of so delicious a prize of which it will be remembered the cunning of Ambrose had deprived his "confreres"

In this attempt Clement was aided by the Superior, who also bitterly lamented his loss, without, however, suspecting the part that Father Ambrose had played.

On this particular evening Clement had posted himself near the house, and seeing an opportunity, set himself closely to watch a certain window which he made sure was that of the fair Bella.

How vain, indeed, are human calculations! While the forlorn Clement, robbed of his pleasures, was relentlessly watching one chamber, the object of his desires was bathed in salacious enjoyment between her two vigorous lovers in another.

Meanwhile the night advanced, and Clement finding all quiet, contrived to raise himself to the level of the window. A faint light was burning in the room, by which the anxious "cure" could detect a lady reposing by herself in the full enjoyment of sound slumber.

Nothing doubting of his ability to win Bella to his desires, could he only gain her ear, and mindful of the bliss he had already enjoyed while revelling in her beauties, the audacious scoundrel furtively opened the window and entered the sleeping-chamber. Well wrapped in the flowing frock of a monk, and disguised in its ample cowl, he stole across to the bed; while his gigantic member, already awake to the pleasures he promised himself, stood fiercely up against his hirsute belly.

Madame Verbouc, roused from a pleasant dream, and never doubting but that it was her faithful spouse who thus so warmly pressed her, turned lovingly towards the intruder, and, nothing loath, opened her willing thighs to his vigorous attack.

Clement on his side, equally sure that the young Bella was in his arms, and, moreover, not unwilling to admit his caresses, pushed matters to a crisis, and mounting in hot haste between the lady's legs, brought his huge penis opposite the lips of a well-moistened slit, and fully aware of the difficulties he expected to encounter in so young a girl, thrust violently inwards.

There was a movement, another plunge downwards of his big bottom, a gasp on the part of the lady, and slowly but surely the gigantic mass hard flesh went in, until it was fairly housed. Then, as it passed in for the first time Madame Verbouc detected the extraordinary difference. This penis was at least double the size of her husband's—to doubt succeeded certainty. In the dim light she raised her head; above was visible, close to her's, the excited visage of the ferocious Clement.

Instantly there were a struggle, a violent outcry, and a vain attempt to disengage herself from her strong assailant.

But come what might, Clement was in full possession and enjoyment of her person. He never paused, but, on the contrary, deaf to her cries, he broke in to his utmost length, and strove, with feverish haste, to complete his horrid triumph. Blind with rage and lust he was insensible to the fact of the opening of the door, of the blows which now rained upon his hinder parts, until with set teeth and the subdued roar of a bull, the crisis seized him, and he poured a torrent of semen into the unwilling womb of his victim.

Then he awoke to the position, and fearing the results of his detestable outrage, he rose in all haste, and withdrawing his foaming weapon, slipped from the bed upon the side opposite his asailant. Dodging as well as he could the cuts which Mr. Verbouc aimed at him and keeping the hood of his frock over his features to avoid detection, he rushed toward the window by which he had entered, then taking a headlong leap he made good his escape in the darkness, followed by the imprecations of the infuriated husband.

We have already stated in a former chapter that Mrs. Verbouc was an invalid, that is, she fancied herself one, and to a person of weak nerves and retiring habits my reader may picture for himself what was likely to be her condition after undergoing so indelicate an outrage. The enormous proportions of the man, his strength, his fury almost killed her, and she lay without consciousness on the couch which had witnessed her violation.

Mr. Verbouc was not naturally endowed with astonishing attributes of personal courage and when he beheld the assailant of his wife rise satisfied from the pursuit, allowed Clement to retreat in peace.

Meanwhile Father Ambrose and Bella, following at a respectful distance from the outraged husband, witnessed from the half-opened door the denouement of the strange scene.

As soon as the ravisher rose, Bella and Ambrose both instantly recognised him; indeed, the former had had, as the reader knows already, good reason to remember the huge lolling member which dangled dripping between his legs.

Mutually interested in maintaining silence, a look exchanged between them was sufficient to indicate the necessity for reserve, and they withdrew before any movement on the part of the outraged woman betrayed their proximity.

It was several days before poor Mrs. Verbouc was well enough to leave her bed. The shock to her nerves had been dreadful, and nothing but the kind and conciliatory manner of her husband enabled her to hold her up at all.

Mr. Verbouc had his own reasons for letting the matter pass, and he allowed no considerations beyond expediency to weigh with him.

On the day after the catastrophe I have recorded above, Mr. Verbouc received a visit from his dear friend and neighbour Mr. Delmont, and after being closeted with him for over an hour, the two parted with beaming smiles and the most extravagant compliments.

The one had sold his niece, and the other believed he had purchased that precious jewel: A maidenhead.

When Bella's uncle made the announcement that evening that the bargain had been struck, and the affair duly arranged, there was great rejoicing among the conspirators.

Father Ambrose immediately took possession of the maidenhead, and driving in to the girl the whole length of his member, proceeded, as he explained it, to keep the place warm, while Mr. Verbouc, reserving himself, as usual, until his "confrere" had done, afterwards attacked the same mossy fort, as he facetiously expressed it, just to oil the passage for his friend.

Then the whole of the details were finally arranged, and the party broke up, confident in the success of their stratagem.

CHAPTER X

Ever since the meeting in the green lane with the rustic whose simplicity had so much interested her. Bella had dwelt upon the expressions he had used, and the extraordinary avowal of his parent's complicity in his sensuality. It was clear that his mind was simple almost to idiocy, and from his remark; "Father's not so clever as me," she assumed that the complaint was congenital, and wondered if the father really possessed the same, or—as declared by the boy—even greater proportions in his organs of generation.

I plainly saw, by her habit of thinking partly aloud, that Bella did not reckon upon her Uncle's opinion, or stand any longer in fear of Father Ambrose. She was doubtless resolved to follow her own course, whatever it might be, and I was not, therefore, at all astonished when I found her wending her way the following day at about the same hour in the direction of the meadows.

In a field hard by the spot where she had beheld the sexual encounter between the horse and his mate, Bella discovered the lad engaged in some simple agricultural operation, and with him was another person, a tall and remarkably dark man, of about forty-five years of age.

Almost as soon as she saw them, the lad observed the young lady, and running toward her, after apparently a word of explanation with his companion, he showed his delight by a broad grin.

"That's Father," said he, pointing over his shoulder, "come and frig him."

"For shame, you naughty boy," said Bella, much more inclined to laugh than to be angry. "How dare you use such language?"

"What did you come for?" asked the boy. "Did you come for fucking?"

By this time they had reached the man, who stuck his spade into the ground, and began to grin at the girl in very much the same fashion as his son.

He was strong and well built, and by his manner Bella could see the boy had told him the particulars of their first meeting.

"Look at Father, ain't he a randy one?" remarked the youth. "Ah! You should see him fuck!"

There was no attempt at disguise; the two evidently understood each other and grinned more than ever. He seemed to accept it as a huge compliment, but he cast his eyes upon the delicate young lady, the like of whom he had probably never met before, and it was impossible to mistake the look of sensuous longing which shone in his large black eyes.

Bella began to wish she had never come.

"I should like to show you Father's big doodle," said the lad. and suiting the action to word, he commenced to unbutton the trousers of his respectable parent.

Bella covered her eyes, and made a movement in retreat. Instantly the son stepped behind her. Her refuge in the lane was thus cut off.

"I should like to fuck you," exclaimed the Father, in a hoarse voice. "Tim would like to fuck you as well, so you must not go away yet. Stop and be fucked!"

Bella was really frightened.

"I cannot," she said; "indeed you must let me go. You must not hold me like that: you must not drag me along; let me go. Where are you taking me?"

There was a small building in the corner of the field, and they were now at the door. Another second and the pair had pushed her inside and shut the door, lowering a large wooden bar across it afterwards as they entered.

Bella looked round and saw that the place was clean and half-filled with hay in trusses. She saw that resistance would be useless. It would be best to be quiet, and perhaps, after all, the strange pair would not hurt her. She noticed however, that the trousers of both stuck out in front, and doubted but that their ideas were in harmony with their excitement.

"I want you to see Father's cock; my gum! you ought to see his cods, too."

Once more the lad began unbuttoning his father's breeches. Down went the flap and out stuck his shirt with something under it, which caused it to bunch up in a curious manner.

"Oh, do hold still, Father," whispered the son; "let the lady see your doodle."

With that he raised the shirt, and exposed in Bella's face a fiercely erected member with a broad plum-like nut, very red and thick, but not of very unusual length. It had a considerable bend upwards, and the head, which divided down the middle by the tightness of the frenum, bent still further back towards his hairy belly. The shaft was immensely thick, rather flat and hugely swollen.

The girl felt her blood tingle as she looked upon it. The nut was a large as an egg—plump, and quite purple. It emitted a strong smell. The lad made her approach, and pressed her white, lady-like little hand upon it.

"Didn't I tell you it was bigger than mine," continued the boy, "look here; mine is not nearly as thick as Father's."

Bella turned. The boy had his trousers open and his formidable penis in full view. He was right—it could not compare with his father's for size.

The older of the two now caught her round the waist. Tim also essayed to cling to her, and to get his hand under her clothes. Between them she swayed to and fro. A sudden push cast her upon the hay. Then up went her skirts. Bella's dress was light and wide, she wore no drawers. No sooner did the two catch sight of her plump, white legs than they snorted again, and both threw themselves on her together. A struggle now ensued. The Father, much heavier and stronger than the boy, got the advantage.

His breches were about his heels; his big, fat prick was out and wagged within three inches of her navel. Bella opened her legs, she longed for a taste of it. She put down her hand. It was hot as fire, and as hard as a bar of iron. Mistaking her intention, the man rudely withdrew her arm, and roughly helping himself, put the tip of his penis to the pink lips. Bella opened her young parts all in her power, and with several forcible lunges the peasant got about halfway in. Here his excitement overcame him, and a terher. He discharged violently, getting right up rible stream of very thick fluid spouted into her as he did so until the big nut lay against her womb, and he sent a quantity of his semen into it.

"Eh, you are killing me," cried the girl, half smothered, "what is all that you are pouring into me?"

"That's the spunk; that's what that is," remarked Tim, as he bent down and watched the operation delightedly. "Didn't I tell you, he was a good' un to fuck."

Bella thought the man would now get off, and allow her to rise, but she was mistaken; the large member which was now crammed into her only seemed to grow more rigidly stiff, and to stretch her worse than ever.

Presently the peasant began to work himself up and down, pushing cruelly into Bella's young parts at each descent. His enjoyment appeared to be extreme. The discharge which had already taken place caused his truncheon to slip in and out without difficulty, and made the soft region foam with the rapid movement.

Bella gradually became dreadfully excited. Her mouth opened, her legs went up and her hands were convulsively clenched on either side. She now favoured every effort and delighted to feel the fierce plunges with which the sensual fellow buried his reeking weapon in her young belly.

For a quarter of an hour the conflict raged on both sides. Bella had discharged frequently, and was on the point of giving down a warm emission, when a furious spouting of semen rushed from the man's member and inundated the young lady's parts.

The fellow then rose, and withdrawing his dripping prick, from which the last drops of his plentiful ejection were still exuding, he stood moodily contemplating the panting figure he had released.

Still threatening stood his huge rammer in front of him, yet smoking from the warm sheath, Tim, with true filial care, proceeded to wipe it tenderly and return it, pendant and swollen with its late excitement, within his father's shirt and breeches.

This done, the lad began to cast sheep's eyes on Bella, who still remained, slowly recovering herself upon the hay. Looking and feeling, Tim who met with no resistance, commenced to push his fingers about in the region of the young lady's private parts.

The father now came forward, and taking his son's weapon in his grasp, began to frig it up and down. It was already stiffly erected, and presented a formidable mass of flesh and muscle in Bella's face.

"Goodness me. I hope you are not going to put that into me," murmured Bella.

"I am, though," answered the lad, with one of his silly grins. "Father frigs me, and I like it, and now I mean to fuck you."

The father guided this splitter towards the girl's thighs. Her slit, already swimming in the spendings which the peasant had thrown into it, quickly received the ruby nut. Tim gushed it in, and stooping over her, shoved in the long shaft, until his hairs rubbed Bella's white skin.

"Oh, it's dreadfully long," cried she; "you are shockingly big, you naughty boy. Don't be so violent. Oh, you kill me! How you push. Oh! you can't get in any further; pray be gentle; there, it's quite up me. I can feel it up to my waist. Oh, Tim, you horrid, bad boy!"

"Give it to her," muttered the father, who was feeling the lad's balls, and tickling all round between his legs all the time. "She'll take it. Tim. Ain't she a beauty? What a tight little cunt she's got, ain't she, boy?"

"Ugh, don't talk, Father, I can't fuck."

For some minutes there was silence, save for the noise of the two heaving, struggling bodies in the hay. After a while the boy stopped. His prick, though hard as iron and stiff as wax, had not apparently spent a drop. Presently, Tim pulled it right out, all smacking and glistening with moistures.

"I can't spend," said he, mournfully.

"It's the frigging," explained the Father. "I frig him so often that he misses it now."

Bella lay panting and all exposed.

The man now applied his hand to Tim's cock, and began vigorously rubbing it up and down.

The girl expected every moment he would spend in her face.

After a while passed in thus further exciting his son, the father suddenly applied the burning nut to Bella's slit, and as it passed up, a perfect deluge of sperm issued from it and flooded her interior. Tim set himself to work to writhe and struggle, and ended by biting her in the arm.

When this discharge had quite terminated, and the last throb had passed through the boy's huge rammer, he slowly drew it out and let the girl rise.

They had no intention, however, to let her go, for after

undoing the door, the boy looked cautiously round, and then replacing the wooden bar, turned to Bella.

"What fun, wasn't it," he remarked. "I told you Father was good at it, didn't I?"

"Yes, you did, indeed, but you must let me go now; do, there's a good boy."

A grin was the only response.

Bella looked towards the man, and what was her terror to see him in a state of nudity, all save his shirt and boots, and with an erection that threatened another and even fiercer assault upon her charms.

His member was literally livid with the tension and stuck up against his hairy belly. The head had swollen enormously with the previous irritation, and from its tip a glistening drop hung pendant.

"You'll let me fuck you again," enquired the man, as he caught the young lady by the waist and put her hand on his tool.

"I'll try," murmured Bella, and seeing there was no help for it, she suggested his sitting on the hay, while straddling across his knees, she tried to insert the mass of gristly flesh.

After a few heaves and pushes it went in, and a second course, no less violent than the first commenced. A full quarter of an hour elapsed. It was now apparently the elder who could not be brought to the point of emission.

"How tiresome they are," thought Bella.

"Frig it, my dear," said the man, withdrawing from her body his member, even harder than before.

Bella clasped it with both her small hands and worked it up and down. After a little of this excitement she stopped, and perceiving a small spurt of semen exude from the urethra, she quickly placed herself upon the huge pummel, and had hardly housed it before a flood of spunk rushed into her.

Bella rose and fell, thus pumping him, till all was finished, after which they let her go.

At length the day arrived, the eventful morning broke, when the beautiful Julia Delmont was to lose that coveted treasure which is so eagerly sought after on the one hand, and often so thoughtlessly thrown away upon the other.

It was still early, when Bella heard her foot upon the stairs, and the two friends were no sooner united than a thousand pleasant subjects of prattle found their way into their talk, until Julia began to see that there was something which Bella was keeping back. In fact, her rapidity was simply a mask for the concealment of some piece of news which she was somewhat reluctant to break to her companion.

"I know you have something to tell me, Bella, there is something I have not heard yet which you have to tell me; what is it, darling."

"Can't you guess," she said, with a wicked smile playing round the dimpling corners of her rosy lips.

"Is it anything about Father Ambrose?" asked Julia. "Oh! I feel so dreadfully and awkward, when I see him now, and yet he told me there was no harm in what he did."

"Nor more there was, depend upon it; but what did he do?"

"Oh, more than ever. He told me such things, and then he put his arm round my waist, and kissed me, till he almost took my breath away."

"And then," suggested Bella.

"How can I tell you, dearest! Oh, he said and did a thousand things, until I thought I was going out of my senses."

"Tell me some of them at least."

"Well, you know that, after he had kissed me so hard, he put his fingers down my dress, and then he played with my foot and my stocking, and then he slipped his hand up higher, until I thought I was going to faint."

"Oh! you little wanton, I feel sure you liked his proceedings all the while."

"Of course I did. How could I do otherwise? He made me feel as I had never felt in my life before."

"Come, Julia, that was not all—he did not stop there, you know."

"Oh no; of course he did not, but I cannot tell you his next proceeding."

"Away with such childishness," cried Bella, pretending to be piqued at her friend's reticence. "Why not avow all to me?"

"If I must, I suppose there is no help for it, but it seemed so shocking, being all so new to me, and yet not wrong. After he had made me feel as if I was dying of a delicious shivering sensation, which his fingers produced, he suddenly took my hand in his and placed it upon something he had which felt like a child's arm. He bid clasp me it tightly. I did as he directed me, and then looking down, I beheld a great red thing, all white skin and blue veins, with a funny, round purple top, like a plum. Well, I saw that this thing grew out from between his legs, and that it was covered below with a great mass of curly black hair."

Julia hesitated. "Go on," said Bella.

"Well, he kept my hand upon it, making me rub it over and over; it was so large, and stiff, and hot!"

"No doubt it was under the excitement of such a little beauty."

"Then he took my other hand and placed both together on his hairy thing. I felt so frightened when I saw how his eyes glared and his breathing grew hard and quick. He reassured me. He called me his dear child, and, rising, bade me fondle the stiff thing in my bosom. It stuck out close to my face."

"Is that all?" asked Bella, persuasively.

"No, no, indeed it is not, but I feel so ashamed. Shall I go on? Is it right that I should divulge these things? Well then, after I had held this monster in my bosom a little time, during which it throbbed and pressed me with a warm delightful pressure, he asked me to kiss it. I complied at once. A warm sensuous smell arose from it, as I pressed my lips upon it. At his request I continued kissing it. He bade me open my lips and rub the top between them. A moisture came at once upon my tongue, and on an instant a thick gush of warm fluid ran into my mouth, and spurted over my face and hands. I was still playing with it, when a noise of a door opening at the other end of the church obliged the good Father to put away what I had hold of—"for," he said, "it is not for the common people to know what you know, or to do what I permit you to do. His manner was so kind and obliging, and he made me think I was quite different to all the other girls. But tell me, Bella, dearest, what is the mysterious news you have to tell me? I am dying to know."

"Answer me first, whether or not the good Ambrose told you of joys—of pleasures, derived from the object you trifled with, and whether he pointed out any means by which such delights could be indulged without sin?"

"Of course he did—he said that in certain cases such indulgence became a merit."

"As in marriage, for instance, I suppose."

"He said nothing about that, except that marriage often brought much misery, and that even marriage vows might, under certain circumstances, be broken advantageously."

Bella smiled. She recollected to have heard somewhat the same strain of reasoning from the same sensual lips.

"Under what circumstances did he mean then that these joys were permitted?"

"Only when the mind was firmly set upon a good motive, beyond the actual indulgence itself, and that, he says, can only he, when some young girl, selected from others for the qualities of her mind, is dedicated to the relief of the servants of religion."

"I see," said Bella, "go on."

"Then he said how good I was, and how meritorious it would be for me to exercise the privilege he endowed me with, and devote myself to the sensuous relief of himself and others, whose vows prevented them from either marrying or otherwise gratifying the feeling which natnre has implanted in all men alike. But tell me, Bella, you have some news for me—I know you have."

"Well, then, if I must—I must, I suppose. Know then, that good Father Ambrose has arranged that it will be best for you to be initiated at once, and he has provided for it here to-day."

"Oh, me! You don't say so! I shall be so ashamed, so dreadfully shy."

"Oh, no, my dear, all that has been thought of. Only so good and considerate a man as our dear Confessor could have so perfectly arranged everything as he has done. It is designed that the dear man shall be able to enjoy all beauties your witching little self can afford him, while, to make a long matter short, he will neither see your face, nor you his."

"You don't say so! In the dark, then, I suppose?"

"By no means; that would be to forego all the pleasures of sight, and he would lose the rich treat of looking upon those delicious charms the dear man has set his heart upon possessing."

"How you make me blush, Bella—but how, then, is it to be?"

"It will be quite light," explained Bella, with the air of a mother to her child. "It will be in a nice little chamber we have; you will be laid upon a convenient couch, and your head will be passed through and concealed by a curtain, which so fills a door-way leading into an inner apartment that only your body, all naked to the view, will be exposed to your ardent assailant."

"Oh, for shame! Naked, too!"

"Oh, Julia my dear, tender Julia," murmured Bella, as a shudder of keen ecstatic feeling rushed through her, "what delights will be yours; how you will awake to the delicious joys of immortals, and find now that you are approaching that period called puberty, the solaces of which I know you already stand in need of."

"Oh, don't Bella, pray, don't say that."

"And when at length," continued her companion, whose imagination had already led her into a reverie to which outward impressions were quite imperious, "when at length the struggle is over, the spasms arrive, and that great throbbing thing shoots out its viscid stream of maddening delight, oh! then she will join that rush of ecstasy, and give down her virgin exchange."

"What are you murmuring about?"

Bella roused herself.

"I was tinking," she said, dreamily, "of all the joys of which you were about to partake."

"Oh, don't," Julia exclaimed, "you make me blush, when you say such dreadful things."

Then followed a further conversation, in which many small matters had their place, and while it was in progress I found an opportunity to overhear another dialogue, quite as interesting to me, but of which I shall only furnish the summary for my readers.

It took place in the library, and occured between Mr. Delmont and Mr. Verbouc. They had evidently understood each other on the main points at issue, which incredible as they may appear, were the surrender of Bella's person to Mr. Delmont in consideration for a certain round sum to be then and there paid down, and afterwards invested for the benefit of "his dear niece," by the indulgent Mr. Verbouc.

Knave and sensualist as the man was, he could not quite bring himself to the perpetration of so nefarious a transaction without some small sop to stay the conscience of even so unscrupulous a being as himself.

"Yes," said the good and yielding uncle, "the interests of my niece are paramount, my dear sir. A marriage is not unlikely hereafter, but the small indulgence you demand is, I think, well compensated for between us, as men of the world, you understand, purely as men of the world, by a sum sufficient to reward her for the loss of so fragile a possession."

Here he laughed, principally because his matter-of-fact and dull-witted guest failed to understand him.

Thus it was settled, and there remained only the preliminaries to arrange. Mr, Delmont was charmed, ravished out of his somewhat heavy and stolid indifference, when he was informed that the bargain was forthwith to be executed, and that he was to take possession of that delicious virginity he had so longed to destroy.

Meanwhile the good, dear, generous Father Ambrose had been some time in the house and had prepared the chamber where the sacrifice was to take place.

Here after a somptuous breakfast, Mr. Delmont found himself with only a door between him and the victim of his lust.

Who that victim was, he had not the remotest idea. He only thought of Bella.

The next moment he had turned the lock and entered the chamber, the gentle warmth of which refreshed and stimulated the sensual instincts about to be called into play.

Ye Gods! What a sight burst upon his enraptured vision. Straight before him, reclining upon a couch, and utterly nude, was the body of a young girl. A glance sufficed to demonstrate the fact that it was beautiful, but it would have taken several minutes to go over in detail and discover all the separate merits of each delicious limb and member: The well-rounded limbs, childlike in their plump proportions; the delicate bosom just ripening into two of the choicest and whitest little hills of soft flesh; the roseate buds which tipped their summits; the blue veins which coursed and meandered here and there and showed through the pearly surface like little rivulets of sanguine fluid only to enhance the more the dazzling whiteness of the skin. And then, oh! then, the central spot of man's desire, the rosy close-shut lips where nature loves to revel, whence she springs and whither she returns—Ia source—it was there visible in its almost infantine perfection.

All indeed was there except—the head. That all-important member was conspicuous by its absence, and yet the gentle undulations of the fair maiden plainly evidenced that she suffered no inconvenience by its non-appearance.

Mr. Delmont exhibited no astonishment at this phenomenon. He had been prepared for it, and also enjoined to maintain the strictest silence. He therefore busied himself to observe and delight himself with such charms as were prepared for his enjoyment.

Meanwhile no sooner had he recovered from his surprise and emotion at the first view of so much naked beauty, than he found certain evidences of its effects upon those sensuous organs which so readily respond in men of his temperament to emotions calculated to produce them.

His member, hard and swollen, now stood out in his breeches and threatened to burst from its confinement. He, therefore, liberated it, and allowed a strong but gigantic weapon to spring into light, and rear its red head in presence of its prey.

Reader, I am only a flea. I have but limited powers of perception, and I fail in ability to describe the gentle gradations and soft creeping touches by which this enraptured ravisher approached his conquest. Revelling in his security, Mr. Delmont ran his eyes and his hands over all. His fingers opened the delicate slit, over which as yet only a soft down had made its appearance, while the girl, feeling the intruder in her precints, wriggled and twisted to avoid, with the coyness natural under the circumstances, his wanton touches.

But now he draws her to him; his hot lips press the soft belly—the tender and sensitive nipples of her young breasts. With eager hand he firmly seizes her swelling hip, and pulling her towards him, opens her white legs and plants himself between.

Reader, I have already remarked I am only a flea. Yet

fleas have feelings, and what mine were I will not attempt to describe when I beheld that excited member brought close to the pouting lips of Julia's moist slit. I closed my eyes; the sexual instincts of the male flea rose within me, and I longed—yes! how ardently I longed to be in Mr. Delmont's place.

Meanwhile steadily and sternly he proceeded in his work of demolition. With a sudden bound he essayed to penetrate the virgin parts of the young Julia. He fails—he tries again, and once more his baffled engine flew up and lay panting on the heaving belly of his victim.

During this trying period no doubt Julia must have spoilt the plot by an outery more or less violent, but for a precaution adopted by that sage demoraliser and priest, Father Ambrose.

Julia had been drugged.

Once more Mr. Delmont returned to the charge. He pushes, he forces forward, he stamps his feet upon the floor, he rages and he foams, and oh, God! the soft elastic barrier gives way and he goes in—in with a felling of ecstatic triumph; in, until the pleasure of the tight and moist compression forces from his sealed lips a groan of pleasure. In, until his weapon, buried to the hair which covered his belly, lay throbbing and swelling yet harder and longer in its glove-like sheath.

Then followed a struggle no flea can describe—sighs of blissful and ravishing sensations escape his open slobbering lips, he pushes, he bends forward, his eyes turn up, his mouth opens, and, unable to prevent the rapid completion of his lustful pleasures, the strong man gasps out his soul, and with it a torrent of seminal fluid, which thrown well forward squirts into the womb of his own child.

All this time Ambrose had been a hidden spectator of

the lustful drama, and Bella had operated on the other side of the curtain to prevent any approach to utterance on the part of her young visitor.

This precaution was, however, unnecessary; for Julia, sufficiently recovered from the effects of the narcotic to feel the smart, had fainted.

CHAPTER XI

No sooner was the struggle over, and the victorious, rising from the quivering body of the girl, began to recover himself from the ecstasy into which so delicious an encounter had thrown him, than suddendly the curtain was slid on one side, and Bella herself appeared in the opening.

If a cannon-shot had suddenly passed close to the astonished Mr. Delmont, it could not have occasioned him one half the consternation which he felt, as hardly believing his own eyes, he stood, open-mouthed, alternately regarding the prostate body of his victim, and the apparition of her he supposed he had so recently enjoyed.

Bella, whose charming "neglige" set off to perfection her young beauties, affected to appear equally stupified, but apparently recovering herself, she drew back a step, with a well-acted expression of alarm.

"What—what is all this?" inquired Mr. Delmont, whose agitation had prevented him from remembering that he had not as yet even readjusted his clothes, and that a very important instrument in the gratification of his late sensual impulse hung, still swollen and slippery, fully exposed between his legs.

"Heavens! that I should have made such a dreadful mistake," cried Bella, hiding her furtive glances this inviting exhibition.

"Tell me, for pity's sake, what mistake, and who then, is this?" exclaimed the trembling ravisher pointing, as he spoke, to the recumbent nudity before him.

"Oh, come—come away," cried Bella, hastily moving towards the door, and followed by Mr. Delmont, all anxiety for an explanation of the mystery.

Bella led the way into an adjoining boudoir, and closing the door firmly, she threw herself upon a luxuriously disposed couch, so as to exhibit freely her beauties, while she pretended to be too overwhelmed with her horror to notice the indelicacy of her pose.

"Oh! what have I done! what have I done!" she sobbed, hiding her face in her hands in apparent anguish.

A horrible suspicion flashed across the mind of her companion; he gasped out, half choking with emotion.—

"Speak—who is that—who?"

"It was not my fault—I could not know that it was you they had brought here for me, and—and—not knowing better—I substituted Julia.

Mr. Delmont staggered back—a confused sense of something dreadful broke upon him—a distress obstructed his vision, and then gradually he awoke to the full sense of the reality. Before, however, he could utter a word, Bella, well instructed as to the direction his ideas would take, hastened to prevent him time to think.

"Hush! she knows nothing of it—it has been a mistake—a dreadful mistake, and nothing more. If you are disappointed, it has been my fault—not yours; you know I never thought for a moment it was to have been you. I think," she added, with a pretty pout, and a significant side-glance at the still protruding member, "it was very unkind of them not to have told me it was to have been you."

Mr. Delmont saw the beautiful girl before him; he could not but admit to himself that, whatever pleasures might have been his in the involuntary incest in which he had been a party, they had, nevertheless, failed of his original intention, and lost something for which he had paid so dearly.

"Oh, if they should find out what I have done," murmured Bella, changing a little her position, and exposing a portion of one leg above the knee.

Mr. Delmont's eyes glittered in spite of himself his calmness returned, his animal passions were asserting themselves.

"If they should find me out," again sighed Bella, and with that she half rose and threw her beautiful arms round the neck of the deluded parent.

Mr. Delmont pressed her in a close embrace.

"Oh, my goodness, what is this?" whispered Bella,

whose little hand had seized the slimy weapon of her companion, and was now engaged in squeezing and moulding it in her warm grasp.

The wretched man felt all her touches, all her charms, and, once more rampant with lust, sought no better fate than to revel in her young virginity.

"If I must yield," said Bella, "be gentle with me; oh! how you touch me! Oh! take away your hand. Oh! heavens! What do you do?"

Bella had only time to catch a glimpse of his red-headed member, stiffer and more swollen than ever, and the next moment he was upon her.

Bella made no resistance, and fired by her loveliness, Mr. Delmont quickly found the exact spot, and taking advantage of her inviting position, pushed with fury his already lubricated penis into her young and tender parts.

Bella groaned.

Further and further inwards went his hot dart, until their bellies met together, and he was up her body to his balls.

Then commenced a rapid and delicious encounter, in which Bella did her part to perfection, and roused by this new instrument of pleasure, went off in a torrent of delight. Mr. Delmont quickly followed her example, and shot into Bella a copious flood of his prolific sperm.

For several moments both lay without motion, bathed in the exudation of their mutual raptures, and panting with their efforts, until a slight noise made itself heard, and before either had attempted to withdraw, or change from the very unequivocal position they occupied, the door of the boudoir opened, and three persons made their appearance almost simultaneously.

These were Father Ambrose, Mr. Verbouc, and the gentle Julia Delmont.

The two men appeared bearing between them the half-conscious figure of the young girl, whose head, languidly falling on one side, lay on the shoulders of the robust priest, while Verbouc, no less favoured by his proximity, supported her slender form with her nervous arm, and gazed in her face with a look of unsatisfied lust, such as only a devil incarnate could have equalled. Both men were in a state of hardly decent dishabille, and the unfortunate little Julia was as naked as when, scarcely a quarter of an hour before, she had been violently ravished by her own father.

"Hush!" whispered Bella, putting her hand upon the lips of her amorous companion, "for God's sake, do not criminate yourself. They cannot know who has done it; better suffer all than confess such a dreadful fact. They are merciless—beware, how you thwart them."

Mr. Delmont instantly saw the truth of Bella's prediction.

"See, thou man of lust," exclaimed the pious Ambrose, "behold the state in which we found this dear child," and placing his big hand upon the beautiful unflegded "motte" of the young Julia, he wantonly exhibited his fingers, reeking with the paternal discharge to the others.

"Horrible," observed Verbouc, "and if she should be found with child!"

"Abominable," cried Father Ambrose. "We must, of course, prevent that."

Delmont groaned.

Meanwhile Ambrose and his coadjutor led their beautiful young victim into the apartment, and commenced to cover her with those preliminary touches and lascivious pawings which precede the unbridled indulgence in luxurious possession. Julia, half awake from the effects of the sedative they had given her, and wholly confounded by the proceedings of the virtuous pair, appeared barely conscious of the presence of her parent, while that worthy, held in position by the white arms of Bella, still lay soaking on her soft white belly.

"The spunk running down her legs," exclaimed Verbouc, eagerly inserting his hand between Julia's thighs; "how shocking!"

"It is even reached her pretty little feet," observed Ambrose, raising one of her rounded legs, under pretence of making an examination of the delicate kid-boot, upon which he had truly observed more than one gout of seminal fluid, while, with a glance of fire, he eagerly explored the rosy chink thus exposed to view.

Delmont groaned again.

"Oh, good Lord, what a beauty!" cried Verbouc, smacking the rounded buttocks. "Ambrose, proceed to prevent any consequences from so unusual a circumstance. Nothing less than a second emission from another and vigorous man can render such a thing positively safe."

"Yes, she must have it—that is certain." muttered Ambrose, whose state during all this time may be better imagined than described.

His cassock stuck out in front—his whole manner betrayed his violent emotions. Ambrose lifted his frock, and gave liberty to his enormous member, the ruby and inflamed head of which seemed to menace the skies.

Julia, horribly frightened, made a feeble movement to escape. Verbouc, delighted, held her in full view.

Julia beheld for the second time, the fiercely erected member of her Confessor, and knowing his intention from the previous initiation she had passed through, half fainted with trembling fear.

Ambrose, as if to outrage the feelings of both, father

and daughter, exposed fully his huge genitals and wagged his gigantic penis in their faces.

Delmont, overcome with terror, and finding himself in the hands of the two cospirators, held his breath and cowered by the side of Bella, who, delighted beyond measure by the success of the scheme, kept counselling him to remain neutral and let them have their will.

Verbouc, who had been fingering the moistened parts of the little Julia, now yielded her to the furious lust of his friend, and prepared himself for his favourite pastime of watching her violation.

The Priest, beside himself with lubricity, divested himself of his nether garments, and his member, standing grimly all the while, proceeded to the delicious task which awaited him. "She is mine at last," he murmured.

Ambrose immediately seized his prey; he passed his arms around her, and lifted her from the ground; he bore the trembling Julia to an adjoining sofa, and threw himself upon her naked body; he endeavoured with all his might to accomplish his enjoyment. His monstrous weapon, hard as iron, battered at the little pink slit, which although already lubricated with the semen she had received from Mr. Delmont, was no easy sheath for the gigantic penis which threatened her.

Ambrose continued his efforts. Mr. Delmont could only see a heaving mass of black silk, as the robust figure of the priest writhed upon the form of his little daughter. Too experienced to be long held in check, however. Ambrose felt himself gaining ground, and too much master of himself to allow the pleasure to overtake him too soon, he now bore down all opposition, and a loud shriek from Julia announced the penetration of the huge rammer.

Cry after cry succeeded, until Ambrose, at length firmly

buried in the belly of the young girl, felt he could go no further, and commenced those delicious pumping movements, which were to end at the same moment his pleasure and the torture of his victim.

Meanwhile Verbouc, whose lustful emotions had been intensily excited by the scene between Mr. Delmont and Julia, and subsequently by that between the foolish man and his niece, now rushed towards Bella, and releasing her from the relaxing embrace of his unfortunate friend, at once opened her legs, regarded for a moment her reeking orifice, and then at one bound buried himself in an agony of pleasure in her belly, well anointed by the abundance of spunk which had been already discharged there. The two couples now performed their delicious copulation in silence, save for the groans which came from the half-murdered Julia, the stentorous breathing of the fierce Ambrose, or the grunts and sobs of Mr. Verbouc. Faster and more delicious grew the race, Ambrose, having forced his gigantic penis up to the curling mass of black hair which covered its root into the tight slit of the young girl, became perfectly livid with lust. He pushed, he drove, he tore open with the force of a bull; and had not nature at length asserted herself in his favour by bringing his ecstasy to a climax, he must have succumbed to his excitement in an attack which would probably have for ever prevented a repetition of such a scene.

A loud cry came from Ambrose. Verbouc well knew its import, he was discharging. His rapture served to quicken his own. A howl of passionate lust arose within the chamber as the two monsters loaded their victims with their seminal outpourings. Not once, but three times did the Priest shoot his prolific essence into the very womb of the tender girl, before he assuaged his raging fever of desire.

As it was, to say that Ambrose simply discharged would give but a faint idea of the fact. He positively spurted his semen into the little Julia in thick and powerful jets, uttering all the while groans of ecstasy, as each hot and slippery injection rushed along his uge urethra and flew in torrents into the stretched receptacle. It was some minutes ere all was over, and the brutal Priest arose from his torn and bleeding victim.

At the same time Mr. Verbouc left exposed the opened thighs and besmeared slit of his niece, who lying still in the dreamy trance which follows the fierce delight, took no heed of the thick exuding drops which formed a white pool upon the floor between her well-stockinged legs.

"Ah, how delicious," exclaimed Verbouc, "you see, there is pleasure after all in the path of duty, Delmont, is there not?" turning to that dumbfounded individual. "If Father Ambrose and myself had not mixed our humble offerings with that prolific essence of which you seem to have made such good use, there is no knowing what mischief might have ensued. Oh, yes, nothing like doing the thing which is right, eh, Delmont?"

"I don't know. I fell ill; I am in a kind of dream, yet I am not insensible of sensations which cause me renewed delight. I cannot doubt your friendship—your secrecy. I have much enjoyed, I am still excited, I know not what I want?—Say, my friends."

Father Ambrose approached, and laying his big hand on the shoulder of the poor man, he encouraged him with a few whispered words of comfort.

As a Flea I am not at liberty to mention what these were, but their effect was to dissipate in a great measure the cloud of horror which oppressed Mr. Delmont. He sat down and gradually grew more calm.

Julia also had now recovered, and seated on each side of the burly priest, the two young girls ere long felt comparatively at ease. The Holy Father spoke to them like a father and he drew Mr. Delmont from his reserve, and that worthy having copiously refreshed himself with a considerable libation of rich wine, began to evince evident pleasure in the society in which he found himself.

Soon the invigorating effects of the wine began to tell upon Mr. Delmont. He cast wistful and envious glances towards his daughter. His excitement was evident, and showed itself in the bulging of his garments.

Ambrose perceived his desire and encouraged it. He led him to Julia, who, still naked, had no means of concealing her charms. The parent looked on all with an eye in which lust predominated. A second time would not be so very much more sinful, he thought.

Ambrose nodded his encouragement. Bella unbuttoned his nether garment, and taking his stiff prick in her hand, squeezed it softly.

Mr. Delmont understood the position, and the next moment was upon his child. Bella guided the incestuous member to the soft red lips; a few pushes and the half-maddened father was fully entered in the belly of his pretty child.

The struggle that followed was intensified by the circumstances of his horible connection. After a fierce and rapid course, Mr. Delmont discharged and his daughter received in the utmost recesses of her young womb the guilty spendings of her unnatural parent.

Father Ambrose, whose sensual character thoroughly predominated, owned one other weakness, and that was preaching; he would preach by the hour together, not so much on religions subjects as on others much more mundane, and certainly not usually sanctioned by Holy Mother Church.

On this occasion he delivered discourse which I found it impossible to follow, and went to sleep in Bella's armpit until he had done.

How far in the future this consummation would have been, I know not, but the gentle Bella, having obtained a hold of his great lolling affair in her little white hand, so pressed and tickled it that the good man was feign to pause by reason of the sensation she produced.

Mr. Verbouc also, who, it will be remembered coveted nothing so much as a buttered bun, knew only too well how splendidly buttered were the delicious little parts of the newly-convered Julia. The presence of the father also—worse than helpless to prevent the utmost enjoyment of his child by these two libidinous men, served to whet his appetite while Bella, who felt the slime oozing from her warm slit, who also conscious of certain, longings which her previous encounters had not appeased.

Verbouc commenced again to visit with his lascivious touches the sweet and childish charms of Julia, impudently moulding her round buttocks and slipping his fingers between their rounded hillocks.

Father Ambrose, not less active, had got his arm round Bella's waist, and putting her half-nude form close to him, he sucked licentious kisses from her pretty lips.

As the two men continued these toyings, their desires proportionately advanced until their weapons, red and inflamed by previous enjoyments, stood firmly in the air, and stiffly menaced the young creatures in their power.

Ambrose, whose lust never wanted much incentive, quickly possessed himself of Bella, who, nothing loth, let him press her down upon the sofa which had witnessed already two encounters, and still further exciting his skinned and flaming pego, the daring girl let it enter between her white thigs, and favouring the disproportionate attack as much as she could, she received its whole terrible build in her moistened slit.

This sight so worked upon the feelings of Mr. Delmont, that he evidently needed small encouragement to attempt a second "coup" when the Priest had done.

Mr. Verbouc, who had for some time been throwing lascivious glances towards Mr. Delmont's young daughter, now found himself once more in condition to enjoy. He reflected that the repeated violation she had already experienced at the hands of her father and the Priest had fitted her for the part he loved to play, and he knew, both by touch and sight, that her parts were sufficiently oiled by the violent discharges she had received to gratify his dearest whim.

Verbouc gave a glance towards the Priest, who was now engaged in the delicious enjoyment of his niece, and then closing upon the beautiful Julia, he in his turn, succeeded in reversing her upon a couch and with considerable effort thrust his stout member to the balls in her delicate body.

This new and intensified enjoyment brought Verbouc to the verge of madness; he pressed himself into the tight and glovelike slit of the young girl, and throbbed all over with delight.

"Oh, she is heaven itself!" he murmured, pressing in his big member to the balls, which were gathered up tightly below. "Good Lord, what tightness—what slippery pleasure—ugh!" and another determined thrust made poor Julia groan again.

Meanwhile Father Ambrose, with eyes half shut, lips parted, and nostrils dilated, was battering the beautiful parts of the young Bella, whose sensual gratification became evident in her sobs of pleasure.

"Oh! my goodness! You are—you are too big—enormous! Your great thing. Oh! it's up to my waist. Oh, oh! it's too much; not so hard—dear Father—how you push!—you will kill me. Ah! gently—go slower—I feel your great balls at my bottom."

"Stop a moment," cried Ambrose, whose pleasure had become insupportable, and whose spunk was nearly provoked to rush out of him. "Let us pause, Shall I change with you, my friend? The idea is lovely."

"No, oh, no! I cannot move, I can only go on—this dear child is perfect enjoyment."

"Be still, Bella, dear child, or you will make me spend. Don't squeeze my weapon so rapturously."

"I cannot help it—you kill me with pleasure. Oh! go on, but gently. Oh, not so hard! Don't push so fiercely. Heavens! he's going to spend. His eyes close, his lips open. My God! you kill me—you slit me up with that big thing. Ah! oh! come then! spend, dear—Father—Ambrose. Give me the burning spunk. Oh! push now—harder—harder— kill me, if you like."

Bella threw her white arms round his brawny neck, opened wide her soft and beautiful thighs, and took in his huge instrument, until his hairy belly rubbed on her downy mount.

Ambrose felt himself about to go off in rapturous emission right into the body of the girl under him.

Push—push now!" cried Bella, regardless of all modesty, and giving down her own discharge in spasms of pleasure. "Push—push—drive it up me. Oh, yes, like that. Ah, God, what a size! What a length—you slit me, brute that you are. Oh, oh! oh! You are off—I feel it. Oh, God—what spunk! Oh, what gushes!"

Ambrose discharged furiously, like the stallion that he was, thrusting with all his might into the warm belly below.

He then reluctantly withdrew, and Bella, released from his clutches, turned to regard the other pair. Her uncle was administering a shower of short thrusts at her little friend, and it was evident a climax must soon be put to his enjoyment.

Meanwhile Julia, whose recent violation and subsequent hard treatment by the brutal Ambrose had sadly hurt and enfeebled, had not the slightest pleasure, but lay a unresisting and inert mass in the arms of her ravisher.

When therefore, after a few more pushes, Verbouc fell forward in a voluptuous discharge, she was only aware that something warm and wet was being rapidly injected into her, without experiencing any other sensations than languor and fatigue.

Another pause followed this third outrage, during which Mr. Delmont subsided into a corner and appeared to be dozing. A thousand pleasantries now took place. Ambrose, while reclining upon the couch, made Bella stride over him, and applying his lips to her reeking slit, luxuriated in kisses and touches the most lascivious and depraved.

Mr. Verbouc, not to be behindhand with his companion, played off several equally libidinous inventions upon the innocent Julia.

The two then laid flat upon a couch, and felt all her beauties over, lingering with admiration upon her yet un-fledged "motte," and the red lips of her young cunt.

After a time the desires of both were seconded by the

outward and visible signs of two standing members, eager again for a taste of pleasures so ecstatic and select.

A new programme was now, however, to be inaugurated. Ambrose was the first to propose it. "We have had enough of their cunts," said he, coarsely, turning to Verbouc, who had passed over to Bella, and was playing with her nipples. "Let us try what their bottoms are made of. This lovely little creature would be a treat for the Pope himself, and ought to have buttocks of velvet and a "derriere" fit for an Emperor to spend into."

The idea was instantly seized upon, and the victims secured. It was abominable, it was monstrous, it was apparently impossible, when viewed in all its disproportionate character. The enormous member of the Priest was presented to the small aperture of Julia's posterior—that of Verbouc threatened his niece in the same direction. A quarter of an hour was consumed in the preliminaries and after a frightful scene of lust and lechery, the two girls received in their bowels the burning jets of these impious discharges.

At length a calm succeeded to the violent emotions which had overwhelmed the actors in this monstrous scene.

Attention was at length directed to Mr. Delmont.

That worthy, as I have before remarked, was quietly ensconsed in a corner, apparently overcome with sleep, or wine, or possibly both.

"How quiet he is," observed Verbouc.

"An evil conscience is a sad companion," remarked Father Ambrose, whose attentions were directed to the ablution of his lolling instrument.

"Come, my friend—it is your turn now, here is a treat for you," continued Verbouc, exhibiting to the edification of all the most secret parts of the almost insensible Julia;

"come and enjoy this.—Why, what is the matter with the man? Good heavens, why,—how—what is this?"

Verbouc recoiled a step.

Father Ambrose leant over the form of the wretched Delmont—he felt his heart. "He is dead," he said, quietly—and so it was.

CHAPTER XII

Sudden death is so common an event, especially among persons whose previous history has led to the supposition of the existence of some organic deterioration, that surprise easily gives place to ordinary expressions of condolence, and this again to a state of resignation at a result by no means to be wondered at.

The transition may be thus expressed:

"Who would have thought it?"

"Is it possible?"

"I always had my suspicions."

"Poor fellow!"

"Nobody ought to be surprised!"

This interesting formula was duly gone through when poor Mr. Delmont paid the debt of nature, as the phrase goes.

A fortnight after that unfortunate gentleman had departed this life, his friends were all convinced they had long ago detected symptoms which must sooner or later prove fatal; they rather prided themselves on their sagacity, reverently admitting the inscrutability of Providence.

As for me, I went about much as usual, except that for a change I fancied Julia's legs had a more piquant flavour than Bella's and I accordingly bled them regularly for my repast matutinal and nocturnal.

What could be more natural than that Julia should pass much of her time with her dear friend Bella, and what more likely than that the sensual Father Ambrose and his patron, the lecherous relative of my dear Bella, should seek to improve the occasion and repeat their experiences upon the young and docile girl!

That they did so, I knew full well, for my nights were most uneasy and uncomfortable, always liable to interruption from the incursions of long hairy tools among the pleasant groves, wherein I had temporarily located myself, and frequently nearly drowning me in a thick and frightfully glutinous torrent of animal semen.

In short, the young and impressionable Julia was easily and completely broken up, and Ambrose and his friend revelled to their heart's content in her complete possession.

They had gained their ends, what mattered the sacrifice to them?

Meanwhile other and very different ideas were occupying the mind of Bella, whom I had abandoned, and feeling, at length, a degree of nausea from the too frequent indulgence in my new diet, I resolved to vacate the stockings of the pretty Julia and return—"Revenir a mon mouton," as I might say—to the sweet and succulent pastures of the prurient Bella.

I did so, and "voici le resultat!"

One evening Bella retired to rest rather later than usual. Father Ambrose was absent upon a mission to a distant parish, and her dear and indulgent uncle was laid up with a sharp attack of gout, to which he had lately become more subject.

The girl had already amanaged her hair for the night. She had also denuded herself of her upper garments and was in the act of putting her "chemise de nuit" over her head, in the process of which she inadvertently allowed her petticoats to fall and display before her glass the beautiful proportions and exquisitely soft and transparent skin.

So much beauty might have fired Anchorite, but alas! there was no such ascetic there present to be inflamed. As for me, she only nearly broke my longest feeler and twisted my right jumper, as she whirled the warm garment in the hair above her head.

One present there was, however, whom Bella had not counted upon, but upon whom, it is needless to say, nothing was lost.

And now I must explain that ever since the crafty Father Clement had been denied Bella's charms, he had sworn a very unclerical and beastly oath to renew the attempt to surprise and capture the pretty fortress he had once already stormed and ravished. The remembrance of his happiness brought tears into his sensual little eyes, and a certain distension sympathetically imparted itself to his enormous member.

Clement in fact had sworn a fearful oath to fuck Bella in a natural state in her own unvarnished words, and I, Flea though I be, heard and understood their import.

The night was dark; the rain fell—Ambrose was absent. Verbouc was ill and helpless—Bella would be alone—all this was perfectly well-known to Clement, and accordingly he made the attempt. Improved by his recent experience in his geography of the neighbourhood, he went straight to the window of Bella's chamber, and finding it, as he expected, unfastened and open, he coolly entered and crept beneath the bed. From this position Clement beheld with throbbing veins the toilette of the beautiful Bella until the moment when she commenced to throw off her chemise, as I have already explained. In so doing Clement saw the nudity of the girl in full view, and snorted internally like a bull. From his recumbent position he had no difficulty in viewing the whole of her body from the waist down, and as she faced from him, his eyes glistened as he saw the lovely twin globes of her bottom opening and shutting as the graceful girl twisted her lithe figure in the act of passing the chemise over her head.

Clement could restrain himself no longer; his desires rose to boiling point, and softly, but swiftly, gliding from his concealment, he arose behind her; and without an instant's loss of time he clasped her asked body in his arms, placing as he did so, one of his fat hands over her rosy mouth.

Bella's first instinct was to scream, but that feminine resource was denied her. Her next was to faint, and this she probably would have done out for one circumstance. This was the fact, that as the audacious intruder held her close to him, a certain something, hard, long and warm, very sensibly pressed inwards between her smooth buttocks, and lay throbbing in their separation and up along her back. At this critical moment Bella's eyes encountered their image reflected in the opposite toilet-glass, and she recognized, over her shoulder the inflamed and ugly visage, crowned by the shock circle of red hair, of the sensual priest.

Bella understood the situation in the twinkling of an eye. It was nearly a week since she had received the embraces of either Ambrose or her uncle, and this fact had no doubt something to do with the conclusion she formed on this trying occasion. What she had been on the point of doing in reality, the lewd girl now only simulated.

She allowed herself to recline gently back upon the stout figure of Clement, and that happy individual, believing she was really fainting, at once withdrew his hand from her mouth and supported her in his arms.

The unresisting position of so much loveliness excited Clement almost to madness. She was nearly naked, and he ran his hands over her polished skin. His immense weapon, already stiff and distended with impatience, now palpitated with passion, as he held the beautiful girl in his close embrace.

Clement tremblingly drew her face to his, and imprinted a long and voluptous kiss upon her sweet lips.

Bella shuddered and opened her eyes.

Clement renewed his caresses.

The young girl sighed.

"Oh!" she exclaimed, softly, "how dare you come here? Pray, pray leave me at once—it is shameful."

Clement grinned. He was always ugly—now he looked positively hideous in his strong lust.

"So it is, said he, "shameful to treat such a pretty girl like this, but then, it's so delicious, my darling."

Bella sobbed.

More kisses, and a roving of hands over the naked girl. A great uncouth hand settled over the downy mount, and a daring finger, separating the dewy lips, entered the warm slit and touched the sensitive clitoris.

Bella closed her eyes, and repeated the sigh. That sensitive little organ instantly commenced to develop itself. It was by no means diminutive in the case of my young friend, and under the lascivious fingering of the ugly Clement, it arose, stiffened, and stuck out, until it almost parted the lips of its own accord.

Bella was fired—desire beamed in her eyes; she had caught the infection and stealing a glance at her seducer, she noticed the terrible look of rampant lust which spread itself over his face, as he toyed with her secret young charms.

The girl trembled with agitation; an earnest longing for the pleasure of coition took absolute possession of her, and unable longer to control her desires, she quickly insinuated her right hand behind her, and grasped, but could not span, the huge weapon which drove against her bottom.

Their eyes met—lust raged in each. Bella smiled, Clement repeated his sensual kiss, and insinuated his lolling tongue within her mouth. The girl was not slow to second his lecherous embraces, and allowed him full liberty of action, both as to his roving hands and active kisses. Gradually he pressed her towards a chair, and Bella, sinking upon it, awaited impatiently the next overtures of the Priest.

Clement stood exactly in front of her. His cassock of black silk, which reached to his heels, bulged out in front, while his cheeks, fiery red with the violence of his desires, were only rivalled by the smoking lips, as he breathed excitedly in the ecstasy of the anticipations.

He saw that he had nothing to fear and everything to enjoy.

"This is too much," murmured Bella, "go away."

"Oh! impossible now I have had the trouble of getting here."

"But you may be discovered, and I should be ruined."

"Not likely—you know we are quite alone and not at all likely to be disturbed. Besides, you are so delicious, my child, so fresh, so young and beautiful—there, don't withdraw your leg. I was only putting my hand on your soft thigh. In fact, I want to fuck you, my darling."

Bella saw the huge projection give a flip up.

"How nasty you are!—What words you use."

"Do I, my little pet, my angel," said Clement, again seizing on the sensitive clitoris, which he moulded between his finger and thumb; "they are all prompted by the pleasure of feeling this pouting little cunt that is slyly trying to evade my touches."

"For shame!" exclaimed Bella, laughing in spite of herself.

Clement came close and stopped over her, as she sat; he took her pretty face between his fat hands. As he did so, Bella was conscious that his cassock, already bulging out with the force of the desires communicated to his truncheon, was within a few inches of her bosom.

She could detect the throbs with which the black silk garment gradually rose and fell. The inclination was irresistible; she put her delicate little hand under the priest's vestment, and lifting up sufficiently felt a great hairy mass, which contained two balls, as large as fowl's eggs.

"Oh, my goodness, how enormous!" whispered the young girl.

"All full of the beautiful thick spunk," sighed Clement, playing with the two pretty breasts which were so close to him.

Bella shifted her ground, and once more grasped with both hands the strong and stiffened body of an enormous penis.

"How dreadful, what a monster!" exclaimed the lewd girl. "It is a big one, indeed; what a size you are!"

"Yes, isn't that a cock?" observed Clement, pushing forward and holding up his cassock the better to bring the gigantic affair into view.

Bella could not resist the temptation, but raising still higher the man's garment, released his penis entirely, and exposed it at full stretch.

Fleas are bad measures of size and space, and I forbear to give any exact dimensions of the weapon upon which the young lady now cast her eyes. It was gigantic, however, in its proportions. It had a large and dull red head, which stood shining and naked at the end of a long grissly shaft. The hole at the tip, usually to small, was, in this instance, a considerable slit, and was moist with the seminal humidity which gathered there. Along the whole shaft coursed the swollen blue veins, and behind all was a matted profusion of red bristling hair. Two huge testicles hung below.

"Good heavens! Oh, Holy Mother!" murmured Bella, shutting her eyes, and giving it a slight squeeze.

The broad, red head, distended and purple with the effect of the exquisite tickling of the girl, was now totally uncapped, and stood stiffly up from the folds of loose skin, which Bella pressed back upon the great white shaft. Bella toyed delightfully with this acquisition, and pressed still further back the velvety skin beneath her hand.

Clement sighed.

"Oh, you, delicious child," "he said gazing at her with sparkling eyes; "I must fuck you at once, or I shall throw it all over you."

"No, no you must not waste any of it," exclaimed Bella; "how pressed you must be to want to come so soon."

"I cannot help it—pray, remain quiet a moment, or I shall spend."

"What a big thing—how much can you do?"

Clement stopped and whispered something into the girl's ear, which I could not catch.

"Oh, how delicious, but it is incredible."

"No, it is true, only give me the chance. Come, I am longing to prove it to you, pretty one—see this! I must fuck you!"

He shook the monstrous penis, as he stood in front of her. Then, bending it down, he suddenly let it go. It sprung up, and as it did so, the skin went back of its own accord, and the big red nut came out with the hand-open urethra exuding a drop of semen.

It was close below Bella's face. She was sensible of a faint, sensuous odour, which came up from it and increased the disorder of her sense. She continued to finger and play with it.

"Stop, I entreat you, my darling, or you will waste it in the air."

Bella remained quiet a few seconds. Her warm band still clasped as much as she could of Clement's prick. He amused himself meanwhile in moulding her young breasts,

and in working his fingers up and down in her moist cunt.
The play made her wild. Her clitoris grew hot and prominent;
her breathing became hard and her pretty face flushed with
longing.

Harder and harder grew the nut, it shone like a ripe
plum. Bella's was crimson with desire; she furtively regarded the ugly man's naked and hairy belly—his brawny
thighs, thickly covered also with hair like an ape. His great
cock, each moment more swollen, menaced the skies, and
caused her indescribable emotions.

Excited beyond measure, she wound her white arms
around the stout figure of the great brute and covered him
with rapturous kisses. His very ugliness increased her
libidinous sensations.

"No, you must not waste it, I cannot let you waste it,"
and then, pausing for a second, she moaned with a peculiar articulation of pleasure, and lowering her fair head,
opend her rosy mouth, and instantly received as much of
the lascivious morsel as she could cram into it.

"Oh! how nice; how you tickle—what—what pleasure
you give me."

"I will not let you waste it. I will swallow every
drop," whispered Bella, raising her mouth for a moment
from the glistening nut.

Then again sinking her face forward, she pressed her
pouting lips upon the big tip, and parting them gently and
delicately, received the orifice of the wide urethra between
them.

"Oh, Holy Mother!" exclaimed Clement, "this is heaven!
How I shall spend? Good Lord? how you tickle and suck."

Bella applied her pointed tongue to the orifice and licked
it all round.

"How nice it tastes; you have already let out a drop or two."

"I cannot continue, I know I cannot," murmured the Priest, pushing forward and tickling with his finger at the same time the swollen clitoris that Bella put within his reach. Then she retook the head of the great cock again between her lips, but she could not make the whole of the nut enter her mouth, it was so monstrously large.

Tickling and sucking—passing back in slow delicious movements the skin which surrounded the red and sensitive ridge of his tremendous thing, Bella now evidently invited the result she knew could not long be delayed.

"Ah, Holy Mother! I am almost coming; I feel—I—Oh! oh! now suck. You've got it."

Clement lifted his arm in the air, his head fell back, his legs straddled wide apart, his hands worked convulsively, his eyes turned up, and Bella felt a strong spasm pass through the monstrous cock. The next moment she was almost knocked backwards by a forcible gush of semen, which rushed spouting in a continuous stream from his genitals, and flew in torrents down her gullet.

In spite of all her wishes and endeavours, the greedy girl could not avoid a stream issuing from the corners of her mouth while Clement, beside himself with pleasure, kept pushing forward in sharp jerks, each one of which sent a fresh jet of spunk down her throat. Bella followed all his movements, and held fast hold of the streaming weapon until all was done.

"How much did you say?" muttered she, one "tea-cup full—there were two."

"You beautiful darling," exclaimed Clement, when at last he found breath. "What divine pleasure you have

177

given me. Now it is my turn, and you must let me examine all I love in those little parts of yours.''

''Ah, how nice it was; I am nearly choked.'' cried Bella. ''How slippery it was, and, oh, goodness, what a lot!''

''Yes. I promised you plenty, my pretty one, and you so excited me that I know you must have received a good dose of it. It ran in streams.''

''Yes, indeed it did.''

''Now I am going to suck your pretty cunt, and fuck you deliciously afterwards.''

Suiting the action to the word, the sensual Priest threw himself between Bella's milk white thighs, and thrusting his face forward, plunged his tongue between the lips of the pinky slit. Then rolling it around the stiffened clitoris, he commenced a titillation so exquisite that the girl could hardly restrain her cries.

''Oh, my goodness. Oh, you suck my life out. Oh! I am—I am going off. I spend!'' and, with a sudden forward movement towards his active tongue, Bella emitted most copiously upon his face, and Clement received all he could catch in his mouth with the delight of an epicure.

At length the Priest arose; his big weapon which had scarcely softened, had now resumed its virile tension, and stuck out from him in a terrible erection. He positively snorted with lust, as he regarded the beautiful and willing girl.

''Now I must fuck you,'' said he, as he thrust her towards the bed. ''Now I must have you, and give you a taste of this cock in your little belly. Oh, what a mess there'll be!''

Hastly throwing off his cassock and nether garments, he compelled the sweet girl like-wise to denude herself of

178

her chemise, and then the great brute, his big body all covered with hair and brown as a mulatto, took the lily form of the beautiful Bella in his muscular arms and tossed her lightly on the bed. Clement regarded for a moment her extended figure as, palpitating with mingled desire and terror, she awaited the terrible onslaught; then he looked complacently upon his tremendous penis, erect with lust, and hastily mounting, threw himself upon her, and drew the bed-clothes over him.

Bella, half-smothered beneath the great hairy brute, felt his stiff cock interposed between their bellies. Passing down her hand, she touched it again.

"Good heavens! what a size, it will never go into me."

"Yes, yes—we will get in, all of it, up to the balls, only you must help, or I shall probably hurt you."

Bella was saved the trouble of a reply, for the next moment an eager tongue was in her mouth and almost choking her.

Then she became aware that the Priest had raised himself slightly, and that the hot head of his gigantic cock was pressing inwards between the moist lips of her little rosy slit.

I cannot go through the gradations of that preliminary conjuncture. It was full ten minutes in the accomplishment, but in the end ungainly Clement lay buried to the balls in the pretty body of the girl, while with her soft legs raised and thrown over his brawny back she received his lascivious caresses, as he gloated over his victim and commenced those lustful movements with the intention of ridding himself of his scalding fluid.

At least ten inches of stiff nervous muscle lay soaking and throbbing in the little girl's belly, while a mass of coarse hair pressed the battered and delicate mount of poor Bella.

"Oh, my! Oh! my, how you hurt," moaned she. "My Good! you are splitting me up."

Clement moved.

"I can't beat it—you are too big, indeed. Oh! take it out. Ah, what thrusts."

Clement pushed mercilessly two or three times.

"Wait a second, my little devil, until I smother you with my spunk. Oh, how tight you are. How you seem to suck my cock,—There, it's in now, You have it all."

"Oh, mercy."

Clement thrust hard and rapidly—push followed push—he squirmed and writhed on the soft figure of the girl. His lust rose hot and furious. His huge penis was strained to bursting in the intensity of his pleasure, and tickling, maddening delight of the moment.

"Ah, now I am fucking you at last."

"Fuck me," murmured Bella, opening still wider her pretty legs, as the intensity of the sensations gained upon her. "Oh, fuck me hard—harder," and with a deep moan of rapture she deluged her brutal ravisher with a copious discharge, pushing upwards at the same moment to meet a dreadful lunge. Bella's legs were jerked up and down, while Clement thrust himself between, and forced his long, hot member in and out in luscious movements. Soft sighs, mingled with kissings from the set lips of the lusty intruder, occasioned moans of rapture, and the rapid vibrations of the bedstead all bespoke the excitement of the scene.

Clement needed no invitation. The emission of his fair companion had supplied him with the moistening medium he desired, and he took advantage of it to commence a radid series of in and out movements, which caused Bella as much pleasure as pain.

The girl seconded him with all her power. Gorged to repletion, she heaved and quivered beneath his sturdy strokes. Her breath came in sobs, her eyes closed in the fierce pleasure of an almost constant spasm of emission. The buttocks of her ugly lover opened and shut, as he strained himself at every lunge into the body of the pretty child.

After a long course he paused a moment.

"I can't hold any longer, I'm going to spend. Take my spunk, Bella, you will have floods of it, pretty one."

Bella knew it—every vein in his monstrous cock was swollen to its utmost tension. It was insupportably big. It ressembled nothing so much as the gigantic member of an ass.

Clement began to move again—the saliva ran from his mouth; with an ecstatic sensation. Bella awaited the coming seminal shower.

Clement gave one or two short, deep thrusts, then groaned and lay still, only quivering slightly all over.

Then a tremendous spout of semen issued from his prick and deluged the womb of the young girl. The big brute buried his head in the pillows and forced himself in with his feet against the bedsteadend.

"Oh, the spunk," screamed Bella "I feel it. What streams, Oh, give it me. Holy Mother! What pleasure it is!"

"There, there, take that," cried the Priest, as once more at the first rush of semen into her, he pushed wildly up her belly, sending at each thrust a warm squirt of semen into her.

"There, there. Oh, what pleasure!"

Whatever had been Bella's anticipations, she had had no idea of the immense quantity this stalwart man could discharge. He pumped it out in thick masses, and splashed it into her very womb.

"Oh, I am spending again," and Bella sank half-fainting beneath the strong man, while his burning fluid continued still to dart from him in viscid jets.

Five times more that night Bella received the glutinous contents of Clement's big balls, and had not daylight warned them it was time to part, he would have recommenced.

When the astute Clement cleared the house, and hastened, as the day broke, to his humble quarter, he was forced to admit he had had his belly full of pleasure, even as Bella had had her belly full of spunk. As for that young lady, it was lucky for her that two protectors were incapacited, or they must have discovered in the painful and swollen condition of her young parts, that an interloper had been trespassing on their preserves.

Youth is elastic—everyone says so. Bella was young and "very elastic." If you had seen Clement's immense machine you would have said so. Her natural elasticity enabled her not only to sustain the introduction of this battering-ram, but also in about a couple of days to fell none the worse for it.

Three days after this interesting episode Father Ambrose returned. One of his first cares was to seek Bella. He found her, and invited her to follow to a boudoir.

"See," cried he producing his tool, inflamed and standing at attention, "I have had no amusement for a week, my cock is bursting, Bella, dear."

Two minutes later her head was reclining on the table of the apartment, while, with her clothes thrown completely over her head, and her swelling posteriors fully exposed, the salacious Priest regarded her round buttocks, and slapped them vigorously with his long member. Another minute and he had pushed his instrument into her from behind, until his black frizzly hair pressed against her bottom. Only a few thrusts brought from him a gush of spunk, and he sent a shower up to her waist.

The good Father was too much excited by long abstinence to lose his rigidity, but drawing down his stalwart tool, he presented it, all slippery and smoking, at the tight little entrance between those delicious buttocks. Bella favoured him, and well-amointed as he was, he slipped in, and gave her another tremendous dose from his prolific testicles. Bella felt fervent the discharge, and welcomed the hot spunk, as he discharged it up her bowels. Then he turned her over on the table, and sucked her clitoris for a quarter of an hour, making her discharge twice in his mouth, at the end of which time he employed her in the natural way.

Then Bella went to her chamber and purified herself, and, after a slight rest, put on her walking dress and went out.

That evening Mr. Verbouc was reported worse, the attack had reached regions which caused serious anxiety to his medical attendant. Bella wished her uncle a good night and retired.

Julia had installed herself in Bella's room for the night, and the two young friends, by this time well-enlightened as to the nature and properties of the male sex, lay exchanging ideas and experiences.

"I thought I was killed," said Julia, "when Father Ambrose pushed that great ugly thing of his up my poor little belly, and when he finished I thought he was in a fit, and could not understand what that slippery warm stuff could be which kept splashing into me, but, oh!''

"Then my dear, you commenced to feel the friction on that sensitive little thing of yours, and Father Ambrose's hot spunk spurted all over it.''

"Yes, that it did. I am always smothered, Bella, when he does it.''

"Hush! What was that?''

Both the girls sat up and listened. Bella, better accustomed to the peculiarities of her chamber than Julia could be, turned her attention to the window. As she did so, the shutter gradually opened, and there appeared a man's head.

Julia saw the apparition, and was just about to scream, when Bella motioned her to keep silence.

"Hush! Don't't be alarmed,'' whispered Bella, "he won't eat us, only it's too bad to disturb one in this cruel fashion.''

"What does he want?'' asked Julia, half hiding her pretty head under the clothes, but keeping a bright eye all the time upon her intruder.

All this time the man was preparing to enter, and having sufficiently opened the shutter he squeezed his large figure through the opening, and alighting on the middle of the floor, disclosed the bulky form and ugly sensual features of Father Clement.

"Holy Mother! a Priest,'' exclaimed Bella's young visitor, "and a fat one, too. Oh! Bella, what does he want?''

"We shall soon see what he wants,'' whispered the other.

Meanwhile Clement had approached the bed.

"What? Is it possible? a double treat,'' he exclaimed; "delightful Bella, this is indeed, an unexpected pleasure.''

"For shame, Father Clement,''

Julia had disappeared under the bed-clothes.

In two minutes the Priest had stripped himself of his raiment, and without so much as waiting for an invitation, darted in the bed.

"Oh, my!" cried Julia, "he's touching me."

"Ah, yes, we shall both be touched, that is certain," murmured Bella, as she felt Clement's huge weapon pressing close up to her back. "What a shame for you to come in here without any permission."

"Shall I go then, pretty one?" said the Priest, putting his stiff tool into Bella's hand.

"You may stay, now you're here."

"Thank you," whispered Clement lifting one of Bella's legs, and inserting the big head of his cock from behind.

Bella felt the thrust and mechanically seized Julia round the loins.

Clement thrust once more, but Bella, with a sudden bound, jerked him out. Then she rose, turned back the clothes, and exposed both the hairy body of the Priest, and also the fairy form of her companion.

Julia turned instinctively, and there, right under her nose, was the stiff and standing penis of the good Father, looking ready to burst with the luxurious proximity in which its owner found himself.

"Touch it," whispered Bella.

Nothing daunted, Julia grisped it in her little white hand.

"How it throbs! It is getting bigger and bigger, I declare."

"Swing it down," murmured Clement; so—oh! lovely!"

Both girls now sprang out of bed, and eager for the fun, commenced stroking and skinning the Priest's huge penis, until he was almost with his eyes turned up, and a slight convulsive spending.

"This is heaven!" said Father Clement movement of his fingers, which betokened his pleasure.

"Stop now, darling, or else he'll spend," remarked Bella, assuming an air of experience, to which no doubt, her previous acquaintance with the monster she considered fairly entitled her.

But Father Clement himself was in no humour to waste his shot, while two such pretty targets were ready for his aim. During the fingering to which the girls subjected his cock, he had remained impassive, but now, gently drawing the young Julia towards him, he deliberately raised her chemise and exposed all her secret beauties to view. He allowed his eager hands to pat and mould her lovely butocks and thighs and opened with his thumbs her rosy chink; he thrust his lewd tongue within, and sucked exciting kisses from her very womb.

Julia could not remain insensible under such treatment, and when at last, trembling with desire, and rampant with lust, the daring Priest threw her back upon the bed, she opened her young thighs and let him see the crimson lining of her tight-fitting slit. Clement got between her legs, and throwing them up, he touched with the big top of his member the moistened lips. Bella now assisted, and taking the immense penis in her pretty hand, skinned it back and presented the tip fairly at the orifice.

Julia held her breath and bit her lip. Clement gave a hard thrust. Julia, brave as a lioness, held firm. In went the head, more thrusts, more pressures, and in less time than it takes to write it, Julia was gorged with the Priest's big member.

Once fairly in possession of her body, Clement commenced a regular series of deep thrusts, and Julia, with indescribable sensations, threw back her head and covered her face with one hand, while with the other she clasped Bella's wrist.

"Oh! it is enormous; but what pleasure he is giving me!"

"She's got it all; he is in up to his balls," exclaimed Bella.

"Ah! how delicious! She'll make me spend—I can't help it. Her little belly is like velvet. There, take that—".

Here followed a desperate thrust.

"Oh!" from Julia.

Presently, a fantasy seized the salacious giant to gratify another lecherous idea, and carefully drawing his smoking member out of little Julia's tight parts he pushed himself between Bella's legs, and lodged it in her delicious slit. Up her young cunt went the big throbbing thing, while the owner slobbered out the ecstacy his exercise was giving him.

Julia looked on with amazement at the apparent ease with which the Father thrust his huge prick up into the white body of her friend.

After a quarter of an hour spent in this amatory position, during which Bella twice hugged the Father to her breast and emitted her warm tribute upon the head of his enormous yard, Clement once more withdrew, and sought to case himself of the hot spunk which was consuming him in the delicate person of the little Julia.

Taking that young lady in his arms, he once more threw himself upon her body, and, without much difficulty, pressing his burning prick upon her soft cunt, he prepared to deluge her interior with his wanton discharge.

A furious shower of deep and short pushes ensued, at the end of which Clement, with a loud sob, pressed deeply into the delicate girl, and commenced to pour a perfect deluge of semen into her. Jet after jet escaped from him, as, with upturned eyes and trembling limbs, the ecstasy seized upon him.

Julia's feelings were roused to the full, and she joined her ravisher in the final paroxysm with a degree of fierce rapture no flea can decribe.

The orgies of that lascivious night are past my powers of description. No sooner had Clement recovered from his first libation, than in the grossest language he announced his intention of enjoying Bella, and immediately attacked her with his redoutable member.

For a full quarter of an hour he lay buried to the hairs in her belly, spinning out his enjoyment until Nature once more gave way, and Bella received his discharge in her womb.

Clement produced a cambric handkerchief, on which he wiped the streaming cunts of the two beauties. The two girls now took his member in their united grasp, and with tender and lascivious touches so excited the warm temperament of the Priest, that he stood again with a force and virility impossible to describe. His huge penis, made red and more swollen by his previous exercise, menaced the pair as they pawed it first in this direction and then in that. Several times Bella sucked the hot tip and tickled the open urethra with her pointed tongue.

This was evidently a favourite mode of enjoyment with Clement, and he quickly pushed as much of the big plum into the girl's mouth as he could insert.

Then he rolled them over and over, naked as they were born, glueing his fat lips to their reeking cunt in succession. He smacked and moulded their round buttocks, and even pushed his finger up their bottom-holes.

Then Clement and Bella between them persuaded Julia

to allow the Priest to insert the apex of his penis into her mouth, and after a considerable time spent in tickling and exciting the monstrous cock, he ejected such a torrent down the girl's throat and gullet that it nearly choked her.

A short interval ensued, and once more the unwonted enjoyment of two such tempting young and delicate girls roused Clement to his full vigour.

Placing them side by side he thrust his member alternately into each, and after a few fierce movements withdrew and entered the one unoccupied. Then he lay on his back, and drawing the girls upon him, sucked the cunt of one, while the other lowered herself upon his big prick, until their hairs met. Again and again he spouted into them his prolific essence.

The dawn alone put an end to the monstrous scene of debauchery.

But while such scenes as this were passing in the house, a very different one was rapidly approaching in the chamber of Mr. Verbouc, and when, three days afterwards, Ambrose returned from another absence, it was to find his friend and patron at the point of death.

A few hours sufficed to end the life and experiences of this eccentric gentleman.

After his decease, his window, never very intellectual, began to develop symptoms of insanity; in the paroxysm of which she perpetually called for the Priest, and when an aged and respectable Father had on one occasion been hastily summoned, the good lady indignantly denied that he could be an ecclesiastic, and demanded "the one with the big tool." Her language and behavior having scandalised all, she was incarcerated in an asylum, and there continued her ravings for the big prick.

Bella, thus left without protectors, readily lent ear to the solicitations of her Confessor, and consented to take the veil.

Julia, also an orphan, determined to share her friend's fate, and her mother's consent being readily given, both young ladies were received into the arms of Holy Mother Church upon the same day, and when the noviciate was past, both accordingly took the vows and the veil.

How those vows of chastity were kept, it is not for me, a humble flea, to dilate upon. I only know that after the ceremony was over, both girls were privately conveyed to the seminary, where some fourteen Priests awaited them.

Hardly allowing the new devotees the necessary time to divest themselves of their clothing, the wretches, furious at the prospect of so rich a treat, rushed upon them, and one by one satisfied their devilish lust.

Bella received upwards of twenty fervent discharges in every conceivable fashion; and Julia, hardly less vigorously assailed, at length fainted under the exhaustion caused by the rough treatment she experienced.

The chamber was well secured, no interruption was to be feared, and the sensual Brotherhood, assembled to do honour to the recently admitted sisters, revelled in their enjoyment to their heart's content.

Ambrose was there, for he had long seen the impossibility of attempting to keep Bella to himself, and, moreover, feared the animosity of his "confreres."

Clement was of the party, and his enormous member made havoc of the young charms he attacked.

The superior also had now the opportunity of indulging his antiphysical tastes; and not even the recently deflowered and delicate Julia escaped the ordeal of his assault. She had to submit, and with indescribable and hideous emotions of pleasure, he showered his viscid semen into her bowel.

The cries of those who discharged, the hard breathing of those labouring in the sensual act, the shaking and the groaning of the furniture, the half-uttered, half-suppressed conversation of the lookers on, all tended to magnify the libididinous monstrousity of the scene, and to deepen and render yet more revolting the details of this ecclesiastic pandemonium.

Oppressed with these ideas, and disgusted beyond measure at the orgie, I fled. I never stopped until I had put some miles between myself and the actors in the hateful drama, nor have I since cared to renew my familiarity with either Bella or Julia.

That they became the ordinary means of sensual gratification to the immates of the seminaty, I know. No doubt the constant and vigorous sensual excitement they endured, tended very soon to break up those beautiful young harms which had so worked upon me. Be that as it may; my task is done, my promise is performed, my memoir is ended, and if it is out of the power of a Flea to point a moral, at least it is not beyond his ability to choose his own pastures. Having had quite enough of those of which I have discoursed, I did as many are doing, who, although not Fleas, are, nevertheless as I reminded my readers in the commencement of my narrative, Bloodsuckers;—I emigrated.

THE END

PARISIAN NIGHTS

PART I

I

A lady, young, fresh, extremely pretty and stylishly though quietly dressed, tripped daintily along a street in the neighbourhood of the Madeleine, in Paris, then disappeared into a respectable house, ran quickly up the stairs to the first floor and nervously pressed the button of the electric bell.

The tinkle had hardly ceased when the door was open by a neat maid who ushered the visitor into a handsome drawing-room in which were assembled sundry other ladies, all young and fashionably dressed, but all wearing the preoccupied air of persons about to have an interview with, say, their doctor or their solicitor.

Presently, as if awaiting the newcomer, the

mistress of the house appeared — tall, slender, exquisitely attired in black silk with a dainty head-dress of the style adopted by many English ladies of a certain age, possibly because of the undoubted air of distinction it confers. She smiled pleasantly at her young visitor as she shook hands with her; then with a murmured apology, she turned towards two of the other ladies and said: "Your friends have arrived and are awaiting you" — whereupon they rose and retired, smiling their thanks.

Turning again to her young visitor, she said affectionately: — "My dear, some one is waiting also to see you, a gentleman, one of my best friends. If you are willing to let him make your acquaintance, I shall be happy to introduce him to you."

This "good friend" was none other than myself! The house belonged to Madame de Saint-Edme, the most obliging of women and also the most tactful of her sex in the delicate mission of creating and establishing the most intimate of relations between persons of opposite sexes who desired to avail themselves of such services. To pretty women pressed for money or inconvenienced by their sexual appetites and desires, to mistresses "en titre" seeking to increase or supplement their alimony, and to married women who found their allowances insufficient or their husbands' powers not equal to the marital duties desired from them, Mme de Saint-Edme's discreet chambers offered the safest and pleasantest of opportunities for the acceptance incognito of financial or other assistance from gentlemen. Similarly she was ready to provide for gentlemen of amorous proclivities satisfactory opportunities of satisfying their carnal desires by the favours of impecunious ladies — thus avoiding on the one side a lengthy pursuit and on the other resistance before surrender.

Further again, those who loved to indulge in Lesbian practices found at her house a convenient *rendez-vous* where they could revel in the enjoyment of their sweet fantasy with the wished-for object of their desire, or (in her absence) they could there without difficulty come across girls who understood and shared their tastes, and who desired nothing better than to bestow or receive the lingual caresses so dear to tribades, lending themselves adorably to either of the two functions.

To old and trusted *habituées* (the younger fry being absolutely debarred unless there was not the slightest doubt as to their fidelity and discretion) she allowed the privilege of assisting at Lesbian-Priapus fêtes and representations to which were also invited such ladies as wished to be present and whose discretion was assured —

the lively feminine contingent knowing they had nothing to fear on such occasions where modesty was conspicuous by its absence.

She for who I was waiting was, according to Mme de Saint-Edme, a debutante in libertinage who had so far honoured her house once only with her presence. Said Mme de Saint-Edme to me:

— "I wanted you to be first to enjoy her, but you were unfortunately in the country when she finally plucked up her courage to visit me, having disappointed me twice previously. I wished very much that one of my good friends had been then on the spot, but alas, there were none! — And from fear of letting her slip away again, I introduced a casual visitor to her and she let him enjoy her! It was a rare good piece of luck for him, but now, at all events, we have caught our little bird."

Despite her cynically immoral principles, this excellent woman had the considerate delicacy to let her lady clients have a peep in secret at their respective proposed male companions, to decide whether they were pleased with them. Some fancied dark men, others fair — some admired beards, others preferred the simple moustache. Hot blooded and passionate woman sought for muscular strength coupled with distinction; cold blooded ones were more solicitous about the price they would receive for their favours. To these latter, the preliminary peep was only a formality of secondary importance.

It is no use to run counter to tastes — to clash with caprices. The ladies that were satisfied by their preliminary peep were forthwith conducted to the destined chamber and the introduction effected, a similar privilege and opportunity of inspecting his proposed lady companion having been accorded to the male client.

But as a rule these preliminaries were purely formal — thanks to the care that Mme de Saint-Edme took to bring together suitable partners, — thanks also to the skill with which she described to each in turn the charms of the other. And when the happy man was conducted to the allotted chamber (carefully furnished with every requirement a loving pair could desire) and introduced to the lady (who invariably made a pretence of doing needlework or reading when he was ushered in) Mme de Saint-Edme would disappear, the sequel not concerning her.

But when it was a case of a debutante she took care never to be far away! — for it was at the critical moment that the courage of the former failed them. "No! no! — not now! — not today! —" they would not unfrequently exclaim — and run out of the room. Then Mme de Saint-Edme would intercept them in the corridor, — and by means of her soothing caresses and persuasive words, she would induce them to stay. Then she would take them to another room and induce them to undress, — then whisper soothingly and encouragingly "Now dear, you are all right — I will go and bring him myself to you!" — and the episode would terminate with a bout of love made all the more delicious by the ardour imparted to the lover by a resistance that could only indicate that the girl he was about to enjoy was a novice in such matters!

But it must not be supposed that all the debutantes gave this trouble. After their second — and very often on their first visit — the majority of girls would not make any serious resistance to even the most audacious and libertine actions of their male companions. Very often indeed, instead of resorting to airs of startled innocence in order to stimulate their partner's lust, they would endeavour to attain to the same end by arraying themselves in the most provocative and decolleté costumes! Among her other virtues, Mme de Saint-Edme was able to give of the best advice as to the toilette to be adopted towards this end. It was not for nothing that she had been for years in one of the leading Parisian modistes establishments. In this situation, she had amassed much by pecuniary gifts from the clientele, both for her suggestions and still more for her services as a "broker-in-love", and the friendly relations she thus inspired invariably remained unimpaired.

On this occasion the lady whose favours had been retained for me had simply removed her hat, and I held mine respectfully in my hand while being introduced to her in the following words — "My dear, let me introduce to you the gentleman and friend regarding whom I have spoken to you!"

She turned to greet me, when — good Heaven! — I recognised a young cousin of mine! In our preliminary peeps we had seen each other but imperfectly, — her face had been in a great measure hidden by her matinée hat while it was no doubt my beard that made her fail to recognise me, for many years had passed since we had seen each other.

"Why? — it is you, Gilberte!"

Mme de Saint-Edme at once saw that she had unwittingly created an awkward situation — that she had "put her foot" into it! She stood dumbfoundered! I begged her to leave us to ourselves.

The situation was piquant! This cousin was the "*petite cousin*" of authors, the "*petite cousine*" of youthful amorous indiscretions and yearnings which had not come to anything owing to her early marriage and the subsequent impossibility of rendez-vous, — and further, at such a time a woman does not lend herself to amorous adventures. I now found her grown into a beautiful woman, — and under surroundings that (to me, at least) afforded an opportunity of reviving our youthful mutual passion and of carrying it to a satisfactory denouement.

She dropped her eyes in confusion! I took her hands gently in mine, and while assuring her that she could absolutely rely on my discretion I added that if she would like to go away she was at perfect liberty to do so and that I would never breathe a single word as to this meeting. But as my noble and chivalrously virtuous declaration did not produce any response, the mere man in me began to assert itself — and imperiously too! — as I contemplated the tumultuous heaving of her breasts under her dainty corsage and the betrayal by them of her emotions!

"Speak, Gilberte!" No answer. "Would you like me to go away?" Still silence.

I was puzzled to know what to do! Would it be advisable straightway to respect her and give up any attempt to induce her to accord to me favours she had evidently come prepared to accord to a stranger? Or should I treat her as if she was of easy morality, and without circumlocution address to her proposals that I would have made to any other woman I met under similar circumstances, and which I was justified in assuming would not be unwelcome to her? But women are so odd, their ideas of morality so extraordinary!

— and some who would in occasions submit themselves without hesitation to the grossest lubricity would on other occasions resent the least attempt at a liberty! At all events ladies that came to Mme de Saint-Edme's chambers could hardly expect to be considered as strictly virtuous — and Gilberte must rank herself with them! But our cousinly relationship — which at an ordinary society function would have assisted me — here was a positive handicap to both of us: I represented to Gilbert her family, her respectability, her past life, her girlish days!

I must confess that the memories of these latter were such as afforded to both of us a pretext for reviving the past in the present. In our youthful amusements we had not troubled to respect our mutual modesty! Stolen kisses, caresses of tongue against tongue, indiscreet ramblings of inquisitive hands under clothes, — all had brought us to the very threshold of the supreme pleasure. One day, when hidden in a barn with her, my hand had found its way to her little girlish cunny which it strove to excite by an active finger — while her little hands were amusing themselves with my prick as it stood rampant and stiff in her honour! But nothing else had transpired, and we had not met again, until now.

I reminded her of this, — she smiled, and little by little let fall her constraint, whether real or simulated.

"Don't speak of it!" she said — "we were sillies!"

"We certainly were, because we did not take advantage of our opportunities! But now that we have so unexpectedly met! . . ."

"Tell me, — didn't you know who I was when you came in?"

"Honestly, I did not."

"Well, suppose that you had made me out, would you then have come in?"

"It is possible that I might have considered it better in your interests to disappear, — but I should have done so with great regret, for you were looking so lovely! And you? — if you had recognised me?"

"I should have run away!"

"But why? Do you think I cannot appreciate your charms as well as any one else?"

"Oh! . . . But you and another man are two very different things! — you are a relative — and I had not come here for the purpose of meeting my family."

"I don't suppose you did!" I replied laughing. "But it is so easy for us to forget that we are relatives. I have only to think of you as a charming young lady I have for the first time met, — and you have only to allow me to make to this charming young lady declarations and proposals to which I am sure she would like to listen much more than to remonstrances she might fear!"

"It seems to me so strange that I should be here at all with you! — I feel my presence here is so extraordinary — so upsetting!"

"Then, if we were to go on with our last meeting in the old barn, the sin (if any) would seem to you to be less grave and less piquant, — in fact almost allowable, as in marriage?"

"You're talking nonsense! . . . Of course not! . . . But to be seen by you here makes me feel as if everybody I know is also looking at me!"

"Then you don't care about doing this sort of thing before the world?"

Gilberte laughed frankly. I saw at once to what extent I should have adopted a false policy and how weak I should have been had I treated with an excess of respect a girl who, although my cousin, had of her own accord come to a house resorted to only by those who wished for a gratification of their sexual passions and desires! In fact, with any one else but her, I would before now have put myself in possession of charms which would have been surrendered to me kindly, — while had she been with any one else but me, she would not have concealed them from the eyes and no doubt the kisses of her happy companion!

"Well," I continued, "I don't know who you

19

are, — it is the first time I have seen you. Mme de Saint-Edme told me that she would introduce me to a charming girl who was visiting her for the first time, who proves to be even prettier than I could have anticipated, and who will, I trust, prove not less unkind than the others to whom Madame has introduced me and who have been good enough to amuse themselves with me here. May I ask what is your Christian name?"

"Gilberte," she replied laughing.

"Gilberte! What a pretty name! Well now, Gilberte, let me help you to take off your hat and cloak."

When I had hung these up, I passed my arm around her waist and kissed her on her mouth clasping her to me as I did so.

"You come here very seldom, I understand?" I said, — "I have not had the good fortune to meet you before."

"This is my first visit, Monsieur," she replied, entering into the spirit of the game.

"Really! But I think it cannot be the first time that you have left your husband in the lurch — for you look to me like a young married woman?"

"You are indiscreet, Monsieur!"

"Well — I won't press my curiosity any further! — at all events it is very sweet of you to allow others to share with him in enjoying your charms."

Seating myself on a sofa, I drew her gently on to my knees, — I repeated my kisses on her mouth while my hand wandered inquisitively over her corsage. She laughed, — then exclaimed "Oh! Monsieur!" in the most natural way.

Then my hand descended a little, and pressed against and between her thighs over her dress. Her hand tried to push mine away! I yielded, — but only to pull up her skirts, in order to touch the bare flesh of what I had been feeling over her clothes! Gently I groped her calves, knees and thighs.

"Oh! . . . what are you doing, Monsieur?"

"Only trying to learn if you wear your garters above or below your knees."

"Above, always!"

"You have such sweet calves!" My hand climbed a little higher, — her skin was so soft and sweet!

"Oh! . . . oh! . . . you're tickling me! . . . No! . . . no! . . ."

"Why! . . . your drawers are closed in front! . . ."

"Ha! . . . ha! . . . oh! take away your hand! . . . you're tickling me! . . ."

"Oh! . . . now I've got to it! . . . Oh! . . . what a lot of hair you have! Ever so much more than you had in the barn!"

"What barn?"

"Ah! . . . pardon me! . . . I was forgetting!"

In spite of the re-appearance of the cousin under the lover, she did not stop or even hinder my delicious rovings among and over her most secret charms! This proceeding no doubt pleased her better than any sentimental modesty on my part, — it also pleased me better! Arranging her comfortably on my knees, my hand set to work to explore the delightfully rounded contours of her bottom — which I found plump, firm and springy.

"Madame," I said — "what lovely globes you have — real Maps of the World! . . . Very few girls have anything like your bottom, — so hard and so elastic!"

"What a comical name, Map of the World! Why?"

"Because there are there the two half-globes of the world. Do let me see them. Let me take off your corset! Oh! what a troublesome corset! Ah! now it is off! Oh! what lovely breasts! so nice and firm, as firm as your bottom!"

"Hush! you mustn't talk like that!"

"You are simply charming — delicious. I am charmed to make your acquaintance! No woman has ever inflamed me with desires to such an extent."

I seized her hand and placed it on the unmistakable proof of the desires with which she had inspired me! She called me "*polisson*," which in the mouth of a woman is an encouragement to go still further, — and declared that I had not improved, I whom she had considered sentimental! I confessed to her that I was no longer so — that sentiment between men and women only tended to waste time and delay the pleasures of love.

"You then no longer are sentimental?" I asked.

"As you find me here you can see for yourself. Anyhow, all women sentimental or not, who talk about it, manage to finish in the same way, either sooner or later."

"You are making nice distinctions. You make me think you are a little student in love matters."

"Well, as to that, I fancy, I shall be still more so as soon as I escape out of your arms. You have a way of effecting this: I shall emerge from this truly accomplished."

This phrase spoken with a delicious smile, with that look that a woman knows how to use when she wishes to undress a man with her eyes and say to him, "Now come, let me see your," — this passage of words transported me with desire in indicating to me a horizon of endless pleasures with my lively cousin. I clasped her lovingly in my arms, exchanging, tongue-kisses with her, — then prayed her to undress herself.

I assisted her, seizing opportunity for deliciously touching her bare flesh, intoxicated by the sweet fragrance emanating from her undergarments which she had carefully selected — for every woman knows that the charms of her person are a treasure to be placed in a suitable frame to fairly show its beauty to the eyes privileged to view it.

Very soon she only had on her chemise! — in a jiffy I was in a similar costume: then after the necessary toilet we laid ourselves on the bed, closely clasped in each others arms, and abandoned ourselves to the sweet preliminaries to bliss.

"You will be discreet, eh?" said my cousin as she surrendered herself to me. To be so was of course as much to my interest as to hers.

Very soon she allowed herself to be invaded by symptoms of pleasure. Her lovely breasts began rapidly to heave, — her eyes half closed languorously. Was it real, or was she only pretending as part of her assumed role of a woman of pleasure? As she afterwards admitted that she had perfectly recognised me at the first and had allowed me to be introduced to her fully knowing the reason of my presence, it is quite possible that my handling and fingering of her naked body had the same rapid and sweet effect on her as when we indulged in our youthful escapades. As a matter of fact, it is the restless women who feel most sensitively the hand that caresses them. Gilberte, I recollect, used to go off at once, like a thorough-bred to the least pressure of the bit, — and now she had become a woman, she evidently had preserved this precious quality. Anyhow, on my part, I was soon burning with the hottest lust. The girl I held in my arms inspired me at one and the same time with a craving for orgies such as one would indulge in with ladies of professed easy virtue, and the rage for such forbidden fruit gained additional piquancy from the fact that she was my cousin.

At my request she took off her chemise and displayed herself to me, naked, her lovely body relieved by the thicket of silky hairs that formed a triangular shadowing at the extremity of her rounded stomach, her nakedness being emphasized by her shoes and stockings which she had kept on, by her garters which she adjusted above her knees when pulling her stockings tight. The little coquette knew well how a naked girl can heighten the effect of her nudity!

Then I felt and handled her all over, — I kissed and sucked her breasts. I thrust my nose under her arm-pits, diving amid the tufts of hair. There is nothing that imparts to one's desires so alluring a frenzy as the breathing of the "odor di femina" of the sweet body that has surrendered itself to you. My fingers nevertheless employed them-

25

selves in curling and twisting and playing with the mossy covering of her plump cunt, one of them caressing the delicious slit into which it soon forced its way, for the first time since our adventure in the barn. At that time, this cunny and slit were virgin! but my pleasure lost but little through this detail — for then her breasts were not so sweet a handful, her thighs were not so fat and round, her hips were not so full and plump, while the little hand that I had taught to play with my prick (oh! so timidly) was not so clever and soft. Her mouth then was not so skilled in the art of kissing, — while her chaste little ears would have closed themselves if I had whispered to them all that I was now softly murmuring to them while I gently agitated my finger over her clitoris.

"And what about this little pussy, this sweet little pussy? Does it love catching and eating mice? I will gladly give it mine!"

"It is a very big mouse, this one!"

"Girls like large pricks in their cunts! They are also charmed when a male tongue is applied. I want to apply mine to your cunt, — I want to do *minette* to you! You know what that is?"

She answered me simply with a smile. Promptly I placed my mouth on her closely clustering hairs (Gilberte was a lovely brunette) — I nibbled them with my lips, inhaling delightedly their fragrant perfume tempered with

26

rice-powder and Eau de Lubin. Even as a young girl, this was her favourite scent, but then she did not apply it to this part of herself, no doubt in ignorance of the arts of provoking and spicing the audacious kisses that make the coldest girls faint with pleasure. But cold she never was, — and when my mouth settled itself on her cunt, when my tongue insinuated itself gently between its lips in search of the little spot in which a woman's sexual pleasure is concentrated, unmistakable symptoms indicating the most exquisite delight gave me to understand that she knew well how to taste this caress. One of her legs was thrown across my back and held me firmly to her, and I could feel the little heel of her dainty shoe dig into my ribs like a spur: the other foot she extended right down my front and against my prick and I could feel the soft leather that was rubbing against it.

Oh! what ecstacies! I could hear the broken breathings of my voluptuous companion, — I could feel her body quivering under the thrusts of my tongue, and the cheeks of her bottom wriggle in .my hands as they gripped them. I felt her frenziedly press down my head between her thighs so as to let her taste every tongue-thrust. And I, twenty times was I on the point of flooding my cousin's shoe with the torrent of my discharge, — but I preferred to dispose of it otherwise. So at length, I released myself from her sweet clasp and placed myself again alongside of her on the sofa.

"Was it good? — did I do it properly?" I whispered to her.

"Very sweet indeed, you naughty man! It is very evident that you were not doing it for the first time!"

"And you? — is it the first time that you? . . ."

"You are horrid!"

"Ha! ha! Then you like having it done to you, eh!"

"All women do! But what do you think of one of my friends who declares she commits no infidelity towards her husband when she lets a man do her in this way?"

"I think I know her. Is she not a tall fair girl called Angela?"

"Yes. So you know her?"

"She comes here!"

"But how do you know that she is the one I mean?"

"Well! it is the same name, and she won't let a man do anything else to her but this."

"And have you then done it to her?"

"Yes! — I must admit it! — and it was well worth my while! But did she not also tell you that she confines her ministrations to her husband to this same one way?"

"Which way?"

I placed my finger softly on her mouth. Gilberte broke into laughter and asked if I had let Angela do me in the same way.

"Of course! — and what's more, I begged her to do it as she did not do any other way."

"Oh you men! — you dreadful men! Monsieur Henri!" (my Christian name). "I would not have believed you to be so . . . so . . ."

"So naughty? But in love many things that are naughty are also nice. But tell me — has no one ever asked you nicely to do it?"

"If I could say that no one had ever made such a request of me, I would not be able to say so for long — for I can read your intention in those eyes that are sparkling with lust!"

"Ah! — so I have missed also the virginity of your mouth! And so you have already committed this sweet sin! Was it in this house? Tell me all about it?"

"I don't remember!"

"Oh yes you do! — now do tell me, — whisper in my ear as if you were with your confessor!"

"You're a fine confessor."

"At all events not a cruel one! Listen:

Ma fille pour pénitence,
Et ron, ron, ron, petit patapon,
Ma fille, pour pénitence,

29

Nous recommencerons.

"Come, I'll give you a start! — you've done it once, twice, thrice, the first time out of curiosity, the second . . ."

"Oh! once will do! . . . I think I was mad that day! . . . A girl friend had invited me to supper with her and her lover, — and after dessert we all were a trifle squiffy! They told me all sorts of naughty stories, and they didn't mind what they did before me! In short, I watched them do all sorts of things till I was completely upset and excited beyond my self-control! . . . till unable to stand their teasing and challenges I let myself go in rivalry of my friend's libertinage and let her see me do with her lover all that she herself had just done with him!"

"And your friend was not jealous? And this is how you learnt this sweet little vice?"

"Alas! yes, — I must admit it!"

It is a well established fact that it is by their own sex and not by men that women are initiated into the most ingenious refinements of lust: and Casanova correctly recognised the fact when he maintained that a gallant who could manage to bring to one and the same rendezvous two girls hitherto enjoyed my him separately, would realise with the two together the most erotic of debauches. But as far as I was concerned, I was going to take

30

advantage of what I had so happily found out, — and so continued to play my part as Gilberte's Father Confessor.

"Very good, my daughter!" I said to her. "And since then, how often?"

"I haven't done it since, Father," she replied laughing.

"My daughter, you must be nearly a saint! But nevertheless you must do penance!"

> Et pour pénitence
> Nous recommencerons, ron, ron,
> Nous recommencerons.

She resisted a little, saying that she was not worked up as on that occasion, that she didn't wish to do it again, that she had promised herself not to repeat the performance ... But the example of her friend which I recalled to her soon overcame these feeble hesitations — coming as they did from her head and not from her inclination.

"Oh!" she exclaimed, as she bent down towards the object that stood rampant and stiff, burning to receive her caress. — "I don't think Angela would have waited till she was asked twice! — she loves doing it! Say!" she added with a malicious smile, "when we were in the old barn we didn't get as far as this, eh?"

31

Her soft hand guided my pego towards her lips and I felt it enter into her mouth, the moist warmth of which caused a delicious quiver of pleasure from my thighs to my loins. For a beginner she acquitted herself divinely: she took my prick well into her mouth, and with the recollection of her friend's methods in her mind, she set to work to give me the most intense pleasure in her power! Oh! my exquisite bliss! . . . my delirious sensations! Twenty times I was on the point of spending! . . . twenty times did I make her moderate her sweet suction so as to avoid spending, to postpone for the moment the ecstatic crisis! . . . twenty times did I ask myself in my rapturous transports whether I might let myself go! whether I might not expire deliciously in the mouth of the sweet girl whose fair head I could see as it rose and fell in cadence with the agitated movements of my body!

When a man is being thus blissfully ministered to by a woman who has a taste for this method — a taste that is more common than people believe, and which sometimes betrays its votaries when they are in the act of eating thick asparagus — and has reason to guess it, he can fairly let the sweet operation pursue its natural course and deposit his spermatic nectar on the pretty lips or in the dear mouth that has extracted it from him. But it is not less delicious to pour it, tripled in quantity by such a caress, into a cunt prepared by a similar caress and burning to receive it! And I shrewdly believe that while women may be willing on subsequent occasions to receive in their mouths the tribute of their lover's ardour, they are reluctant to do so on the first occasion on which they consent to effect this sweetest of ministrations!

Accordingly, placing my hand softly on her forehead, I reluctantly arrested the up and down movement of my cousin's head as she sucked my prick with a frenzy that seemed to indicate that she was fully sharing the pleasure she was giving me!

She looked at me in surprise, as if astonished at being stopped before the appearance of the unmistakable indication that her sweet duty had been accomplished! — the fact being that her friend (whose performance she had witnessed and was not following) never stopped her sucking until the "situation had been liquidated!" — as good Mme de Saint-Edme put it. And possibly on that memorable evening Gilberte also had . . .! Not having the skill of her Father Confessor, my interrogatories on this point had not been sufficiently direct and her confession remained complete!

So Gilberte, with a flushed and rosy face and moist lips, got up, and placing herself by me asked me if she had done it properly.

"Most charmingly, dearie, — quite as well as your friend!" I murmured as I kissed her on her mouth and passed my tongue over her lips all wet and humid! "Now darling, come! . . . on me, eh!"

Without a moment's delay she placed herself on top astride of me, — and quickly I shoved into her cunt my prick all moist with her kisses!

Suddenly, while lying on me thus transfixed and clasped in my arms, quivering with pleasure and jogging herself up and down in rhythm with my movements, she whispered, "But when you were . . . with my . . . friend . . . how . . . did you . . . do it . . . for she won't do . . . what we . . . are now doing . . .?"

"You must know! . . . a pretty woman . . . is . . . all cunt! . . ."

"You . . . dreadful man! . . . So . . . it was in her . . . mouth . . . always? . . ."

"Well! . . . Yes! . . . But you . . . are forcing . . . secrets . . . out of me."

"Then why . . . didn't you do so . . . with me? . . . I . . . was doing . . . the same thing . . . to . . . you? . . ."

"Are you . . . sorry . . . I didn't? . . ."

"No! . . . I only . . . wanted to know!"

"Well, because . . . I fancied . . . you didn't care . . . only . . . for this . . . like Angela!"

"That was very kind of you! . . . Well . . . one won't get . . . children . . . that way . . . that's something! . . ."

"So . . . next time . . . you wish me . . . to . . . spend . . . in your mouth . . . like . . . Angela does?"

She smiled, nodded her head slightly, — then closed her eyes voluptuously as if not to lose a single particle of the pleasure that was now thrilling through her whole person. For a moment I had an idea of resuming the sweet exercise we had just abandoned, — but the keenness of my present pleasure retained me at my delicious post beneath her! For the most exquisite of crises was approaching! Our tongues intertwined, our lips met, our movements accelerated! . . . oh! . . . now! . . . now! "Oh!"

Just at the critical moment, I took the precaution to swing Gilberte from the danger of presenting me with more cousins! I spent wildly outside her, my discharge shooting up into the air and falling like hot rain on her bottom and loins!

We had half-dressed ourselves again when we heard a knock at the door. It was Mme de Saint-Edme, who had come to see if we wanted anything. We asked her to bring us some refreshments. She seemed delighted and relieved to note from our deshabillé that not unpleasant sequel had followed her mistake in introducing us

35

to each other.

In due course my cousin, now fully dressed and gloved, gave me a parting kiss through her veil, — and before leaving me arranged with me a further rendez-vous, — at which I promised myself (with a thrill of concupiscence) the pleasure of treating her as I did her friend Angela. I then called a carriage for her, a concluding attention that a woman appreciates after an amorous escapade.

"Well," said Mme de Saint-Edme to me after Gilberte had gone, "so you are satisfied! I was terribly afraid of scandal when I saw you knew that lady! Is she a relation of yours?"

"No. I used to know her when she was a young girl!"

"Oh! Well, I was very afraid of a scene!"

"Thanks to me, dear lady, there wasn't one!"

"I do thank you, — but some how I felt sure that you would arrange the matter without any scandal: another thing that reassured me was the air of distinction the lady had, — a woman of that caste hates a row. I feel the same also: do what you like, — amuse yourself as you may wish with the ladies, — all this concerns nobody else, and does harm to no one!"

"Rather the contrary," I rejoined.

"But do it in the proper way, — maintain appearances!"

36

"Pleasure coupled with discretion — that's my rule!"

"Oh! I'm not referring to you, — it's a pleasure to do anything for you! But all the same, when you asked me to leave the room, you looked a little afraid!"

"But now, you are reassured?"

"Oh! now she has once passed through your hands, she will be all right."

On the day arranged between Gilberte and myself, I attented at Mme de Saint-Edme's house. She escorted me to the chamber she had got ready for us, where she left me alone. I was the first at the rendez-vous, — and I must have waited some little time when she came in to tell me that my fair cousin had just arrived but that just at that moment a lady "habituée" had stopped her in the corridor and was expressing surprise at meeting her here.

"Why, Gilberte!" she had exclaimed — "I never thought of meeting you here! — you always used to say you dared not come! Have you come then to meet somebody?"

As Gilberte, surprised unpleasantly, hesitated — not knowing what to say, Mme de Saint-Edme came up and told her that her visitor had already arrived, — whereupon the other lady had remarked that it was a pity, but nevertheless continued her conversation.

This lady (I had very little doubt) was the blonde friend of Gilberte, Angela de Valençay, an adopted name, as I learnt later on, without my having done anything to pierce the veil of anonymity with which she (like the rest) strove to hide her visits for the purposes of satisfying and gratifying her secret passions.

"At all events, she does not seem to be jealous!" I asked Mme de Saint-Edme.

"Not in the least. She would not mind lending her lovers to her friends. But she objects strongly to any one being jealous of her. That seems fair enough."

Gilberte had not yet appeared.

"If she lets herself begin chattering with her friend, you may have to wait a long time," said Mme de Saint-Edme. "But it is all right — here they come, both of them. Ladies, you are being anxiously waited for!"

"Oh! no one's waiting for me!' exclaimed Mme de Valençay, — "all have made their arrangements for their fuckings and fun, for I notice the refreshments all over the place."

She indicated a table on which stood afternoon tea already laid out, which I had ordered in anticipation of Gilberte's arrival. I invited her to join us.

"But shan't I be in the way?" she replied. "Two turtle-doves like best to be alone! Very well — if I shall not be in the way, I will join you with pleasure, — only you must tell me when I am to disappear. You will respect my modesty, I am sure!"

But as she spoke she looked at me in a way that sufficiently indicated that her wishes were the very opposite of her words: her ardent glances seemed intended to recall to me past pleasures shared together and to invite me to the further joys she was evidently ready to give me. Dressed simply in a black costume, and carrying herself in a quiet manner but with an air of distinction, there was nothing about her to betray the lascivious desires that had brought her here, or the lecherous fashion in which she was ready to conduct herself — unless it was that peculiar glance that allowed one to detect, beneath the woman dressed, the naked woman, and behind perfect Society manners the intimate familiarity with the most daring libertinage.

While she was apologising to Gilberte for the liberty she was allowing herself to take, I had called for another plate and had dismissed her cab: for she had said that she hesitated to rejoin a cab that had been waiting at the door so long, — a feeling and accession of shame that a woman on an amorous escapade will well understand and which is often experienced when the time comes for her to quit the sweet seclusion in which she has been surrendering herself to her lust.

Then when the ladies had removed their hats and mantles we sat down at the table. Thus I found myself between the two pretty women, one a blonde, the other almost a brunette — a charming contrast! Each of them had been enjoyed by me separately — but this fact did not in the least diminish the power of their charms over me — and their joint presence, the sweet proximity of these two appetising feminine bodies to me aroused in my flesh the wildest lust which I hoped in turn to communicate to them.

The idea that each of them had been previously enjoyed by me made them both somewhat constrained at first, especially Gilberte, who seemed almost jealous: but very soon, under the soothing influence of "five o'clock tea" skilfully prepared, snatched kisses and licentious handlings, this slight constraint disappeared like dew under a morning sun. My mouth hotly attacked theirs alternately, — my tongue greedily sought theirs in turn, finding them only too ready to respond. Finally, when I was busily occupied with Gilberte, sucking her tongue, while my hands actively wandered all over her, unbuttoning her dress and stealing up her legs under her clothes till it reached the silken-haired centre of attraction which my finger then sought to inflame, I felt Mme de Valençay's hand pass over my trousers and attempt to drag into the air my torch of love, now fully alight and getting stiffer and stiffer in her fingers! Then away went all reserve! I begged them to undress or at all events to throw open their clothes so as to let me see, feel, handle and kiss more at my ease the two pairs of lovely breasts of which now I could only get a glimpse.

"But I say," exclaimed Mme de Valençay laughingly, "if you're going to ask your guest to undress herself, your invitation in place of being a simple one to lunch will be one including a dance!"

"When a lady is invited to dinner," I replied, "she naturally expects to stay and see the fun that is sure to follow."

"Ah! a play for three, eh?" she rejoined gaily, "but not arranged by the ballet-master of the Opera! Well, there's no reason why it should prove any the less entertaining, is there Gilberte?"

Gilberte smiled, half-pleased, half-vexed, — not from any sense of offended propriety but from a sort of feeling that as a comparative novice in amorous orgies she might have to play second fiddle to her friend! But her semi-hesitation only added a piquancy to her final surrender of herself, and did not hinder a woman of my cousin's disposition from letting herself go freely to learn fresh experiences in lust.

Mme de Valençay was already busy (in accordance with my request) to release from their confinement the two prisoners whom I had begged her to set at liberty. To effect this she had taken off her light blue silk stays, — and my lady readers will fully comprehend how the removal of a corset causes the dropping of petticoats unless held up by the hand: Mme de Valençay did not bother to do this, and so when the exciting rustling noise made by feminine garments being hurriedly taken off and thrown on a chair had ceased, she had on only a half-transparent chemise when she returned smiling to my side! Gilberte, after a little pressing, followed suit, and soon was similarly attired. As for me, I rapidly divested myself of all my clothes, — and Mme de Valençay's hand — Gilberte's also — was able to learn without hindrance the state in which I had been driven by the sight of the charms they were now exposing naked to me!

Then we set to work to play the fool! to commit a thousand erotic follies! We took chocolates from each others mouths: with my lips, I set to work to nibble one balanced on the nipple of one of their breasts, tickling her delightfully in so doing. Then I made a minute and close inspection of my companions' breasts, of the hairs under their armpits, also of what grew on their hills, light and golden on Mme de Valençay's, auburn and plentiful on Gilberte's. They both lent themselves to these games with a grace and freedom that was simply charming. At each fresh indecency that she found herself committing, Gilberte blushed shamefacedly, her bashful modesty being increased by the presence of a witness. Having kissed with ardour all the charms that I had been comparing, dividing my admiration and tribute equally between my fair companions, I proceeded to cover with kisses the two mossy hills of Venus they were exhibiting to my delighted eyes. Kneeling in turn before each one and between her legs, my mouth played lovingly with their curling hairs, every now and then touching with my tongue the sweetly hidden slit, and eliciting from them little shrieks of pleasure. Suddenly, under a libertine inspiration, I took from the table two chocolate creams, and having slipped them into each of their cunts to their great surprise, I announced my intention of eating them there, and proceeded to do so taking Gilberte first.

"Oh! what an ideal," she exclaimed, quivering and palpitating with pleasure as my tongue discovered the fondant between the lips of her cunt and having dislodged and rolled it over her clitoris!

"Oh! make haste! make haste!" cried Mme de Valençay, "mine's beginning to melt!"

And truly, when I planted my mouth between her thighs on the lovely slit that she impatiently presented to me, my tongue had really to hunt for her chocolate, to dive and burrow deeply in the charming cleft, only to find a trace or two and the aroma of the flavouring. Oh! how delicious her flesh tasted, thus sugared!

With such erotic pranks and antics our desires increased and grew stronger. Mme de Valençay, now quite wild with lust, took a candied cherry in its paper covering, and having removed the envelope she made me sit down — then kneeling before me she pulled up my shirt, seized my priapus with one hand, and with the other balanced the cherry on the cherry coloured gland which was rivalling its complexion. With smiles of delight she contemplated the result, — then suddenly, with sparkling eyes and heaving breasts, she moved her mouth forward and engulfed the cherry — and with it the head of my member, thus bestowing on it that most delicious of caresses which makes the happy recipient long to employ his mouth in a similar fashion and which impels the loving pair to satisfy their mutual cravings in a sweet "*soixante-neuf*"! Burning with this desire, I clutched hold of Gilberte who was busy kissing me and sucking my tongue, and was just going to propose to gamahuche her when she exclaimed: "Come it's my turn now,

Angela!"

Forthwith Mme de Valençay rose reluctantly, her lips moist, her face flushed. Gilberte immediately slipped into her place, and had already put my pintle (still wet with her friend's kisses) into her mouth when the latter cried out. "Why! you've forgotten the cherry!"

Quickly Gilberte, blushingly repaired this omission, and then I felt my prick again put into her mouth and sucked with ardour! Mme de Valençay had come back to her old place at my side, and while she finished eating the cherry she had taken, she watched with curiosity, whose pretty head was now bent down between my thighs. I slipped my arm round Mme de Valençay's waist, — our lips and tongues met in kisses into which I strove to put the burning pleasure that I was tasting from Gilberte! But I wanted something more! I wanted with my mouth to pass on to her exquisite sensations that were thrilling through me!

"Do let me do '*minette*' to you!" I murmured.

"All right," she replied, "but not here, as we now are! Let's go to the bed!"

This forced Gilberte to interrupt her ardent suction, — and when she had risen from between my thighs, I lovingly kissed her lips still fragrant with the scent of the fruit she had just eaten. And so we moved towards the bed. As we reached it, I

45

begged the ladies to take off their chemises.

"No!" replied Mme de Valençay, "but this will be better still!"

Cognisant of Mme de Saint-Edme's fore-thought in matters erotic, she opened a drawer and took out two dressing-gowns made of the thinnest and most transparent material possible to image, one black and the other rose-tint.

"The black one will suit me as I am blonde," she said, — "don't look!"

She let her chemise slip down and replaced it by the dressing-gown, the transparency of which seemed to heighten the brilliant hue of her skin without in any way veiling the nakedness, but making it more piquant still! Moreover she did not fasten it in front, — but on the contrary she allowed it to float open on each side of her — thus displaying her lovely body naked from her stockings to the velvet ribbon round her throat! In this adorable costume, she placed herself in front of me and saluted me in military fashion.

"All in order, Monsieur!" she said — "see! I'm naked — yet I'm — not!"

My cousin slipped on the rose-tinted dressing-gown.

"I'm absolutely naked in this!" she exclaimed laughing!

"That is exactly as you ought to be!" I replied smiling.

Being then stretched out on the bed between my two pretty guardians whom I kissed and felt all over while their little hands contended for the control over my member, I was trying to decide which one of them I would choose in which to extinguish the fires of my concupiscence — when Angela who then was holding my prick tightly with her fingers, said:

"Who is to have this first?"

"Better draw for it!" I replied, "guess how many?" — and I took in my hand a lot of hairpins. Gilberte's guess was the nearest.

"Don't forget me, Gilberte!" said her friend, — "leave a little for me!"

But as I began to place myself between Gilberte's legs so as to put my prick into her cunt and fuck her, she appeared surprised, — then declared that she understood that she was to do what she had been doing to me on the sofa, viz, suck my prick!

"For you know," she explained, "Angela won't do anything else!"

"Oh! don't give me away like this, silly!" exclaimed her friend.

"Do you know that you are a charming and ravishing naughty little girl, just as she is?" I said, kissing her lovingly. "Well, do you also prefer . . .?"

Her response was to gently slip out from under

me and to lay me on my back in her place, — and as soon as she had got me properly extended on the bed, she, without loss of time, lowered her face towards the God Priapus. I felt her lips kiss the burning head, then her mouth envelop it, engulfing it deeply! Then I took up the thread of my caresses with Mme de Valençay; I drew her to me, kissed her lips, and let her tongue play on mine.

"Let me do *minette* to you," I murmured.

"Yes, dear."

Smiling lovingly at me, Mme de Valençay placed herself in position by straddling across my upturned face, arranging herself so that her cunt rested on my mouth, her face being turned towards Gilberte who had not stopped her sweet employment and who she watched at work intently. My tongue attacked her cunt eagerly, plunging deeply into it. I sucked her excited clitoris! — I licked passionately her warm and throbbing slit from end to end! Many times before this, had I enjoyed this privilege and pleasure, but always without the accompaniment of the spicy sucking that was doubling my transports and was impelling me to pass on to her the delirious fury that was agitating me!

Oh! the indescribable ecstasy! — to be sucked by one lovely woman while sucking another! Oh! the delightful postures of this doubled "*soixante-*

neuf" which permitted my lascivious fair friends to taste the most piquant voluptuousness equally with myself! But soon I felt that the torrent of my sperm would overcome my efforts to restrain it so as to prolong my present bliss!

"Gilberte! Gilberte!" I gasped brokenly, ceasing for the moment my sweet intentions to Mme de Valençay's cunt — "Gilberte! . . . I'm going to . . . spend . . . in your mouth . . .!"

I saw her head quickly nod a sanction which after all was perhaps superfluous after our recent meeting. My mouth returned to Mme de Valençay's cunt, my tongue resumed its voluptuous occupation with an ardour now unfettered by my efforts to retard my pleasure! Then came the ecstatic crisis! In my paroxysms of rapturous pleasure, my hands closed on my cousin's head, stopping the movements of her mouth! — I thrust my prick wildly down her throat! — my tongue madly darted deeply into Mme de Valençay's cunt! — . . . Oh! . . . Oh! . . . I spent! . . . I spent!! . . .

My boiling discharge shot in jets into Gilberte's mouth, making her retire in the middle of the eruption! Mme de Valençay, half fainting with pleasure, dropped limply on me! . . . We lay motionless till our energies revived. Then Gilberte wiped her mouth with her dressing-gown.

"I believe I've swallowed some of it!" she exclaimed laughing.

Mme de Valençay's head happened to be close to Gilberte at the moment when the latter drew back with filled mouth in the middle of my discharge, and she got the rest of it on her face, — which made her laughingly tell Gilberte that the latter had kept her promise to leave a little for her. Then she slipped off the bed and hurried off to the dressing-room, picking up her dressing-gown and holding above her waist as a woman does when she fears that her chemise may get compromising traces! Of course in this case there was no such fear, — but the result was to exhibit the most charming contours! Gilberte in turn went off also to wash off the traces of her recent occupation, for which purpose she did not require to use the bidet! I also imitated them, for my mouth, my lips, my moustache, all bore evidence of Mme de Valençay's warm feminine essence!

While I was thus occupied, Gilberte returned and lay down carelessly on the sofa. Mme de Valençay went to her, and placing her hand laughingly on her pretty calves began to amuse herself by running her fingers softly up and down Gilberte's legs. But when she got above the knee, Gilberte stopped her.

"Chut! . . . Not here! . . . Not before everybody!"

"It isn't before *everybody*!"

"Please don't trouble about me!" I said.

This little gust of passionate affection concluded for the time with a kiss from Angela to her friend, which clearly meant a great deal. There was no doubt about it! — my delicious companions were worshippers at the shrine of the Lesbian Venus! This revelation did not surprise me as far as Mme de Valençay was concerned, — to so voluptuous a woman nothing that was connected with sexual pleasures would be unknown to her, — but I never imagined that my naughty little cousin also had this fantasy! I was far from being displeased at this discovery, and I had the curiosity to ask since when had they mutually enjoyed each other. Then to my surprise, I learnt that it was Gilberte who had in the first instance seduced Angela! As girls they were great friends, — and one day, or rather night, an overflow of guests at a country house at which they were staying compelled their hostess to ask them to share the same bed. And oddly enough, it then came out that I must also have been a guest on that very occasion! Among my dancing partners was a certain Mlle B..., the fiancée of a happy mortal introduced to me as Monsieur R..., a Colonel in civil employ in the War Office. This girl had become Madame R..., and her husband

51

having obtained rapid promotion (as well may be imagined) was now one of the pillars of the Administration! As for her, after that valse with me, she had under an assumed name executed dances of quite a different nature, — and I had often had the pleasure of being her partner without either of us recognising the other!

"So after all, there is no reason why you should be so particular today, Gilberte!" I said, as I played gently with her bottom and her pretty white breasts. She only laughed and hid her face in her hands. We asked what was the cause of her merriment.

"Now, I come to think of it," she replied, "it must have been the very night on which you danced with Angela that she and I did! . . ."

"Of course in honour of myself and of all the partners that had pleased you!"

"But my dear," exclaimed Mme de Valençay, who continued to use this name, "you really are very indiscreet to tell Monsieur who I am! Fortunately he is your cousin instead of simply one of your lovers, and so the knowledge will not go any further. However, Monsieur, you must allow me to continue to be an entire stranger to you, should we ever happen to meet anywhere outside. Here I shall be delighted to continue on our old footing, and to place at your disposal myself and any talent I may have."

I promised, I swore to obey faithfully all her wishes, — and this little interlude did not divert the ardour that began to assert itself in our senses.

The thought that my cousin's friend, this lady whose naked charms I was enjoying, was really Mlle B . . . and now Mme R . . . the wife of a man high in office, — and that she came to this asylum of elegant immorality and discreet prostitution as a *habituée*, to yield herself to the most unrestrained demands of her lust, to the most erotic fantasies, — this thought did not tend to allay my concupiscence! Every sensation is heightened by contrast. A fair valley is doubly delicious after a painful toiling along burning rocks. The possession of a woman outwardly of rigid virtue seems to some preferable to having a beautiful courtesan! It is simply the idea of contrast that makes certain lovers dress their mistresses as nuns before rogering them! So with this woman, already so desirable while I thought she was simply a fast member of good Society (an opinion quite justified by her bold ways, her science in provocative arts, her freedom from prejudice as to the ways of enjoyment) what additional piquancy her favours acquired now that I knew that the lovely body she delighted to surrender to my licentious caresses was that of a well-bred and beautiful member of Society, respected in her circle, but who knew how to become debauched, naughty, almost as if she wished to make up for the time she was compelled, under the dictates of polite society, to behave as a "virtuous and godly matron!"

It was an agreeable sequel to my surprise when Gilberte, instead of manifesting by tears, refusals, etc. her dislike to seeing her position as a woman of respectability compromised in the eyes of some one that knew who she was, did not hesitate to be persuaded by the calls of her flesh and blood, — and resolving to see in me only a lover, lavished on me the pleasures of her person with an ardour and abandonment I could not have dreamt of!

So I renewed to both my fair friends my vows of discretion etc., adding that I swore on what I considered to be my most precious possession, viz, my prick, — which now was asserting itself boldly under the caresses of their delicate hands.

"Egoist!" they exclaimed, — "so what we have is not so precious according to your ideas!"

"What you girls have is to me the dearest of possessions and what I have to enable me to enjoy yours is to me the most precious."

"That is sweet of you! But I'm afraid that we are wasting good time!"

"And in a costume that in itself makes one wish to employ the time more sweetly!" added

Gilberte.

"Just listen to her!" exclaimed Mme de Valençay.

"Who loves me will follow me!" cried Gilberte, throwing herself on the bed.

And very shortly there raged between the three of us a storm of kisses, interspersed with exciting touchings and gropings and all the delicious preludes to a fresh bout of love! My hands wandered over two pairs of bubbies, two pairs of thighs: my mouth and my tongue played on theirs, deserting them at times in favour of two other mouths lower down and sweetly hairy — desertions which their charming owners did not seem to mind if I might judge by the sweet murmurs that came from the former as I licked and tickled the latter! Oh! if I only had two tongues so that I could gamahuche them both at the same time!

When at length I ceased and rose, I saw they both were on fire from the ardent way in which they kissed each other! Thereupon, I passed my arms round them, and drawing them close to me so that their lips and mine were touching I murmured "Oh! you two darlings! what a delicious and adorable pair of *gougnottes* you would make!"

A gentle cuff on my head told me that the word was not strange to my fair friends — but the smiles that their faces wore showed me that they were not displeased by my audacity.

"Won't you then do it before me?" I whispered — "do let me see you!"

"Oh! what a mad idea! . . . Well, what do you say, Gilberte?"

"Oh! I daren't! — I really couldn't! . . . see, we aren't by ourselves!"

"He won't look at you! . . . Come! . . . I want it! . . . I'll do it to you!"

Mme de Valençay slipped across me and gave my cousing several long clinging kisses, — then quickly placed her head between Gilberte's thighs, and soon the latter began to quiver under the action of the former's tongue! Leaning over my pretty cousin as she lay deliciously happy, I kissed her rosy lips, introducing my tongue between them as I revelled at the sight of these two naked lovely women surrendering themselves to their lesbian passions before me! Suddenly, Mme de Valençay stopped, raised herself, then flushing with delight, turned herself round and straddling across Gilberte, she placed herself on Gilberte, reversing herself. Her lovely backside sank down and hid her friend's face, — then settling herself down with a movement or two she placed over Gilberte's mouth the cunt that sought the lingual caresses which she recommenced on Gilberte's cunt! As for me, I delightedly contemplated the curtain of flesh which masked my cousin's face, the two plump and white buttocks which already had begun to agitate themselves in sweet tremors under the caress that had commenced. My hand passed lovingly over the rounded contours, — my lips deposited a hundred kisses on them, — and my tongue passing along the valley that separated them, travelled downwards till it nearly met Gilberte's, now in full operation on Mme de Valençay's cunt. But by this time it was not only a gentle tremor that agitated those charming globes of flesh, — it was a veritable storm of quivering heavings that indicated the approaching burst of her voluptuous discharge. I also, horribly excited, felt myself ready to spend, — but with a desperate effort I restrained, and eagerly watched my sweet pair of lesbians in the spasms of their spending! waiting impatiently for the finish of their ecstasy to beg one or the other of them to put out the fire that was blazing within me.

But no! They continued in their charming posture! . . . were they going to begin again? . . . oh! the naughty darlings! . . . they started afresh! I bent down towards Mme de Valençay, whose lips were playing on the lowest portion of the dark silky fleece on Gilberte's cunt. On seeing me she discontinued for a moment her charming employment.

"Are you going to do it again?" I asked eagerly.

"Well . . . yes! it's all your fault, you know! you've so excited us!"

"You naughty girls! O you're a pair of naughty, naughty girls!" I exclaimed — then kissed her luscious lips all moist and impregnated with Gilberte's spendings!

Before allowing her to resume her duties, I amused myself by playing with the hairs on my cousin's cunt. She began to do the same with one of her delicate hands!

"What lovely fur Gilberte has!" she murmured — "and pretty thighs!" she added as she passed her hands lovingly up and down over the satiny skin from the top of Gilberte's cream-coloured stockings right up to the sweet junction with her abdomen. I in turn did the same.

"Now, I begin to understand," I remarked "why one loves to get one's head between a girl's thighs even though one should be a girl!"

"Rather say because one is a girl!" she replied laughing, "for it is all that a girl can do unfortunately!"

"Now tell me," I continued seriously, "which gives a girl the intensest pleasure — to be sucked by a man or by a girl?"

My pretty companion laughed amusedly,

tickled at the idea of such a conversation being carried on in the silent presence of Gilberte's cunt. But at all event, she recognised that here was a chance to test the pleasing experiment.

"Gilberte!" she called out — "we are both going to do it to you, — tell us who does it best! you go on!" she whispered, pointing to Gilberte's cunt lying temptingly ready.

Her increasing agitation as betrayed by her voice clearly indicated that the fair judge was getting impatient and had recommenced her sweet ministrations to her friend's cunt! Quickly, I thrust my tongue into the charming slit so impatiently awaiting it, my salute being received with violent and rapturous transports! After a few moments, I made way for Mme de Valençay, who before long stopped for Gilberte's verdict. But the latter remained silent! — her tongue was too much occupied with Angela's cunt! and the fair owner, no longer able to restrain herself, stopped talking philosophy with me to give herself up to the imperative call of fast increasing pleasure. Thus the interesting experiment remained unsolved, ample opportunity being now available for some fair seeker after truth to test the efficiency of the male and the female tongue on her cunt! But I felt I could no longer remain an idle spectator of so voluptuous a combat! . . . I must cut in somehow!

"Would you like all you can get now?" I whispered in Mme de Valençay's ear.

"Yes! . . . yes! . . ." she answered, her tongue hard at work!

"You would? O you naughty thing! . . . You would like . . . *feuille de rose*?"

"Yes! . . . yes! . . . yes! . . .? she murmured with difficulty!

Promptly my tongue commenced to wander up and down between the firm yet elastic twin globes of her bottom, traversing the depths of the mysterious valley that separated her buttocks, thrusting, tickling, and working her into erotic fury. The naked bodies of the two girls plunged and twisted to the accompaniment of broken murmurs and inarticulate ejaculations! And I? Their lascivious transports sent me into a state of lustful excitement impossible to describe! — it was veritable torture! I could stand it no longer! — I must have something, some hole — a mouth, a cunt! I rushed behind Mme de Valençay as she lay astride across Gilberte's face, — I caught a glimpse of the cunt the latter was licking and sucking, — I slipped my rampant and furious prick between her nose, her lips and the grotto of love, — I drove her tongue away, — and rammed myself in! O the exquisite pleasure! — O the cunt, so soft, so deliciously warm and moist, so exquisitely lubricated by my cousin's minis-

trations! But I was soon forced to beat a retreat!
— it was contrary to the principles of my voluptuous partner to allow her cunt to be invaded in
this way, and in spite of my endeavours to the
contrary and the grip of her posteriors I had
effected in my desperation, she managed to dis-
lodge me!

"O, you are very disobedient!" she exclaimed,
shaking her finger at me, "we must bring you to
order! O look at it! how angry it is, poor thing!"
— it was my raging prick that she was addressing
— "come! we'll soon calm you, Sir! Lie down!"
she added to me.

I released Gilberte, whose head had been imprisoned between my legs.

"You were in a funny position!' Mme de
Valençay said to her.

"You at all events cannot say that he didn't
have you, dear! At all events I could see! He went
into you up to your hair! O yes, you were
properly had that time, my love!

"As a matter of fact, you ought to have kept
him out!"

But by now, I was on my back. Mme de
Valençay, after some tender kisses, directed her
mouth to where a different function was eagerly
awaiting her. "After the cunt of the girl-cousin,
naturally comes the turn of the male-cousin's
prick!" she said, laughingly. I suggested to

Gilberte that she should let me suck her, and although she had already spent plentifully with her friend, she was none the less ready to commence anew! "Gladly! gladly!" she exclaimed, as she slipped across my face and adjusted her cunt so as to rest on my mouth!

I plunged my tongue wildly into it, though I was almost swooning with ecstatic rapture as Mme de Valençay devoted herself to my prick — kissing, sucking and tickling the gland with the tip of her warm tongue and her burning mouth, then allaying the poignant sensations thus excited by ardent and passionate suction. Then she would remain passive, retaining her prick in my mouth and letting me work it up and down deliciously between her lips! and when I stopped, she would resume the entrancing motion! It was a taste of Paradise that I would gladly have prolonged indefinitely! But this was impossible! I simply couldn't contain myself any more! My tongue redoubled its activity on Gilberte's clitoris! — my hands clenched Mme de Valençay's head! — between her delicious lips my prick worked itself faster . . . faster! . . . with a frenzied upward heave, I shoved it into her throat! — I surrendered myself wildly to my pleasure! . . . then spent . . . spent . . . spent . . . nearly swooning as I shot my three burning discharges into her mouth!

Without the least flinching, Mme de Valençay received and retained in her mouth this unceremonious homage to her charms, and also held as a prisoner the object that had caused the deluge, — while Gilberte (who had spent equally deliciously on me) fell breathless and panting on me with a gasp of pleasure, — and thus we rested for some instants in rapturous oblivion.

*   *   *   *

"What's the time?" asked Mme de Valençay, who had slipped on her chemise again and was engaged before the mirror with a powder puff. "Six o'clock".

"Heavens! And I have to dine out to-night! I shall hardly have time to get back and dress! My husband will be cross!"

"The same with me!" exclaimed Gilberte. "My husband will scold me!"

Quickly and hurriedly, the two ladies picked out their belongings from the mass of garments lying all over the room, — and soon put on their drawers (the most useless things where love is concerned) corsets, skirts, etc., and very soon were fully attired and ready to appear in public. I called carriages.

Just then Mme de Saint-Edme asked for a word

with Gilberte and whispered something to her.

"Not this afternoon! — I've no time" she replied.

"Only tell me if you would be willing and when."

"I would like it, — but I'll write."

Mme de Valençay caught her arm and asked what it was all about. Gilberte whispered something. I in turn asked for information, but the two ladies went off in fits of laughter.

Later on, I learnt that what had been asked of her and what she had accepted was to be introduced to a young and pretty actress who was well-known as a high-priestess of Lesbians, and who had desired to make my cousin's acquaintance and to cultivate her in the charming intimacy necessary to the cult. I venture to say that she will not be disappointed.

II

"Well? And your loves? Have you brought your last conquest to a successful termination?"

The person who was thus questioning me was Madame de Liancourt, who I was about to accompany in her carriage at the close of a Charity Ball given at the Hotel C.

"What new conquest?" I asked.

"You know! The lady with whom you were seen in the Bois the other day! It was most imprudent on your part to thus compromise her! Now, was she not the wife of Maitre B., the lawyer?"

"What? Did you really see us? Do you know her? I assure you . . ."

"My dear man, you are defending yourself

very badly! But otherwise, my compliments to you! She really is very nice! And has she been . . . kind? She has the air of being a trifle too un-sophisticated for you, but she is in excellent hands and will soon learn . . . eh? Tell me, have you already educated her to humour your . . . caprices?"

"Dear Madame! I assure you . . ."

"Come, come, — you needn't tell me this, me, your old pupil! You know I won't be jealous!"

"A pupil who has graduated with honour to her teacher and now possibly exceeds him!"

"Be polite, if you please! You men are really too awful! You teach a poor innocent girl all sorts of naughty things, and then you reproach her if she should put your lessons into practice!

"I reproach you? — on the contrary! I prefer you as you now are, so knowing, — so charmingly naughty!"

"Then tell me."

"Here comes your carriage! Haven't you changed your coachman?"

"Yes and no! Baptiste drives when I go out in domestic state in the company of my lord and master, my husband. But when I go by myself, I drop the family coachman and the family state and take a hired carriage. It is better in case of any . . . adventures, — for then I have nobody's indiscretions to fear! Baptiste for instance, knows

66

you."

"Without knowing my successors!"

"You rude man! Come, open the carriage door for me!"

"May I not have the honour of accompanying you?"

"Oh, yes! I know what you mean! You don't deserve to be allowed! But you must behave properly! Tell the man to drive to Rue de Suresnes."

Since the termination of my liaison with Madame de Liancourt, a liaison which terminated without any rupture or unpleasantness, she (so she told me) had been leading a life without restraint and unfettered by any ties. She amused herself by studies in the physiology of Love, selecting her subjects for comparison how and where she pleased. Further, we had agreed to confide to each other the result of our various amatory adventures, and we did not interdict ourselves from renewing our former intimate relations if we so desired — if our electric currents should attract us to each other and if their tension should become such as to make the contact of our naked bodies bring about a "discharge" (truly, a scientific word, but one most appropriate for the occasion)!

This evening, we were in such a condition. Speaking for myself, the act of dancing, the sight of bare shoulders and breasts emerging from their lace surroundings as if to challenge men to consider whether what was hidden was likely to correspond with what was being shewn, all this had greatly excited me; and it did not make me any the calmer to be seated beside a lovely woman of about thirty, luscious and voluptuous to the degree at which a touch of maturity adds such spice to the charm of youth!

As for tell-tale eyes (which seemed to say "Do you remember?" and "Shall we re-commence?"), the gentle friction of her knees against mine as the carriage swayed, and a thousand other signs, showed me clearly that she was quite willing to satisfy with me the warm desire, the longing for a man which a hot-blooded woman feels after inhaling the masculine odour emanating from her dancing partners and after having abandoned herself to their more or less lascivious embrace. We could not but concentrate our ardent desires one for the other, — she, with all the burning longings of an erotically excited woman; I, with all the lustful ideas which riot through the brain of a man as he looks at pretty women and mentally undressing them imagines their appearance without clothes!

It was not therefore very surprising that before we had got half way to our destination, I threw my arm round Mme de Liancourt's waist, brought my face against hers, and set to work to kiss her on her mouth and with my tongue to seek hers. My disengaged hand slipped up under the frilly flounces of her ball-dress, crept along over her silk clad legs and over her garters, and little by little reached her drawers and found the opening — through which it passed and commenced to touch and play with the close clustering and mossy forest of silky curly hairs.

"Wretch!" gasped my companion, as she abandoned herself to the voluptuous sensations that my finger was communicating to her as it sought to bury itself in the warm moist slit! In kindly reciprocation, her white-gloved hand travelled over my trousers, till it found the unmistakable proof of my excited condition! Quickly sundry buttons yielded, — and then I felt against my sensitive skin the touch of dainty gloved fingers which promptly began their delicious manoeuvres, returning service for service, pleasure for pleasure!

Not a word passed! — only the sound of sighs, breathings, gaspings, as fingers and tongues busied themselves in their salacious duties! Oh, why is man not physically able (as a woman is) to sacrifice to Venus over and over again with hardly a pause, as women can? — Why must there as a rule be a break between one sacrifice and the next? With what delight would I have surrendered myself to the exquisitely maddening sensations communicated to my rampant prick by those gloved fingers and their subtle compression, even at the risk of ruining those white kid-gloves! But as I looked and hoped for a more completely satisfactory gratification of my lust before long, I managed to retain my burning ardour and keep it in reserve! More fortunate than me, Mme de Liancourt, whose soft smooth thighs kept squeezing my hand, let herself go! — gasping, panting, quivering, she clung to me, spasmodically agitating her heaving hips and bottom — then inundated my hand with the creamy dew of her ecstatic discharge!

Just then the carriage stopped. Hastily we adjusted our dress, and after sending the carriage away, we entered the house in which Mme de Liancourt's suite was located. A dim light had been left burning for her. As she passed the concierge's den she gave her name as Mme Germain, telling me after we had passed inside that this was the name by which she was known here.

The suite was on the first floor. Mme de Liancourt unlocked the door herself and ushered me into a handsomely furnished vestibule in which a rose-shaded lamp shed a soft light quite sufficient to illuminate the place. She remarked that she had done the furnishing, and that besides this there were a few more rooms.

"Here's the Temple!" she exclaimed, leading me into the bedroom, the best room of the suite. In it was a bed, large and low with thick curtains, a veritable theatre of Love! In one corner was one of those long and low easy chairs which accommodate so delightfully the form of a woman, especially when she is surrendering herself to furtive fondling and groping under her clothes! Numerous cushions were scattered all over the place; in another corner was a dainty stove; against one wall stood a full length mirror. A smaller room opening into the bedroom had been furnished as a dressing and bathroom; here one saw displayed and ready for use the whole of a woman's mysterious toilet equipage, low divans, bidet, douche, basins, jars of essences, bottles of scent; a third room also communicating with the bedroom served as a boudoir, but for the moment fulfilled the office of a supper room, as the table had been laid with a cold supper for two persons. Thick close carpets covered the whole of the floors, and each room was fitted after the convenient English fashion with gas heating and lighting apparatus, thus enabling the occupant to practically dispense with servants.

"Does your maid Justine attend on you here?"

"No, only the concierge's wife and her sister."

"But what do they think when they see you here?"

71

Madame de Liancourt smiled with a significant glance from her eyes and a gesture that plainly said that the presence of a gentleman would not occasion any surprise!

"Then they must have queer ideas about you?"

"My dear man, I have made the position quite simple and easy by not attempting to hide anything, but to pass as a *cocotte*. You see this cuts short all suppositions!"

Undoubtedly she had freed herself from traditions since I last had the honour of being entertained in her arms; and her candid admissions constituted in her quite a new attraction for me!

"Then this evening you are going to be my little cocotte!" I replied as I amorously kissed her mouth. She nodded, with a smile.

Then I proceeded to utilize with her to its best advantage her luxuriously equipped installation. I began by taking off her shoes, — and under the pretence that her high laced uppers rendered it necessary, I lifted the frilly flounces of her ball-dress and petticoats till the bewitching sight of a pretty woman's dainty underclothing was displayed to me, — the neatly shod tiny feet, the delicately rounded silk covered calves, the tempting garters above her knees, the strip of naked flesh just above them, her semi-transparent drawers with their frills, — all framed by the surrounding waves of her petticoats!

"What are you about? . . . come, do take off my shoes!"

But in spite of protests, I managed to deposit sundry hot kisses on the tempting bare flesh just above the garters; then in reluctant obedience I took off her shoes and helped her out of her ball-dress, — but not without permitting myself sundry libertine and wanton touches! How delicious it is to feel a girl's naked flesh under its gauzy covering, to pass one's hands over her back and loins, her lips and haunches, her bottom, when protected only by a thin chemise! — then turning one's attention to her front, to draw the light folds tightly round her so as to reveal her shapely round belly and thighs, to press the light material well in between her legs! O what delicious preliminaries! — and what riotous desires they kindle! And how girls always pretend to try and prevent the taking of such liberties, pleading shame as an incentive to induce the tickling which invariably results and which draws from them the inflaming little screams and wriggles they know so well how to give! My pretty companion did not disappoint me in this respect!

"Wait, wait!" she ejaculated as she freed herself from my audacious hands and ran towards the dressing-room, pausing at the door to say softly but significantly "I have danced a lot to-night, and . . . I have not forgotten your . . . caprices!"

Could one be paid a more delicate attention or be given a more discreet invitation? Promptly I undressed myself, — then when Mme de Liancourt had quitted the dressing-room, I passed in, and presently I joined her on the bed on which she had laid herself.

"Let us stay as we are on the top and not under the sheets!" she suggested, — "it is warm."

"By all means, — and we can also see each other better!"

"You are just the same, — or rather worse than ever! You have already seen me all over, — you know every bit of me!"

"Yes, — but a man can't see too much of a pretty girl."

"You're very complimentary today! Well, if you must . . ."

She had on only a light dressing-gown, and nothing under it! not even a chemise! One by one, I undid the fastenings in front, and soon there was nothing to hide her naked beauty from her garters to her neck, round which she had retained a loop of velvet. Her white satin-like skin lay open to my sight interrupted only by the tawny gold patch that covered the lowest extremity of her belly with its clustering curls.

"You have grown a little fatter, my love," I

remarked as my hands passed over her naked flesh!

"Too much so?" she asked regarding herself.

"Oh no, — you're just perfect, just delicious!"

"And what about you? . . . The same as before?" With her soft hand she began to feel me, and little by little she approached the organ she had already so deliciously honoured during the drive, — then gently took hold of it!

"How stiff it is!" she said softly — "how it swells! — it seems quite pleased to meet its old friend! Eh? . . . You're very pleased, old chap, aren't you . . . eh? . . . eh? . . ." (she spoke as if to her pet dog). And you've seen cunts of every shade of hair since you last saw mine."

"As to hairs, yes," I replied, — "but nothing so adorable as this!" — (my readers can guess where my fingers now were!) What a lot you've got!"

"More than Madame Beaupré?"

"I haven't yet seen hers!"

"Come, come, what nonsense! Haven't you then even touched it?"

"Hers couldn't possibly be more lovely than yours!"

After many a burning kiss, many a thrilling tongueing, my mouth in its turn visited and explored all that my eyes had been feasting on, — my hands meanwhile playing with her neck, arms, shoulders, haunches, and then her saucy breasts — the nipples of which I playfully bit gently as I watched the lovely owner as she lay pleased and smiling. Then going a little lower, I pressed my lips through her hairs with the intention of working my way along her tender slit, with the result that my tongue was soon inside her cunt! Madame de Liancourt no longer smiled, she was now too much absorbed in the sensations of the moment — as was conclusively evident by her broken breathing and the wriggling movements of her loins, haunches, hips and bottom!

"Together! . . . both together!" she presently murmured, — then disengaged herself for a moment to pull back a curtain and reveal a large mirror in which one could see everything that passed on the bed!

"Isn't it shocking?" she laughed.

Then without further delay I placed myself on my back, my head between her legs, our bodies forming that delightful posture known as *soixante-neuf* . . . Reflected faithfully in the mirror, I could see the back of Mme de Liancourt, the adorable curves of her loins, her superb hips and haunches, the magnificent globes of her bottom — between which was visible my head framed by her plump round thighs, — while my thighs in turn flanked my voluptuous companion's bent down head, of which I could only see a few on the curls of her neck!

O what pleasures we tasted! what ecstatic quiverings thrilled through our bodies as our mouths emulated each other in their efforts to communicate to each other the most poignant and rapturous bliss! Mme de Liancourt devoted herself divinely to her sweet function! Although her mouth was small, she succeeded in making it large enough to get into it nearly the whole of my swollen and rampant prick, her fingers supplementing her lips as regards the portion left outside and making me feel exactly as if the whole of my organ was buried inside her mouth! On my side, my tongue (admittedly agile and clever by every woman who had allowed herself the experience) excelled itself in its efforts to drive Mme de Liancourt into indescribable ecstasy, ecstasy shared also by me, — for nothing can be more heavenly to the man than to feel the rapturous thrillings of pleasure as they vibrate through the woman to whom he is endeavouring to impart the most exquisite pleasure she is capable of tasting, and who is ready to forgive the immorality of the act so long as she is maintained in a heaven of blissfulness!

Having thoroughly teased, worried and tickled her clitoris with my tongue and excited it by tender nibbles of my teeth, I attacked the quivering lips of Mme de Liancourt's cunt, thrusting my tongue deeply between them and arousing in her a hitherto unfelt depth of pleasure, so keen and so voluptuous as to cause such violent agitation of her hips and the globes of her bottom, that although I was gripping the latter with my hands, I could scarcely restrain their plunging movements sufficiently to maintain my mouth on the dear object of its worship!

Finally we disengaged ourselves, and adopting the ordinary position I extended myself on the bosom of my voluptuous companion; she clasped me closely to her with her lovely arms, and in silence we united the parts of ourselves that our lips and our tongues now finding themselves together again sought mutual pardon for the lascivious caprice which had temporarily separated them! Oh! how delicious is the passage into a grotto that one has been kissing and sucking till the sweet interior has lubricated itself by successive spendings! — The heavenly up-and-down joggings are so delightfully facilitated, the pleasure becomes doubly sweet owing to the more intimate contact and union of sexual parts, while the girl now provoked into the highest pitch of erotic desire, quivering with unsatisfied lust and deliriously enjoying her position under her lover and the clasp of his arms, abandons herself ecstatically to the sensations of the moment in furious unison with him!

Presently, I saw Mme de Liancourt's eyes turn

upwards and half close as the first spasms of pleasure began to thrill through her.

"Gently! . . . gently! . . ." she gasped! . . . "Oh! . . . it's just heavenly! . . . gently darling! . . . oh! . . . oh! . . . wait! . . . wait! . . . I'm . . . just coming! . . . coming! . . . oh! . . . oh! . . ."

Our tumultuous plungings and heavings quickened frenziedly, then ceased in a storm of kisses!

* * * *

"O darling, what a deluge! I'm absolutely full of it!" And she rushed off to wash and purify herself.

After a visit in my turn to the lavatory, we were ready for supper: pâté de foie gras and old Sauterne are most excellent auxilliaries to Venus!

Mme de Liancourt had placed herself at the table with only a dressing-gown on. This did not remain fastened for long, — and then the spectacle of her naked charms and the sensations excited mutually by our inquistive and wandering hands quickly put us in train for more erotic scenes, which soon began to be reflected in the mirror.

"Tell me," said Mme de Liancourt, "have you ever done this with Mme de B."

"No."

"I can hardly believe you! Then for this particular caprice of yours you have come to your old pupil, your present one not yet being educated up to it! But no doubt you will before long gently break her to it, — just as if you were newly married husband and wife! I should like to see you at it! You might do much worse than to let me have her for a time to polish and finish her in these matters!"

"You're very kind! Only you would inspire her with desire for girls, not for men. You know you thus seduce all your girl friends in this particular way!"

"Come, come, — don't you speak evil of this fancy of mine, you of all people! — for except for it, you would never have met me! But don't you know that a woman can and does love to . . . amuse . . . herself with women as well as with men? I can, for instance!"

"Yes! that may be! — but there aren't many like you! Most girls go after either girls or men. You are essentially a woman of pleasure, devoted to pleasure, loving pleasure for the sake of pleasure, — ready to taste it in any form, with complete indifference to the sex of the person that is communicating pleasure to you!"

"I am not worse than you, my friend!"

"I'm not reproaching you! I'm simply stating a fact, which explains why we understand each other so splendidly! You have learnt how men can induce pleasure and how women can impart it, — and so you go from sex to sex audaciously experimenting, without being able to decide which you like the best!"

"I'm exactly like you in this respect, my friend!"

"Yes! but with this one important difference, — the feminine sex satisfies my exigencies and my curiosity and generally in every direction in which I may be tempted to pursue my researches!"

"Prettily spoken, my friend! — Still, had I your present sweetheart as a pupil, I would soon inculcate in her quite as excellent principles only more in accord with my tastes; I would impress her with myself as an example and also to keep her from concentrating herself on any one person, be it male or female! More over, unless I am deceived by the look of her eyes, she possesses the right temperament for my teaching; and I fancy it would not be long before your little innocent friend is ready and willing to lend herself to all sorts of salacious variations of carnal love, — and who knows? — may become the mistress both of yourself and of myself!"

Mme de Liancourt laughed merrily, then continued, — "But I won't ask for so much! I would like just to give her one lesson for your special benefit, — and I would even allow you to listen behind the door, so that you can judge for yourself whether I overstep the bounds of what a girl ought really to know!"

I fell in with her fantasy and I agreed to her suggestion. In my secret heart, the idea of having a woman as my rival in the affections of another woman was to me exceedingly piquant, — and I gladly left her to carry out her caprice.

*　　*　　*　　*

Mme de Liancourt accompanied me one day when I had arranged to meet Martha; and as soon as we discovered the latter she went forward by herself to meet her as from me, while I slipped off to her chambers. Mme de Liancourt told Martha that the latter's husband was suspicious, and was endeavouring to have a watch kept on her. — And this was why I had not come to the rendezvous, — that I had asked her to come instead to explain and to bring her to where I was awaiting her. After a little hesitation, Martha consented to accompany her to the Rue de Suresnes.

Presently (hidden in the small boudoir) I saw them come in and pass into the bedroom.

"You're quite safe here! You're in my own rooms! Here you can bill and coo as much as you please with your lover!"

Martha coloured to the tips of her little ears.

"But, Madame, Monsieur R. isn't my lover! We have never . . ."

"Really? My child, you have done well to tell me this, — you need fear no indiscretion on my part, for I also have a lover! The danger you were running has made me take an interest in you, and this is why I gladly brought you here at the request of Monsieur R... Really it was almost heroic of me to do so, for there are not many women who would go out of their way to bring to a mutual male friend another woman younger and prettier than herself! But it is so, dear, for you are certainly prettier than me!"

She kissed Martha. Then she invited her to take off her wraps and to make herself at home. But when she observed that Martha remained fully dressed with the exception of her mantle, she said to her.

"Don't be afraid, dear! do make yourself at home and do as I do! You mustn't remain as you are and receive your lover so, — for men like to see their sweethearts in some déshabillé when they come to visit them, — besides this, I have to change my dress for my evening's engagements. It will be pleasant to take advantage of this and see how some of my dresses will look on you, — an excellent idea — for should any one have followed us here and finds us so engaged, it will completely throw them off the scent!"

I admired the cleverness of the argument!

Mme de Liancourt rapidly divested herself of her dress, corset, and petticoats till she had on her chemise only; then she proceeded to reduce Martha to a similar condition of undress, in spite of the latter's hesitation especially as to removing her corset, as she alleged that she should keep this on if she was to try on any dresses! This Mme de Liancourt would not agree to!

"You wear very pretty under-clothing, dear! — no doubt you study his tastes in such details?"

This was a good guess, — for Martha had put on the corset we had bought together, also the lace petticoats and the delicately trimmed chemise. How delicate is the female instinct in the matter of attracting the male amorous desires!

"I do not know whether my dress will fit you, dear," continued Mme de Liancourt. "I think I am bigger than you are in the bust!"

Under this pretext she threw open her chemise and exhibited her breasts, which she set to work to compare with those of Martha, after having first unfastened and opened the latter's chemise.

"What deliciously white and firm little bubbies you have, dear! I expect you have often been complimented on them! A very fortunate man is your lover, — of course I don't mean your husband, — for if the latter saw you thus, I suppose

84

he would trop to spoil these little darlings, where as your lover would know how to show his appreciation of them by his caresses."

"Suppose he should suddenly turn up and catch us as we are!

"I should rush off into any corner that I could!" replied Mme de Liancourt with a smile she endeavoured vainly to repress! She added:

"But at a ball we women show quite as much of ourselves as you and I are now doing! I, at all events, have my dresses cut low enough to let my nipples be seen! Besides, it is only a woman with a bad figure that objects to be found naked or practically so! I'm not one of that lot! — see!"

With a touch, she caused her chemise to fall to her feet, and stepped forward out of it in all her glorious nudity, the effect being heightened by the contrast caused by the triangular patch of tawny golden hair at the junction of her belly and thighs and her black silk stockings with their rose-tinted garters worn above the knees!

"This is how I meet my lover!" she said.

Martha became scarlet!

"How you are blushing, dear! Is it because of the sight of me standing naked? If so, you remind me of one of my girl friends who declares that the sight of me naked excites her much more than the sight of a naked man would do! Every time she comes to see me, she insists on my undressing myself completely in front of her! — and then you should see how she kisses and embraces me just as if she was playing with a naked man! Then she will go and do a thousand and one improper and indecent things to me which at first used to make me feel horribly ashamed, but which now I really like — even to the length of paying her back in the same coin! Oh! it's lovely! And mind you, we're not deceiving our husbands! Strange, but true! isn't it, eh?"

She kissed the blushing Martha, and continued?

"Ever since, I have had lovers and . . . enjoyed them; I still recollect how delicious those tête-à-tête with my girl friend were! We used to caress and kiss each others breasts, like this . . ."

"Oh! you're biting me!"

"Doesn't your lover do this to you? . . . Oh! see how the pretty little nipples are stiffening and standing out!"

"Oh! Madame, you're tickling me! . . . Oh! take away your hand! . . . Oh! what are you doing! . . . No! . . . no! . . . I don't want it!"

Mme de Liancourt had seized Martha and was passionately clasping her against herself, holding her tightly with one arm round her waist while she slipped her other hand between Martha's thighs! The latter, utterly surprised by this sudden attack, could only struggle feebly!

"Oh! . . . but Madame, what . . . are you going . . . to do . . . to me?"

"Make love with you, darling! I'm gone on you! Don't you know how one woman can adore another? — how two women can mutually prove their love for each other? — Let me show you! But you surely must know all about it! At school, didn't one of the bigger girls take charge of you, and teach you . . . this? Ah! — you're blushing now. Oh! you little humbug! . . ."

"That was so long ago! . . . I quite forget it all! . . ."

"No, one never forgets that sort of thing! Your girl friend must have had a sweet time! Come, dear little humbug, what was it you used to . . . do together? . . ."

"Really I don't know!"

"Really and truly? . . . Well, I know! . . . Come, you'd like to do it again, wouldn't you? . . . with me?"

"No, — no! Suppose . . . he came in! . . ."

"He can't, without our hearing him! . . . Come, you pretty little coward, come! Place yourself against me! . . . so! Take off your chemise! . . . you can have a dressing gown if you like!"

She gave Martha one.

"No, don't fasten it! . . . leave it quite open! . . . I want to have a good look at you! . . . your

87

breasts — your belly — your hairs! . . . Oh! how they curl and cluster!"

Suddenly she knelt and applied her lips to the dark triangular patch that luxuriated at the end of Martha's stomach, the latter still offering a shame-faced resistance!

"No, no!" she cried, squeezing her legs closely together.

It had been however decreed and registered in the Book of Lesbian Venus that Mme de Liancourt should sacrifice yet another victim on the altar dedicated to tribadic love! I didn't think it was advisable to intervene! I felt sure that my turn would come before long, — and in the meantime here was Mme de Liancourt preparing for my delectation the most charming spectacle one could desire, one which the famous Regent would gladly have had performed before him at the Palais-Royal, yes, and paid cheerfully for it also!

Martha, now half-willing and still half-reluctantly, passively allowed herself to be placed on the sofa. Mme de Liancourt seated herself at Martha's side, passed one arm round her and slipped her other hand between Martha's thighs while she passionately kissed her, darting her tongue into Martha's mouth! Her finger, directed by both art and passion, soon produced the desired result! Martha's breath began to come brokenly, her eyes half closed, her bosom and breasts heaved agitatedly! At this moment Mme de Liancourt, no longer content to play only the part of the communicator of pleasure, caught hold of one of Martha's hands and gently conducted it to her own cunt with a mute demand for reciprocity! And Martha did not draw it back! — she recognised the silent request, and her gentle little hand began to do its untutored best!

What a charming picture the pair made! — what a glorious group worthy of Fragonard or of Boucher! I would have paid gladly a long price for a series of photographs representing them thus! Both girls intertwining their lovley white thighs and slender legs, then separating them only to interlace them in some other way in the midst of a storm of kisses and broken ejaculations, principally from Mme de Liancourt, who by now was simply mad with lust, her hips and haunches quivering, her body rapturously becoming more and more rigid!

"Martha! . . . oh darling! . . . keep on! . . . oh! . . . keep on! . . . You're . . . doing it . . . beautifully! . . . Oh! . . . Oh! . . . I'm coming! . . . Oh! . . . Oh! . . . I'm spending! . . . Ah! . . . a — h! . . ."

A moment of silence followed this ecstatic crisis, Mme de Liancourt still keeping her hand on Martha's slit!

"Oh! how wet you are! . . . You've also spent, you naughty thing! Darling, we've done it together! . . . Wipe yourself!" She gave Martha a handkerchief.

"Now, wasn't it good?"

"Yes!" replied Martha, timidly.

"Then let's do it together!"

"If you like!"

Immediately, our two lascivious heroines recommenced their lubricious caresses! Martha extended herself flat on her back on the sofa, and while her seducer, bending over her, looked her all over and felt and handled her as the spirit willed her, and freshly aroused in her new lust (as was manifest from the agitation of her bosom and breasts), Martha's hand, without invitation, stole to Mme de Liancourt's cunt and resumed its loving ministration. She had caught the fancy, she, so timid with me!

Nevertheless, she began to protest when, after having tenderly sucked her breasts, her mistress in lesbian pleasures carried her lips lower down!

"No, no, — not there!" she panted, trying to raise herself.

"Yes, yes! — I wish it! let me kiss your sweet cunny with its pretty hair! I'll do it just as well as your lover can!"

"But he has never . . . kissed me there!"

"Then he doesn't know his duties as your

lover! So much the better for me! I shall now be the first to do it to you! You'll see how delicious it is! I used to be just like you at first, — but now I simply adore this way! — and you'll always do it this way in future whenever you get the chance! . . . So! . . . Let me arrange you, open wider these pretty thighs! . . .

Then in the twinkling of an eye, the desired spot was covered with her lascivious and skilful mouth!

"No! no! . . . not there! . . . not down there! . . ." panted Martha as she felt Mme de Liancourt's tongue wandering over her cunt still virgin to such treatment and to the accompanying sensations!

For response, she was dragged down to the foot of the sofa, her thighs widely pulled apart, as Mme de Liancourt falling on her knees between them murmured almost unconsciously:

"Oh! what a lovely sweet fresh little cunny! . . . Oh! the beauty!" Then, like the swoop of hawk on a chicken, her mouth attacked it and remained there as if glued to it! Completely defeated, Martha fell on her back again and resigned herself as best she could to abandon herself to the voluptuous sensations that now were thrilling through her, induced by the ardent tongue of her passionate friend! Some minutes thus passed! At last Mme de Liancourt raised herself, red, flushed, panting, almost delirious!

"Together? . . . together? . . . Will you? . . ."

"What?" gasped Martha.

"This! . . . Let's do it together! . . . Will you? . . ."

"If you wish it! . . . But how? . . ."

"I'll show you, darling! . . . Now watch!"

She got on the sofa, turned her bottom towards Martha's head, straddled across Martha, then placed herself astride of her face, her belly resting on Martha's breasts and her cunt seeking the same lingual caress which she was recommencing on Martha's one now lying below her lips. Her thighs hid half the face of my sweet little mistress, and I could only see a bit of her forehead and her pretty hair emerge from between Mme de Liancourt's buttocks. As the latter wriggled and waggled her charming globes of flesh in lascivious undulations, I noted that Martha had accommodated herself to her position, and that her mouth as docilely as her hand comprehended and daintily executed the delicate function demanded from it!

But as for Mme de Liancourt, she was simply mad with passionate lust! What a strange thing it is that a woman can thus procure for herself such keen and ecstatic enjoyment in thus caressing another woman! I was splendidly placed for contemplating her, — and also the object of her delirious worship! I saw her face in profile, her chin resting on the hairs, her mouth poised on the lips of Martha's slit between which her tongue was playing! These secret charms of Martha, hitherto unknown to me, made me envy Mme de Liancourt both her place and the game she was playing! Time after time I was on the point of bursting out of my hiding place, and planting my mouth on the sweet spot she was attacking! — (our convention would have authorised the act) but I refrained! The charm of the spectacle fascinated me!

Sometimes Mme de Liancourt seemed as if she wanted to get the whole of Martha's cunt into her mouth! — sometimes amused herself by administering little touches to the clitoris with her tongue! — then she would pass her tongue right along the tender slit from top to bottom, — sometimes she would, with her fingers, separate the sensitive lips and thrust her tongue between them as deeply as she possibly could! Frequently she stopped, inspected attentively the sweet object of her admiration with eyes blazing with lust unsatisfied, then ejaculating frenziedly in her passionate adoration. "Oh! this cunt! . . . this sweet cunt! . . . this delicious darling cunt! . . ." She would shower kisses on it! How Martha must have revelled in bliss! I would have liked to have been able to watch her tell-tale face! She evidently was acquitting herself most satisfactorily in reciprocating Mme de Liancourt's attentions, if one might judge by the plungings and joggings of the latter's body as she brokenly ejaculated. "Oh! . . . oh! . . . you do it well! . . . I can feel your tongue! . . . now, do you feel mine? . . . wait . . . I'm going to shove it right inside this sweet cunt . . . as far in . . . as . . . it will go . . . There! . . ."

It is impossible to indicate the accent of these words as pronounced by a mouth the tongue of which was endeavouring to talk and lick at one and the same moment! What a terrible state of nervous excitement must have possessed Mme de Liancourt, a woman so reserved and correct in ordinary life, especially in language! But the ecstatic crisis was fast approaching! . . . the breathings became more and more broken!

"Martha . . . oh! Martha! . . . oh! darling . . . I'm coming! . . . Ah! . . . Ah! . . . I'm spending! . . . are you? . . . spend! . . . together! . . . wait a moment! . . . now! . . . now! . . . Oh! . . . I'm spending . . . again! . . . spend also! . . . s.p.e.n.d!!!"

Their bodies stiffened, constricted, — I heard a deep sigh of unspeakable pleasures! . . . They had finished!

Mme de Liancourt slowly slipped off her position and then proceeded to give her pupil kiss after kiss of approbation and satisfaction.

"Darling! your face is all wet with what you have drawn out of me! . . . And I've drunk you! . . . Use my handkerchief! . . . How flushed and red you are! . . . Now, wasn't it good?"

"Oh! yes . . . much better than I could have believed!"

Was it not now time for me to put in an appearance? But what could I do with two women whose lust had thus been satiated! Nevertheless I decided to show myself, and opened the door, regretting that I had delayed so long!

Two piercing cries saluted me! Martha leaped on her piled up garments and covered herself as best she could with the first she could snatch, then hid herself behind the bed curtains Mme de Liancourt caught up a velvet mantle trimmed with fur and threw it hastily round her, but it reached only to her fleshy buttocks and did not even cover the fur of her belly.

"What do you mean, sir," she exclaimed with a fine pretence of anger and outraged modesty, — "what do you mean by thus rushing into a lady's room without first knocking? It is a piece of the greatest impertinence! You are a mannerless brute! . . . You might well have waited! We were changing our dresses so that we might with the greatest safety leave the house! I had forgotten to lock the door, — but I really considered you knew better . . ."

"Madame, I humbly and earnestly beg your pardon for having surprised you in this way," I replied suppressing as best I could the desire to laugh — "but I came in trusting in your promise to give a kind refuge to this lady and myself!"

"Yes! — but Madame has been waiting for you for some time now; we had given you up! Is this your idea of the proper way of keeping an appointment? But I will abide by my promise; you can have my room and my bed. Only be prudent! I know your secrets now and if I choose I can be nasty!"

She winked at me out of the corner of her eye as if to qualify her menace, then walked past me towards her dressing-room.

"Take care about the sheets!" she added with a meaningly wicked smile!

I watched as she walked her lovely plump and round bottom, quivering and waggling with every step, — I would dearly have liked to have put myself into her! But I went and dragged Martha out of her hiding place.

"What makes you so red, dear?"

"I've been laughing so much! Madame has been telling me the funniest stories . . ."

"You look simply charming in that dressing gown! — but don't fasten it up, it's quite unnecessary!"

"Oh! . . . very well. But wait a minute. Don't look!"

She disappeared into the lavatory, and while she was engaged in clearing away all traces of her recent pranks, I undressed myself; then when she re-appeared I took her in my arms and carried her to the bed, on which I gently laid her. Her desires which I had feared were by now dormant were quickly restored to life again, having another promise of satisfaction in a different way! Her modesty after so rude an experience had become less troublesome, — and I did not meet with any marked resistance on her part when after bestowing a thousand kisses all over her body, I did to her what Mme de Liancourt had so sweetly inaugurated — the deliciousness of which she now fully appreciated as with her two little hands she pressed my face against her slit so as not to lose a single movement of my tongue!

I thought of Mme de Liancourt, and wished she could see us! But she did even better than this; she stood stark-naked by the side of the bed and while I was busy between Martha's thighs, she kissed her lips and squeezed her breasts, — while the former, having within her reach her friend's thighs, slipped her hand between them and let it disappear under the plentiful cluster of curling hairs, without interrupting my ministrations.

Excited, inflamed, burning with hot desire, I

rose to throw myself on Martha and quench in her the fire that was raging in my veins! But at that moment Mme de Liancourt carried her hand to the lowest point of my belly and seized the object she found there in a state of furious erection!

"Look, Martha!" she exclaimed, "look at it! Have you ever seen it before? isn't it splendid! See, how stiff it is! — that's in honour of you, my dear! Oh! I must . . . I can't help it! . . ."

I was then kneeling on the bed. With a single quick movement she seated herself with her head at the required height, — then covered with hot kisses my member which she found just on a level with her lips. She kissed and re-kissed the gland, the hairs, the testicles, murmuring endearments, then she took my prick into her mouth and sucked it madly in front of Martha, who in utter astonishment was watching her!

"Now, Martha, you take it, — it's your turn! Suck it! Do as I did!"

"I don't know how to!" stammered Martha, — it's so big!"

Now redder than fire she approached it, kissed the tip and tried for some time in vain to take it into her mouth — when all of a sudden it slipped in, as if in spite of her, completely filling her mouth, and she then proceeded to suck me violently! Oh! my raptures! It was Martha! Martha herself that was sucking me! It was not with the lascivious skill of Mme de Liancourt, — but her inexperience itself gave to her caress a special and indescribable spice of pleasure!

Finally I put Martha flat on the back, — I let myself fall between her arms and legs, and shoved my prick into her burning cunt! — tasting delights hitherto unknown, divine, delirious! Already I could see Martha's eyes slowly turning upwards and half-closing, indicating her approaching ecstasy — when Mme de Liancourt, no doubt jealous of our transports, put herself astride across Martha's face, blindly seeking for her cunt a further caress which it was impossible to refuse to her! Being thus suddenly driven away from Martha's lips and tongue I transferred my kisses to the two luscious globes of flesh which I had at my mouth's command, kissing them, nibbling and playfully biting them in spite of their squirming and constant agitation!

Dear readers, I will confess that my tongue at times lost itself in the furrow which separated these temptingly superb buttocks, so much did the sight of them and the subtle perfume which emanated from them madden me!

But everything must end! We three spent simultaneously! The blissful ejaculations of sperm calmed us! One by one we came to our senses and rose to purify and refresh ourselves!

"My gracious! I've got it all over me!" cried

Martha in pretty confusion, — "even on my stockings! . . . they're quite wet!"

"Well, dear," said Mme de Liancourt to her, you've done very well for one time! You must be very tired! By the time you get home, your eyes will have dark rings round them, — and then what will your husband think, eh?"

"Ah! I'll risk that! That won't stop me from . . . doing it again."

"What, today?"

"Why not? . . . When one has tasted the forbidden fruit, one must bite it well!" she replied, dropping her eyes. "Now I know what it is to be libertine! And I fancy it won't be long before I am nearly as clever at this game as Madame, your old pupil, with whom you evidently have been practising, eh?"

"How do you know?"

"By this!" she replied, pointing to an article that stood on the toilet table, which she and I had bought together and which I had left at Mme de Liancourt's.

"But I didn't want this proof after what I have seen today!" Martha continued chaffingly, — now if I had been jealous . . ."

"Your jealousy would have deprived us from the delicious time we have had together!" replied Mme de Liancourt.

"I quite agree with you!" said Martha with a

smile.

Mme de Liancourt showed herself a good teacher, and rapidly she educated her apt pupil, till it only remained to put her lessons into practice and delight her "amant" and her "amante"! And after the cares of the toilet had been attended to and a few glasses of champagne taken, we arranged that all three should meet at Mme de Liancourt's chambers on the first day that Martha was able to come, and we separated with longing for the time when we should next find ourselves in Mme de Liancourt's delicious boudoir for a *séance à trois!*

III

On a warm summer morning, a young lady of elegant appearance was strolling in a pretty park, selecting the narrower paths when possible and every now and then looking behind her over her shoulder as if she was on the way to some love-tryst and feared that she might be followed. As a matter of fact she was being followed by a gentleman who did not lose sight of her for a single minute as he slipped along, hiding himself in the brushwood like an Indian in a jungle!

My fair readers, do I hear you say, what is he going to relate to us? — a scene of jealousy? — a husband surprising his wife just as she is about to enjoy with the sweet help of her lover a supplement to the monotonous conjugal attentions?

Oh no! Please be reassured! Should anything drip it certainly won't be blood, — and if you should be affected by the fortune of our heroine it will be only with the most delicious of emotions!

The young lady quietly made her way to a sort of summer-house, then after a final look round she picked up her skirts (thereby revealing prettily shod feet and shapely calves), pressed through the surrounding herbage to the door, opened it quickly and disappeared within.

Sic vos non vobis . . .

For it was no other than myself who was thus taking a share in this adventure, a poacher in conjugal preserves!

Since I first met Mme de Baisieux in Paris and obtained an introduction to her, and above all at the Chateau de C . . . when kind fortune had made us guests together, I had made assiduous siege to her with a certain hope of success as her husband was away on a long sea trip. But up to date I had been frustrated, — and now my want of success seemed to be explained, the place I desired was already occupied!

I thought of withdrawing, but I wished first to make certain of the position; and may I confess that I was also seized with the desire of being a spectator of the piquant scene which no doubt was about to take place and which would finally and convincingly show me the uselessness of further pursuit.

"How shocking!" my lady readers will no doubt exclaim! Well, perhaps so, but I ask them to deal not too hardly with me in a matter of curiosity!

Thereupon I sought for the means of seeing without being seen. A little garret-window afforded me the desired assistance, and through it I obtained a view of the interior, full of hay, a suitable furnishing to a rustic boudoir. Mme de Baisieux was still alone; after having carefully closed the door, she seemed to be choosing a suitable spot for the sacrifice. I held my breath in my absorbed attention, quivering at the idea of being able to witness the scene which the principal actress was preparing against the arrival of the leading actor. Only I could not understand why she had so carefully fastened the door!

As soon as she had found a suitable place, Mme de Baisieux seated herself, took out of her pocket a little book and hurriedly turned over the pages. At last she seemed to find what she was seeking. Forcing the book open so that she could easily hold it so in one hand, she stretched herself out voluptuously, supported herself on her elbow, — while her disengaged hand . . .

My dear lady readers, have you guessed? Need I draw a curtain over a picture which you all must recognise? Will you not prefer to take a naughty peep at the sin your sister is about to commit?

This hand with a graceful movement raised her dress and the white petticoats beneath it. In consequence of the heat, she had not put on any drawers, and so my eager eyes were able to travel delightedly over all the charms I so ardently coveted but which so far I did not possess! And all I saw only inflamed me all the more, — for her charming exterior had not lied and her naked person was all and more than all I anticipated would be found under her clothes. All was rounded, plump! Above the dainty shoe came a slender shapely leg with a delicately rounded calf, a neat knee, then higher up a thigh underlined prettily by her blue garter, — the whole issuing from out of a wave of lace frillings! A fold of her chemise had dropped and so hid the part to which her hand had stolen! It was a living representation of Boilly's picture "MIDI" only with all the movement in it!

So far I had never been privileged to witness this solitary feminine pastime! It was therefore with strangely concentrated attention that I followed every movement of her hand — as it first began to rove from one end to the other of her slit, sweetly and caressingly, as if to gently flatter and excite the deity it sought to tame.

She read a few lines, — then her movements quickened! There was a gentle tremble, as if a tremolo was being executed on the charming instrument on which she was playing, — then quicker, and still more quickly . . . The book slipped out of her hand . . . her body and her head fell back . . . her eyes half closed, showing the whites . . . while her lips half opened, displaying her pearly teeth . . .

Between her widely extended legs her hand continued its tender gymnastics. She jerked her stomach upwards in violent up-heavings, which allowed me momentary glances of blond clustering hairs, but not of the dainty tickling finger which had been entrusted with the delicate mission of awaking and exciting the sources of her pleasure . . . Ah! now it was over . . . the delicious crisis had come and gone!

Mme de Baisieux raised herself, put the precious book into her pocket, brushed the dust off her garments, inspected herself in a pocket mirror, — and satisfied with the result, slipped prudently and cautiously away.

I quitted my peep-hole in a state of excitement more easily understood than described. My brain seethed with fresh desires and with them the hope of being able to enjoy them in the company of her whom I coveted, all the more so as it was evident now that she had no means of obtaining for herself a more solid and satisfactory way of solace.

I made a long round in the park timing myself

so as to meet her on one of the pathways where she was amusing herself with plucking wild flowers. The action was natural enough as was our meeting, nevertheless she blushed, — for a woman will betray herself thus under such conditions. And she was not any more at her ease when I remarked that she was looking pale and tired. All the evening, I harped on this theme, leading her to think that I suspected her of having kept an amorous rendez-vous, a teasing she accepted in good temper in the impression that she had completely thrown me off the scent as to her real occupation of the morning. Nevertheless, it was many days before she went out by herself. Was this the result of distrust, or prudence, — or was she able to solace herself in the house? I learnt the truth later on; the poor girl occupied a room that communicated with that of the lady who owned the house, her aunt, — and it was a regular school-girl's room in which she had no privacy whatever; hence her visits to the summer house.

The recollection of my delicious vision was always with me.

I dearly would have loved to have witnessed again the charming scene, to plan so that I could turn up at precisely the right moment, — at all events to get a chance of a talk with her by ourselves!

One day, the owner of a neighbouring estate invited the gentlemen of our party to his place for some rabbit shooting. I loved the sport, but what were my feelings of regret that I had accepted the invitation, when I saw that Mme de Baisieux, strawhatted, was on the point of going out by herself while we were filling our cartridge pouches! Hardly had we started, when I pretended that I had forgot mine (as a mere pretence for getting back to the house).

"We'll lend you some," my friends exclaimed.

"They won't do," I explained, — "I use no. 12."

"I believe I saw the gentleman place his cartridge pouch in the waggon," said a servant.

The gentleman had carefully taken them out again quietly!

"Shall we wait for you?"

"No, no, — I'll follow on foot. Begin without me. You may as well take my gun along with yours though."

Off they all went! And now for the park!

The summer-house had its back on the wall of the roadway. I took the quickest cut to it by not entering the park by the side gate, and soon I was at the gable end. Perhaps Mme de Baisieux had already begun to . . . to . . .! In a desperate hurry, I scrambled over the wall and jumped down on the other side.

Crack went something! Oh, bad luck! A confounded nail had caught in my breeches and had ripped one leg open from waistband to knee! And I wasn't wearing drawers! What was I to do!

Just then, I caught sight of Mme de Baisieux at the foot of the little slope on which the summerhouse stood, evidently making her way to it. She was leading her little cousin by the hand, from which I came to the conclusion that she did not propose today to satisfy the cravings of sexual desire. — I was rather pleased than otherwise, for now I could slip in and hide there till the evening or until I managed in some way to mend my torn breeches.

So in I slipped, and was hardly among the bundles of hay and certainly not full of voluptuous ideas, when the door suddenly opened, and I saw Mme de Baisieux enter, leaving the little child outside.

"Don't you come in," she said, — "I'm going to see if there are any rats here and to kill them. So don't come in, for they may bite you."

"Don't be long, cousin!"

"No, no." And she set to work to find the spot she occupied on the last occasion.

I had taken off my breeches and I had them in my hand, greatly embarrassed. Here was the much desired *tête-à-tête*, and a stupid accident was preventing me from benefiting by it! But the

110

sight of Mme de Baisieux, looking more charming than ever inspired me with the most voluptuous ideas and re-aminated my somewhat chilled desires and gave me the necessary audacity that the situation demanded. The recollection of the charms which I could still imagine under her clothes and which I perhaps was again going to see in their lovely nudity soon produced on me the effect that no pretty woman can help producing on any man worthy of the name. Rather than appear after the conclusion of the little play she was preparing for herself (and which would make her die of shame if she thought I had been a spectator of her actions) I showed myself without further delay.

A cry of startled modesty, quite natural, greeted me.

"What are you doing here, Monsieur? — I thought you had gone off with the shooting party!"

"I did start with them, but I left my cartridges behind and came back for them, — and chose the quickest way; and in climbing over the garden wall I have torn my breeches badly. I saw you coming along and so took refuge here, — and was horribly astonished when you came in! Now will you do me a great favour? Can you somehow get me a needle and thread so that I can repair this disaster as far as may be possible, at all events sufficiently to allow of my getting out of my present extremely unfortunate and inconvenient position!"

Mme de Baisieux broke into hearty laughter, no doubt relieved to find that I had not been spying on her; my accident thus saved me from suspicions which would have entirely spoiled my chances!

Briefly, so as not to tire my readers with conversations and explanations, after some hesitation on Mme de Baisieux's part, we arranged that I should hide in a corner and throw my breeches over to her; she then would mend them as much as possible and throw them back to me. She had the necessary needle and thread with her and in a few minutes she completed her work.

"There you are, Monsieur," she exclaimed as she threw the breeches back to me, and which I quickly slipped on, — "now good morning!"

"Oh please, wait a moment to let me thank you!"

"No, no. — good-bye! If any one should find us together here! . . ."

But by this time, I was alongside of her and had slipped my arm round her waist while I begged for a sweet kiss! — I then stole one.

"Enough! enough! no more!" she protested, — suppose any one should come in! . . . And my cousin?"

"Only one word, please! I must tell you!"

"Quickly then!"

"I didn't scramble over the wall to get my cartridges, — I wanted to get here without exciting anyone's suspicions, for I saw you on your way here. I wanted to tell you that you are the prettiest girl I know, that I adore you . . ." And I rained kisses on her cheeks.

"Oh! oh! — Monsieur Henri, how can you! . . . I couldn't have believed it . . ."

"I adore you! you are so pretty, so sweet! Oh! Bertha, my darling, my love! . . . you will? . . . — you will? . . . won't you? . . ."

"What! . . . do you know my name?"

"It's the first thing a man learns about the girl he loves, — and I've known it for a long time!"

All the time I continued to shower kisses on her as I held her tightly clasped in my arms against me. I could feel how her flesh was quivering through her thin summer dress, as I covered her cheeks, the nape of her neck, her throat, her mouth and lips with my ardent kisses. She let herself sink down on the straw murmuring "Enough! . . . enough! . . ." then, as if to conceal her surrender of herself now commencing, she fell into a half-swoon, closing her eyes which I kissed, and half-opening her lips, between which my tongue promptly slipped without however getting any reciprocal response from hers! One of my arms supported her body, the other hand crept under her dress and petticoats and caressed gently her dainty calves, then after a pause crept higher up to her garters where when a woman's leg is bent one can so deliciously lodge one's hand between the swell of the calf and the skin of the thigh! From this point of vantage, getting bolder, my hand crept still higher! Oh! what a sweet thrill ran through both of us when my fingers touched the soft warm bare flesh of her plump rounded thighs which she was vainly squeezing against each other.

This time also she had no drawers on! From the top of her dainty shoes to her smooth satin belly, the hairs on which I now gently was playing with, there was no obstacle to my full view!

"No! . . . no! . . ." she murmured as she felt my fingers invade her slit, — "not there! . . . not there! . . ."

But in spite of this flicker of rebellion, this last effort of expiring shame, my finger settled itself on her tiny clitoris and commenced the ecstatic function which Mme de Baisieux hitherto had reserved for her own little fingers! Under its sweetly mysterious influence, her body began to stretch itself out, her faintness increased, her tongue began to respond to mine! And then her legs commenced to open out! She was mine! — she had surrendered herself to me! — I now only had to take possession of her!

In one's first amorous encounter with any fresh woman, it is always most advisable that one should go slowly at first, watching her carefully and defeating every attempt at resistance, — to pretend to be seized with delirious passion for her — until your sweet combatant yields herself under the repeated thrills of pleasure you have communicated to her, — then let yourself go and indulge to the utmost your concupiscence and your desires.

I was now burning to look closely at all the charms that so far I had seen from a distance only. Quickly I threw up her clothes so as to get a good look — and as I did I thought of the piquant spectacle we would afford any one who might have his eye where I had mine on the previous occasion!

All I saw were now mine! . . . mine! these lovely legs, these slender, dainty calves. She was wearing the same underclothing as on the last occasion, — tiny kid-shoes, cream-coloured silk stockings, blue garters. On her right thigh was a tiny brown molemark! Oh! how I longed to kiss everything! — that lovely satin skin, that silky chestnut triangular patch of curls which formed so adorable a contrast to her blonde beauty! — how I would have liked to put my mouth on the delicious little slit which was now beginning to open its pouting lips! But I hadn't the time now! I had to keep holding her clothes up! Another time I would repay myself with interest!

Recalled thus to the sweet reality, I placed myself between her charming legs, I pulled her clothes still higher up, I rapidly undid the front of my breeches and freed my imprisoned member — then shoved it still and burning into the sweet opening that was impatiently awaiting its introduction, — while at the same time I thrust my tongue as deeply as I could into the mouth of my pretty victim.

"Bertha! . . . oh! Bertha! . . . oh! how heavenly! . . . your're delicious! . . . divine! . . . oh! you angel! . . . you angel! . . ."

Women as a rule do not let their lovers who are rogering them for the first time understand how they appreciate the pleasure that is wildly rioting through them all the time, for they love to behave as if they were being violated! Mme de Baisieux only departed from this policy to murmur as we were approaching the sweet ecstatic conclusion. "Oh! . . . please . . . please . . . take it out! . . . not inside me! . . . no! no! please!" Although I was mad with pleasure I had sufficient control of myself to obey her. Unfortunate results might otherwise arise from our pleasure. Oh! mysterious decrees of Providence! — without you how much more amiable and obliging women would be, — and also how deliciously libertine!

It comes back to me how I was kissing her tiny ear ornamented with a single pearl as I awaited the moment when I must withdraw my prick from inside her in accordance with her prudent request. The moment arrived, — everything shot on to her white petticoat!

I offered her my handkerchief.

"But then you won't have a handkerchief!" she exclaimed.

"Oh, yes! — I'll preserve it in memory of the delicious use you will have made of it!" I replied with a smile. She blushed prettily.

While we were exchanging the loving kisses which follow so tender an encounter, we heard a little voice at the door!

"Cousin, cousin, haven't you finished killing the rats yet?" We had absolutely forgotten all about the child that was patiently waiting outside!

"Yes, yes!" called out my lovely companion raising herself hurriedly and flushing scarlet — "I'm just coming! — I've killed the last I think!"

We couldn't maintain our seriousness at the plaintive trouble in the little voice that had thus interrupted us.

"Here I am, dear, I'm just coming. Don't come in!"

"Good-bye Bertha, my darling!" I whispered, — when again?"

"Oh! — never, never!"

"You little humbug! Shall we say tomorrow?"

"No, no! . . . I'll tell you, later!"

"One last kiss then!" She gave me a delicious one in which her tongue and mine also said good-bye! "Now goodbye! . . . *Au revoir!*"

As she neared the door, she brushed and dusted herself, took a glance in a pocket mirror she had with her, waved her hand lovingly to me, said goodbye again with her eyes, — then slipped out.

As soon as I considered she would got to a safe distance, I in my turn crept out, hurried off to my bedroom and quickly changed my things, as they carried evident traces of our sweet combat! Then I picked up my cartridge pouch and set off to rejoin the shooting party, my absence being hardly an hour. How one can employ time some-times!

From that day, for Mme de Baisieux and me, the term *to kill a rat* became synonymous with "have a turn". In spite of her innocent air, she was full of mischief, and did not hesitate to let herself loose in her love-letters to me. In memory of the adventure she adopted the following for-mula in her *billets-doux*.

"Mon cher Monsieur, will you give the pleasure of your company at a rat hunt on . . . next at the usual place." She continuted to send me these invitations after we had returned to Paris, even when her husband was there; he did not stay there long, but his presence nevertheless was a nuisance as it of necessity reduced the frequency of our "hunts" and the consequent opportunities of satisfying our desires!

When our liaison had become very intimate I told her that one day I had surprised her in the act of "frigging" herself! I was sweetly scolded for thus playing the spy on a "poor lone woman", but I was soon pardoned, and she consented to let me see the book which seemed to arouse the desires which she strove thus to satisfy. She had found it among her brother's papers. It was *The Confessions of a Woman of the "World"*, illustrated in the most lascivious way, — enough to excite anyone's senses!

"On the day we first killed the rat, what bit were you reading?" I asked softly.

In pretty embarrassment she pointed out to me the following lines, which we then read together:

"As I lay on my back on my sofa, stretched out at full length with my legs widely parted, my lover fell on his knees in front of me and in the most delicious way sucked me till I spent in thrilling delirium!"

Needless to say we did not read any more that day! And I take this opportunity to express to the amiable author and to his clever illustrator my sincere thanks for having thus aroused a fire which I was able to extinguish in the pleasantest way possible!

IV

If from time immemorial the French woman, especially the Parisienne, has enjoyed the reputation of being in love affairs the most agreeable and the most sprightly of her sex, and of knowing how to impart to her favours a piquancy which greatly augments their value, I venture to consider that the Vienna ladies should be allowed to participate in this praise, especially such as have had the benefit of Parisian education, — for their elegance, their air of distinction, their coquetry, their talent for being discreetly provoking, in no way ranks behind their Parisian sisters whom often they surpass in beauty of form and figure. Full of curiosity in all matters appertaining to sexual love, they delight to make a study of them and to lose themselves in dream eroticism, in meditations of the most refined lubricity, — after which they will resume in the easiest manner possible the outward appearance of the most virtuous and well-behaved woman.

Such at all events was Mme de Schoenfutz. Transplanted from the banks of the Danube to those of the Seine, she had there found so many subjects for amorous study that she did not long live in accord with her legal lord and master; the latter, like a wise man, avoided any scandal by quietly letting her live as she chose while he in turn did as he also pleased.

It was I who was the privileged mortal with whom she took her first lessons in the Art of Love, with whom she made her first studies, — which we did not hesitate to carry on to extremes!

She was a delicious pupil, so full of enthusiasm! I could conduct her and teach her the most outrageous method of unrestrained lust as long as I did so by agreeable and picturesquely amusing paths! — and there was little doubt that I had hit off the right way, as very soon she became most expert!

But everything comes to an end, even such delightful refinements of amorous pleasure. She began to put into practice with others the lessons I had taught her, — while I passed on to the education of other pupils. Since then we had often met — but Our Lady Venus did not receive any sweet sacrifice from us, partly because the occasions were not propitious and time was wanting. Now the attractions of the hunting season had brought us together at the Château de V . . .

My Viennese charmer had become even more beautiful than before; to the charms of her face and figure was now added a certain trick in the way she looked at you, which under the air of distinction nevertheless indicated she was not wanting either in enterprise or audacity. In short I found myself ready if she should indicate that she was willing. But do not think that I imagined that I had only to ask her to let me have (so to speak) my latchkey again. — To have done so would have been both foolish and fatal, for a woman requires to be re-conquered by any man whose caresses she has forgotten. Accordingly I laid siege to her in the regular way, but at first all the encouragement I got lay in vague half-promises, such as "Perhaps! . . . if you're very good!" But little by little I made progress, — now snatching a hasty kiss, now a significant pressure of her corsage, sometimes a hand slipped under her clothes but not permitted to! . . .

One day, we went out fox-hunting. Mme de Schoenfutz both rode well and looked well on horse-back, having something of the elegance of seat and style of the late Empress Elizabeth of Austria, whom indeed she resembled in more ways than one.

The atmosphere was heavy and thunderous, the heat stifling. The sport was poor. Twice the hounds had to be whipped off a false scent. A state of confusion prevailed, and the riders formed little groups as they watched the proceedings and held themselves ready to gallop off as soon as the signal was given. Presently the sky began to be covered with black threatening clouds which presaged a serious storm. Was it good enough to go on? — wouldn't it be as well to get shelter? But before any general decision was arrived at, a roll of thunder shook the air and large drops of rain began to fall.

Immediately there was a general skedaddle, — a wild rush for the carriages. Several riders galloped off to the kennels not far off, others to the village of T... The men ceased to chat with their lady friends and with each other, concerned now to make the best of their way to shelter. But M. de Z. (who I suspected to be in Mme de Schoenfutz's high favour) remained by her and asked her what she proposed to do.

"I'm going back home," she said.

"You'd much better come to T..., the rain will soon be over and we can then resume hunting."

"Many thanks! in the forest, all dripping! I've

had enough for one day already!"

"But really it is not going to be wet."

"Please don't let me keep you from hunting! I'm going off, I hate rain!"

"Then let me come with you! You don't know the road and you will most likely take the longest way round . . ."

But Mme de Schoenfutz had galloped off as he spoke! And now I recognised why old Ovid had included the chase among his Remedies for Love! M. de Z . . . did not insist on following. The lady riders all dismounted quickly and crowded into carriages to drive back to the Château, while the men unanimously allowed them to go off unescorted while they themselves made the best of their way to T . . . to wait there till the rain was over and the hunt could be resumed.

"This is much jollier than with all those petticoats hanging about!" remarked F . . ., a womanhating sportsman. "Come along to T . . . — there's a good hotel there, a good stable, and a good billiard table on which we can have a game while we wait."

"Sorry I can't come, old chap," I replied, — "I must go off to see one of the keepers about a dog. We'll meet presently."

It had stopped raining, but the sky was more threatening than ever. My intention was not to stop at the keeper's but to get off to the Château and try and find Mme de Schoenfutz, — for in such panics, it is seldom that an enterprising gallant does not have some luck, because everybody is too busy looking after himself or herself to notice what any one else is doing. So after a few minutes at the keeper's house, I galloped down a bridle path which was a short cut to the Château and led into the road Mme de Schoenfutz had taken.

As I joined the road I saw some way down a lady riding slowly by herself. It was she! I soon caught her up.

"What! not home yet?" I exclaimed.

"No," she replied, "My horse has a stone in his hoof and I have nothing to get it out with. So I am forced to go slowly."

I had with me the necessary implement and soon put matters right, then remounted.

"Are they all coming this way?" she asked.

"Yes, the carriages are just behind, with all the women inside them."

"Then let us get out of their way, — for if they see me with you after the way I rushed off, they will conclude that our meeting was premeditated."

"You are quite right! Let us ride down here."

As soon as we had got out of sight of any one on the road, I drew alongside my fair companion and slipped my arm round her slender waist, then

drawing her quickly to me I kissed her lips
ardently.

"Enough! . . . enough!" she exclaimed, trying
to release herself, "here comes the rain!"

"I don't mind the rain as long as I have you!"
And I renewed my amorous assault, clasping her
passionately against me as I kissed her furiously,
darting my tongue into her mouth, squeezing her
waist with one hand while the other attacked her
bosom, her knees, her thighs which I felt and
pressed through the cloth of her habit. So impetuous was my attack that I nearly caused her to
fall off her horse.

"Oh! . . . oh! . . . what are you doing! — is it
the storm that has made you so mad?"

"Yes! . . . yes! a storm of love and desire! I am
full of love's electricity, like the clouds."

"And so you want me to be your lightning-
conductor! but I thought I had become incapable
of electrifying you to such an extent."

"You know well that you are to me what no
other woman can be. And if you would like a
proof of your power over me . . ."

"As a matter of fact, folk that have known of
our old liaison suspect me now to be with any one
but you."

"But you haven't answered my question! Do
let us take advantage of our security! Let me
prove to you that you have electrified me to the

uttermost of my capacity! Will you? . . . may I? . . ."

"Well . . . yes! . . . but you're not allowing for the storm!"

As a matter of fact the rain now had begun to come down heavily, rain that clears the air but which is a horrible nuisance to an out-of-doors *rendez-vous* without any curtains beyond the kindly trees!

We went off at a gallop down the path. Was it never coming to an end? Soon I noticed that we were going away from our proper course, the fault of our hasty flight. I was somewhat upset by this, but said nothing. We continued to gallop. Presently a signpost came in sight, I rode up to it — the château was a good three miles from where we were.

"Where are we?" she asked.

"Oh, not far off."

"Then which is the road? This way?"

Just then I caught sight of a shanty (or hut) hidden in the forest. It was a sort of hunting shelter with a lean-to for the horses. The sight put a droll idea into my mind, — here was a nest for an amorous pair!

At all events, it would be only prudent to avail ourselves of this unexpected shelter. We tied the horses under the lean-to, and forcing open the locked door we went inside. We found ourselves in a fair sized room, quite bare except for one or two strawseated chairs and a fireplace. In the ceiling there was a trap door which evidently communicated with a hay-loft.

Hardly had we entered when the rain began to come down in torrents. What we had experienced was nothing to what was now falling, a veritable deluge! I kindled a fine fire in the hearth with the debris and straw I found lying about, — then I took off my coat and hung it across the back of a chair in front of the fire. Mme de Schoenfutz slipped out of her riding-habit and did the same.

She looked deliciously piquant as she stood thus, décolletée, her pretty arms bare, with her riding-breeches, her dainty riding-boots and little man's silk hat!

I gently caught hold of her and drew her against me, — then slipped my hand under her chemisette and getting hold of one of her round full breasts, I drew it out of its hiding place and kissed it passionately. "Suppose some one should come!" she whispered.

"Wait a moment!" I replied, and went out. I brought the horses inside, then barricaded the door, — now no one could possibly suspect our presence, for even the fire (now reduced to a glowing mass) did not throw off any smoke to call attention to human habitation.

"Now we're at home!"

Seated on a chair with Mme de Schoenfutz on my knee, I surrendered myself to my desires! On her part she abandoned herself entirely to me, returning me kiss for kiss, laughing delightedly at the originality of our situation. She simply adored such situations! By now I had pulled both of her sweet little breasts out of her corset and was kissing them fiercely, — under my burning lips, the pretty little nipples began to swell up and get hard.

"I really believe they recognise you!" she said laughingly.

"Then what about my third little friend, the sweetest, the sauciest, the wickedest of them all!" — and my fingers unbuttoned the front of her riding breeches and slipped inside!

"It's an odd sensation," I remarked maliciously, "to find a cunt inside a man's breeches!" And my happy hand set to work to caress and play with the sweet feminine hairs it found, then stole between a pair of soft plump satin-like thighs which it felt and handled, — and then my finger made its way into a certain opening already warm and moist and commenced to play on her little quivering clitoris! . . .

As her pleasure crept over her, my pretty companion began to become sweetly agitated. Her hand stole towards me; I delightedly guided it. Quickly unbuttoning my trousers I helped her to drag out what she was seeking and what she now had got hold of!

"Just suppose that you had found something like this when you put your hand inside my riding breeches!" she remarked laughingly.

"What an idea!"

"He recognises me, I'm sure! He wants to see his old friend!"

The way in which we had placed ourselves was not propitious or convenient for the prosecution of our adventures. True pleasure demands horizontal position, — and I, at all events, consider that one only cheats Venus if one sacrifices to her in the odd positions which are only allowable when there is absolutely no help for it. So instead of making her sit astride on my knees (as she seemed to expect) I suggested that I should climb into the hayloft to see whether we could not build for ourselves a more comfortable nest up there.

The ladder was rather ricketty, — however I got up all right. The loft was full of hay, sweet-smelling. I quickly persuaded Mme de Schoen-futz to join me, — but as the ladder was a little short for her I had some little difficulty in raising her off it, she all the time laughing and revelling in the adventure.

"Now, where?" she asked, looking about her.

O delicious question, "Now, where?" As much as to say "where shall I place myself so as to let you have me, — to yield myself to you — to let you do whatever you like to me!"

I collected some bundles of hay and soon improvised as excellent couch on to which I gently placed her.

"The mice will see us!" she exclaimed playfully. Then "Oh! this hay is pricking me awfully!"

This I soon remedied by means of my horse rug, — and then we were comfortably installed!

Outside the tempest continued to rage unabated, with loud claps of thunder and torrential rain. My pretty companion however had no alarm, and abandoned herself afresh to me. In the midst of our toyings and handlings of each others persons, I whispered: "Do take this off, — it's only a nuisance!" And I pointed first to her stays, then to her riding breeches.

"You'll do the same?"

"Yes, of course. And at once."

Gracefully she consented to satisfy my prayer, and set to work to take off her breeches, or rather her cloth knickers buttoning at the knee. When she had let them fall I helped her to draw her legs out of them and to pass them over her little patent-leather riding-boots, a task I took care not to accomplish without availing myself of the opportunity to effect sundry little ticklings and indiscreet touchings which provoked from her little screams of laughter.

"I'm going to keep on my hat," she said, "for my hair is damp and I would never be able to get it into order again!"

Oh! how bewitching she then looked! — and what a piquant costume! She stood in her chemise with her silk riding hat on, and her patent-leather riding boots halfway up her calf, the rest of her leg being covered with a grey silk stocking fastened above the knee with a rose coloured garter!

I dropped on my knees in front of her and pressed my lips upon a forest of golden hairs through which I tried to insert my tongue . . .

"No, no," she exclaimed, drawing herself back a little, — "not standing upright!" Then she lay herself down, — and pleasure invaded the pair of us!

Her chemise I had turned back and the whole of her lovely body was now exposed! I showered kisses all over it, but especially all about her thighs, between which I then recommenced my sweet occupation in a less unfavourable posture than before. My skilful tongue soon sent out of herself! — her stomach heaved agitatedly, then jogged itself spasmodically upwards as if loth to lose a single touch of my tongue!

Pleasure communicated demands reciprocity! This was always our rule and practice in the days when she was taking lessons from me in the Art •

and Practice of Love. Without arresting my ministrations, I placed myself in a position that I knew would recall to her our old conventions! Her soft hand showed me that she understood, as it gently seized the object I had placed at her disposal; I then brought myself still nearer, so that her mouth had even less distance than before to travel in order to carry out its sweet duty.

"No, no! that won't do!" she softly exclaimed, — "you will disarrange my hair! Let me come on top of you!" — and she gently freed herself in order to do so.

She took my place, put herself on top of me, turned without hesitation her lovely bottom towards my face, — and then lowered herself till her delicious slit rested on my mouth! And immediately I felt my member kissed, caressed, — handled, — then sucked in the most delightful fashion, I responding by furiously thrusting my tongue as deeply as I could into her throbbing quivering cunt!

The storm, the hunt, — all were completely forgotten! What ecstacies we were revelling in! . . . what delirious transports! . . . what zest she was putting in her suction of me! My lessons had borne wonderful fruit! . . . And I, with what fury I thrust my tongue into the grotto of love that was palpitating on my lips! . . . how I licked, sucked, nibbled! . . . But I began to feel I was . . .

"Diana! . . . Diana! . . . stop! . . . stop! . . .
I'm coming! . . . coming!"

Alas! — too late! A suction more subtle and
overpowering than anything that had preceded it
deprived me of the power of moving! — and my
boiling discharge shot into the sweet mouth of my
companion!

Shocked by such a catastrophe, I feared a
legitimate punishment. But nothing happened!
To cover my fault, I continued to pass my tongue
into and over Mme de Schoenfutz's cunt till she
lay motionless! Perhaps my now somewhat
calmed ardour was expressed by my tongue! Perhaps my lovely companion herself had spent
deliciously! Presently I began to make my
apologies.

"My sweet Diana, really I beg pardon . . ."

She made no reply, — but raised herself off
me, rosy red, approached me as if to kiss me, —
put her lips on mine . . . and spat into my mouth
the liqueur she had been storing so carefully in
hers! Then shaking with laughter she remarked
wickedly, "There, you've got it all back!"

Delighted by so happy a solution, I caught hold
of her, captured her bottom, raised her chemise,
and set to work to slap her playfully, but not for
long — for I bent down and covered her charming
hemispheres with numberless kisses.

Before long, thanks to a thousand erotic

follies, the standard-bearer of my desires — the "Leader of the shocking party" (as a witty English girl once called it) became again rampant and erect. This time we gave the preference to a sacrifice to Venus in the ordinary method; for however delicious may be other postures and the other ways of performing the act of fucking, they are more or less *hors-d'oeuvres*, tit-bits, rather than a substantial meal. — But owing to her hat my partner took the upper place, — and very soon, clasped in each others arms, lips against lips, my prick penetrated into the sweet opening already lubricated by my kisses and tongueings!

Just then the rain came down with an intensity hitherto unequalled, as so often happens towards the end of a storm. Mme de Schoenfutz began to squirm and wriggle in a most extraordinary way, — it was with the greatest difficulty that I managed to keep her impaled on my prick in spite of my hands being firmly pressed on the two charming rotundities which women so love to exaggerate in their toilettes.

"The rain is coming through," she explained, I can feel some drops just in the small of my back. Oh! there's one!

"Shall we change places?"

"No! . . . No! . . . oh! there's another, just between the cheeks of my bottom! Oh! how it tickles!" And again she squirmed and wriggled in the most voluptuous way as she lay on me!

The rain was really coming through the roof. But what did we care! The blissful ecstatic crisis was approaching! — our breath mixed with our humid lips! — I began to feel that I could not hold back my boiling discharge for long! Among our mutual understandings, it was decreed that I was not to deposit my tribute of love inside the shrine (whichever it might be) into which I had been permitted to perform my worship. My recent infraction was one which would carry no grave after-consequences, — it was only perhaps an offence to shame; but if I now should repeat it the result might be most serious and in fact might damage Mme de Schoenfutz's reputation! So I murmured in her ear softly that I was getting to the end of my powers of self-control, that I must soon . . . spend! . . . that something was just . . . coming! and that I must withdraw my prick while I was sufficiently master of myself to do so!

"Wait! . . . wait! . . . one moment! . . . I'm . . . finishing . . . also! . . ." she gasped brokenly as her movements on me accelerated, accompanied by convulsions of pleasure! . . . A few ecstatic thrills, and then the sudden relaxing of her body announced that her blissful crisis had come and gone! — that she had spent! . . . Then promptly I withdrew my prick out of its sweet nook and . . . discharged! . . . not wasting my

137

ammunition however, as I slipped my rampant prick between the quivering globes of her bottom and inundated the charming valley that lay between them with a deluge of another sort to what had come from the roof!

"Oh! . . . oh! . . ." she ejaculated, "it has reached right up to my back! . . . it's much warmer than the rain!"

*　　*　　*　　*

After we had crept down again, we found our garments quite dry. I helped my companion to dress.

"Is my hair much tumbled? I expect you've rumpled it horribly!"

"No, not at all. It's all right." And I kissed her tenderly.

She drew out of her pocket a little powder box and passed the puff lightly over her face.

"You Viennese ladies are very fond of rice powder!" I said.

"O yes. I use it all over me!"

"Don't I know it?" I replied maliciously.

"Oh! you wretch!"

We remounted our horses. The rain had ceased; the forest was full of the delightful fragrance which leaves give out after a shower.

Our road back took us close to a keeper's

house where we made enquiries about the hunting and were told that it had not been recommenced. Just then a group of horsemen came from T... where they had taken shelter; among them was M. de Z... We joined them.

"So you took refuge here?" he enquired of me.

"No, not I, Mme de Schoenfutz did. I came by just as she was remounting. I stopped with the keeper, Jean."

* * * *

In the drawing-room the same evening, the conversation turned on the storm and the interrupted hunt, and everyone told how he or she had fared while sheltering.

"In the house I was in," said Mme de Schoenfutz, "they made me taste a sort of white sauce . . . You know it!" she added looking at me!

"Oh, yes!" I stammered, staggered by her audacity, — "as I was passing you called me in!"

"Yes, that was so, and I made you try it, but you did not seem to fancy it!"

Her coolness simply dumbfounded me!

Then they all began to discuss what it could have been; every one expressed some opinion, but an old maid insisted that she knew it.

"Of course it was only milk thickened with

maize powder! When it is warm and not too thick, it is very nice!!"

PART II

I was fifteen years old when my mother was seized with an illness which proved to be fatal. After eight months of suffering, she left this life. Realizing the depth of my sorrow at the loss, my father cherished me all the more, and I returned his tenderness with all my heart.

I was continually the object of his caresses. Not a day passed without his cuddling me and covering my face and lips with the most passionate kisses.

I remember that my mother had reproached him one day for the liberties he was taking with my body.

'What are you complaining about, Madame?' he had replied. 'I am doing nothing wrong. If she were my daughter, the censure would be justified. I am no Lot.'

This incident never left my memory, although I did not understand until some time later. I clung to him, however, since I knew I owed everything to him. It was not hard to do, for he was the soul of affection and solicitude.

So favoured was I by nature that he believed that the deity of love had fashioned me. He never tired of telling that to me. From my infancy, I showed promise of a pleasing, svelte figure and a face with regular features. The vivacity of my brown eyes was tempered by the sweetness of my glance. Although I was lively and gay, I had a tendency to be reflective.

My father studied carefully my tastes and inclinations, which he cultivated and developed with the greatest diligence. One thing that he was insistent on was that I hold nothing back from him. It was a condition I found no difficulty in meeting. His tenderness for me was such that on the infrequent occasions when he thought I deserved to be punished, the blows were caresses.

Some time after the death of my mother, he took me in his arms.

'Laurette, my dear child,' he said, 'It is now time to think of your education.'

With my father as my sole teacher, I received the most brilliant training imaginable. He was familiar with everything – drawing, dancing, music, literature and the sciences.

Although my father was occupied with my upbringing, I noticed him often sunk deep in thought and perturbed. It was obvious that something was bothering him. After my mother's demise, we had left our home in the country to live in the city. Since he had few other interests, I became the centre of his life and the object of all his affection.

The caresses he lavished on me seemed to animate him, for his eyes sparkled, his face turned red, and his lips became dry and hot. He liked to take my buttocks in his hands and massage them. Or he passed a finger over my thighs while he kissed my mouth and breast. Often, he completely undressed me and lowered my naked body into a bath. After having dried me and rubbed oils and essences into my skin, he put his lips to every part of my body excepting one. As he contemplated me, he shook all over. Then his hands were again on me. How I liked this delightful game. Then suddenly he ceased his fiery manipulations to run and lock himself in his study.

One day, when his kisses were more impassioned than usual, kisses I returned with my usual tenderness, and our mouths were glued together with his tongue moistening my lips, I suddenly felt strange sensations. The flame of his embraces had slipped into my veins. He then escaped me when I least expected it and great was my chagrin. Also, I was curious to learn what had attracted him to his room, but when I tried to open the door, I found it latched.

The following day, he was given a letter which seemed to please him. After having read it a second time, he spoke to me.

'My dear Laura, it is time for you to have a governess. One is arriving tomorrow. Although she comes with the highest recommendations, I have to see her for myself to make my own judgment if they are exaggerated or not.'

I was totally unprepared for such news which, for some reason, greatly saddened me. Without knowing why, I was uncomfortable at her presence and I did not like her even before I had seen her.

Lucette arrived the day before she was expected. She was a big girl around nineteen or twenty with an opulent bosom, extremely white skin, a good but not unusual figure, a pretty mouth with carmine lips, and two perfect rows of enamel teeth. Immediately my preconception of her was changed. In addition, she had an excellent character, an abundance of gentleness and kindness, and a winning way. I was completely taken by her, and we soon became the most intimate friends. It was evident that my father was more than satisfied with her.

Envy and jealousy are strangers to my soul. Besides, what arouses the desire of men often is not our beauty or our merit. Thus, for the sake of our own happiness, it is wisest to let them alone and not to worry. More often than not their infidelity is nothing more than a slight fire that goes out as soon as it is lit. Consequently, it is folly to torment oneself about it.

Although I was not yet capable of reasoning in such a way at that time, I still felt no animosity towards Lucette. Besides, there was no diminishment in the signs of affection that my father bestowed on me. The only thing I perceived was his reserve when she was present but I put this down to mere shyness. Some weeks passed in this fashion until I finally noticed the attentions he was paying her. He never let an opportunity escape to reveal his feelings towards her. It was not long before I shared his sentiments for her.

When Lucette expressed her desire to sleep in my room, my father readily gave his consent. When he awoke in the morning, the first thing he did was to enter our chamber in which our beds were side to side. This arrangement enabled him to make advances towards Lucette while pretending that he had come to see me.

It was obvious that she was not rebuffing him, but she did not respond to his urgings as quickly as I would have liked her to, and I could not figure out the reason for her dragging feet. Loving my father as much as I did, I was of the opinion that everybody should feel towards him as I did. I could not help but chide her for her indifference.

'Why don't you like my Papa?' I asked her one day. 'He seems to have such warm feelings for you. I think that you are very ungrateful.'

She merely smiled at these reproaches, assuring me that I was doing her an injustice. She was right, for in a short time the apparent coolness vanished.

One evening after supper, we retired to a salon where my father had coffee and liqueurs served. In less than half an hour, Lucette was sound asleep. At that, my father took me up in his arms and carried me to my room where he put me to bed. Surprised at this new arrangement, my curiosity was instantly aroused. I got up a few moments later and tip-toed to the glass door, whose velvet curtain I slightly pushed aside so that I could look into the salon.

I was astonished to see Lucette's bosom completely uncovered. What charming breasts she possessed! They were two hemispheres as white as snow and firm as marble in the centre of which rose two little strawberries. The only movement they showed was from her regular breathing. My father was fondling them, kissing them and sucking them. In spite of his actions, she continued slumbering. Soon he began to remove all of her clothing, placing it on the edge of the bed. When he took off her shift, I saw two plump, rounded thighs of alabaster which he spread apart.

19

Then I made out a little vermilion slit adorned with a chestnut-brown tuft of hair. This he half opened, inserting his fingers which he vigorously manipulated in and out. Nothing roused her out of her lethargy.

Excited by the sight and instructed by the example, I imitated on myself the movements I saw and experienced sensations hitherto unknown to me. Laying her on the bed, my father came to the glass door to close it. I saved myself by hastening to the couch on which he had placed me. As soon as I was stretched out on the sheets, I began my rubbing, pondering what I had just viewed and profiting from what I had learned. I was on fire. The sensation I was undergoing increased in intensity, reaching such a height that it seemed my entire body and soul were concentrated in that one spot. Finally, I sank back in a state of exhausted ecstasy that enchanted me.

Returning to my senses, I was astonished to find myself almost soaked between my thighs. At first, I was very worried, but this anxiety was dispelled by the remembrance of the bliss I had just enjoyed. I fell into a deep sleep filled with dreams of my father caressing me. I was not yet awake when he came the next morning to awaken me with kisses which I eagerly returned.

Since that day, my governess and he seemed to have a secret understanding, although in the morning he did not remain with us as he formerly did. Of course, they had not the slightest suspicion that I was *au courant* as to what was going on, and lulled into a false security, during the day, they shamelessly flirted before retiring to my father's room where they remained for long periods of time.

With justice, I imagined that they were going to repeat what I had already seen, and my ideas did not go any further than that. Nevertheless, I was dying to view the same spectacle again. The reader can picture to himself the violent desire that was tormenting me. Finally came the moment when I was to learn everything.

Three days after the event I have just described, I took advantage of my father's absence to satisfy my burning curiosity. While Lucette was engaged in some task in another part of the house, I punctured a little hole in the silken curtain of the glass door.

I had not long to wait to profit from my stratagem. On my father's return, he immediately donned a flimsy dressing-gown and led to his room Lucette, who was in equally casual attire. They were careful to close the door and draw the curtain, but my preparations frustrated their precautions, at least in part. As soon as they were in the room, I was at the door with my face glued to the glass by the lifted curtain. The first person to meet my eyes was Lucette with her magnificent bosom completely bare. It was so seductive that I could not blame my father for immediately covering it with quick, eager kisses. Unable to hold himself back he tore off her clothing, and in a twinkling of the eye, skirt, corset and chemise were on the floor. How temptingly lovely she was in her natural state! I could not tear my eyes from her. She possessed all the charms and freshness of youth. Feminine beauty has a singular power and attraction for those of the same sex. My arms yearned to embrace those divine contours.

My father was soon in a state similar to his part-

21

ner's. My eyes were fixed on him, because I had never seen him that way before. Now he placed her on the divan, which I could not see from my observation post.

Devoured by curiosity, I threw caution to the winds. I lifted the curtain until I could see everything. Not a detail escaped my eyes, and they spared themselves not the slightest voluptuousness.

I was able to perceive clearly Lucette stretched out on the couch and her fully expanded slit between the two chubby eminences. My father displayed a veritable jewel, a big member, stiff, surrounded by hair at the root below which dangled two balls. The tip was a scarlet red. I saw it enter Lucette's slit, lose itself there, and then reappear. This in-and-out movement continued for some time. From the fiery kisses they exchanged, I surmised that they were in raptures. Finally, I noticed the organ completely emerge. From the carmine tip which was all wet spurted a white fluid on Lucette's flat belly.

How the sight aroused me! I was so excited and carried away by desires I had not yet known that I attempted, at least partially, to participate in their delirium.

So entranced was I by the tableau that I remained too long and my imprudence betrayed me. My father, who had been too preoccupied with Lucette, now, disengaging himself from Lucette's arms, saw the partially lifted curtain. On spotting me, he wrapped himself in his robe as he approached the door. I hastily withdrew, but he raised the drape and discovered me trying to beat a retreat.

He stationed himself at the door while Lucette was

dressing. Seeing that he remained motionless, I fancied that he had not noticed anything. Still curious to know what was going on, I returned to the curtain. My astonishment when I met his face on the other side can be imagined. I was thunderstruck with fright.

By this time, Lucette had her clothes back on. My father pretended that nothing was amiss. Reminding Lucette of certain errands she had to carry out, he dismissed her, and I was alone with him.

When he came up to me, I was trembling and pale with fear. But, to my great surprise, instead of castigating me, he took me in his arms and covered me with a hundred kisses.

'Calm yourself, my dear Laurette,' he comforted me. 'Who in the world could have inspired the terror I see in your eyes? You need have no fear, my darling. You know that I have never harmed you. All I ask of you now is the truth. At this moment, I want you to consider me a friend rather than your father. Laura, I am your friend, and I beseech you to be sincere with me. Don't conceal anything from me. Tell me what you were doing when I was with Lucette and the reason for your peeking around this curtain. If you are honest, you will not have any reason to repent. If you aren't, my warm feelings for you will vanish and you can count on the convent.'

The mere mention of the final word had always filled me with dread. What I had heard of the life in those retreats! I mentally contrasted life there to that with my father. Besides, I had no doubt that I had witnessed everything. Finally, from past experience, I knew the wisdom of avowing everything to him, and I blurted out the entire truth.

23

Each detail I told him and each tableau I retraced, far from igniting his wrath, was repaid with kisses and caresses. I hesitated, nevertheless, at confessing the new, delicious experiences I had procured by myself, but he suspected them.

'Darling Laurette, you still haven't told me all,' he remarked, as he passed his hands over my derriere and kissed me. 'You should not hide anything from me. Give me the whole story.'

With some reluctance, I admitted that I had imitated his friction movements with Lucette, which had produced in me the most wonderful sensations. Even though I got all wet from doing it, I had repeated it three or four times, always with the same pleasure.

'But, dear Laura,' he cried, 'seeing what I put into Lucette, didn't you get the idea of inserting your finger into yourself?'

'No, Papa, the thought never crossed my mind.'

'Don't try to deceive me,' he warned. 'You can't hide anything from me. Come over here so I can see if you are telling the truth.'

'Honestly, Papa, I have told you the truth,' I protested.

Using the most endearing words with me, he led me into his bedroom, where he stretched me out on a couch. He lifted up my skirt and examined me carefully. Then, slightly opening my narrow slit, he tried to penetrate it with his little finger. The screams from the pain he was causing me made him stop.

'It is all inflamed, my child. Nevertheless, I recognize that you have not lied to me. The redness undoubtedly is due to the friction you committed on yourself while I was with Lucette.'

Now that I had lost my fear, I even told him that I could not obtain the pleasure I was looking for. The sincerity of my mouth was rewarded by a kiss from his. Then he lowered it, and with his tongue, tickled a certain spot that made me squeal with delight. I found this kind of caress new and heavenly. To bring my raptures to a peak he produced that member I had seen before. Involuntarily, I took it with one hand, while with the other, I opened his robe. He made no objection. I regarded with admiration and fondled that joyous instrument that I had seen disappear into Lucette's interior. How pleasing and unusual it was! From the first moment I touched it, I instinctively realized that it was the originator of pleasure. It went up and down in rhythm with the movement of my hand, which covered and uncovered the skin of the tip. Imagine my surprise when, after several moments of this sport, I saw gush out the same fluid that had flooded Lucette's thighs. As the last drops oozed, I noticed that he was trembling all over. I was happy that I had given a pleasure which I partially shared.

When I released my sticky hand, he resumed his previous game with his tongue. I was dying of an ineffable bliss. I was suffocating, but he continued.

'Dear Papa, stop it!' I pleaded. 'I can't stand it any longer.'

I fainted in his arms.

From that time on, everything became clear to me. What I had guessed before became a certainty. It seemed that the instrument I was touching was the magic key to understanding. Because of that organ, my father became even dearer to me. And my sentiments for him were returned in like measure.

He led me back to my room, where my governess appeared a few moments later. I did not have the slightest idea of what he was about to say to her.

'Lucette, from now on it is senseless to watch our step with Laura, for she knows everything.'

Then he repeated to her everything I had related to him and showed her the curtain. She appeared very disturbed, but I threw my arms around her neck, and my embraces, along with the reasons I gave her, quickly dissipated the embarrassment she had evinced. Kissing us both, he told Lucette not to leave me out of her sight. He left, returning an hour later with a woman who, as soon as she was in the room, made me completely disrobe and took my measurements for a sort of garment, the form of use of which I could not guess.

When it came time to go to bed, my father put me in Lucette's bed, admonishing her to keep an eye on me. Once again he departed, only to return a few minutes later and crawl in the same bed with us. I was between the two of them. My father held me in a tight hug. Covering with his hand the space between my legs, he prevented me from putting mine at that spot. I took his instrument, which surprised me because it was so limp and moist. I had never seen it in this pitiable state, imagining that it was always swollen, stiff and erect. But in my hand it was no longer slow in regaining the condition in which I knew it.

Lucette, who perceived what we were doing, was shocked.

'What you are doing with Laurette is outrageous,' she reproved him. 'Especially since you are her father.'

'You are partially right, Lucette,' he replied. 'But it is a secret that I wish to confide to you. It is to Laura's own interest that she keep her silence. Circumstances make it necessary that I tell you both.

'I had known her mother only fifteen days when I married her. The very first day after the wedding, I discovered her condition, but I considered it the wisest course to pretend not to notice it. In order that dates could not be put together, I took her to a distant province. After four months, Laura entered the world with all the vigour and health of a normal nine month infant. For six months more, I remained in that province, after which I brought the two back home. Now you recognize that this child who is so dear to me is not my own daughter in the strict sense of the word. Although she is not bound to me by flesh and blood, she is as dear to me as if she were.'

Then I immediately recalled the reply he had made to my mother's reproaches. The silence she maintained no longer appeared strange.

'But how could you have acted in such a way towards your wife?' Lucette wanted to know.

'Oh, I was never close to my wife,' my father nonchalantly answered. 'The Count de Norval, to whom Laura owes her entry into this life, is a likeable nobleman, a fine figure of a man with a handsome face, possessing those qualities that interest women. I wasn't the least bit surprised to learn that my wife had

27

succumbed to his attack. However, she was unable to marry him, for her parents did not find him wealthy enough for her. But if Laura is not my daughter by blood, the affection I have conceived for this adorable child renders her perhaps even more dear to me.

'Nevertheless, because of the mother's falsity I never approached her. I had an antipathy for her that I could not overcome. That is why I turned all my love to the innocent child.'

Lucette lavished on me hugs and kisses which told me that all her prejudices had been effaced. Warmly I returned her tokens of affection, even taking her enticing breasts and kissing and sucking the pink tips. My father stretched his hand to her and met mine, which he passed over Lucette's stomach and her thighs. Now my hand was guided over the fleece, the *mons Veneris*, and the crevice. I soon learned the names of all these portions of the female anatomy. Then I put my finger on the spot where I thought I would cause her pleasure. There I came across something rather hard and distended.

'Good, Laura!' my father complimented me. 'You are holding the most sensitive part. Move your hand without relinquishing the clitoris while I stick my finger in her little cunt.'

Lucette, her arm about me, caressing my buttocks, took my father's prick and introduced it between my thighs, but he did not put it in nor did he make the slightest movement. Soon my governess was at the peak of pleasure. Her kisses multiplied and her sighs became moans.

'Stop! That's enough!' she moaned. 'Faster! Put it

in all the way, my dearest. My God, I am coming! This is the end.'

How these expressions of voluptuousness delighted me. I felt that her cunt was all damp. My father's finger came out, all covered with what she had discharged. I was beside myself with excitement. Taking Lucette's hand, I brought it to between my legs so that she would do to me what I had done for her, but my father, covering my mound with his hand, stopped her. He was too much of a libertine not to be sparing of his pleasures, and he moderated his desires, leaving me up in the air by recommending us to calm ourselves. We fell asleep, our arms interlaced, plunged into the sweetest intoxication. I had never spent such a delicious night.

When the rays of the morning sun brought us back to life, Lucette and I looked at each other. Then I noticed a note pinned to the chair. It was from Papa who wrote that he would be away all day, but he knew that Lucette would take good care of me. Excitedly, I reminded my companion that it was the servants' day off and we would be alone. We beamed at each other with radiant smiles.

I nestled closer to her for I loved to sniff the sharp odour that came from her svelte body. I nuzzled my nose between her breasts to breathe it in more deeply. It reminded me of carrots, and every time I smelled it, I quivered with excitement.

'I think I am too fat,' she remarked. 'Don't you think so?'

She lifted up her nightgown as if to prove her point. I wondered why she thought she was so fat. Her legs were lovely and well-rounded, and her buttocks dimpled and charming. There was not the trace of a bulge on her body. The magnificent breasts were so heavy that I wondered how they could jut out as they did. And I could not keep my eyes from the clump of luxuriant hair under her armpits. When she turned her back to me, I saw her derriere, two superb hemispheres that must have been fashioned in heaven.

'You are not too plump,' I affirmed again. 'On the contrary, it seems to me that you are just right.'

She gave me a pleased pout as she got out of bed and walked to the desk with the cheeks of her bottom swaying seductively from side to side. She returned to the warm bed with a large album of art reproductions, many of them of nude women and in co!"ur.

'Look,' she said, pointing out one to me. 'She is far more slender than I.'

'Yes, but on the other hand, this woman by Rubens is far plumper than you.'

'That may be so, but I still should lose some weight. A massage does the trick, and you can help me if you wish.'

'I? . . . Massage you? I have never done that before. . . .'

'There's nothing difficult about it. It's just the sort of favour one does for a friend. And you are my friend, aren't you?'

I puffed up with pride at that. But I felt a certain uneasiness not unmingled with anticipation.

'And I have just the thing for a massage,' she added with a slight blush.

'What do you mean by that?' I asked her in some puzzlement. 'I always thought you massaged with the hands.'

'There are also appliances that are helpful in removing excess flesh. . . . I'll get mine.'

She went to her room and came back with a rubber glove covered with bumps. It reminded me of the skin of a toad. Lucette ran it up and down my arm. It gave me goose-pimples but the sensation was not unpleasant.

'How do you like it, Laura?' she asked with a glint in her eyes.

Then she applied it on her shoulders, her arms and above her breasts. I felt a twinge of envy.

'I hope I'll be able to use it correctly and not hurt you. I have never seen anything like that before. If I am clumsy, please forgive me.'

'There's no danger, but I'll have to lie down.'

Now she was on her stomach, lovelier than ever, particularly since her lush body was reflected in the wall mirror.

'Now start at the top of my back,' she ordered.

This promised to be fun. The skin quivered and turned pink where I touched it with my gloved hand. Lucette remained motionless, her head between her arms and her hair over her ears. After vigorously treating the glorious buttocks, she suddenly turned over.

'And now the breasts, Laura.'

Nervously, I did as I was bid. The gorgeous globes shivered as much as my hand. Taking my hand, she made it descend to one of the rosy nipples.

'Look,' she said.

To my astonishment, I saw it dilate, swell, get hard and jut out. It became a crimson mountain peak. Then she made me put it on the other. As I rubbed

31

the mound, there occurred, to my uneasiness, the same phenomenon.

'I'm in heaven,' Lucette blissfully sighed. 'That's the way nipples become when they are handled that way. Now the belly, Laura, and the hips. It is so wonderful when you do it, and I can't tell you how grateful I am.'

My eyes were glued to the hard breasts, the hollow navel, and the dark triangle whose hair extended almost all the way up to her waist. Mentally, I compared myself with her. I had only a pitiful little fleece there, while hers was a carpet, a beautiful luxurious Persian rug.

I revolved the glove on her stomach around her navel. I did not dare get too close to the triangle, for I was afraid that it might get tangled in the matted hair and hurt her. She was lasciviously wiggling her hips with her eyes shut. It was obvious that she was in an incipient ecstasy. Her toes contracted and sometimes her knee twitched when I got too close to the erogenous zone.

'Now between the thighs,' she murmured without opening her eyes. I observed that her nipples were straining more than ever.

Reassured that I was giving her pleasure, I redoubled my efforts as I rubbed the glove on the silky skin. But I could not keep my eyes from the luxuriant thicket. I wondered how what it was concealing would look like.

I was sure that mine would be put to shame in comparison.

The more I kept at it, the more pleasure it gave me. I was not a little disappointed when she told

32

me to stop. Reading my feelings in my face, Lucette laughed.

'I can see that you are unwilling to give up, dearest Laura,' she said. 'But don't be disappointed, I need a bit of a breathing spell, for that puts my nerves on edge. Why, you are perspiring! Take off your night-gown. You'll be much more comfortable. I don't think you are bashful after last night.'

'A little,' I confessed, but I followed her suggestion.

'Completely nude, that's the way I want you,' she breathed. 'I adore nudity. I can never get enough of looking at myself naked in a mirror. I never feel alone when I can regard my reflection in the mirror. We were so excited last night that I did not notice what adorable little breasts you have. And what promise your delicate figure shows!'

The compliments gave me so much pleasure that I could not conceal my blushes. I wanted to bury my face in her arms. Hurling myself at her, I feverishly kissed her cheeks. She looked at me straight in the eyes, holding my gloved hands in hers.

'Continue,' she commanded.

Eagerly, too eagerly I resumed my task. She promptly rebuked me.

'Not so fast and not so hard,' she scolded. 'Just run it gently over my whole body. Do you understand?'

Now I did not press down so hard. Lucette closed her eyes in contentment.

'It's like a lover's caress,' she murmured.

In the mirror I could see the bed, the naked body of my new friend, and mine which was trembling and twitching. At the same time, I regarded my little, rounded, apple-like breasts with their tawny tips, and

33

came to the conclusion that I was not too bad. Perhaps I was not as abundant as Lucette, but I was not her inferior. My charms were just on a smaller scale.

Now her mouth was agape and her breathing laboured. I twisted the glove on her stomach and breasts. Each time I touched a nipple, she gave a start, convulsively lifted a knee, and spread her legs. When I took the rubber glove away, she became motionless.

'Farther down, Laura,' she whispered as if I were neglecting her spread thighs. I massaged the inside of them. From the knees, the glove gradually ascended to the groin and the buttocks.

It was then that I noticed a curious movement of her pelvis. She kept lifting and dropping it in fits and starts. At the same time, she was rattling in her throat and trying to catch her breath.

Going up still farther, I put the glove on the hairs of her mound. Her jerky movements became more agitated and vehement. Suddenly, she grasped my hand and spread her legs as far apart as she could.

'There . . . there!' she panted. 'Don't take it away. Keep it where it is. How good it feels!'

I was a little afraid at the way she was flopping about. Her legs shot up in the air and then limply dropped. I watched her face. It was livid, contorted in a grimace that deformed her features. Horrified, I tried to take away the glove, but she held it firmly in position. I wondered what was wrong with her. After more convulsions, both her body and face relaxed. For several minutes she remained without life or movement.

When I took off the glove, wondering if I had hurt her with it, she opened her eyes and smiled sweetly at me.

'It was sheer bliss,' she said dreamily.

I was dumbfounded. How could she say a thing like that when I had seen how she was suffering?

'You don't understand, I see,' she told me. 'And I can't explain. It is something that you have to experience yourself. Do you want me to massage you in turn?'

'But won't it hurt?' I timidly asked. 'You were groaning and moaning so, and the words you said, I was really afraid.'

'Do you love me that much, Laura?'

'Yes, yes, I love you . . . more than anything.'

In such gambols we spent the day and night.

When Lucette and I awoke, we were still locked in each other's arms. My father entered, bringing with him the woman who had come the previous day. My surprise and chagrin were great when she put on me morocco leather shorts which descended from my hips to slightly above my knees. They were loosely fitting and not constraining at all. The girdle fitted me perfectly around the waist and two straps holding up the shorts passed over my shoulders. They could be loosened or tightened at will. The girdle had an opening in the front that extended four inches down. Along this aperture, there were eyelets on both sides through which my father passed a little chain of delicately worked silver gilt which he locked with a little key.

'My dear Laura, adorable child, I am greatly concerned about your health and your preservation.

Chance has instructed you already in that which should only have learned at the age of eighteen. Consequently, I have to take precautions against your premature knowledge and the inclinations you have by nature and love. In time, you'll come to share my judgment, but nothing you will say now will change my mind.'

At first I was infuriated, and I could not conceal my ill temper, but on reflection I realized the gratitude I owed my father.

He had foreseen everything. At the bottom of these shorts was a little silver gondola the size of the space between my thighs. In this my little mound was completely encased, while on either side it covered my little cunt and my asshole. It was not uncomfortable. It was so fashioned that I could perform my natural functions without any inconvenience, but it was impossible to insert my finger into the narrow aperture to masturbate, which was what my father desired to prevent above all things.

Since that time, I have often seen such contraptions on boys to keep them from wasting their virility before their time, for no matter how one keeps an eye on them, they go their own awkward way, much to their regret in later years.

For two years, my father removed the shorts every evening, which Lucette cleaned after washing me. After ascertaining that the chastity contrivance was not hurting me, he put it back on. From that day until I was eighteen, I had to wear the thing night and day. But during that period I learned a great deal, for I was curious by nature. Each year saw my knowledge increase, and I was indefatigable in my studies.

I had become used to my imprisonment, and the thought that one day I would be rid of it made it bearable.

Among the questions I most frequently asked him was the reason for my restraint and what were the precautions he was taking with regard to me, for he kept postponing my freedom until I was older. It was on my eighteenth birthday that he finally satisfied my curiosity.

'Now I think it is about time, dear Papa, for you to tell my why I have to wear this horrible thing, especially since you keep telling me how much you love me. Lucette is happier than I, and surely you care for her less than you do for me. I insist on knowing why you have done this to me.'

With that, I stamped my foot and shook my curls in determination.

'I have to agree that you are no longer a child, and it is time that I should give you an explanation. With men, nature starts to manifest itself around the age of fifteen or sixteen, but it reaches its peak at seventeen or eighteen. When one diverts its operations by premature and numerous discharges, so that this development is weakened, the results are felt for the rest of one's life.

'It is the same with women. If they waste their resources at too early an age, they will die early, become enfeebled and languid, and suffer from depression. They become so thin that they fall easy prey to tuberculosis. As a result, they are not able to enjoy the sweetest pleasure life has to offer.

'Because of my deep and tender love for you, dearest Laurette, I wanted to keep you from such a terrible fate, and what I did to you was for your own good.'

Although I had a deep-seated penchant for pleasure and voluptuousness, I had no desire to obtain them at such a price, and the prospect, as painted by my father, frightened me.

'I recognized such inclinations in you,' my father continued, 'and I knew that reason would have no power against your innate sensuousness. That is why I wanted to protect you against yourself, and I have to tell you that it is not yet time to set you free, for there are still many dangers lurking which you cannot cope with now.'

The thought of impaired health and the fear of an early death were vivid in my imagination. Nevertheless, what I had seen him do with Lucette and the way he lived with her weakened somewhat the impact of his dire predictions. I could not help but express to him my doubts.

'Why don't you take the same precautions with Lucette as you do with me, Papa? Why do you give her so often what you absolutely forbid me?'

'Why, my daughter,' he replied, 'Lucette is a fully formed woman. Besides, if she retains within her too much fluid of life, it would ravage her health by stagnating. Moreover, it would hinder the circulation of her blood. When that happens, a woman becomes dizzy, demented, exhausted and delirious. You can see horrible examples in certain nunneries where the sisters are so closely watched that they have no outlets for their natural desires. Remedies have been attempted, but the results have been worse than the cure.

'With some women, the ardour of temperament is quenched earlier than with others, and I want yours to continue as long as possible. When the time is right, you will have no cause to repent of your long continence and you will receive the life-giving fluid as copiously as Lucette does. Now you can understand my behaviour towards you.'

'Papa, for that is how I shall always call you,' I protested, 'I can understand your reasoning, but how long do I have to wait until you do with me what you do with her? I can hardly wait for that moment, since I am so eager to satisfy your desires to the fullest extent.'

'Wait until nature speaks more loudly,' he counselled me. 'Wait just a little longer when you will have the force. Then, Laurette, I shall receive the full measure of tenderness you have for me. You will allow me to pluck that rare blossom that I have been so carefully cultivating, but that moment has not ·yet come.'

His words were etched in my memory, and his reasoning seemed based on such a sound foundation, his readiness to answer my questions openly prompted me to query him further. I had always wondered about Lucette, who was in such a profound sleep the first time I found them together. To me, it was a mystery that I wanted cleared up. Finally, one day, I asked him.

'Papa, why was Lucette sleeping so soundly the first day you bared her breasts and why didn't she wake up while you were doing everything you wanted with her? Was she really asleep or was she just pretending?'

'She was really asleep,' he replied. 'It is a secret, but I am going to let you in on it, for it will be a lesson to you. I'll admit that for some time I was torn with desire. I became excited with you, but you could afford me no satisfaction. I liked Lucette at first sight, and I found her agreeable in every way. But seeing that she was hesitant about giving in to me, I determined on a bold step. I put some sleeping powder in the glass of liqueur that I offered her. You saw the effect. But I was not satisfied with that. I was afraid that if she woke up, surprise and anger would ruin all my plans. In order to prevent that, I had prepared in advance a potion designed to arouse all her sensuousness. That is what is called a love philtre. After I had put you in my bed, I went back to get several drops which I rubbed on her mound, her clitoris and her lips. This liquid has the power to excite even the most enfeebled and give him an erection if he smears it on his organ shortly before he enters combat.

'Lucette had not been asleep an hour before she awoke, feeling an itching, a burning, and a passion which nothing could extinguish. She did not seem surprised to see me in her arms, for she passed hers around my neck. Far from opposing my caresses and desires, for she herself was deeply moved, she voluntarily spread her legs wide. It was a matter of seconds before I was revelling in the most exquisite delights that I made her share. I was attentive to the consequences that could ensue, for at the moment when I sensed rapture ready to shoot out like a flame, I withdrew, inundating her mound and belly with a copious

40

libation, an offering to the altar at which I was then worshipping.

'From that time, Lucette has always lent herself to my desires. It was because of her complacency, my inattention, and the curiosity I did not suspect in one your age that you discovered our secret. She does not know what I have just taught you, and you must keep my confidence.'

'You need have no worry on that score, dear Papa,' I assured him. 'But please finish your story. Aren't you afraid of getting her with child if you don't always pull out in time? Are you always in control of yourself? Aren't you sometimes carried away by ecstasy? And the fear that one has for the consequences, doesn't that diminish the pleasure?'

'Ah, my dear child,' he sighed, 'where your imagination doesn't take you! I recognize fully that I should not conceal anything from you. I don't run any risk with you, for you are intelligent beyond your years.'

'First of all, semen which is not shot into the matrix bears no fruit. There are ways to prevent it from reaching its goal, but you will learn about this when you are older. I use an infallible method with Lucette which enables her to give herself up to her passions without any worry. Before we start our lovemaking, she fits herself out with a special device which makes it impossible for her to produce children.'

I nodded in understanding.

Such were some of the conversations we had, mostly for my benefit. It goes without saying that they were frequently interrupted by kisses and caresses. Libertine books of all kinds were freely placed in my hands for me to peruse, but those that pertained to my sex

41

were stressed. We discussed religion, and according to my father, God is 'incomprehensible; he is felt rather than known. He demands our respect and despises our speculations.' My father reduced morality to, 'Do unto others as you would have them do unto you,' or 'Do not do unto others what you would not have them do unto you.'

As I pursued these studies, my figure was filling out; my pointed breasts had acquired an admirable amplitude. Every day I showed their progress to Lucette and my father, who gladly kissed them at my request. I put their hands on them to show them how firm and full they were. Finally, I made no secret of the fact that I was at the end of my patience. Never having had to curb my temper, I no longer listened to or followed anything but the voice of nature. I could see that this banter was arousing my father.

'You're getting an erection, dear Papa. Come over here,' I ordered, and placed him in Lucette's arms.

Although I was deeply aroused, I still found enjoyment in their pleasures. She and I lived in the closest intimacy; she cherished me as much as I loved her. I slept ordinarily with her, and I never failed her when my father was absent. I fulfilled my role the best I could. While hugging her, I sucked her lips and the buttons of her Junoesque breasts, and I kissed the cheeks of her derriere and her smooth belly and her delicious *mons Veneris*. I stroked her entire body. Often my fingers took the place that I could not supply her with, and I plunged her into agonies of rapture which was a delight to see. My good will and complaisance caused her to feel for me an affection that is impossible to describe. During our lovemaking, many times she.

had noticed me violently animated and she assured me that she ardently desired to procure for me the same ecstasies I was giving her.

'Yes, my dear Laura,' she breathed, 'when the great moment arrives, I plan on having a grand celebration. I can't wait for it. I have the feeling that the time is not far off. Your delightful breasts are just about perfectly rounded. Your arms and legs are shapely and your mound, already covered with a soft fleece, is rising. Your pretty little cunt is now a rosy pink. In your eyes, I see that something which puts you in the ranks of womanhood. Last spring, you saw some preludes of eruptions which are going to be a fact very quickly.'

Indeed, in a short time I felt more sluggish, my head was heavy, my eyes lustreless; I had pains in my back and attacks of colic. After eight days of this, Lucette found the gondola covered with blood. My father, on seeing this, did not put it back on me, for they had foreseen this. I was told of my situation. For about a week, I remained almost in a stupor, after which I was as gay and full of health as I had been before.

My happiness at my newfound freedom was indescribable. I was beside myself with joy as I threw my arms around Lucette's neck.

'How happy I am going to be!' I cried.

Then I ran to my father, whom I likewise embraced, and exultantly told him: 'Here I am in the state in which you desire me. How happy I shall be if I can arouse your desires and satisfy them! My bliss is to belong entirely to you. My love and tenderness are the goal of my felicity.'

Taking me in his arms, he sat me on his knees. With

what passion he returned the embraces I bestowed on him. He squeezed and kissed my woman's breasts; he sucked my lips; his tongue sought mine; and my buttocks and my cunt were both victims of his feverish hands.

'The moment has finally come, dearest Laurette,' he panted, 'this blessed instant when your tenderness and mine are going to be united in the breast of voluptuousness. I want to have your maidenhead this very day, to pluck the flower that has just blossomed. I owe it to your love, and your sentiments towards me put an inestimable value on the offering you are about to make. But I should warn you that if ineffable bliss follows our embraces and kisses, the moment when I become master of that charming rosebud, you will be pricked by some thorns that will cause you pain.'

'What does it matter?' I exclaimed. 'Make me suffer. Slash me until I bleed if you wish. I cannot make enough sacrifices for you. Your pleasure and your satisfaction are the sole object of my desires.'

My eyes were sparkling. The ever-helpful Lucette, wishing to cooperate in the bloodletting of the victim, showed herself as eager as if she had been herself the executioner. They lifted me up and carried me into a chamber that they had prepared for the time when I would be ready. The light of day was completely banished from it. In a recess surrounded by mirrors was a bed covered with a blue satin covering, and on it was a cushion of fire-red silk which was to be the sacrificial altar.

Quickly, Lucette exposed all the charms nature had bestowed on me. I, the sacrifice, was adorned only with crimson ribbons which she knotted above my elbows and waist. I resembled another Venus. Another ribbon was woven in my loose hair. Without any hesitation, I threw myself on the couch.

Regarding myself in the mirrors, I found myself more beautiful than I would be had I been wearing any ornaments. I felt very satisfied with myself. My skin was of a dazzling whiteness; my little but firm pink nipples rose proudly from the enticing breasts; a delicate fleece shaded the plump little mound, which, slightly open, revealed a clitoris stuck out from between two lips called pleasure and voluptuousness. Add to that a svelte, shapely figure, slender legs ending in dainty feet, buttocks like little apples, and a small of the back with all the freshness of Hebe. If I had been competing against the three goddesses, Paris certainly would have bestowed the apple of victory on me. Such was the praise that Lucette and my father vied in heaping on me. I was bursting with pride. The more I thought myself lovely, the more they encouraged me in the belief. My father in particular could not get over my charms. He examined and admired me. His hands and ardent lips were all over my body. We were like two young lovers who up until now had met only with difficulty and who were going to get recompense for their patience and affection.

I so wanted to see him in the state I was. At my insistence, he quickly ripped off his clothing with the assistance of Lucette. He arranged me on the bed so that my derriere was on the cushion. In my hand I held the sacred blade that in an instant was to immolate my virginity. This prick that I was passionately caressing was of a stiffness to prove to me that it would surely pierce the rose that he had so carefully tended for such a long time. My imagination was burning with desire. My cunt was on fire and calling for that dear prick which I immediately set on its path.

We were locked in each other's arms, glued to each other. Our mouths and tongues devoured one another. I noticed that he was holding himself back, but passing my legs over his rump and squeezing as hard as I could, I gave an upward thrust with my backside so that he went in as far as he could go. The pain I felt and the scream that escaped from my lips were signs of his victory.

Inserting her hand between us, Lucette stroked my cunt and with the other hand tickled my asshole. The melange of pain and pleasure, and the flowing fuck and blood raised me to paradise, to an ineffable sensuousness.

I was suffocating; I was expiring. My arms and legs became limp and my head sagged. I was no longer among the living. But I took a delectation in these excesses that I could barely stand. What an exquisite state! Soon I was roused from my sweet lethargy by renewed caresses. He kissed me, sucked me, and massaged my breasts, the cheeks of my derriere, and my mount. He lifted my legs into the air to have the pleasure of regarding from a different angle my backside, my cunt and the ravages he had committed. His prick that I was still clutching and his testicles which Lucette was stroking were soon restored to their former rigidity. The former he quickly inserted into me. Now that the passage had been made easier, his penetration was nothing but sheer joy. Goodhearted Lucette renewed her titillations, and I again fell back into the lascivious apathy I had just experienced.

My father, proud of his triumph and delighted at the willingness with which I had succumbed, took the bloodstained cushion that was under me and embraced it as the trophy of his victory.

'Dear Laura,' he said as he tenderly lay down on the pillow, 'good Lucette has multiplied your pleasures. Don't you think it would be the right thing to do to let her join in our frolics?'

I threw my arms around her neck and pulled her down with me on the bed, where I lifted up her skirt and found her all damp.

'How aroused you must have been,' I said understandingly. 'Now I wish to give you at least a portion of the bliss I have just enjoyed.'

Taking my father's hand, I introduced one finger into her and he pushed it in and out while I caressed her. It was a matter of instants before she was in that state of ecstasy from which I had just emerged.

By now, we were soaked in sweat, and Papa suggested we all take a bath together. Lucette and I enthusiastically agreed. The three of us rushed to the large tub which Papa had foresightedly filled with lukewarm water beforehand. Papa and Lucette were the first to get in and then I. Being the youngest, it was I who soaped them down. Papa complimented me on my enthusiasm for my task, which I did not find irksome in the least. I paid special attention to the opulent breasts and Junoesque derriere of my governess and the shaggy hair on the chest and at the bottom of the stomach of my supposed sire. His sex was the particular object of my care. As a joke, I inserted the bar of soap into Lucette's slit. This caused general merriment.

After I bestowed a filial kiss on Papa's virility, it was my turn to receive their attention. First smearing me from chin to knees, he started a systematic fondling to which I reacted with ardour. Then we rinsed ourselves with fresh water to get rid of the mucous irritations caused by the soap. Once we were dried, Papa felt in a jovial mood.

'Lucette, let's show little Laura some games she has not seen.'

'Oh yes, let's,' Lucette cried, clapping her hands. 'But Laura has to help.'

'Indeed she does.'

Papa sat on the bidet, which I was ordered to fill with water up to the brim. His testicles and backside were completely wetted. Then I had to sit behind him with my arms around his waist. Under Lucette's guidance, my right hand began to stroke his masculinity while the left squeezed and released the testicles. Finally, my finger was led into his rear aperture. He gave a start and squeal of joy.

Lucette went back into the bedroom and returned with two thick books which she placed before Papa's feet, one on each side of the bidet. Then she stepped on them, placing her hands on his shoulders. In this position, the matted shaggy mound, already moist with desire, was directly in front of his face. Without hesitation, he darted his tongue into the inviting grotto. For better penetration, he firmly clutched the two callipygian hemispheres of his lovely Lucette.

Releasing one of them, he dipped his finger into the vagina which he vigorously stirred.

Now the only sounds heard were the grunts of the lovers and the slipslop of Papa's tongue lapping the vulva and the clitoris to the tempo of my hands fondling his sex and swollen sacks. So that I could take part in the sport, Papa withdrew his hand from Lucette and began to titillate my excited inflamed button.

It was Papa who reached bliss first. His initial jet was so powerful that it splattered the wall and drenched Lucette's thighs. The succeeding spurts plopped into the bidet water like hail stones on a pond. The sound triggered Lucette and myself to release our fluids, which we did with long lingering sighs.

We were so exhausted that some repose was necessary. Lucette and Papa were soon dozing in the bed, while I went to my room. When I came back, I saw that they were just awakening. I hid behind the curtain. Lucette was smiling affectionately at Papa and her affectionate embraces soon produced another erection. At the sight of the angry organ, she felt overwhelming desire. With a jerk of her powerful derriere, she threw off the sheets and blankets, pressed her fleshy lips on the hirsute torso, nibbling the nipples, and slid her mouth down to the navel. One of her hands blindly clutched the pulsating virility. Getting off the bed and kneeling on the rug, she thrust her head between Papa's dangling legs.

When Papa espied me, I gave a little cry of surprise, covered my eyes with my hands, and taking off my shift, clambered into the bed with Papa. I shoved a

49

pillow under his head and put my thighs over him. I dug my hands into his wavy hair.

Papa was unable to resist the temptation of the delicious slit, which I had slightly perfumed, right in front of his nose. As his tongue automatically thrust itself into it, I gave a shriek of delight and squeezed his head tightly between my two legs. I was beside myself with pleasure at the cadence of his tongue which I regulated with the up-and-down movement of my pelvis. I took particular joy in rubbing my irritated clitoris on his nose.

Abandoning her fellation, Lucette got up and bestrode Papa on the edge of the bed. This change of position somewhat cooled Papa's ardour, for he was on the verge of ejaculating in Lucette's mouth if only she had continued her oral activity. After several downward thrusts, she was unable to hold back her orgasm and collapsed on my shoulders, gasping with pleasure. At that, I went into an almost uncontrollable spasm and gushed my inner glycerine into Papa's mouth.

Breathless, Lucette and I fell back in a near faint. Of the three of us, Papa was the only one who felt cheated, and he demanded recompense. He nodded at Lucette, who shook her head in refusal. There was only myself left, but I could see that he was reluctant to re-enter my cunt, still tight and narrow in spite of my recent defloration. But he began to caress the labia and tickle the clitoris. He whispered a few words into Lucette's ear.

She promptly stretched out on the sheets and ordered me to get on top of her, back to belly. Then Lucette put her legs on mine, spreading her knees as far apart as she could. With this manoeuvre, she so widened my cunt that the interior gaped open. It was now child's play for Papa to insert his weapon into the still damp aperture.

I was delighted and more than ready for another bout. But still the memory of the first pain caused me worry. But like a skilled tactician, Papa launched a surprise attack. His first rhythmic thrusts were barely perceptible. It seemed that the hymen had again erected its barrier. He stopped for several seconds before starting again his methodical boring, gradually gaining a few centimetres at a time. When I relaxed, he pursued his advantage to win a little more ground. Now he was at the halfway mark with another victory in sight if he did not make a misstep.

Now he employed another method of ingress, this time a corkscrew movement. In my delirium, I could see the expression of triumph on his face when he felt that it was succeeding.

Success crowned his efforts. The fleshy sword was in to the bottom of me, in spite of the narrowness of the contested valley.

I was groaning with a pleasure I had never before experienced – the first time the pain had blunted the bliss – and marvelling at the sensation in the depths of my stomach. It was a victory that Papa could well be proud of. The look on his face seemed to say: 'Ah, my little one. I finally got you. You got me to stick my tongue in your cunt, but in turn you got a prick that is going to give you a squirt you'll never forget.'

I was conquered.

I was dripping wet inside and it eased the action of his piston. Now he went at his work in a rage. His belly slapped the victim's with every jab. Sensing the approach of the supreme moment, Lucette released my lips and inserted her finger to Papa's slimy rear hole.

The reaction was immediate. In a roar of triumph and voluptuousness, Papa stopped his frenzied injections and stiffened as he shot the hot jets of his sperm into the ecstatic womb which answered his stream with one of hers.

Ah, how many charms that day held for me! It was the most wonderful one in all my life and the first in which I savoured the delights of sensuousness to the full. This memory which causes me so much pleasure brings at the same time the bitterest regrets. But I want to forget about that for the time being.

There reigned in the room an agreeable sultriness, and I was so comfortable the way I was that I did not want to put anything on. I was in such a gay mood that I wanted to have supper naked. Lucette, always on the alert, had had the good sense to dismiss all the servants, and she prepared the meal herself after locking all the doors. Still I was not satisfied. I wanted her to be as we were, and without further ado, I tore off her few garments. She made an enchanting picture. Thus we sat at the table. Seated between the two of us, my father was the object of our fondlings which he gave back in good measure. The mirrors multiplied the charm of the tableau we formed. Our moods and attitudes were varied by our sallies inspired by a delicate wine.

Under its influence our cunts became inflamed and Papa's prick resumed its old stiffness and firmness. In the state of mind we were in, the table no longer pleased us and we hurried back to the bed. During that day, which was consecrated to me, I was plunged once again into the delights of supreme voluptuousness. Papa lay on my left, his legs under my raised ones, and his prick proudly presented itself to the entrance.

Lucette stretched herself out on me, my head between her knees. Her delightful little cunt was just above my eyes; I half-opened it and tickled it while I stroked her buttocks which were stuck up in the air. Her stomach was grazing my breasts and her thighs were between my arms. All was calculated to ignite the flame of passion.

She spread wide the lips of my cunt which was now a deep red. I urged her to put the contraceptive into it so that my father could enjoy me and discharge into me without any worry.

My cunt hurt like anything, and the pain became even worse as soon as it was touched. In spite of this soreness, I endured the procedure with the knowledge that it would be succeeded by sensations more agreeable. Lucette conducted my father's prick onto the path from which she had removed all the dangers and which was now strewn only with flowers. He rushed along it, and quickly sank into the aperture. Her finger was also inside at the same time. I rendered her a similar service while my father was doing the same thing in her cunt with his finger that his prick was doing in mine.

These variations, these positions, and this multiplicity of personages and sensations in the preliminaries enhanced infinitely their delights. Simultaneously we felt them approaching, but ready to escape us like a flash of lightning, and we savoured them to their fullest extent. Now we began to feel fatigue. Lucette, who was the first to get up, set everything in order. As soon as she was back, we returned to the bed and, wrapped in one another's arms, fell back to sleep.

My disappointment that such joys were not to be had every day can be imagined. My father, always solicitous about the state of my health, ordered me back into the chastity belt.

'My dear Laurette,' he explained to me, 'I do not hide from you that I have misgivings about you and all of us. Your character is not yet sufficiently formed so that I can leave you to your own devices, and you are too dear to me for me not to guide your steps for a while longer. Nonetheless, you will have your pleasure from our lovemaking. You'll do it with us, and, in a certain manner, you will share our pleasure. Also, from time to time, we'll reserve for you a similar night, which you will find much more agreeable if you have to wait for it. Finally, if you wish to please me, you will lend yourself to what I desire of you, and you will comply without argument.'

That was his method of rendering my new imprisonment less unbearable.

Nineteen months had passed since that memorable evening when I learned to my sorrow that Lucette was leaving us. Her father, who lived in the provinces and was mortally ill, had summoned her for a last meeting. Her departure caused us the greatest regret. Our sincere tears mingled with hers. As for myself, I could not hold back my sobs, which finally subsided when she said she would return to us as quickly as she could. But shortly after the death of her father, she went into a decline from which it took two years for her to recover. Her father had left her a comfortable inheritance which made her much sought after by the young bachelors of the region, but she would have nothing to do with them. According to her letters, they formed such a contrast with my father that all those who paid her suit, she found absolutely revolting. Marriage was the furthest thing from her mind and her greatest wish was to return to us.

Nevertheless, urged by her mother and other relatives who praised the advantages to be found where she was, and the need that her infirm parent had of her, she was finally persuaded to remain with her family, much against her will, but only after consulting with my father in whom she had the greatest confidence.

Since the suitor who presented himself offered numerous advantages, my father felt himself obliged out of a sense of principle to advise her to accept him, a decision which he found extremely repugnant to make, for he confided in me several times that he had a presentiment of misfortune for her, but to which he could not lend credence, regarding it as a weakness. His foreboding was correct, however, for she died in her first childbirth.

Often I regretted the departure of Lucette, whose loss I regarded as my own, but I consoled myself in the arms of my dear and tender father. I had finally rid myself for good of that detestable attachment I had so often cursed. But what had happened to Lucette because of her excesses weighed heavily on me and made me realize how careful I would have to be because of my delicate constitution. I confided my misgivings to my father, with whom I slept every night. He was never far from me and he watched over me like a guardian angel, stopping me when I yielded to my desires with too much ardour.

After Lucette's departure, he had made some changes in his suite. For example, one could only enter my room by passing through his. Our beds touched against the same wall. Thus not even the servants had the slightest inkling of our frolics.

It was during one of those delightful nights that he enabled me to enjoy a new kind of pleasure, one of which I didn't have the slightest idea. It was marvellous.

'Dearest Laura,' he began. 'You have given me your first flower, but you possess another blossom that you owe me, one you cannot refuse me if you hold me dear.'

'Oh, Papa, you know the depth of my love for you,' I exclaimed. 'What do I have left that you want? Whatever it is, I give it to you with all my heart, and nothing would give me greater pleasure than for you to have it. Your happiness is my only goal.'

'Dear girl,' he replied, deeply moved. 'I am so delighted with you. Your generosity and nobility match your beauty and grace. The soul of voluptuousness resides in you. It presents itself in myriad forms on every part of your body. Your hands, mouth, armpits, breasts and derriere are all cunt.'

'Take your choice. You're the master, and I lend myself to your slightest desire,' I cried.

He made me turn on my left side with my buttocks

facing him. Moistening my asshole and the head of his prick, he inserted it, so very gently. The difficulty of the passage gave us nothing but a new path strewn with accumulated pleasures. Supporting my leg with his raised knee, he masturbated me, sticking his finger in my cunt from time to time. I was almost wild from this exhilaration on both sides. When he sensed that I was on the verge. he quickened his movements, which I seconded with mine. Then I felt the bottom of my backside inundated with a boiling fluid which produced, on my part, an abundant discharge. I relished an ineffable delight. It seemed as if all the parts of my body were fused into one spasm of lust. My convulsions and transports were all due to that incomparable sharp-pointed virility belonging to a man whom I adored.

'What a ravishing pleasure,' sighed my father. 'What do you have to say about it? Judging from your moans and movements, you must have enjoyed it as much as I.'

'Ah, Papa,' I breathed. 'It was infinite, new and strange. How can I put into words all the varied raptures I experienced? What happened before was as nothing to what I just now enjoyed.'

'In that case, my dear child, another time I will employ a dildo to give you new pleasures, ones that you never dreamed of.'

'Papa, what is a dildo?' I innocently asked.

'You'll see,' he mysteriously replied. 'But you'll have to wait until another day.'

The following day, the only thing I talked about was a dildo. I absolutely insisted on seeing one. My persistence was such that he finally acceded to my wishes. I was dumbfounded when he produced it, but I demanded that he try it out on me that very evening. I had to admit it was a poor substitute for the real thing.

There was not one variation of pleasure he did not show me and initiate me into. Sometimes he lay on me, his head between my thighs and mine between his knees. With his open, hot mouth, he covered the lips of my cunt and noisily and greedily sucked them. Then he stuck his tongue deep down between them or with the tip tickled my clitoris. In return, I sucked the head of his prick. Squeezing it with my lips, I soon had it all the way in my mouth. I wished I could have swallowed it. At the same time, I caressed his testicles, his belly, his thighs, and his rump.

'Everything is pleasure and delight, when two people love each other as tenderly and passionately as we do,' he was accustomed to say.

Such was the joyous existence I led after the departure of my beloved governess. Eight or nine months rolled by before I knew it. The only clouds on the horizon were the souvenirs of Lucette. I spent happy days and happier nights in the arms of my adored father whom I overwhelmed with my kisses and embraces. How he cherished me! My soul was united to his, and I loved him in a way no words could express.

If the heart remains constant and is filled with the same sentiments, there is always some phantom caprice which pushes us beyond the limit which we should not exceed and carries us much farther than we ourselves desire to go. I was a striking example of that. Do I dare make that confession? Yes. Nothing must remain hidden. I blush at revealing it to my reader.

We have seen the bounty and goodness of my father towards me, the justness of his spirit, and the steadfastness of his character. In other words, he showed how much he merited my love and heart. His image will never be effaced from my heart.

In our house also lived a kindly, devout, aged widow, who spent the greater part of the day in the neighbouring churches. She had three children, the oldest a debauchee in the fullest sense of the word whose companions were of the lowest order. We scarcely ever saw him. He amused himself by squandering the money he had inherited from his father. His younger brother was about sixteen when he left school to join his mother. He was as adorable as a cherub, with a cheerful temperament and a kindly, gentle character.

As for the sister, she was a honey blonde, with pink-tinted cheeks, sparkling eyes, turned-up nose, vermilion smiling mouth, luscious figure, but petite in build, a madcap if you ever saw one, and possessed of an amorous temperament which she cleverly kept concealed. She constantly joked about the sermons her pious mother gave her from time to time.

I became very close to her after Lucette had left, and I made the acquaintance of her younger brother on the few occasions when he accompanied her. Later, there did not pass a day when they did not come to see me and spend the afternoon or evening with me. Their mother was particularly happy at these visits, for she held me up as a model of virtue to her daughter. It is quite true that I had a reserved air that was both inborn and strengthened by my father's example.

I noticed that my father was studying and making up his mind about Vernol and his sister. One day, he told me that Rose knew more than her nanny had ever taught her, and that if she was less instructed than I in sexual matters, which he doubted, she was eager to learn. Also, he mentioned that if I was curious to find out the extent of her knowledge, I was free to do so. The banter Rose and I exchanged afterwards led me to the same opinion as my father, but I could not figure out Vernol.

My talents had been perfected. I was a good musician, playing the harp with taste and singing with feeling, reciting with feeling and consequently, Rose, Vernol and I formed a little society. During our meetings, he made known the depth of his feelings for me. He sought me out on the slightest pretext and followed me ceaselessly. When he was with me, he was in turn attentive, submissive and impertinent, but all his actions told me what he did not dare say. When I became aware of it, I informed my father. My tone was mocking.

'Laura, the first time I saw him, I guessed. When he is with you, his eyes and cheeks become animated. He does his best to hide his embarrassment, but he is not very successful. You can see right through him. Now that you know his love for you, what feelings do you have for him?'

I had never asked myself that question. Up to then, I had considered Vernol merely my friend, and I always addressed him in such a fashion. But my father's query made me think and, on reflection, I had to admit that I was not unsusceptible to Vernol's presence, and that when he was not with his sister, I sorely missed him. When he was absent, I always eagerly asked Rose where he was and what he was doing. It was a mystery to me how a caprice for the likes of him, who was so unlike me, could have taken hold of me. His handsomeness attracted me, to be sure, and his good manners and his winning ways added to his charms.

From my father's look, it was not hard to see that he had discovered in me what I almost did not dare admit to myself. He went for some time without speaking to me about it. I loved him more than ever for his silence, if that were possible. My admiration and affection did not diminish in the slightest, and as a child of truth and simplicity, I was unable to dissimulate. It is claimed that we women are false by character, but I am of the opinion that this so-called sham is acquired and not inborn. Finally, feeling able to sacrifice everything for my loving father, I made up my mind to avoid the pursuit and attentions of the handsome young lad. I was unable to reconcile in my fantasy the feelings I had for Vernol with those I had for my father.

Apparently, my father wanted to put me to the test (for which I was totally unprepared), because one day he took me aside.

'Laura,' he said to me rather sternly. 'I am not very fond of your new friends. Would you please not see Rose and her brother any more?'

I did not hesitate for an instant. Throwing my arms around his neck and pressing him to my bosom, I sobbed:

'If you say so, dear father. Of course, I won't have anything more to do with them. If you wish, you can send them away, or we can go to the country where I won't be able to see them. Let's leave tomorrow. I'll be ready to go.'

Indeed, I started off to pack my things. I was busy at my task when he called me back. Seating me on his knees, he hugged me tightly and affectionately.

'My dear Laurette,' he stammered with emotion in his voice, 'I am overjoyed at your tenderness and affection for me. Your dry eyes tell me that you are willing to make this sacrifice without any pain. Tell me that it is so, I beg of you. Open your heart to me, for there is no doubt that fear is not at the bottom of your resolution. You have never had to be afraid with me.'

'No, father,' I answered simply, 'I have never been afraid of you. I am just following my feelings. I agree that Vernol has given birth within me to an illusion, a caprice, if you wish, which I cannot explain. But my heart is filled with you. When it comes to you, there is not a moment of indecision. I don't want to see him any more.'

'No, my child,' my father quietly declared. 'I just wanted to learn the nature of your sentiments for me, and now I am satisfied. Vernol excites in you sensations that your imagination enhances. You will enjoy them. Also, you will learn the full extent of my tenderness for you, and you will feel that you cannot stop loving me. And that's all I want. Go ahead. I am only jealous of your heart, the possession of which is so precious to me.'

I was stunned. I fell at his knees, my face bathed

in tears and my bosom heaving. I was sobbing so violently that I could barely speak.

'Dearest Papa,' I stuttered, 'I love you and I adore you. In my heart, there is only room for you.'

He was deeply moved at my grief. Raising me up and pressing me to him in turn, he covered my face with kisses.

'Console yourself, my child. Don't you think that I know nature and its immutable laws? Follow your heart, for, as you know, I am not hard-hearted. It is time for you to learn the difference between fatherly love and the love of a lover. I promised you that you will enjoy pleasure with Vernol. As you well know, I keep my word. Besides, he is a nice lad, good-looking and well-mannered. That I have to say for him. If your heart had not gone out to him, it would have turned to someone else, perhaps not as worthy as he. That is the reason for my decision.'

From that day, I felt myself much freer with Vernol. After spending one night in my father's arms, I awoke to hear him telling me between the kisses I was raining on his cheeks that I should pay a call on Rose's mother.

'Tell her to allow her daughter to spend the day in the country with you, and mention, too, that she should not worry if she does not return in the evening for we'll bring her back the next day. As an excuse, we'll say that the coach is being repaired, and you'll keep her here until tomorrow. When you are alone with her, you can find out her inclinations and what she does. She seems to trust you. Once you have wormed your way into her confidence, let me know.'

For a moment, I thought he had designs on her,

but I did not ask any questions. I merely did what I was bidden. For some time, I suspected that Rose was as knowledgeable as I, or almost.

Everything went as my father planned. She came and the door was locked to all comers. All alone, we spent the day in the maddest follies. I played a hundred mischievous tricks on her. She returned them with interest. I bared her budding bosom and made my father kiss the pink-nosed puppies. Her buttocks, her *mons Veneris* and her cunt suffered my playful tortures. I held her in my arms so that my father could repeat my performance, at which she laughed and giggled. Although at times she pretended indignation at some unexpected prank, she lent herself willingly to everything we could think of. Her eyes were glistening and her cheeks flushed.

I partook only sparingly of the collation that was served, but I kept filling her glass to stoke the flames that were already consuming her. After rising from the table, we renewed our frolics. Rose, no longer capable of any resistance, was turned over with her face down on a settee. I raised her skirts, and her bared behind presented a perspective that no painter's brush could reproduce. My father helped me to get revenge for all the tricks she had played on me. I was curious to learn what effect these games would have on her, and when I looked more closely, I found she was almost dripping between her thighs. No doubt about it. She had enjoyed herself immensely during our madcap pranks.

Finally, Rose and I went to my room where we got ready to go to bed. As soon as she saw me in my chemise, she tore it off me. I did the same to her, hurling the last garment to the floor. Dragging me to the bed, she gave me long drawn-out kisses as she fondled my straining breasts and damp matted mount. Immediately, I put my finger on the spot which I guessed would give her the most pleasure. I was not mistaken. She spread her legs and kept cadence with the movement of my finger. Still curious, I inserted my finger into her cunt, and the ease with which it entered left no doubt as to the use she had made of it.

Now I was burning to find out how and when she had lost her maidenhead. I was just about to question her when my father entered the room to kiss us goodnight before retiring. With a sudden jerk, Rose threw off the covers, revealing us completely in the nude with our hands on each other's centres of voluptuousness. She put her arms around his neck, drew his head down, and made him kiss my breasts. Not to be outdone, I forced him to do the same to her seductive gloves. Then I promenaded his hand all over her body, stopping it only at her Venus mount. I could see that he was aroused, but he left us abruptly, wishing us an amusing night.

The clock was striking ten when, the next morning, my father returned to our room and asked, as he awakened us, if we had had a pleasant night.

'We stayed up long after you left, Papa. You saw the mood we were in when you left us.'

Rose, whom our diversions had calmed and sleep had refreshed, blushed and clapped her hand to my mouth. I promptly removed it.

'No, Rose,' I declared, 'you will never prevent me from telling my father everything we did and all you told me. I never conceal anything from him, for I trust him implicitly, as he does me.'

Placing her arms and legs around me, she allowed me to continue.

'When you left us, Papa, Rose was already at a high pitch of excitement. As soon as we were alone, she kissed me passionately on the mouth and began to suck hard on my nipples. She drew me close to her, on top of her. Our legs were interlocked so that our cunts were rubbing one another. My breasts were dangling and grazing hers, and we were belly to belly. Demanding my tongue, she cuddled my buttocks with one hand and with the other tickled my clitoris. By the action of her finger, she invited me to do the same to her. I put my finger on the spot where she was waiting impatiently, and soon we experienced the delights of these amusements. But she refused to let me withdraw it until she had enjoyed ineffable transports four times.'

While I was rendering an account of our gambols, Rose, aroused again by the description and the recollection, had inserted her hand between my thighs and performed what I was telling. I immediately grasped what she was desiring. We had remained in the nude, and I uncovered her. Then I grasped my father's hand which immediately took possession of all her charms. All he was wearing was a dressing-gown which half opened at his movements. From the protuberance straining against the cloth, I could see the effect that the touch of his hands on her body was producing on him. Pointing it out to Rose, I advised her to take off his robe and lay him at our sides. Unhesitatingly, she got up, threw herself at him, stripped him and, enveloping him in her arms, pushed him on the bed.

I was not idle, for I lifted one of her legs on him, and passed the other through his. In this position, his prick naturally was face to face with her cunt, and it goes without saying that I guided the member on its proper route. Her anticipation was so great that she began to quiver like a willow in the wind. With an upward thrust of her derriere, she precipitated the entry into the venereal temple. I fondled her most sensitive parts, an activity she seconded with perfect rhythm. From her passionate transports, we could perceive the excessive pleasure she was undergoing.

My father, who was experiencing the keenness with which she was sucking his prick, was unable to hold himself back. He hurriedly withdrew, and with my hand I finished off the libation that he feared to empty into Rose's cunt. In a delirium, Rose moaned that she had discharged five times while he was in her. Her stomach was inundated with the fuck he was spreading on her. It went all the way up to her breasts. While I was attending to these various duties, she took hold of my cunt which she began to titillate. This little game, together with the emotions caused by the sight of their bliss and the fondlings I was lavishing on them, soon put me in a state of violent agitation.

Now I fervently desired the fire that was devouring me to be quenched. Rose was quick to notice it, and she soon enabled me to join in the merriment.

When we had somewhat recovered from our exertions, I found enough breath to address my father.

'Listen, Papa,' I murmured. You are probably as astounded as I was at Rose's skill, and I won her promise to tell me where and how she had received her training. Now I am going to repeat to you her story, but, no, it is from her mouth that you are going to hear it, and I hope that she is agreeable. What you have just done with her puts her in just the mood to tell you everything without embarrassment and to confide in you all of what she said to me.'

Embraces and kisses were sufficient to overcome her feeble protests.

'Well, all right. Since Laura knows everything already, I have nothing to lose. From what I have gathered, even if I did not impart my story to you, you would get it from Laurette. Moreover, I trust you completely after what we have been through. Yes, it is better that I tell you myself.'

PART III

'I was sixteen years old when my mother sent me to one of her sisters in the provinces, where I spent six months, mostly in the company of her daughter who was a year my senior. Until that time, I had led a secluded life, always with my mother who is so pious that she never mixes with other people. Since my brothers were away at school, I was either alone or at church with my mother. As you can imagine, I was bored to tears.

'Nevertheless, I liked it better in church than at home, because, although my mother and I sat in the most remote corner in the house of worship, I was aware that someone now and then would have his eyes fixed on me.

'Quite some time before, my mother had promised her sister to send me to her for a stay, since she had often said she would like to have me. I was very eager to go, because I knew that my aunt was the exact opposite of my stuffy mother. It was, however, an unforeseen turn of events that finally caused my mother to keep her word. My oldest brother, who was at home at the time, had contracted the pox, and it was imperative that I leave the house as quickly as possible.

'My aunt and cousin welcomed me with the utmost cordiality. Immediately after a warm exchange of hugs and kisses, Isabelle, for that was my cousin's name, insisted that I share her bed. Although I may have constrained her at the beginning, she embraced me tenderly every night before we went to sleep, and in the morning, when we awoke, I returned her tokens of affection.

'It was not two weeks until we were such warm friends that in the evening in bed, she tucked up our nightgowns to press her buttocks against mine and then give me the four sisters' kiss.

'One night, when I could not fall asleep, although I pretended to, I felt Isabelle's arm make a slight movement. Now her hand was on the upper part of my thigh. Her breathing was heavy and spasmodic, while her derriere gave little twitches. Finally, after a deep sigh, she calmed down and went to sleep.

'Bewildered by her strange behaviour, I at first thought that there might be something wrong with her. The next morning, however, she was her cheerful self, and my anxiety vanished. From that time on, I was aware that she was acting the same way every night. It was a mystery to me, but it was not long before I was to be enlightened.

'My aunt had a chambermaid of about twenty with whom Isabelle was often alone in her room, ostensibly because Justine embroidered beautifully and Isabelle was taking lessons from her. My cousin told me never to disturb her when she was with Justine, for the work required the greatest concentration. At first, I swallowed the story, but when I noticed that she had become as skilful as her teacher, I became suspicious.

'To tell the truth, I was also piqued at being excluded from these tête-à-têtes, and I determined to get to the bottom of the matter. For a young girl, curiosity is the tormenting demon to whom she has to yield lest she succumb herself.

'One day, I found myself all alone in the house, my aunt having gone out with Isabelle, and Justine away doing some errands. Taking advantage of their absence, I went into Isabelle's room to see if I could not find some way whereby I could learn what was going on in there when they were by themselves. After exploring the room, I spied near the foot of my cousin's bed an almost hidden door that I was able to open only after several vigorous jerks. It led into a dim chamber filled with old furniture heaped up almost to the ceiling. The only free space was a narrow passage going to another portal which opened onto a concealed staircase that descended down to a little courtyard from which one emerged into a deserted alley.

'If my aunt thought that she had shut off this part of the house, Isabelle or Justine undoubtedly had discovered the keys. In the furniture-jammed room, I noticed in the wall a bit of drapery that seemed to cover some aperture into my cousin's room. Climbing up on a dusty chair to investigate further, I found a little hole in the cloth through which I could look into the adjoining room. Since it was too small to afford a clear view, I took my scissors and enlarged it so that nothing obstructed my vision. Delighted with my stratagem and determined to take full advantage of it, I beat a quick retreat, closing the door behind me. As I returned to my room, I recalled that when Justine went to Isabelle's room, it was almost always after lunch.

'The opportunity I was waiting for finally came when my aunt went to pay a call on an old friend. Since the matter she wished to discuss was of a delicate nature, she did not take Isabelle or myself. When she was gone, Isabelle made a point of telling me that because she had some new intricate stitch to learn with Justice, I was to feel free to do as I wished as long as she was not disturbed. That was all I needed.

'I made as if I were going for a stroll, but in reality I stealthily made my way to the unlit room, where I hid myself among the discarded pieces of furniture and fastened my eye to the opening. Not long after, I saw my cousin come in with some embroidery in her hand. At the sight of that my heart sank, for I was sure that I was going to spend a boring afternoon and I repented of my curiosity.

'But my hopes rose when Justine appeared and immediately asked where I was. Isabelle replied I had gone to see some friends in the vicinity. Reassured, the maid quickly latched the bedroom door and opened the one of the room in which I was concealed, continuing to the hidden staircase.

'I shook with fright at the thought of being discovered, but she apparently did not notice me as she groped her way down the passage. On her return, Isabelle put aside her work and went to the mirror to arrange her hair. When she began to readjust her scarf and blouse, Justine snatched them off, revealing my cousin's snowy bosom. Taking one of the pink-tipped globes in her hands, she complimented my cousin on their roundness and firmness. Then, baring her own full hemispheres, she compared them to Isabelle's.

'As they were thus amusing themselves, I heard somebody coming up the staircase. Because of the way I was crouched down, I could not see him as he passed by my hiding place. On hearing a scratch at the door, Justine opened the door and then quickly closed it again.

'As soon as the stranger was in the room, I immediately recognized him. He was a tall young fellow slightly related to the family and he paid us an occasional call. His name was Courbelon. Isabelle was not at all embarrassed when he went up and kissed her still uncovered bosom. At the same time, his hand went up under her skirt. When he had finished, he gave Justine the same greeting.

'Taking Isabella up in his arms, he lay her at the foot of the bed where he threw up her skirt to reveal her all. From my vantage point, I could see her flat stomach, her slightly plump thighs, and her rose-lipped slit. She did not have much hair down there, but what there was of it was pitch black. Putting his mouth to the orifice, he tickled its upper part with his finger which soon disappeared in its depths.

'In the meantime, Justine unbuttoned the front of his trousers and brought out an organ of astonishing dimensions which my cousin shamelessly grasped. As he began to replace the finger with it, I heard Justine scold him: "No Courbelon, that I won't allow. If I were to get pregnant, I would know what to do to avoid unpleasant consequences, but if Isabelle ever got into that condition, where could the two of us hide ourselves? Caress and fondle her as much as you like, but just don't you dare put that into her."

'That discourse, which I heard distinctly, was a complete enigma for me. I saw Courbelon reluctantly withdraw the member and grumblingly titillate Isabelle, who was clutching his masculinity as she had before.

'A short time after he had resumed the game with his fingers, I heard and saw the same sighs and motions that she made when we two were in bed together.

'Now I had a glimmering of what had been happening. She had been doing to herself what Courbelon was now doing to her. Now that it was over, Isabelle rose from the bed, and Justine, who had been watching them like a hawk, threw herself in turn on the couch. With one arm she embraced the small of Courbelon's back, and with the other she gripped the truncheon as she dragged him down on her. In a twinkling of the eye, her skirt was up to her navel. Resting on her stomach, he massaged the pearl-shaped breasts which he then covered with feverish kisses. Judging from the convulsive movements of her flanks and derriere, I gathered he was inserting his member into her. I would have given anything to see it go in.

'From behind, my cousin passed her hand between his bucking buttocks, either to fondle his testicles or to measure how deep the member had penetrated.

Now both were seized by spasms. They must have been in seventh heaven. It seemed that Courbelon was dying after a violent explosion. When he pulled out his instrument, it was no longer its proud self, but a humble, self-effacing creature diminished in length and thickness. I thought it rather resembled an earthworm. Exhausted, they paused for several moments on the bed, after which the kisses and embraces were resumed.

'This opening scene, which thoroughly delighted me, was soon followed by a second act which aroused my emotions even more.

'Impatient with their hampering garments and aware that my aunt would not be back until dusk, Courbelon tore off their clothing, and in an instant they both were as naked as the day they were born. In proportion, Justine's figure was not the equal of Isabelle's, but her skin was whiter and more satiny and her body more rounded and contoured. Playing no favourites, his lips alternated rapidly between the bodies of his two enticing partners. And their bottoms, breasts and slits were his to do with as he wished.

'What I regarded avidly for more than half an hour lit fires within me and excited emotions I had never before experienced. The caresses of the intertwined trio became more animated. Now Courbelon made his two lovely partners lie on their backs, side by side, then on their bellies, with their legs spread wide apart. I saw as clearly as Courbelon all that met his eyes. He examined them carefully, kissed their slightly arched buttocks, and stuck a finger of each hand between their thighs. In the meantime, his instrument was restored to its pristine condition.

'Because Justine could not see him from the position she was in, Courbelon took advantage of the situation to introduce the monstrosity into Isabelle. Suddenly, however, Justine became mistrustful and abruptly sat up. When she saw what he was doing, she grabbed the miscreant by the neck, nearly choking him, and dragged him off of his willing victim.

'I was furious, for I was following the course of the implement with the deepest interest, and Justine had to ruin it all.

' "No, no," she stated firmly. That is not permitted. I've told you the reason a hundred times, and you're just going to have to give up the idea."

'Since I could hear as clearly as I could see, I did not miss a single word or phrase.

' "Come now, my dear boy!" Justine said in a conciliatory tone as she took hold of the offender. "Why don't you just put your prick into my cunt? They are old friends, and you don't run any risk with me!"

'She was too late, though. Before inserting it in her, she gave it two or three shakes. At that, I saw Courbelon lean on her shoulder, holding one of her breasts and kissing it, as he spilled out a white liquid I had never seen before. The spurts were accompanied by a series of convulsions that marked the depth of his rapture. For some unknown reason, the sight nearly drove me out of my mind.

'Without realizing it, I had been irritating the upper part of my slit in the same fashion I had seen Courbelon do to Justine and Isabelle. I was engaged in this stimulating occupation which gave me nothing but unalloyed pleasure. Suddenly, Justine and my cousin, undoubtedly animated by the caresses he had lavished on them, put him in the same state they themselves were in, namely, complete stark nudity. From head to toe, there was not a stitch of clothing on his body.

'This new perspective attracted my eyes to him with a delicious curiosity, for unknowingly, that is just the way I had wanted to see him. As I regarded them, it seemed that their enjoyments were all that I had ever desired. Justine and Isabelle were caressing him, kissing him, fondling the now lifeless virility, and cuddling his testicles and buttocks. In return, he kissed them, massaged and sucked their nipples, turned them over on their backs, looked minutely at their rear cheeks, and excited them by inserting and withdrawing his fingers in and out of their apertures.

'As this went on, I noticed his instrument slowly regaining all its former pride. The organ, with which he playfully menaced the laughing girls, looked like a pike about to be stuck into the body of a ferocious beast. There was no mistaking Courbelon's desire for my cousin, but Justine, taking a firm hold on him, forced him with her back down on top of the bed. For a moment, I thought he was going to split open 'her stomach, but she was not to be daunted.

' "Let's wait a moment," he suggested to her, "so that we may enjoy our raptures simultaneously."

'Placing Isabelle on the bed, he spread open her knees and thighs between which Justine put her legs, also spread apart. Since there was nothing to hinder my view, I was able to see Courbelon's truncheon sink into her aperture, only to reappear, vanish again, and so on.

'It seemed inconceivable that such a fearsome object could ever enter my opening, which was so tight I could barely get my little finger into it. And I never dared push it too far because of the sheer agony it caused. But Justine's example lent me courage, and I determined not to worry about the consequences, no matter what they would be.

'While Courbelon had his prick in Justine's cunt, his finger was ensconced in Isabelle's. He turned my cousin's head by telling her that she possessed the most charming Venus mount he had ever beheld. After saying the same about her slit, he recommended her to stimulate her clitoris, a suggestion she promptly followed as he slipped his finger in and out in regular cadence with his thrusts into Justine.

'Steadfast in my determination to follow their example, at least in part, I took a deep breath and plunged in the forefinger of my left hand as deep as I could, all the while stirring it around in imitation of the movement of Courbelon's prick. Gradually, a delicious sensation invaded my whole being, and I now realized why my cousin took such a pleasure in a repetition of the game.

'It was not long before the trio was wallowing in utter ecstasy. Isabelle, still on her back, was wiggling her backside like a shimmy-dancer from the South Seas. Witnessing her transports, Courbelon suddenly shouted in glee: "Darling, you're coming!"

'Scarcely had he finished uttering these words than he fell almost senseless on Justine's bountiful bosom after sighing deeply and mouthing oaths to describe his bliss. Justine, after agitatedly twitching her rump, also remained prostrate.

'These evidences of impassioned enjoyments roused me to such a pitch of excitement that I, too, sank back exhausted against a piece of furniture, undergoing at the same time an ineffable gratification. What an excess of delight to feel for the first time such a hitherto unknown voluptuousness, a delight never dreamed of. Such bliss lifts one out of this world and, for too brief a period, it is the only thing that really exists.

'During the subsequent period when I was savouring to the full my complete contentment, the three performers in the adjoining room were starting to put back on their clothes. As soon as they were decent, Courbelon tenderly embraced the two girls and made his way out as he had come in. A few moments later, Justine and Isabelle also left the room. As for myself, I waited a while longer to emerge from my place of concealment and, taking the same route as Courbelon, I regained the inhabited part of the house. Shortly afterwards, my aunt returned in company with Isabelle, who had gone out to meet her.

'From that time on, I thought and dreamed of nothing but what I had witnessed. Their words were still ringing in my ears and their actions were still before my eyes. Not for a moment were my reflections far from that living tableau.

'That very evening when I was in bed with Isabelle, I pretended that I was sound asleep and Isabelle fell in a profound slumber. Since it was apparent that she was not going to do anything to me, I had to seek resources within myself, and I followed her example. But the following evening was an entirely different affair.

'As soon as we were in bed and my cousin thought I was asleep, I became aware that she was starting her little game again. Knowing now full well what was going on, I turned over and, placing my thigh on hers, I put my hand where I knew she had her finger. I slid it under and immediately had her whole mound in my palm. As I fondled her tenderly, I kissed her budding breasts and inserted my finger into her slit. Then I withdrew it to tickle the spot where I had found hers. When she spread her legs and let me have my way with her, I heard her abruptly heave a deep sigh and, to my amazement, I found her all wet in the area where my hand was.

'Now overcome with the urge for the same to be done to me, I gripped her hand and covered my own hillock with it. Forcing her digital extremity to do its duty, I soon found myself returning sigh for sigh.

'She was not a little surprised at all I was doing, for she believed me as innocent as the day I was born. Knowing that I had been raised in a strait-laced puritanical home, she had been wary about imparting to me any of her secrets for fear I would blab everything to my aunt or mother.

' "Well, Rose, how is it that you are so experienced?" she asked curiously. "I am really amazed."

' "That I can believe, my dear cousin, and I'll tell you on the condition that you won't be angry with me and that you will keep on loving me," I replied.

'The moment I said it, I regretted having opened my mouth and was reluctant to continue until Isabelle, taking me in her arms, tenderly pressed me to go on and tell her all.

' "You aren't afraid of me, are you?" she asked. "I

assure you that you can count on my discretion, and I solemnly promise never to say a word, particularly not to our mothers."

'Reassured, I recounted all I had witnessed and how I was able to be a witness. When I had finished, she was aghast at what I had learned.

' "Oh, Rose, my dear Rose, I beg you never to reveal my secret. If you betray me, I'm lost."

'I vowed to be as silent as the grave, and my cousin said she was not even going to tell Justine that I knew. After I had calmed her fears, she rained kisses on my face and body, all the while questioning me closely on what I had seen and heard and the impression it had made on me. I gave her a full account, including my own reaction. Now that she knew of my own misdeeds, her last lingering doubts vanished. Now it was my turn to satisfy my own curiosity.

' "But tell me, Isabelle, how did you happen to fall in with Justine and Courbelon?"

' "I'll do so gladly, cousin," she replied. "Since you know everything, there is little point in holding anything back, and besides, I am sure that you will not break your promise.

' "About four or five weeks before you came here, I had gone out with my mother to pay some calls, but having forgotten my bag in my room, I went back alone to get it. After I found it, I went to Justine's room for some reason or another. Since the door was partially open, I entered without knocking.

' "What met my eyes nearly stunned me. I was stupefied to find Courbelon on top of her in the strangest position. When he noticed me, he quickly got off his mount, but not before I saw his organ which he hurriedly tried to conceal at the same time he was lowering Justine's skirts that were up to her navel. Although she was dismayed at being discovered, she was relieved that it was not my mother who had found out her guilty secret. I began to leave right away, but Justine, fearing that I would tell what I had seen, ran after me, got on her knees, and begged me with tears in her eyes not to reveal her shameful disgrace. Her pleas were so heart-rending that I promised all that she wanted and kept my word.

' "I'll admit to you, dear Rose, that the incident gave rise to many thoughts and conjectures which kept running through my head. From that time on, Justine often came to my room under the pretext of giving me embroidery lessons, but, in reality, the instruction was of a completely different sort. She taught me things I had never dreamed of. She bared my bosom and played with my breasts as she depicted in the most vivid colours the delights of sensual pleasure. I have to admit that I was all ears.

' "Finally, one day, her descriptions so aroused my curiosity and latent sensuousness that my cheeks were flaming, my breath was coming in short gasps, and my bosom was rising and falling. The eager questions I threw at her enabled her to sense that the moment she had been waiting for had come. She took me in her arms, lifted me up, and bore me to the bed, where she raised my skirts. Vaguely sensing that she wished to play forbidden games, I feebly tried to stop her, but she was undeterred, telling me that any handsome young cavalier would be overjoyed to be in her place and regard and touch the beauties she was gradually exposing. His organ would swell and then he would expire rapturously, giving me at the same time the most unimaginable delights. Her flattery, lascivious descriptions and caresses had completely reduced my defences, and I let her do with me as her fancy dictated.

' "Then she placed the tip of the finger of her left hand between the lips of my opening which she titillated, while with the right she rubbed my clitoris."

' "My dear cousin," I interrupted her, "why don't you call a spade a spade and use the terms I heard Justine and Courbelon employ?"

' "You're right, Rose," she conceded. "I should have remembered that I don't have to be careful about my language with you.

' "After some moments of this treatment, I finally experienced that supreme sensation she had described in such glowing terms, even though she told me that the pleasure would be tenfold greater with a gallant young man. Ever since then, we have often been playing this delightful game, much to my satisfaction. One day, she went so far as to stick her finger in me. I felt some pain at first, but it soon went away. It was not long before she was teaching me how to return the favours she was bestowing on me, which I did, and not simply out of a sense of gratitude.

' "A week or so before your arrival, my mother went to make some calls without me, enabling Justine and me to resume our joyful diversions, but this time we were completely in the nude. I did not know it, but Courbelon was hidden behind a curtain witnessing all our merry pranks. As I was to learn later, it had been planned between him and Justine.

' "As he emerged from his place of concealment,

also in the nude, Justine nearly burst her sides laughing to see him in such a state, but I nearly fainted when my eyes caught his enormous erect sceptre. I wanted to flee, but my feet refused to move. Besides, bare as I was, I could hardly leave the room. Trembling and filled with shame and fright, I tried to take refuge behind the curtain, but as I made for it, the two of them stopped me in my tracks. After what Courbelon had seen Justine and I doing, I could scarcely put up an effective resistance.

' "Courbelon held me tightly in his arms, passionately kissed me, and ran his hands and lips all over my quivery body. Finally, my shame gave place to desire. He put the baton in my hand, but it was so thick that my fingers could not encompass it. The fire of his kisses and caresses and the sight of Justine fondling his muscular body set me ablaze, and I was in no state to refuse him anything he wanted. The joys into which he plunged me were so profound that I almost lost consciousness. Justine acted as his able assistant.

' "But the two of them did not stop there. Dragging me to the bed and holding me down with one hand, she made me look at Courbelon's prick which was losing itself in her cunt. From the vivacious expressions on their faces, I had a fair guess of the bliss they were undergoing.

' "Yesterday was the sixth time they allowed me to have the pleasure of their company. You can imagine that we would have had more gatherings had it not been for the fear of discovery. When I learned of your forthcoming visit I was overjoyed, for I hoped your being here would give me more freedom. I confess I was mad to have Courbelon do to me what he always did to Justine, even though Justine had repeatedly warned me of the dangers of pregnancy and I was still awed by the proportions of the desired object.

' "But on closer reflection, I noticed that it caused her no pain. The suffering must be less than the pleasure. Consequently, I decided that my fears were groundless, particularly when Courbelon reassured me on that point. Justine was adamant, but it was hard for me to believe what she said when she was always doing exactly that which she prohibited me."

'When she paused for breath, I urged Isabelle to gratify me as she had been. At first she refused, but I used every argument my innocent mind could come up with. I know that they were not very convincing, but I did not let up. Whether from curiosity, fantasy or coincidence of desire, I do not know, but she finally yielded. From that time, we enjoyed almost nightly what we called our "secret", and we became inseparable.

'A little later, we were invited to a wedding in the village, the bride being a relative of Justine who would be sure to attend. Isabelle laughingly mentioned that it would be a good opportunity to put one over on her Cerberus, for I had been continually urging her to find a way to realize her ambitions with Courbelon. Now was her chance, I told her, and she should not let it go by. I added that my aunt, believing we would be at the celebration together, would take advantage of our absence to visit with friends. All Isabelle had to do was stay in her room, while I went to the wedding, where I surely would find Courbelon. As soon as I saw him, I would tell him that Isabelle was waiting for him to discuss an important matter and that he should go to her room.

'At first, she shook her head and said blushingly that she could not do such a thing. But I kept after her, and with my caresses which stimulated her desires, I prevailed in the end.

'My aunt had already left when I walked to the village. The first person I saw among the merry throng in the banquet room was Courbelon, to whom I gave unnoticed the message from Isabelle. As soon as I had finished, he was gone in a flash. Momentarily, I regretted not being at my observation post, but I consoled myself with the thought that Isabelle would render me a detailed account of all that took place and abandoned myself to the pleasures of the ball.

'When Justine spotted me alone, she immediately inquired why Isabelle was not with me. I replied that I thought she was with her mother for a while, but that she would surely return soon to take part in the festivities. Justine swallowed the story hook, line and sinker, but as time went by and there was no sign of Courbelon, she became suspicious. It was obvious that Courbelon's absence and Isabelle's tardiness were causing her to smell a rat.

'When she seemed at the end of her patience, Courbelon made his appearance, followed by Isabelle a few minutes later. At the sight of them, Justine immediately vanished. I guessed that she had surmised Isabelle had just come from the house. When she came back, there was nothing to be read on her face, but, as we later learned, she had made some inquiries, the answers to which gave her all the information she needed.

'Isabelle turned down all invitations to dance, and when she whispered in my ear the reason, I loudly declared that I, too, was tired from the exertions and was ready to go home. After asking our farewells, we walked back together to my aunt's house. You can imagine my impatience at hearing what had happened, and it seemed an eternity until we were in bed.

'When I tried to put my hand on the spot which should have undergone the assault, she pushed it rudely away, saying that it hurt too much to be touched. There was a moment of silence before the whole story poured forth like water rushing over a dam.

' "Ah, my dear Rose, my curiosity has been satisfied,' she said in a woeful tone. 'Courbelon came promptly to my room when I was eagerly awaiting him. As soon as he opened the door, I flung my arms around his neck and wet his face with my kisses. In turn, he fondled and explored every corner and recess of my body, without my putting up the slightest semblance of resistance. After these preliminaries, he inserted his hard baton in my hole that he had lubricated with his saliva, but you have no idea of what torture it was. That monstrous member was tearing me apart. Not daring to scream, I burst into tears.

' "He tried his best to comfort me by assuring me that the next time I would experience nothing but pure unadulterated bliss, but he deceived me again the second time. His following attack resulted in nothing but redoubled anguish for me. I suffered the unbearable. When he presented himself the third time, I refused him outright, but he was so insistent with his kisses and embraces that I had to yield to his entreaties. He was as gentle and tender as he could be, but it did not help. I could not stand the torment any longer. The stabbing pains along with the fear of getting big with child so terrified me that I shoved him from me with such violence that he did not dare try again. Right now, it feels as if there is fire burning between my thighs. That is why, as I told you, I just could not dance."

' "My darling cousin," I told her consolingly, "since you are younger that Justine, it is quite natural that yours is much tighter and narrower than hers."

' "That's what Courbelon told me. He said that with time and practice my slit would get wider, but in the meantime I am suffering the agonies of hell."

'When she had finished, it was late, and we were so tired that we fell into a deep sleep almost immediately.

'The next day Justine called Isabelle into her room where she simply told her that Courbelon had been in my cousin's room the night before and that the door to the hidden staircase was not locked as it should have been. Moreover, on the rug she had found some petals of the boutonniere he had been wearing. If that were not enough, she found the bed rumpled as if two people had romped on it. Finally, she had learned that Isabelle had not been with her mother, as I had said, but had remained in her room before she left the house more than two hours after I had.

'Although she realized Justine knew what had gone on, she refused to admit it. But the evidence was so damning and Justine was so persistent that she finally made a clean breast of it.

'Either fearing what the consequences might be to

Isabelle or angry at Courbelon for his behaviour, Justine put so many obstacles in their way that they scarcely had a chance to speak to each other, let alone to be by themselves. There was no doubt that Justine was also jealous. Whatever the case may have been, she employed every means at her disposal to break up the affair and watched over their every movement.

'Because of these blockades placed on the road of true love by Justine, Courbelon finally became irritated with his mistress, with whom he soon had a falling out. When he had to move to a remote province, he quickly forgot her as well as Isabelle. Shortly thereafter, Justine left both my aunt's service and the village. Isabelle suspected that she had given up her post to rejoin Courbelon, for whose sake she would have made any sacrifice.

'At first, Isabelle was almost inconsolable at losing him. Whenever we were alone, she always turned the conversation to him. Although I was getting sick and tired of hearing the same old thing day in and day out, I comforted her the best I could and in the end, I succeeded. The pleasures we shared enabled her to bear her loss with more fortitude, and finally she had dismissed him completely from her mind. I have to admit that I was sorry at losing him, for I had entertained high hopes of participating sooner or later in their gambols. But her ever-growing affection for me soon effaced his memory.

'All together, we spent four delightful months in each other's company. During this time, she instructed me in everything she had learned from her former teachers and soon we were able to add a few embellishments of our own.

'Thinking back on this period of my life and the answers Isabelle gave me to the many questions I plied her with made me realize that Courbelon probably had had designs on Isablle from the very day she discovered him with Justine. It seems likely he had persuaded Justine that the best way to guarantee Isabelle's silence was to admit her into their games, and she fell into the trap. If it had not been for her jealousy and mistrust, he most likely would have gained his ends.

'The time that I spent at my aunt's sped by all too quickly. I knew it had to come sooner or later, but I almost burst into tears when my mother wrote saying that she wanted me back with her. My departure was a lachrymose one on all sides. My aunt was so touched that she promised to do everything she could to have me return. Since Isabelle and my aunt knew how to enjoy life, their hearts went out to me, because they envisaged my spending bleak, dreary days with my devout mother who had no social life whatsoever. That was what I thought, also, but the way things turned out proved us all wrong.

'Once back with my mother, I turned to account everything chance and Isabelle had taught me. Like her, I was able to procure for myself the most delicious pleasures every day. More often than not, I allowed myself a double measure. My stimulated imagination was concentrated on one thing, and on one thing only: a man. Every time I came near one, I could not keep my eyes from him. It mattered not if he were young or old – I wanted him to quench the flames that were consuming my entire being.

'Just about that time, my brother Vernol came

home for his vacation. The first thing I noticed was how handsome he had become. That surprised me for apparently his charms had escaped me before. It is true that we always had a good brother and sister relationship, but now I found that my feelings for him had changed completely. In him were united all my yearnings, embers that unknowingly he was stoking. I had eyes only for him.

'For a long time I itched to have him touch and fondle that which I had only let Courbelon glimpse, but I was humble enough to believe that I was too young to be able to attract the attentions of an older man. Besides. I was positive that his male organ had grown in size during his absence, and the thought of Isabelle's trial momentarily frightened me. But that cloud on the horizon quickly passed: and I determined that I was going to have Vernol.

'His room was behind my mother's where I also slept, and when that devout woman departed for church where she spent two or three hours every morning, I quickly locked the door after her. The servants, believing that we were still sleeping, never bothered us. That was my opportunity to go to his room while I was still in my nightgown and tease and annoy him in a thousand ways while he was still in bed. I kissed and tickled him. Other times I would yank off the blankets and sheets so that he was almost naked and then playfully spank his backside which was as soft and tender as a girl's.

'When he had enough, he would leap out of bed and start chasing me. Usually, I let him catch me, whereupon he threw me back on his bed where he paid me back in full for the slaps I had given him.

'We had given ourselves up to these games for two mornings when, on the third, the sport took a different turn. That time, when he hurled me on the bed, my nightgown flew up to my waist (with a little help from me). He looked at me and then at my little cunt. He seemed stunned. Recovering himself after a few moments, he first feasted his eyes on my thighs, gingerly touching them with his hands, and then spread them apart. I made no protest.

' "Ah, Rose," he exclaimed. "This is the first time I have noticed what a difference there is between us."

' "What do you mean, difference?" I innocently replied, feigning ignorance.

' "Take a look for yourself," he cried excitedly as if he had just made a great discovery. With that, he pulled down his trousers and showed me his little implement that I had only half seen before. Under my gaze, it grew in length and rigidity.

'Taking the lance in my hand, I stared at it carefully, tenderly stroked it, pulled the foreskin back and gently rubbed the tip.

' "Let me look at you some more," Vernol begged, impatient to do the same to me.

'More than willing to grant his request, I lay back again on the bed. Raising and spreading my legs, he scrutinized my private parts with the attention of a scientist peering into a microscope, but it was obvious that he had not the faintest idea of their functions. Now he was on his knees, bent over me. Running my hand between his thighs, I grasped the pretty pigmy and amused myself by taking off and putting back on the hat covering the coral head.

'The pleasure I perceived I was giving him

augmented mine, and I was all agog. Straightening up, I reversed him on his back as I completely bared the toy to my view. I kissed it, I nibbled it, and I caressed its little olives. Finally, by means of rubbing my hand up and down on the erect baton, I succeeded in releasing that white fluid I had seen Justine's hand produce with Courbelon. I could not get over the delightful sight of the jets making an arc in the air. He looked as if he did not believe what was happening. In his regard astonishment was mingled with bliss. His hand on my thighs became crisp and then remained motionless.

'Reclining on the pillows, I put my arms around him and made him do a little thing he was totally ignorant of but which I was dying to have. He obliged, and I was soon in that state of ecstasy in which I had put him.

'I was delighted at how extraordinary he found all that was happening, for I had led him from surprise to surprise. I resumed my sweet attack on his innocence by fondling again his instrument, which I then began to kiss and suck. I had it all the way in my mouth. If I could have swallowed it, I would have cheerfully done so. Now he was back again in that state which every normal woman dreams of.

'Up to then I had not dared to teach him how to put it where I most wanted it, but I became bolder and more shameless and snatched off his nightshirt as I pulled mine over my head. Now there was nothing to prevent me from contemplating his charms in their entirety. I covered them with my hot hands and lips, while he gratefully returned the favour. When his boyish prick was as hard as it ever was going to be,

I made him get on top of me and guided the member to its proper home.

'What an apt pupil he was! Although I was tight, he was not big. Energetically, we shoved ourselves against each other. Now straddling him, I finally succeeded in getting all of it into me with the ineffable satisfaction of realizing that I was going to get what I had so passionately desired for so long. With shudders that ran through both of us, we simultaneously and reciprocally rid ourselves of our not exactly intact virginities.

'Dear heaven! What sensuality we enjoyed! Vernol was almost out of his senses with ecstasy. We experienced that unadulterated felicity which comes only once in a lifetime and which cannot be described in mere words. Our bliss was at its peak. He was the first to savour that glorious excess when he discharged. As he gushed into me, his arms which had held me as if in a vice suddenly became limp.

'Quickening my tempo, I reached the goal instants after, and as I collapsed like a punctured balloon, he knew that I was in the same state of wonderment as he. Glued to each other, we tasted to the dregs that magnificent annihilation which is no less exhilarating than the transports that caused it. Being the first to recover from our swoons, I found that I had immediate need of his hand and finger again.

'Every morning we indulged in this most delightful of all diversions, either in his bed or mine, and during the rest of the day, anyplace where we felt ourselves secure from prying eyes. At night, when we could not be together, I resurrected by myself the day's pleasures while he did the same in his chamber. I knew that because he told me himself. Every morning we exchanged confidences during the realization of our nocturnal illusions.

'Impressed from the very first by all that I had taught him, he urged me to tell him where and how I had acquired my knowledge. At first deeming it imprudent to say anything about my stay with my cousin, I skirted the question with vague generalities, but as our intimacy deepened and my confidence in him grew, I told him the whole story.'

When Rose finished her tale, which she had told me before in more vivid detail, especially about Vernol, I took the floor.

'Dear father, you don't know what else Rose confided in me. She didn't tell you everything.

' "My dearest Laura," she said to me, "Vernol is head over heels in love with you. I saw it right away, and he even admitted it to me. Now, I am not jealous at all, for I love both of you tenderly. You are lovely and he is charming, and nothing would give me greater pleasure than to see you in his arms. Yes, my dear, I would even put you there myself, for his happiness means all the world to me." Don't you think she is slightly out of her mind, Papa?'

'Not very,' my father replied after some thought. 'As a matter of fact, I really am not surprised at all.'

It was easy to see that Rose adored pleasure with a fury. When we told her that, she readily agreed. The tableaux that she had summoned up from the past animated her as they did us. The effect on my father produced an eloquence which Rose immediately seized upon. To show us the delight she found in the beloved object, she slid it into her sanctuary with a prolonged sigh.

After she had reached her climax seconds before my father, she resumed her reflections.

'If you feel that you cannot confide in me after what I have told you about my brother, please disabuse yourselves of the notion. Because of our intimacies since yesterday, I feel free to tell you everything that is in my mind and heart.'

'Come, Papa, and sit next to your daughter,' I interrupted. 'I'll take Rose's place and prove to you that I am every bit her equal. But put that thing in her so that she can experience at the same time the joys you have given me.'

'Well, Rose, you are going to play a new role,' he declared as he rose to fetch the dildo, which he then fastened to her waist.

Rose was ecstatic at the intrument, the likes of which she had never seen before. Making me mount her, Papa guided it into my cunt while telling her to bestir herself like a man and titillate me at the same time. Also, he instructed her how to discharge it when she felt that I was on the verge. Then he got on me in turn and introduced my old playmate into the rear aperture.

As Rose wiggled most lasciviously, she held my breasts as I fondled hers, and when she sucked my tongue, I thought I was dying. Just as I was about to lose consciousness, she released the dildo's contents. My cunt was inundated. At the same time, the fuck that my father spurted into my rear lifted me to new raptures. Rose was not left out of the general bliss, for the rubbing of the dildo against her clitoris had produced an orgasm. I finally succumbed completely, slain by sheer bliss.

My father soon came to, and when I was revived, we all three got out of bed since it was almost noon.

When we were back on our feet and in our clothes, Rose could hardly wait to examine more closely the marvellous strange contraption. After explaining that it was an exact replica, if slightly oversize, of the male organ, I pointed out its features, chiefly the mechanism which jetted hot water or milk so cleverly that the recipient could not distinguish it from real semen.

When I was through, Rose promptly tucked up her skirt and tried to introduce it into her cunt. Her awkward attempts were so comical that I could not help but laugh. My peals were so loud that my father came back into the room to learn what was up. When he saw Rose fumbling with the instrument, he shared my amusement.

'Leave it alone, Rose, because it is not functioning for the time being,' he advised her. 'Besides, we have better things to do.'

When she desisted and began rearranging her dress, he took me by the hand and led me out of the room.

'Laura,' he earnestly began, 'Rose will be the victim of her own passion and fiery temperament. There is no holding her back. Already she is abandoning herself to pleasure with a fury that I have never before seen in a woman. You can bet your last franc that she will pay a heavy penalty for her excesses. The same goes for that poor Vernol whom she has started down the same path. But I wish to take advantage of it in order to carry out some plans that I have in my head.'

Leaving me, he went to find her in my room. Naturally, I put my ear to the door.

'Rose, what you said about your brother's feelings for my Laura is evidence of the deep friendship you two girls have for each other. But can we count on Vernol's discretion as we can on yours? It is absolutely necessary to be sure of this, as you can well imagine.'

'I don't think you need have any worry on that score,' she assured him. 'What could he gain by blabbing except expulsion from our society, which would be unthinkable in view of his sentiments for your daughter. I'll vouch for Vernol, and I beseech you to let him join in our fun. If he were prevented from pouring out his heart to Laura, he would die of grief.'

'All right,' my father consented. 'It seems that everybody is in league against me. For the time being, however, I don't want him to have the slightest inkling of our activities, and I demand your promise that you will not breathe a word. If he knew, he would consider me well compensated, but I insist on his paying me himself for the sacrifice I am making for him. Just forewarn him that he can expect anything and that he will have to consent to anything we demand of him.'

'I'll answer for him as I would for myself,' Rose warmly replied, 'and you can be sure that he won't learn a thing from me without your consent.'

'One thing more,' my father continued. 'I want both of you to know that Laura is my daughter in name only. She is not my flesh and blood, but she is no less dear to me for all of that. Nobody but you and your brother must know of this.' My father's voice was stern as he gave that warning. 'Now, go to your mother with Laura and tell her that we are going to spend the day in the country tomorrow. With her permission, we would like to take you and your brother with us. And promise me that you and Laura will behave yourselves until the time when we can give free reign to our fantasies.'

When the colloquy, of which I did not miss a word, was over, Rose came to get me. We hurried to her mother who readily granted my father's request. Leaving my friend to her own resources, I spent the rest of the day with a cousin who lived nearby. In the meantime, my father was supervising the arrangements for the next day's project.

At night, when I was nestled in his arms, I asssumed he was going to tell me about his talk with Rose and the excursion the following day, but he fell asleep without saying a word. Disappointed and frustrated, I soon followed his example.

Early the next afternoon, there stopped before our gate a coach which carried us to a charming villa at some distance from the city. Since I had never seen it before, I suspected that it belonged to one of his friends who had placed it at his disposal. Vernol had done his best to improve on his native attractions, and Rose and I were wearing fetching summer dresses in the latest style. Since Rose had explained certain matters to him, he was more at ease and self-assured. When we finally arrived about four, the weather was still perfect.

We made several turns in the gardens whose natural beauty was not crushed by the artificiality so in style today. From among the shrubbery and the flower beds, we gazed at the horizon whose iridescence

101

seemed to be in accord with our mood. After the promenade, we entered the house and went through the suites of rooms. In the main salon where my father led us a delicious repast was being readied for us. As we consumed the appetizing dishes, my father was not sparing with the superb wines he poured.

Whether it was the juice of the grape or some other stimulant, I do not know, but we soon felt its effects. Our heads were whirling as we pelted each other with the petals from the flowers of our garlands. When father noticed the state we were in, he dismissed all the servants with orders not to return until they were summoned. Now we were by ourselves.

We were almost staggering as he led us to an apartment which we had missed on our tour, for it was situated in the most remote part of the villa. From there he ushered us into an intimate salon illuminated on all sides by candles in holders at a height at which they could be easily extinguished by hand. Below them and all around the room ran mirrors with drapes hung in festoons. Scattered around the chamber were big easy-chairs, very low and almost without backs, which were covered with large soft cushions.

On the walls hung various paintings, but what paintings they were! Heavens! In his wildest flights of fancy, Aretino himself could not have conjured up such images. Also, there were statues of figures in highly suggestive positions. In an elaborately decorated niche was to be seen a piece of furniture which sensuousness and voluptuousness had converted into their throne. The surroundings and the wine now dispelled the last of our inhibitions. We were seized by a sort of delirium, with Bacchus and Madness leading the frenzied dance.

Rose, inspired by her favourite deity, Venus, gave the pitch and commenced the hymn of pleasure by flinging herself at my father's neck, embracing Vernol, and hotly kissing me with an invitation to follow her example. Snatching the scarf that covered my bosom, she threw it to her brother and then sailed hers to my father. She made the men kiss her rosepointed globes and then transferred their lips to my welcoming hemispheres.

These frolics reflected infinitely in the mirrors around us aroused us to dizzying heights of lubricity. Our cheeks were flushed, our lips parched and burning, our eyes glittering, and our hearts pounding madly. Vernol, whose clothes were already in disarray, appeared to me as beautiful as the dawn with his glowing complexion and dancing eyes. I regarded him with the adoration of a god, all of whose attractions were concentrated into a single object in the centre of his body, it being the object of all my desires. Although he was unaware of what condition it was in, my father perceived its gradual growth.

In trying to force me down on one of the settees, Rose called for her brother to help her. By parting and lifting my robe, she enabled him to see that for which he was pining. I tried to get revenge by reversing her on her back in turn, but she beat me to it. She threw herself down on it, and kicking her legs up in the air, she unashamedly displayed all the gifts nature had endowed her with – her fetching cunt, her rounded bottom, her flat belly and her satiny thighs – all were visible to the eye.

Immediately, the three of us were at her side to lavish on her the caresses she made clear she so ardently desired. Scarcely had we placed our hands on her buttocks than, with two or three spasms and a roll of the eyes, the fountain of pleasure gushed. Rose and I soon perceived that my father and Vernol had erections straining at their bonds. With an abrupt movement, Rose was at my father's side.

'Dear Papa, I threw you my scarf. That means you will be my husband, and I shall be your wife. Give me your hand!' she imperiously commanded.

'Willingly, my dear Rose,' my father answered, 'but the ceremony only takes place at the end.'

'That is all right with me,' she assented. 'But Vernol caught Laurette's. We have to bring them together, don't you think?'

'Just as you wish.'

She hurriedly took our hands which she clasped in each other's. When she made us kiss, our mouths obediently obeyed the order. Placing her hand on my bare bosom, she pronounced us man and wife. If our senses were overheated, Rose was on fire.

'How refreshing it would be to have a bath. Right now,' she exclaimed. 'I feel as if I were burning up.'

My father rose to pull a cord in the alcove. When he did so, the throne slid back, revealing a pool with three taps that sprayed cool, warm, or hot water.

'Isn't this marvellous?' Rose chortled gleefully. 'It's an enchanted palace. I'm going to be a naiad, but not all by myself.'

In a flash, she appeared wearing the usual costume of water fairies, namely, nothing at all. Grabbing hold of me, she urged my father and Vernol to aid her in stripping me to a similar state. Before I could utter a word, I was down to the buff. When Rose made a signal, Vernol pranced out like a satyr. That left only my father, whom Rose and I were busily disgarbing.

My furtive eyes were already scrutinizing Vernol. What a handsome and seductive figure he cut! He bloomed with the freshness of youth, and in the middle of all the alabaster whiteness of his skin, skin that a young girl would have envied, proudly rose the distinguishing mark of a man.

Consumed by devouring flames, we were like those furnaces which sizzle when water is thrown on them and then only burn hotter. Two pointed lances were aimed at Rose and myself, but the prospect of combat did not daunt us. Our bodies prey to the frisky hands and lascivious lips of the Tritons, Rose and I happily returned their advances instead of rebuffing them and toyed with their arrows as they manipulated our quivers. At that moment, my father was prudent enough to shove a sponge into mine when I was least expecting it.

Vernol wanted to enter the lists against me, but with the adroitness so natural to women and so calculated to stimulate desire, I nimbly stepped aside and sprang out of the tub. When Rose followed me, the men were soon out, too. The effect that the dip had on them was visible from the condition of their crests. Their temporary humiliation gave us a chance to dry ourselves and don diaphanous robes which concealed nothing from their larcenous eyes. Then we all stretched out languorously on the easy-chairs. Hardly had we settled ourselves than my father, giving a jerk on another cord, had lowered before us a table heaped with delicacies and wines like those that had intoxicated us shortly before. All was there to augment the ardour which was rising again in us.

Vernol was so impatient that he was twitching as he reclined on his chair. What surprised me was Rose's seemingly unabated exuberance. As for myself, for whom voluptuousness was a more refined enjoyment, I preferred to wait and watch before attaining the goal. The anticipation gave me almost as great pleasure as the realization. My father was also firmly of the opinion that the postponement of satisfaction gave it more spice when it was finally tasted.

Consequently, Vernol and Rose had to chafe under the yoke of unrequited desire. It was easier for Rose who, under our touches and fondling, had reached bliss three times already, according to her own admission. She called the collation a wedding banquet, even though no maidenhead presided over it. But what did it matter? Voluptuousness held sway, and we were content under her rule. Crowned by the sylvan deity, she was to be seen in the centre of the table with the sceptre in her hand. In the four corners of the alcove were entwined pairs in the most lascivious positions. Flitting among them were old envious satyrs making their pitiful offerings which the nymphs scornfully refused, for here all was merriment and animation.

The impetuous Rose, with a bottle and a glass in her hand and robe open to reveal her seductive conniceties, sent flames racing through our veins. What she poured us became a torrent of fire. Now I was boiling inside, and our partners were in the same state of lust, judging from their virilities.

No longer able to restrain herself, Rose lifted her

glass and cried out: 'Vernol, take your bride?' Then, throwing herself into my father's arm, she again shouted: 'And here I have my husband!'

She had firm possession of his prick, which she was getting ready to insert into its proper slot, and Vernol had one arm around my waist and the hand of the other on my cunt, when my father put a stop to the proceedings.

'Just a moment, children!' he announced. 'There is a condition I am laying down for my consent to continue, and it is only right that it be met. If Vernol is to penetrate Laura, I insist on following the example of that courtier who, after coupling his wife with a young page she was sleeping with, did in the lad's rear what the latter was doing in the lady's front. Therefore, if Vernol wants to fuck Laura, I demand that his bottom be at my disposition.'

So, I thought, Vernol's charms had attracted my father as much they had me. At first, I felt a twinge of jealousy, but then I reflected that I would be freer with Vernol if my father was not watching me, and I did my best to enhance the pleasure of their game.

Roughly ripping off Vernol's robe, I made my father an offering of his rump, the rounded cheeks of which I spread wide. Oblivious to my actions, the boy was preparing to plunge his prick into my chasm.

'No, no, Vernol,' I chided him as I would a naughty child. 'Don't deceive yourself into thinking that you can put it into me without fulfilling that stipulation my father made.'

'Oh, Laura!' he panted. 'You can put any obstacle in my path and I shall overcome it. I have been in hell

107

for an eternity, and there isn't anything I wouldn't do to have you and expire in your arms.'

'We can't leave Rose out of our little party,' my father said, interrupting Vernol's impassioned declaration.

The table was whisked away, and a thick soft mat covered the flooring over the pool. Now the alcove was a true sanctuary of lust. In a flash, we relieved ourselves of all that we had not entered the world with. Adorned only with what nature had seen fit to give us, we made obeisances at the altar to the divinity we all worshipped from the bottom of our hearts.

On all sides the mirrors reflected endlessly our various charms. When Vernol cast admiring glances on mine, he swept me into his arms and covered me with kisses and caresses, while his prick, which I was firmly clutching, stood as firm as a rock. My father was massaging his buttocks with one hand, while with the other, he was busy with Rose's breasts or slit. She, in turn, was all over us.

Finally yielding to his amorous frenzy, Vernol turned me on my back, widened the space between my thighs, kissed my Venus mount and valley, darted his tongue into it, sucked my clitoris, mounted me, and finally jabbed his prick into me up to the hilt.

In the meantime, my father had taken his position behind him. Rose, on her knees and supporting herself on her elbows, and with her fur-fringed cavern before my face, spread still wider her brother's rear cheeks, noistened the entry with her tongue, and guided my father's prick along the path she had cleared. While they were bucking up and down in rhythm, she impartially was tickling the testicles of each. In her cunt I had my finger, which I energetically kept pushing in and out. Again, it was she who first came to bliss, but Vernol was not far behind. When my father noticed his victim's sudden stiffening and relaxation, he redoubled his efforts which added greatly to my pleasures. Keeping time with his quickened tempo, I plunged down the dizzy descent of ecstasy along with him, and we landed at the bottom side by side. The three of us were now, one could say, a single unit which Rose was bathing with her wet lips.

When it was over, we paused to catch our breath. Still breathing heavily, Vernol asserted that he had never experienced such raptures in his life.

'What you have received you should give,' my father drily remarked. 'Come, Laura, let's see what he can do. Although he is not so well equipped as I, I am quite sure that you will not be dissatisfied with him. While he and I taste of your delights. Rose will repeat her performance, but this time she will stimulate your clitoris with her hand from behind.'

Jumping on my sire, I feverishly caressed his body as Rose introduced his prick into my cunt. After this task was performed, she parted the cheeks of my derriere and took her brother's virility into her mouth. When the organ was sufficiently hardened and moistened, she led it to its goal. She titillated me as she massaged her brother's buttocks. At the same time, my father, his finger in her slit, was nearly driving her out of her mind with lust.

When the sublime presence was announcing himself, we all flew after it and caught it. Oh, how magnificent and superb he was! We all spurted, drenching ourselves with the fluid that began dribbling down the sides of our bodies. I was in such a rapture that I could barely contain myself. After floundering around like a drowning swimmer, I felt come over me a calm, that was no less voluptuous than the climax itself. The contraction of my muscles and the friction of all the sensitive, delicate parts where sensuousness reigns were almost too much.

There was no question but that we had to get some rest. We were able to persuade our male partners to put back on their robes, if only for the time being, but that did little to soothe our taut nerves. Our eyes, hands, mouths, and tongues all bespoke desire, and our conversation concerned nothing else. Rose's and my breasts, buttocks and cunts were massaged and reverently kissed, tokens of affection which we returned on their pricks, nipples and testicles. There was no mistaking the reaction – the vanquished members had risen proudly to renew the struggle with our distended clitorises.

Now Rose had a role with more meat than those she had played before. After I had made her lie down with her knees raised, my father rested himself along side of her, and passing his thighs under her legs, he aimed his prick at the target.

Joining the fray, I got on top of her with her head between my knees and those of Vernol, who was doing it to me in the fashion of a dog. I put my father's instrument into her slippery slit where it went in and out like a piston. In turn, he played first with my breasts and then with her opulent pendants. As he was thus engaged, Rose and I amused ourselves by irritating each other's rosy buttons. She could not keep her fascinated eyes off Vernol's prick which was rising and falling in time with the swaying append-ages. It produced such a powerful effect on her that during the time we were striving for the initial ecstasy, she had savoured in four times. Four times she moaned in a dying voice, 'I'm coming! I'm dying!' She was an inexhaustible fountain. A fifth copious overflow blended with my father's boiling jet, one that flooded her.

With their pleasure prodding us, Vernol and I reached the summit almost simultaneously. This time, Rose seemed as if she were parting this life. The bliss she had been chasing had not escaped her eager grasp. Her cunt was a morass of fuck and no wonder, for she had three or four orgasms to our one. After writhing and biting and scratching, she fell into that prostration in which one feels nothing but the most delicious fatigue.

When she came to, she could not praise highly enough the variation and she made up her mind that she could study it more closely. As soon as we came to, we changed places. I took her place, with her on top of me, while she was being fucked by her brother. Since my head was between their thighs, I was able to follow at close range all their motions. At the same time, my father gave free rein to his fancy with me.

When this fourth act was over, we were so broken that it was imperative to take time out again. After we unsteadily got to our feet, my father had the table lowered again and we gulped down the food as if we were famished. Sleep was also a necessity. As soon as the table was lifted away, the four of us lay down on the matting, one on top or beside the other, our arms and legs interlaced, and each clutching the object of his desires.

After an hour of respose, Rose, awakened by a sultry dream, shook us out of our lethargy. Our gambols commenced anew, but instead of rushing headlong into the maelstrom of sensuousness, we toyed with our urges in order to make them last longer and enhance their intensity. We made advances to pleasure and then pushed it away but, aroused in turn, it pursued us. Only Rose allowed herself to be captured, and she surrendered two or three times before it abandoned her to catch up with us. We were just as helpless before its might. It is not a thing to be trifled with. We finally ended the day with a fifth act, in which Rose played the leading role.

As she was lying on my father who was taking the main highway on her body, Vernol presented himself at the rear gate. I assumed her former position, rendering them the same services I had received. At the same time, my father had his wandering hands all over the hills and dales of my body. Perhaps for the sake of change, Vernol from time to time took different roads. He veered from the one I had started him on to join up with my father on his path. Rose was overjoyed to see them united in such a way, side by side on the same narrow way which barely accommodated the two of them, but at the last moment, he returned to the thoroughfare I had chosen for him. She found this, too, utterly divine. It was not difficult to please Rose.

'Death would be sweet if it came at such a delicious moment!' she cried enthusiastically.

Although we smiled at her flight of fancy, we found

it quite in keeping with her temperament and mentality.

Before dressing, my father made the pool appear again. Without any ado, I immersed myself in its refreshing water. The others promptly followed me. I pulled out the sponge and vigorously washed the hole it had occupied. This second ablution calmed our nerves, and since it was getting late, we made preparations for our departure. The coach appeared at eight, and we were back in the city an hour or so later.

During the ensuing days, Rose kept after me to play similar games with her. I finally yielded, and I have to admit I enjoyed them. But after a while, the sport palled, a fact which my father noted with his sharp eyes. He was not displeased. And I began losing interest in Vernol. My initial infatuation with him merely resulted from the impression made on my eyes and hands. I felt nothing in my heart for him. If you took away his good looks and manners, there was not much left. Finally, it was over and I had few or no regrets.

From then on, I followed only the dictates of my heart which led me back to my father, whom I loved and adored more than ever. I considered him an extraordinary man, unique, and a true philosopher far above the mundane, but at the same time appealing and seductive to a woman's sensitivities. He had the qualities that hold our fair sex in fetters and that can clip the wings of our inborn inconstancy. Thinking men make no protest when they are faced with it, but they are able to put a stop to it. Finally,

I was in reality the sole object of his affection, just as he became to me. These feelings for him, and several incidents, caused me to break off completely my tenuous liaisons.

An adventure during which Rose snapped several lances with too much insolence caused my final alienation from her and Vernol. Added to that was the account of a particularly loathsome adventure they confided to me. Now I was convinced that fastidiousness was not to be found in either of them and that their emotions were ruled only by unbridled lust and passion. Their way of life and thought was not in accord with mine at all.

Since I rarely saw them, they took their pleasures where they found them, and their favourite hunting ground was the public park. One day, as Vernol was taking a stroll on the promenade with his sister, he came across four of his old school comrades, the oldest of whom was about twenty. Joyfully, they recognized each other, embraced, and hurled questions and answers back and forth.

'Where are you coming from? What are you doing? Where are you going? Who is this bewitching creature?'

Rose, of course, did not take their flattery and compliments amiss. Once their curiosities were satisfied, they insisted that Vernol and his sister join their party and go with them to an inn where they had planned a light meal.

At the outset, the young people obeyed social conventions, but the oldest, who was also the craftiest, began to exert his wiles for his underhanded purposes. As they briskly paced to their destination, the polite language turned into double-entendres and off-colour jokes and stories.

Once in their room, Rose flounced on the bed saying that she was hot. As she did so, she revealed her snowy bosom and a well-turned leg. Such praise was rained on her charms that she nearly reeled with delight. After the meal had been consumed and while the wine was being drunk, heads became giddy. Rose tossed off some more champagne with the others following her example. In the general hilarity, the innuendos became more unmistakable and liberties were freely taken and given. Touches became embraces and embraces led to kisses. The fire was lit and soon was to blaze.

The senior, more brazen and experienced than his companions, took Vernol aside and told him what they had planned. At first, he looked stupefied, but then he held his sides with laughter. Curious as usual, Rose insisted on learning what the joke was about. After succumbing to her wiles and pestering, he told her that before they had met her and Vernol, they had agreed among themselves that the one of the quartet with the biggest prick would pay for the wine and the one with the smallest would pay for the rest.

When she heard that, Rose almost choked with merriment. She was so convulsed with laughter that when she fell back on the bed with her legs up in the air she revealed practically everything that a woman should keep concealed.

'Who's going to be judge?' she demanded when she had recovered from her hysteria.

'Why you, of course,' the senior replied as if it were the most natural thing in the world.

Animated by the wine and flattered by the invitation, Rose declared that she was well qualified to take on the judicial chore.

From that moment, all restraint was cast aside and the inhabitants of the room were shameless in their antics. A valiant and battle-scarred warrior, Rose held her own with the best of them and was prepared and ready for more interesting assaults than verbal ones. Eager to bring matters to a head as quickly as possible, she beckoned Vernol to her, and wrapping an arm around his neck, she forced his head down to kiss the breasts she had flipped out of her bodice. Then sliding her other hand down to his trousers, she undid the buttons and yanked out his straining prick.

In revenge, he slipped his hand up under her skirts where he quickly won possession of her cunt that was already beginning to dribble. When she kicked up a knee, her centre of pleasure was visible in all its glory to the others. The sight so awed the group that they eagerly gathered around her. One took hold of a posterior cheek, another a part of the thigh, still another one of her snowy globes. Each now had a part of her. As she made Vernol rise, she asked if any of them could produce its equal. At that, each immediately had a competitor in his hand. Now before her eyes was the dazzling spectacle of five proudly standing pricks, arrogant and menacing, which dared her to combat, even though they knew they were sure to lose.

Sitting up for a better view of the jousting site, she gave the quintet's pride and joy a quick but careful scrutiny.

'I could come to a decision right now,' Rose

116

asserted, 'but as a judge, I want to take every possible precaution. I'll have to use some sort of measure, even my own if necessary, so I won't be accused of making a biased judgment. Let's begin.'

Using her boot-lace as a tape, she conscientiously took the measurements of each, both in length and diameter, and with the same care weighed their appendages in her hand. Manipulating all these instruments of pleasure affected her so deeply that she fell on her back again. The two or three convulsive wiggles of her derriere were evidence that she was discharging.

It was as if they had heared the starting signals of a race, the way they rushed to mount her.

'Before we proceed,' she said, stopping them by imperiously raising her hand, 'I wish to announce my findings. I hereby order the senior to foot the bill for the wine. If my brother had been a party to your pact, he would have been obligated for the remainder of the bill, but since he wasn't, I bestow that honour on number two.'

Seeing the latter's crestfallen expression, she comforted him by saying that it would grow with his years and that he would be the first to have her, which would be very soon, since all those pricks and testicles had set her aflame.

Stretching herself flat on her back, she beckoned to the lad, who needed no second invitation. He leaped on her and in a flash, his dart was in the ring she proffered him. Vernol followed him in turn, and then came the three others according to the gradations she had measured. The overjoyed Rose was wallowing in fuck and bliss. Spurting almost incessantly, she scar-

117

cely had time to catch her breath, for no sooner had one left the lists than another took his place.

There finally came the moment when she could not any more, and the entr'acte was spent in drinking, laughing and cuddling. She was willing prey to the impassioned kisses and foraging hands of her five gallants. Since they did not tolerate a stitch of clothing on her, she was promptly in the state of the goddesses during the Judgment of Paris.

The ravishing sight revived their forces and desires to a fury. Wistfully, she wished she had five cunts so she could have enjoyed them all simultaneously, but she had to be satisfied with having them in twos.

Always impatient for variety, she made the champion lie on the bed with his head at the foot, and then climbed onto him so that her breasts dangled directly above his mouth. The least favoured youngster got on her between her thighs. When they were in position, they each took the indicated road. Now squeezed in a tight vice, she clutched the envious members of the other two, while she took Vernol's bauble between her lips, alternatively sucking and tickling it with her tongue.

Although sperm was running down all over her body, she remained unconquered after twenty-five engagements during which time she irrigated the field of battle twenty-nine times. She was worn out, but deliciously so.

I saw her the following day. At first, I thought she was on the point of death with her languid eyes and listless body. Surprised at finding her in such a sad state, I questioned her and kept at it until she and Vernol told me all about the orgy.

I did not bother to give them any advice, for I knew how useless it would be. I did not even deign to scold them. The reader is undoubtedly aware that they resumed their former activities as promptly as they could. That was the last time I saw them, but I heard about their ends.

Unable to stop herself in her mad drive for pleasure. Rose finally succumbed to it. When she stopped menstruating, she had an abortion, which took a terrible toll on her. She suffered from agonizing fits of dizziness and her sight began to fail. She more resembled a walking wraith than a human being. The cheerful spirited young woman had vanished. Finally, the lingering illness brought her to the grave.

Vernol, who was his sister's faithful companion in all her escapades, shortly after came down with a virulent fever which nearly carried him off, and no sooner had he recovered than he contracted the pox which permanently disfigured his handsome features. It was not long before he was laid to rest at Rose's side.

My father had foreseen that something like this would happen, and afterwards, we often discussed it. Better than ever, I knew the good care he had given me, and my gratitude knew no bounds at having escaped such a tragic fate. Our relationship gradually deepened, but the feelings we had for each other were more tender, more sensuous and refined than passionate. Many nights we spent together in bed with no sensation other than the quiet satisfaction of knowing that the other was there.

One evening, I suddenly remembered all my past indiscretions, which I now considered acts of infidelity, and I burst into tears. Immediately he was at my side, comforting me and asking what was wrong.

'How can you have any esteem for me after the way I treated you?' I sobbed. 'I'm nothing but a debauchee who was unfaithful to you.'

'Have you taken leave of your senses, my child!' he asked in astonishment. 'What does it matter if a woman has lain in the arms of another lover, if her heart and mind remain true? Is the worth of a woman to be judged by how often she has been used? And wasn't I then unfaithful to you with my dalliances with Lucette, Rose, and even Vernol? And yet you know that there is nobody whom I love as much as I do you. So no more much nonsense.'

I was reassured and comforted.

Then tragedy struck. Its first heartless blow had been the death of dear Lucette, the news of which saddened us, my father even more than myself. Although he was his usual kind self always, I noticed a change in him afterwards. Many times I caught a sombre expression on his face.

I was twenty when my father, the most lovable man who ever walked the face of the earth, for whom I would have cheerfully laid down my life, caught pneumonia, and all the arts of medicine were unable to save him. Day and night I was by his bed which I wet with my tears as he feebly ran his hand through my hair. The end came and his last sigh was breathed on my lips.

What a loss! I was more devoted to him than if he had really been my father. He had introduced me to the Count de Norval, to whose amorous activities I owed the light of the day, and whom I regarded with no emotion other than a slight curiosity.

My grief was such that I nearly went out of my mind. I could not even find surcease in sleep since it never came. Soon I, too, came down with a fever which turned into a serious illness. I wanted to die, but my hour had not yet come, for my youth saved me against my will.

When I regained my health, I determined to bury myself alive. Having lost everything that counted, I loathed life. I entered a convent.

If it had not been for the solicitude of Eugenie, I am sure I would have perished behind those forbidding walls. Without knowing the cause of my sorrow, she was still able to touch the bottom of my heart. Never was she too busy to come and dry my tears and dissipate my apathy. Her tenderness and sympathy lent weight to her consolatory words, but the night toppled all that she had built during the day. That she quickly recognized, and she obtained permission to share my bed. I was surprised at the treasures concealed beneath her wimple and robe. When she found that my spirits had picked up some, she urged me to tell her the whole mournful story.

After her kindness, I could not rebuff her and I began recounting my life piecemeal. I knew that I needed a friend, but I despaired over finding one again. It was at such moments that I realized what I had lost in Lucette. And I never dreamed that I would find a replacement in Eugenie. As our intimacy deepened, I repaid her confidences with mine, and in her arms I found the balm for my pain.

Never shall I forget a certain night when she spoke to me even more tenderly than was her wont.

'Dearest Laura,' she said, squeezing me to her, 'I know that you're suffering, but if I can dull the edge of your grief by confiding in you what I am undergoing and have undergone, nothing would make me happier. Listen, my dear, I love you. I love you with all my heart, even though a cruel fate has decreed that I have to wear a religious habit.

'Hypocritical nuns surrounded my innocent childhood with walls and bars and sucked me into their infernal dungeons. Ignorance and prejudice are my tormentors and desire my executioner. During the night, I am unable to shut my eyes because of the tears that fill them. By day, I am disgusted or bored with all I see and hear. Compare yourself to me. At least, you can leave here whenever you wish to give a lover the charms that I have glimpsed and am now touching.'

The soft hand that she placed on my breast sent a thrill running up and down my spine.

'He has come back to me!' I cried deliriously. 'I lost him to death, but now he has been returned to me.'

As I tightly pressed her to me, it was my father whom I was embracing. Such was the illusion she had produced in me. But as I ran my hand over her body, there was one thing lacking that snapped me back to reality. But her other delicacies that I tasted with my tongue compensated for the lack. Her bosom, her figure, her derriere, her skin and her mound were incomparable.

'What a delight it would be for you if only a lover

could hold you in his arms as I am now,' I ecstatically exclaimed. 'You once said you wanted to know about these forbidden pleasures, and if the raptures were as great as they were claimed to be. Now I shall give you some idea, that is, if you wish.'

Her curiosity and desire, both at white heat, led her to accept my invitation. For my part, the wish to console her and tear away the veil of ignorance made me forget temporarily my own woes. She proved to be an apt and conscientious pupil.

Spreading apart her legs, I grazed with my fingers the lips of her narrow cunt whose roses were just starting to bloom. I did not dare insert a digit, for the initial pain would hardly be a suitable introduction to enjoyment. Soon, however, I won the throne of voluptuousness with its fetching clitoris that I slightly irritated. She was thrown into a spasm of ecstasy from which she had the greatest difficulty in recovering.

'Dearest Laura,' she murmured weakly, 'I never dreamt that there was anything like this in the world.'

She in turn awkwardly made me her lover and my body was covered with impassioned kisses and feverish hands as she tried to return the raptures I had given her. But I was still too sad at heart to be receptive, and I stopped her hand. Instead, I took her back in my arms and, renewing my tokens of affection, I put her on the first step towards bliss.

'This is so wonderful,' she sighed. 'Do anything you wish to me, but never stop.'

When my hand slipped back to her darling little cunt and I started to probe it, she squirmed at the exquisite pain.

'It is I, dear friend,' I whispered into her ear, 'it is

I, happiest of mortals, who plucked your maidenhead, that rarest and most sought after of blossoms.'

Now that she had taken the first sip of sensuousness, I no longer hesitated to open my heart to her completely and I recounted to her all the adventures set down on these pages. If I was able to free her from the yoke of ignorance, it was no problem to rid her of the last vestiges of prejudice. After telling her of my own experiences, the fear of pregnancy no longer troubled her.

'Everything you tell me and do to me runs counter to what the nuns have taught,' she panted.

Her trust in me, my counsel, and my assistance brushed away the last crumbling obstacles on the road of sensuality. The peace of mind she enjoys today was due entirely to my efforts, and her lover owes his victory to me. Yes, my friendship served them both well.

Before completing her education, I wanted to meet the Monsieur Valsay so dear to her heart, make sure of his character, and ascertain if he was worthy of her love, her confidence and her favours.

When I met Valsay, I liked what I saw and heard. I felt no qualms about letting him have Eugenie, rouse and satisfy her yearnings, enlighten her and banish her fears.

Yet, had it not been for me, Eugenie would never have completely overcome her timidity. When he pressed her with the most heartbreaking importunities to make him happy, and she refused him, even though she desperately wanted him, I took his side. At the mment when her ardour was becoming almost too much for her I decided it was time for me to intervene, only too happy with the thought that I was contributing to their felicity.

Now I am going to remove the last of the hindrances,' I informed them. 'Valsay, you will be a pure ingrate, one unworthy of the inestimable prize I am about to bestow on you, if my conduct toward this end lowers me in your esteem.'

Earnestly, he assured me that that would never happen.

In spite of Eugenie's protests, I closed the door of the reception room and then almost dragged her to the grille against which Valsay was pressing his face. I did not forget to tear off her veil. There he eagerly grasped for her saucy breasts, kissed her lips, and sucked the tip of the tongue she stuck out in spite of herself.

His overpowering desire gave him courage to insert his hand up inside her skirt to reach and possess the *mons Veneris*. I pushed her still closer to him, kissing her for reassurance at the same time. Finally, he was able to raise the robe up to her waist and contemplate that delightful little cunt with all its ornaments of untouched youth.

His hands wandering over her yielding body were like tinder on her inner bonfire. Vainly he cursed and kicked the implacable grille that separated us and opposed his desire. My heart was almost breaking at the touching sight.

'What?' I taunted him scornfully, although I did not mean it. 'Are you so lacking in resourcefulness that these bars are going to be an insuperable barrier to what you say you so ardently want? True love always finds a way. But I also love Eugenie, and I

125

shall prove it, for there is nothing more I want than to make the two of you happy.'

The squares formed by the iron bars were larger further up. First, I firmly tucked up the hem of the black religious garb which contrasted so dazzlingly with the alabaster of her firmly rounded rump, which he massaged, kissed, and paid the homage due to it. Then I got down on all fours and made her stand on my back so that the little slit was framed like a picture by the bars of the upper square. Valsay, unable to withhold a gasp of admiration, pulled up a chair on which he stood to be at the same level as she. Almost yanking out the organ in which all his desire was concentrated, he thrust it into her hollow as I slipped my hand through her thighs to assist him. Slowly but surely, that sensation we term passion began to exert its irresistible pressure on her. She was swaying back and forth on my back, when I felt her stiffen. A few hot drops of liquid dropped down on my skin.

Just before he was to emulate her, he discreetly withdrew and spattered my back like a hailstorm. Then I left the happy couple to their own devices.

When Eugenie saw the jewel I had so often described and praised, she took it almost gingerly in her hand and fondled it, but it was apparent that she still did not know quite what to do with it. Bashful about admitting her ignorance, she made muffled laments which quickly brought me back to her side, and when I was there, she beseeched me not to leave her. Generously, I offered to lend whatever further assistance was required. Now she was as gleeful as a child with a new toy.

It was then that I reminded her of the beneficial

sponge, about which I had told her. When she returned with the primitive contraceptive, I had a chair ready for her to supplant my back. Touched by my thoughtfulness, she insisted that I stay to witness the consummation.

With her hand, she exposed to me the divinity between Valsay's legs. Then she revealed to him my breasts, which, to my surprise, I found had retained all their curvaceous charm, and everything else that a decent woman keeps concealed. She even permitted him to touch them. If they only knew what a jerk of emotion they aroused in me.

When I whispered to her how I felt, the little traitoress shamelessly blurted out my secret to him. She was insistent that I, too, enjoy the favours of her lover. She wanted me also to have the most precious thing she owned. When she tried to make me take her place on the chair, I resisted in spite of her pleas and urgings. The blood in my veins had turned to lava, but I still held fast.

'No, Eugenie,' I said firmly. 'I shall never consent to something like that, no matter what you say. After all I suffered, I made up my mind to renounce any intimate relationships with men, and I shall not be shaken from this resolution. In spite of the sensations you have awakened in me. I am happy and content just to lie and rest in your arms at night when you quench the flames that you lit during the day.'

With that, I hurried away to let her lose her virginity without me.

A fate jealous of my contentment decided to destroy it. Eugenie and I were separated when urgent matters concerning my inheritance forced me to leave the convent sooner than I had intended.

As I had promised, I wrote her almost daily during my absence. Even through letters, we remained as close as we ever had been. She knew the attraction she held for me just as I knew how she cherished me.

As I conclude this account, I sigh for the warmth of her arms around me and her lips on mine. Inwardly, I send her a thousand kisses which I hope soon to be able to give her personally. When we meet, I shall have for her a little jewel similar to Valsay's but not so dangerous, but one which will fill a certain gap. Since Valsay has been recalled to his regiment and will be gone for some time, the perilous liaison will fade away and I shall soon be at her side to dry her tears.

Wait for me, my dearest.